The Pleasure Palace

The Pleasure Palace

EVANGELINE ANDERSON

APHRODISIA

KENSINGTON PUBLISHING CORP.

http://www.kensingtonbooks.com

APHRODISIA BOOKS are published by

Kensington Publishing Corp.
850 Third Avenue
New York, NY 10022

All Kensington Titles, Imprints, and Distributed Lines are available at special quantity discounts for bulk purchases for sales promotions, premiums, fund-raising, and educational or institutional use.

Special book excerpts or customized printings can also be created to fit specific needs. For details, write or phone the office of the Kensington special sales manager: Kensington Publishing Corp., 850 Third Avenue, New York, NY 10022, attn: Special Sales Department, Phone: 1-800-221-2647.

Aphrodisia and the A logo are Reg. U.S. Pat & TM Off.

ISBN-13: 978-0-7582-1536-9
ISBN-10: 0-7582-1536-3

First Kensington Trade Paperback Printing: September 2007

10 9 8 7 6 5 4 3 2 1

Printed in the United States of America

1

"C'mon, darlin, I jus' wan' a lil' sugar pussy. I'm only topside on this rock for twenty-four hours. You don't wan' me to go away lonely, now do ya?" He had a thick Centaurian accent and had obviously been drinking all night so the words came out in a drawling slur. Shaina McCullough suddenly found herself pinned against the crumbling gray concrete with the disgusting drunk leering in her face. "Jus' a lil' sugar pussy . . ." he repeated and she turned her head in revulsion as his foul breath, thick with gin fumes, washed over her.

That was it; she couldn't stand it any more. Determined to teach him a lesson, Shaina struggled to get her right hand behind her back and grab the mini-tazer that was taped there. Cursing the stupid skintight design of her skirt that made it impossible to carry anything in the pockets, her fingers wiggled beneath the low-slung waistband of the leather mini, feeling for the small, lipstick-shaped tube. She intended to whip it out and shove it straight into the drunk Centaurian's balls—all three of them. A good sharp jolt in the nads ought to discourage him, since he didn't seem to know how to take no for an answer. At the very least it would teach him not to bother innocent-looking girls who turned out to be Peace Control Officers.

"Hey baby, I knew you'd come around." The drunk had managed to pull the magno-tabs of her crop top apart and was currently trying to get off her demi-bra. His breath was making her want to retch. Shaina fumbled grimly for the tazer. Where was it? She had taped it to the small of her back right before leaving the station, but now her searching fingers found nothing but a smooth expanse of skin—it was gone. The drunk had one hand inside her bra now and was mauling her right breast. Shaina was sure she'd have to take a scalding anti-bac shower that night to even begin to feel clean again.

"Get off me!" she yelled, beginning to feel a little panicky. Okay, it was time to call for backup. The drunk Centaurian might not be the serial rapist she was looking for but she was going to be in serious trouble if she didn't get him off her pronto. One thick knee was pressing between her thighs, trying to spread her legs as Shaina reached for the autojewel, actually a link to her backup, nestled securely in her belly button. But the drunk's potbelly was plastered against her own flat stomach too firmly to admit so much as a micron between them, let alone her questing fingers. She tried to push him away, but he was all over her, a suffocating, reeking flesh blanket.

Oh, this could *not* be happening after all her careful training and months of preparation for a case like this, Shaina thought despairingly. It was supposed to be her big break. What would Ty think if he could see her now?

As if to answer her question, a deep male voice came from the depths of the alley behind them.

"Hey, buddy, I don't think you're this lady's type. Why don't you back off and get out of here?" Shaina's heart sank. She knew that voice. It belonged to Brent Tyson, the senior officer who had trained her not so many months ago. Damn it all to hell, what was he doing here? She'd almost rather be mauled by this disgusting drunk than have her ex-partner witness her failure.

The drunk in question was paying no attention to the commanding voice behind him. "Find yer own, mister. I was here first," he mumbled, still pawing at her bra. He had exposed both breasts now and he was working on spreading her thighs. Thankfully, the tightness of the micro-mini actually worked in her favor there, making it impossible for her legs to part more than a few inches. Shaina continued to try and wriggle free with no success.

"Fine, we'll do it your way," Ty said pleasantly. Suddenly, the drunk was dragged off her and Shaina was left leaning against the cold concrete wall, gasping with effort and off balance in her ridiculous thigh-high imitation lizardskin boots. Not for the first time, she cursed the stupid costume, which was supposed to make her look like a university student out for a night on the town. She stumbled a few steps and fell to the dirty, gravel-strewn ground, cutting her palms in the process, and looked up in time to see Ty's fist connect with the drunk's face. The punch wiped the leering grin off in a sickening crunch of cartilage and bone. Blood that was nearly black began pouring down the Centaurian's face. He dropped his bottle of gin and cupped his nose, bellowing in hurt confusion.

"Whyth you do that?" he gasped, his eyes flaring orange with pain. "That hurth, you thon of a bith!" He added a few choice words in his native tongue that Shaina couldn't begin to make out, although their meaning was pretty clear.

"Wouldn't have had to if you'd backed off when the lady asked you to," Tyson replied, still in that same, pleasant, no-nonsense tone of voice. He casually smoothed back his thick black hair with one large hand and waited to see if the drunk had had enough. Apparently, he hadn't. With an inarticulate howl, he came stumbling forward, clearly meaning to tackle Tyson and take him to the ground. This time, Ty didn't even bother to punch him. He just stepped out of the way and let the Centaurian run headfirst into the opposite wall of the alley, knocking himself out cold.

Without missing a beat, Tyson turned back to Shaina, who was still kneeling on the ground, feeling stunned. "Upsy-daisy, sweetheart." He hooked one capable hand under her arm and levered her to her feet as though she weighed next to nothing. Angrily, Shaina shook him off.

"Damn it, Ty, what are you doing here?" She gazed at her former partner with disgust. As always, he looked immaculate, as though he was about to attend a meeting instead of punching out drunk Centaurians in a dark alley in the seedy port district. Shaina couldn't stop her eyes from traveling up his muscular legs and thighs clad in skintight black trousers, to the broad chest and wide shoulders in a crisp white button-up shirt. He hadn't even gotten dirty in the short fight, she noticed with disgust. Brent Tyson had a striking, hawklike face and his distinctive amber eyes were glinting with amusement and maybe something else as he stared at her in the dim light of the alley.

"What am I doing here? Saving your sweet little ass, McCullough. At least that's what it looks like from here." He grinned at her. That self-satisfied smirk Shaina couldn't stand, showing sharp, white teeth in the half light of the alley. Ty was half D'Lonian. Usually, aside from the amber eyes and golden-tan skin, you really couldn't tell. But when he grinned like that, it showed. That grin made Shaina nervous because it reminded her of all the rumors you heard about D'Lonian males—most of them too incredible to be real and too embarrassing to repeat. All her girlfriends whispered and giggled about it when they heard she was working with a man who was half D'Lonian. People said D'Lonian men were animalistic in their mating habits, that they had uncontrollable, unnatural lust. She tried to push the thought out of her head and concentrate on appearing self-sufficient and professional.

"I had the situation completely under control. There was no need for you to interfere." Shaina lied as forcefully as she could. "This is my case and you shouldn't be here."

"What were you going to do, bludgeon him into submission with these?" Ty cupped her still exposed breasts in large, warm hands and scooped them neatly back into the lacy demi-bra, causing Shaina to gasp. The heat of that brief contact lingered, making her nipples into hard little pebbles as she attempted to close the magno tabs of her crop top, getting them misaligned in the process. She tried to ignore her reaction to his touch and remain professional.

"No, I was just about to stun him with my tazer before you interfered." She looked up at him defiantly. Even with the absurdly high-heeled boots, she was too short to meet him eye to eye. Smoothing down the crooked crop top, she tried in vain to pull the micro-mini just a little farther down her thighs. Having those smoldering amber eyes on her body always made Shaina uncomfortable for reasons she was unwilling to explore, even to herself.

"Oh, you mean this?" Tyson reached into the righthand pocket of his skintight trousers. Shaina's eyes couldn't help but follow the gesture as she noticed, not for the first time, the thick bulge between his legs. Part of her wondered if it was any thicker at the moment as a result of having his hands, however briefly, on her bare breasts, but she pushed the thought resolutely away. Ty pulled his hand out of his pocket and there, lying in the center of his large palm, was her lipstick-sized mini-tazer. It still had a small curl of Stiksalot—*sticks anything to anything*—stuck to it.

"Where did you get that? I taped it to the small of my back before I left the station." She reached for it but Ty pulled it back, gripping the miniature weapon firmly in his fist.

"And you dropped it about three blocks back. It fell right out the back of your skirt in front of the Green Iguana." He mentioned the local dive the serial rapist was thought to hang out in. Shaina had spent a good part of the night there, letting herself be seen, before wandering slowly away to the darker side streets of the port district, hoping to lure the rapist into following. Instead, she had gotten the drunk Centaurian, who was currently out cold and snoring at their feet.

"You were following me!" Shaina was outraged. "In case you hadn't noticed, Ty, my training period is over. It's been over for months and you're no longer my partner or training officer—you're my coworker. That means we're equals and I don't need you breathing down my neck while I'm trying to work. I don't need you to take care of me anymore." Shaina could feel her pale skin flushing red with anger but she was helpless to do anything about it.

"Well, from what I just saw it looks like you need *someone* to take care of you." His deep voice was quiet and calm, but those wide amber eyes flashed dangerously. "And I wasn't following you. I happened to be having a beer at the Green Iguana when I saw you walk out. I noticed the tazer fall out of your skirt and came along to give it back to you. What would you have done if I had decided to leave you to your own devices and return it tomorrow?"

"I could have called for backup." Shaina sounded sullen, even to herself. Why was it that Ty could reduce her from a grown woman to a petulant child with a few choice words?

"With this?" He stepped forward, crowding her a little, and ran one long finger along the soft curve of her abdomen, indicating the autojewel in her belly button, now blinking red moons and yellow daisies. The brush of his warm, callused fingertip along her skin made Shaina shiver. "Where *is* your backup anyway?" He smelled like warm male musk.

"They're back a few blocks." She wanted to move away from him, but, once again, her back was to the wall. Her boots grated against the gravel as she shifted her feet; there was no place to go. "I didn't want to scare the guy off. I'm trolling for the Red-Head Rapist; he's been known to hunt in the port district."

"Yes, I know. They're calling him that because he targets redheads, which, I guess, is how you got involved, even though this isn't technically your area of expertise."

Shaina bristled. "I don't want to be stuck in Domestic my entire career. When Tony from Vice approached me about trying to draw this guy out I jumped on it. My hair just made it easier." She flipped her long, silky auburn hair over one shoulder with a defiant little toss of her head, daring him to say anything about it.

"Is that right?" His amber eyes still glittered dangerously. He took another step forward, deliberately invading even more of her space. Shaina held her ground.

"Yes, it is. As a matter of fact, that guy you punched out might be the Red-Head Rapist, for all you know." She gestured at the Centaurian sprawled at their feet.

"You know he's not." Tyson smiled a little, again showing those sharp, white teeth. "He's just a drunk Centaurian out looking for, what did he call it? Oh, yeah—a little 'sugar pussy' I believe is what he said." He leaned in closer, his warm, cinnamon-scented breath brushing along her neck and the tops of her breasts as he spoke, and Shaina felt herself blushing furiously. Goddess! To think he had heard that too . . . it was absolutely mortifying. She was deeply embarrassed—which must be the reason her heart was pounding so hard and she felt like she couldn't get a deep enough breath.

"So you stood there and watched the whole thing. If you were going to interfere, then why didn't you do it in the first place before he started manhandling me?" She fought not to notice how close he was to her. His slim hips were pressed against her pelvis until she was absolutely sure she could feel the bulge of his hard cock digging mercilessly into her flesh.

The heat in his blazing golden eyes was intense and it was all Shaina could do to meet them without flinching. She didn't want Ty to know how nervous he made her.

"McCullough . . . Shaina . . ." He sighed and took a step back. Running one hand through his thick black hair, he shook his head as he looked at her. "I was trying to leave you alone because I knew how you'd react if I interfered with your sting. But damn it—you left me no choice! I couldn't just stand by and watch him rape you, could I?

"I only stepped in at the last minute when it became clear that you weren't handling the situation and your backup was nowhere in sight. I don't see how I could have done anything else. Now, come on." Ty took her small hands gently in his. "You hurt yourself when you fell. I have a first aid kit in my craft. Why don't you come let me bandage you up? Red-Head's not out tonight or he would have taken the bait already. There's no way he could have resisted you." Those frank amber eyes raked over her again, taking in her barely concealed breasts and the too-short skirt, making Shaina feel hot and cold and completely naked all at the same time. She crossed her legs tightly, trying to ignore the throbbing between her thighs. As always, Ty's effect on her body made her feel nervous and angry—out of control.

"I told you, Ty, I don't need you to take care of me anymore. So why don't you do us both a favor and stay out of my life?" She pulled her hurt hands out of his large, warm grip, taking the tazer as she did. Grimly, she pushed past him, fully aware that he was letting her go, the awareness making her angrier than ever.

"Shaina." He grasped her upper arm and swung her around to face him once more. "I admit I've been watching out for you a little bit. You're still a rookie and I get worried about you, especially when you take on an assignment like this. But if that's really what you want, then I'll do it. I'll stay out of your life."

His voice was calm but dangerous; his fingers dug into the flesh of her upper arm like steel pincers.

"Fine." She didn't know why her voice was trembling or why she couldn't look into those golden eyes while she spoke. "Stay out."

"You have my word." Voice cold, he let her go so abruptly she nearly fell again. Stumbling, Shaina got past him as fast as she could, blinking back angry tears as she wobbled in the spike-heeled boots to the end of the alley. She could feel his eyes on her back like laser beams while she walked, and she fought the urge to look back. The boots were pinching her toes and sending spikes of pain through her arches, and every extremity felt frozen solid except her hands—they were still warm from Ty's touch.

Why wouldn't he just leave her alone and let her prove she could do the job right on her own without always swooping in to rescue and criticize her? Shaina knew he had trained lots of other Peace Control Officers, so why did he always single her out, as though her training would never be done?

Well, now at least he had promised to stay out of her life. She wondered how long that promise would last.

As it turned out, it lasted less than twenty-four hours.

2

"Tony, I need to talk to you." Tyson's entrance into the busy Peace Control station was, as usual, right on time. He looked over at Shaina's empty desk as he called to his friend, noting that she had yet to make an appearance, and sighed inwardly. Punctuality was a concept he had never been able to instill in her when she was an officer in training and now he doubted it was a principle she would ever embrace. But even though she was often disorganized and less than punctual there was something about Shaina McCullough, a kind of brilliance, an instinctual intuition that made her a valuable addition to the force. Tyson had no doubt, given the time and opportunity, she would be instrumental in catching the Red-Head Rapist. He just didn't intend for her to get that opportunity.

"Tony?" he repeated and his colleague's head finally surfaced from the latest batch of reports. Tyson knew he had promised to stay out of Shaina's life, at least directly, but this was different. Shaina was putting herself in danger and he couldn't just stand by and watch her risk her life the way she had last night.

"Tyson, hey, what can I do for you?" Tony—short for

T'onzxlyslr, his Xaxian name, which no one could pronounce—raked one pale hand through his neatly clipped white-blond hair and blinked his pink eyes nervously. He took a small sip from the recycled cardboard cup in his other hand and spit it back immediately. "Man, this stuff is awful. I mean, even for synthesized beans—really awful. You'd think they could afford better brew for New Brooklyn's finest."

"Dream on." Tyson sat on the edge of the Xaxian's desk, casually pushing the reports aside. "Listen, I need to talk to you about Shaina."

"Oh, man . . ." Tony groaned. "How did I know you wanted to talk about her? Look, Ty, she's an officer now and she has the right to steer her own career. You can't keep holding her back."

"I'm not trying to hold her back. I'm trying to keep her safe. You and I both know that Shaina has a great mind—she makes the most amazing leaps of logic sometimes—but she's not good at undercover work. She's too apt to leave her backup behind or lose her weapon, both of which happened last night. Did she tell you?"

"Not in those words, exactly. She more or less just said the night was a bust."

"A bust? It would have been a complete disaster if I hadn't come along when I did. Look, Tony, this assignment is too dangerous for her. I want you to pull her off it *right now*." Tyson rapped the plasti-wood desk he sat on for emphasis.

The Xaxian took another small sip from his cup and grimaced, looking distinctly uncomfortable. "Tyson, I don't know if I can do that. The chief himself approved it. It seemed like a good idea at the time, since she's the only natural redhead in the department and with looks like hers . . ." He trailed off, perhaps seeing the glint of anger in Tyson's eyes. "Ty, you can't protect her forever." His voice was gentle. "You know, you've trained lots of officers. Hell, you even helped train me when I first came on the force, but I've never seen you become so over-protective and paranoid about any of your past trainees. I know you've got a thing for McCullough but . . ."

"We're not an item, Tony." Ty cut him off. "It's just that Shaina's too valuable to waste on an assignment like this." Tyson stood up and began pacing back and forth in front of the desk. "You ought to have her behind the scenes, directing your investigation and putting the pieces together—not out in the line of fire. Now, I don't care what it takes or who approved it, I want you to make some plausible excuse and get her off this case. It's too damn dangerous." He was pacing almost angrily. Stopping in front of Tony, he looked the other humanoid right in the eye. Mild pink was no match for blazing amber and the head of Vice dropped his eyes first.

"Well, I'll see what I can do, although it may be completely unnecessary anyway."

"Completely unnecessary—what are you talking about? I think I just outlined the necessity of getting her off this case very clearly." Tyson slapped the desk angrily.

"Yeah, I know, but right now McCullough's in the Chief's office volunteering her sweet little . . . uh, her very fine *mind* for an extremely dangerous off-planet mission."

"What? But she's not even here." Tyson pointed to her empty desk as evidence. "She never comes in on time."

"Yeah, well, never is a long time. It just so happens she came in early this morning while the Chief was asking for volunteers. She spoke right up. Wait, you can't just barge in . . ." But the rest of his words were lost on Tyson, who was already striding angrily toward the solid real-wood door in the middle of the station.

TO PROTECT AND TO SERVE was written in large, black block letters over the arching doorway. Under the lettering a small digital message was running in a loop: BUSY, DO NOT DISTURB UNDER ANY CIRCUMSTANCES it said in red, spooling holo-type.

Tyson paid no attention whatsoever as he grasped the brass knob and pushed his way into the room.

"Ah, good, another volunteer!" The jovial voice came, not from the Chief, who sat silently at his large glass desk with holo displays showing different parts of the city, but from a small, nattily dressed man in the plush chair across from him.

Beside the little man, in another plush chair, sat Shaina, looking beautiful in the standard jumpsuit uniform of black pleather. Tyson had one on, himself—hell, every officer in the place did—but he couldn't help noticing how well his former protégée filled hers out. The pleather clung lovingly to every lush curve of her ripe body and he couldn't forget that he'd held those luscious breasts in his hands just last night, the creamy mounds and berry-pink nipples straining out of that black lace bra she'd had on . . . God! He wanted her so much. From the first there had been an undeniable attraction between them and yet Shaina refused to acknowledge it.

Right now she looked flushed with excitement. Apparently she'd been picked to go on this "dangerous mission," whatever it was, and just couldn't wait to throw herself in the path of peril.

She looked around now to see who the small man was referring to. When she saw Tyson, her face fell. He could almost see her thinking, "oh no," but he wasn't going to let that stop him. There was no way she was risking herself on some damn-fool, off-planet mission if he could prevent it.

"Chief Hamilton," he began when the Chief, a stocky, balding man whose pleather jumpsuit bulged more than a little in the midsection, interrupted him.

"Officer Tyson, I'm so glad you're here. Let me introduce Minister Waynos. Minister Waynos is a direct emissary of the Chancellor and he's here for a very important reason," the Chief emphasized, giving him a glare. Tyson reluctantly took the hint and held on to his lip—at least for the present.

"Yes indeed, my good officer, and I'm so very glad you've

come to volunteer for the mission." The little man seemed to assume that Tyson couldn't possibly be in the office for any other reason. He had a silver-plated goatee and mustache and he was dressed in a triple-breasted dove-gray suit with platinum buttons and mother-of-pearl lapels. He was clearly excited as he jumped out of his chair and began circling Ty, who stood in center of the room. "And I think you'll do quite well too, just the kind of physical specimen we were hoping for."

"What in the name of . . ." Tyson caught another glare from the Chief, and forced himself to modify his tone. "What does this mission involve, Minister Waynos? In terms of danger and personal risk, I mean," he added, giving Shaina a meaningful glance.

"I'm going, Ty." Shaina glowered at him with her gorgeous green eyes and spoke in a low, intense voice meant only for him, but the little Minister heard her as well.

"Why of course you're going, my dear. You'll be going with our Chancellor's hopes and thanks and you'll be outfitted in style. No expense will be spared; you have my word. As for danger, well . . ." He turned back to Tyson, who was watching him expectantly with a frown growing on his sharp features. "Well, there's no denying that there will be some. Quite a lot, actually. Syrus Six is a lawless place and if you were to be found out . . ." He shook his head mournfully, the silver goatee glinting in the office's overhead glows.

"Wait a minute, Syrus Six? You want us to go to the Pleasure Planet?" Tyson demanded, incredulous. "But why? What's there?"

"The Chancellor's only son, we believe." Minister Waynos looked sadly at him. "As you no doubt know, Syrus Six is at the heart of the illegal slave trade. Paul, the Chancellor's son, was abducted over a month ago by people he believed to be his friends. We tried to keep it quiet at first, hoping for a ransom demand, but there was nothing, just nothing. The Chancellor has been quite beside himself.

"Just this morning we received information that Paul is at the Executor's Palace on Syrus Six. The Chancellor has been forced to accept the fact that the boy is being held there and is possibly even being trained as a pleasure slave. A most reprehensible fate, I'm sure you'll agree." He nodded sagely at the Chief, who, Ty noticed, had put on his most concerned face. He supposed he couldn't blame him. This man represented the Chancellor, as close to royalty as New Brooklyn got.

"There must be a personal motive behind this." Shaina spoke up for the first time. "Surely even a well-trained pleasure slave wouldn't bring as much as the Chancellor could afford to pay in ransom. Whoever took Paul wanted his father to suffer. It wasn't just a random abduction."

"Impossible . . . the Chancellor has no enemies that we know of on Syrus Six." The Minister spoke a little too quickly, Ty thought. "However, I like the way you think, young lady: already on the job." Waynos beamed at her approvingly.

"So the plan is what, to auction ourselves off as slaves in hopes that we might see the Chancellor's son somewhere along the way?" Tyson didn't even try to keep the sarcasm out of his voice. He couldn't believe what Shaina had gotten herself into now.

The small Minister blinked at him in surprise, evidently unable to believe that anyone would be less than overjoyed to risk their lives for the esteemed Chancellor's brat. "Most certainly not, Officer . . . Tyson, was it? No, if you both go as slaves, who will protect you? Slaves on Syrus Six have no legal rights whatsoever. They are chattel to be bartered and bought and sold. Most dreadful, really."

"Not to mention completely illegal," the Chief pointed out drily. "Tyson, one of you will pose as a pleasure slave and one of you will pose as a wealthy owner. The officers who go on this mission will be responsible first and foremost for bringing back the Chancellor's son. As a bonus, it would be nice if they could find out who was behind the abduction.

"So . . ." The Chief had risen from his desk and was staring meaningfully at Tyson. "Officer McCullough has already come on board this mission. Very eagerly too, I might add. Her ambition is a real credit to our station and your own training, Tyson. The ship is being equipped as we speak and we were only waiting for one more volunteer to start. Obviously, from the Chancellor's point of view, the sooner things get under way, the better. Are you in or out?"

Tyson looked at Shaina, who was giving him a stony glare out of those deep green eyes. Obviously she was hoping he would decline the mission and just as obviously she was determined to go herself. Chief Hamilton was sanctioning her decision and making it very clear that he would brook no arguments from an overprotective ex-mentor and partner. The only way to protect her from herself was to go along.

The notion of just letting her go alone never even entered Tyson's head. From the moment she had come into his life, he hadn't wanted to let Shaina McCullough out of his sight. There was an innocence about her, and a passion for life, that made her unlike any other woman he'd ever met. Ty wished he could lock her up someplace and keep her safe, keep her all for himself. He knew that sounded dominant and possessive and overprotective but damn it—those were the emotions Shaina had roused in him from the first. His D'Lonian blood boiled when he even thought of her with anyone else, when she ought to be Bonded to him. He could no more give her up than stop breathing—although he could cheerfully have strangled her for getting them into this position.

"Well?" Minister Waynos was looking at him expectantly

and Tyson realized he'd been taking too long to think over a decision that was no decision at all. The minute Shaina had volunteered herself, she had volunteered him as well, whether she knew it or not.

"Yes. Count me in. Although I can't understand Officer McCullough's affinity for dressing up in skimpy outfits and going undercover lately. I hope her slave-girl costume covers more than the hooker outfit she had on last night." He gave Shaina a sly wink.

"That was a cheap shot, Ty." Shaina glared at him with her arms crossed over her full breasts. Tyson only grinned back, meeting her eyes and baring his sharp white teeth. He let his D'Lonian half show because he knew it made her uncomfortable. As he stared into her green eyes, he was already wondering what her luscious body would look like in a skimpy slave-girl outfit . . . maybe it wouldn't be such a bad mission at that.

Tyson could just imagine getting a handful of that silky auburn hair and holding her down while he sucked her ripe nipples. He wanted to part those long, gorgeous legs and taste her sweet, creamy pussy until she moaned and begged for more. He could almost feel her slender fingers digging into his shoulders, pulling him closer while he pressed his face between her firm inner thighs and tongued the tender cleft between her legs. It was only a fantasy, of course, but a man could dream, couldn't he? Hot amber clashed with ocean-green as he let his desires fill his eyes. A deep blush stained Shaina's cheeks, but she refused to look away.

"I'm afraid you are laboring under a misapprehension, Officer Tyson." Minister Waynos interrupted Ty's lascivious thoughts. He cleared his throat and Ty looked up, dragging Ty's eyes reluctantly from the silent battle of wills he had been engaged in with Shaina.

"What do you mean? I thought you said one of us would be

posing as a slave and one of us would be posing as the owner?" He looked at the Chief for clarification. "You said that," he pointed out.

"Yes, but I didn't say who was going as which." Chief Hamilton said. "You see, the slave quarters at the Executor's Pleasure Palace where you'll be staying are sex segregated. Since the Chancellor's son is male, or was when he was abducted"—he cast an apologetic glance at Minister Waynos, who looked troubled—"a male slave will have the best chance of finding him."

"So you're saying . . ." Tyson hoped against hope that what he was thinking was wrong. But the Chief and the Minister were both nodding. Only Shaina looked surprised.

"Yes, Officer Tyson. *You* will be going undercover as the pleasure slave. Officer McCullough will be going as your Master."

3

Shaina McCullough sat staring in disbelief at Chief Hamilton, trying to process what he was saying. *Ty* would be the slave and *she* would be the Master? By the almost comical look on Ty's face, he was surprised as well. She supposed that she could have accused him of being a sexist porcine for just assuming that he would be playing the Master, but then, she had assumed it as well. From the very first day she'd met him, Brent Tyson had always had the upper hand in their relationship. He had always been the mentor, the senior partner, the seasoned veteran to her green rookie. He was always dominant, and the heat in those golden eyes had been making her nervous from the first moment they met. Despite her speech to him the night before about being equal coworkers, Shaina had known in her heart it wasn't true. Now here was a chance to not only be equal but to be superior—to be his *Master,* no less. Or would that be Mistress?

Shaina felt a grin of pure anticipation begin to spread over her face. She had never been so glad she'd volunteered for anything in her life! Meanwhile, Ty looked like he'd been eating unripe nare fruit.

"Maybe this is more than you bargained for when you came barging in here. Would you like to back out, Ty?" she asked sweetly, casting a "lactose spread wouldn't melt in my mouth" smile his way.

Tyson cleared his throat and shook his head. "No." He met her look with a smoldering one of his own. "If you're going, McCullough, then I'm going too." There was something in those hot amber eyes that made Shaina's smile falter just a bit, something hungry and almost animalistic—D'Lonian. Getting the upper hand over Brent Tyson wouldn't be accomplished just by slipping a pain-inducing slave collar on his neck, she thought uneasily. There was apt to be quite a bit more to it than that . . .

"Of course, the Chancellor is sparing no expense to equip and prepare you thoroughly. Your every possible need is being anticipated." With those words, Minister Waynos broke up the silent staring contest Shaina had been about to lose. He was a funny little man, Shaina reflected, but he seemed utterly devoted to the Chancellor, that was certain.

"What can we possibly need other than a ship, the right costumes, and enough credits to make the scenario plausible?" Ty looked at the Minister with obvious dislike.

"Why, Officer Tyson, I am surprised by your lack of imagination. Much more is necessary, I assure you. For instance, I have a neurobiologist waiting by the *She-Creature*—that is the name of your ship—to inject symbiotes into the both of you so that the two of you can communicate via thought transmission and avoid any electronic or spectrographic listening devices in your quarters."

"Wait a minute, you mean I'm going to have Ty inside my head? And I'll have to be inside his?" Shaina was getting a very bad feeling about this. Suddenly she wasn't quite so glad she'd volunteered. It was Ty's turn to look smug.

"Not to worry, my dear," Minister Waynos said reassuringly, obviously misunderstanding her apprehension. "The technique utilizes symbiotes, a specially bred strain of neurobacteria that allows thought transmission by establishing a neural link with your partner. It's a very exact science but quite easy to learn. You'll have a day before hypersleep and a day or so after to practice the technique involved in thought transmission. Plenty of time."

"Are the symbiotes removable after the mission?" Ty asked the obvious question, Shaina noticed gratefully. It had been on her mind as well.

"Unfortunately, the symbiotes, once introduced into a humanoid host, are completely irretrievable. But . . ." The Minister held up one prim finger, stopping the protests about to burst out of both of them. "But they will degrade with time and eventually their effects will fade. In the meantime, they will keep their hosts—that's you, Officers Tyson and McCullough—in perfect health and give you greatly increased healing abilities and the capacity to communicate via thought transmission. All with no harmful side effects whatsoever." He smiled triumphantly, like a salesman winding up his pitch, and sat back down on the plush chair, stroking his silver goatee.

Besides being inside her annoying ex-partner's head, that is, Shaina mentally finished for him. Out loud she said, "I've only ever heard rumors of symbiote injections before. That kind of technology can't be cheap."

"Right you are, my dear." Minister Waynos looked a little grim. "In fact, this treatment that the Chancellor is giving you free of charge is only available at a few very exclusive spas and clinics around the known universe and has been strictly regulated for years. I won't tell you exactly how much it costs but it can run into the multimillions of credits, especially for advanced packages like the one you'll be receiving."

"We're very grateful, but let's not forget that the Chancellor is doing all this so that we can have a better chance of rescuing his son from a life of hideous servitude as a pleasure slave," Tyson said dryly. Shaina pressed her hand to her mouth in what she hoped was a thoughtful expression, trying to smother a smile.

"Quite so," the Minister acknowledged gravely. "As I said before, the Chancellor has spared no expense to be sure your mission is successful. In addition to the ship, the symbiotes, a more than adequate supply of credits, and a set of impeccable false credentials for you both, the Chancellor is also sending an expert to help you train for your roles—doubtless the most important roles of your lives."

"An expert? Who's an expert on the Pleasure Planet?" Tyson asked skeptically. Privately, Shaina wondered the same thing.

"Why, an ex–pleasure slave, of course," Minister Waynos said, as though it were the most obvious answer in the world. "His name is Faron, I believe. He's a Glameron and he's the Chancellor's personal . . . ah . . . best friend. I'm sure you take my meaning."

Shaina *did* take his meaning and she could tell by the expression on his face that Ty did as well. So the Chancellor had his own private pleasure slave. Everyone knew that Glamerons were never anything else. They were the only known race of humanoids in the galaxy that actually enjoyed servitude—something to do with their genetic makeup. Somewhere she had heard the theory that an older, now extinct, race had played with the Glamerons' DNA sequences until they were perfected as the natural slaves they had come to be.

Owning a Glameron was almost the same as having an estate on one of Jupiter's more exclusive moons or getting your name in the book of the four and forty-four families. No wonder the Chancellor could afford all the expensive symbiote treatments and the ship and line of credit he was giving them. Owning a Glameron meant that he must be fabulously wealthy.

And it also meant that he had ties to the Pleasure Planet and the slave trade that he wasn't admitting. Shaina almost wished she had the symbiotes inside her right now so that she could discuss her speculations with Ty without being overheard. But looking across the room at his darkly handsome face pulled into a thoughtful scowl, she decided that she could wait after all.

"Well," Minister Waynos made a self-important little sound somewhere between a cough and a sniff and stood up. "If you have no further questions, then I would ask that you both present yourselves at gate three of the private sector of the port tomorrow morning at eight sharp. I realize that doesn't give you much time to say good-bye to friends and family, but as I think I pointed out earlier, time is of the essence. Needless to say, please keep the details of this mission completely confidential. Oh, and I almost forgot the small matter of remuneration."

"Remuneration?" Shaina heard herself asking. She was still trying to work out how she could say good-bye to her mother without giving away the nature of her dangerous and somewhat kinky assignment. Her mom had never wanted her to be a Peace Control Officer in the first place. If she heard Shaina was off to the Pleasure Planet to play sex-mistress to her annoying if fascinating ex-partner's pleasure slave, she might lose it altogether.

"Yes my dear, compensation, payment for services rendered," Waynos explained pompously. For the first time, Shaina began to dislike him a little.

"Yes, we know what it means." Ty's impatient tone said that he had been disliking the dapper little man with the silver-plated facial hair for quite some time now. "Officer McCullough is just asking you to get on with it. If we've only got one night to get ready we need to move. Packing alone . . ."

"Oh no, you needn't pack, not so much as a sonic toothbrush," the Minister interrupted him. "Clothing and toiletries are completely taken care of. Don't even bother to pack a book to read or a vid to watch. I assure you that all your spare time is going to be wholly consumed with mastering the symbiotes and the customs of Syrus Six."

"Remuneration?" Ty reminded him, pointedly. "You brought it up, not me," he reminded the offended-looking Minister.

"Certainly," the little man agreed stiffly. "When I came to your chief"—he nodded at Chief Hamilton who, apparently feeling that his part of the negotiations was done, sat at his glass-topped desk doing paperwork—"I told him I was only interested in officers who volunteered freely, but that when the volunteers were chosen I would discuss monetary matters with them. I have here"—he whipped out a small, sharkskin briefcase that Shaina had not previously noticed and produced two sets of legal-looking documents—"a contract for each of you to sign." He handed them each a copy of the fat document.

"This merely states that you will do your best to rescue the Chancellor's son. If you try and fail you will still receive the tidy sum of twenty-five thousand credits apiece. If, however, and this is our sincere hope, you bring back Paul alive and hopefully unharmed, you will be given the sum of five million credits apiece, considerably more, as I'm sure you'll note. News or capture of the heinous beast who perpetrated this travesty in the first place will double your fee in either case.

"And now, Officers, Chief Hamilton, I must go. The Chancellor would like to see me once more before I see you off at the port. Just bring the completed documents along with you when you come. Remember, nothing else is necessary. Good-bye, good-bye, a pleasure, an absolute pleasure my dear." He patted

Shaina's hand once more, pumped the Chief's, and waved austerely at Tyson as he left by the office window. Stepping into a hovering, iridescent blue racer that was waiting for him outside, he roared away in a cloud of aesthetically pleasing pink dust.

"Spread your legs, sweetheart. That's it, a little wider. Let me in." *Shaina did as he asked, watching the molten gold eyes flaring above her in the semidarkness. Smooth golden-tan skin brushed against hers, making her aware of her nakedness and her defenseless position pinned beneath his masculine bulk.*

"Ty, we shouldn't . . . I've never . . ." she gasped, but he didn't let her finish. Bending over her, he took her mouth in a hungry kiss that left her breathless, unable to protest his assault on her senses. The warm scent of him filled her head and his mouth tasted like cinnamon.

"Been wanting to do this for a long time, Shaina. Been wanting to fuck you," he growled low in her ear and she gasped to feel the head of his heavy cock brushing along one inner thigh, searching for her center.

"No . . . please . . ." she begged even as she spread her legs wider, trembling, feeling the pulsing heat and wetness between them as her sex prepared for his invasion.

"Can't stop now. Can't wait to be inside you." She felt the broad head find its target and part her slippery folds, nudging into her wet heat. Goddess, he was so big . . . She cried out in terror and need.

"Please . . ." She didn't know if she was begging him to stop or go on.

"Gonna ride your sweet pussy hard tonight, Shaina. Gonna fuck you all night long," he whispered as the thick shaft of his cock slid home inside her quivering, defenseless sex, taking her, making her his . . .

* * *

Shaina woke up gasping and drenched in sweat. It took her a moment to assure herself that she was in her own room on her familiar gel mattress. Just a dream, it had been just a dream. But it had been so real that she could taste Ty's mouth on hers, still feel the weight of his body on her . . . inside her.

No, she thought. *It won't be like that. Just another undercover assignment, that's all this mission is . . .*

An undercover assignment where she had to play Mistress to Brent Tyson's sex slave . . . Goddess, what had she let herself in for?

Shaina rolled over and tried to get back to sleep. The mission started tomorrow and she would need her rest. But the dream wouldn't leave her mind and sleep was a long time coming.

4

Tyson was right on time at Gate Three in the private sector of the space port, which was considerably cleaner and more luxurious than the port proper. The huge, arching white shield wall looming above him was meant to protect the privacy and safety of the ultra-rich and famous, the only people who could afford to own their own ships.

Shaina was only five minutes late. She arrived a little out of breath from having run all the way from the main gate. She was carrying a small velour knapsack despite the Minister's instructions. Tyson wasn't surprised. Shaina always had about a hundred items she absolutely couldn't do without and couldn't possibly find in her purse at any given time.

"Is it good?" She nodded at the sheaf of paperwork, the only item he had brought with him as per instructions. Tyson smiled a little. Of course Shaina knew him well enough to know that he would have spent his time getting the contract checked out. The only real family he had to say good-bye to was his younger brother, Brad, who was out on his own and doing well in university.

She, on the other hand, had probably been placating her mother with wild lies and half-truths. Ty had met her mother once and he liked Mrs. McCullough immensely, mainly because she shared his views about keeping Shaina out of harm's way.

"It's good." He nodded confidently at the large contract. "You can sign it. Lawyer says it's airtight but fair. The Chancellor must be really desperate to get his son back."

"Wouldn't you be?" With no warning she changed tacks. "Ty, why are you coming on this mission with me? Really."

Tyson thought about it. He could say he was coming to take care of her, to keep her from getting her fool self killed. This was no training exercise; it was flat-out espionage and death was a real possibility. He wondered if Shaina knew that. Really understood it in her bones the way he did. Yes, he could lecture her about putting herself willfully into danger but that would only start another argument, and that was a bad way to begin a mission where they would have to trust each other with their lives. So instead he said as lightly as he could, "I'm coming for the five million credits, of course. After this I can quit my job and live in the lap of luxury,"

Shaina gave him a skeptical look and shifted her flowing mass of silky hair from one slender shoulder to the other with that defiant little toss of her head. In the afternoon solarshine, it looked like a mass of molten copper running down her back and Ty had to restrain himself from reaching out to touch it.

"You love the job." She gave him a direct, serious look. "You're a great officer; you'll never give it up. So why are you really coming? What is it about if not the credits?"

He decided to drop the pretense. "It's about you, Shaina." His voice was quiet and he looked directly in her eyes. "Maybe I just wanted to spend some time as your personal pleasure slave. Did you ever think about that?" He grinned at her to lighten his words, but she blushed and dropped her eyes. Unable to help himself, Ty moved in closer and leaned down, whispering into the pink shell of her ear. "Maybe I just want to serve you, want to be on my knees before you, pleasuring you in whatever way you command, *Mistress* . . ."

He saw a shiver go through her, and when she raised her eyes to his again, the pupils were dilated and drowning deep with some emotion he couldn't read.

"Don't . . . I can never tell when you're teasing." Her low voice trembled slightly.

"I'd never tease about something so important." God, she smelled good. She was wearing some light, floral fragrance but underneath it, Ty swore he could smell her heat, an intoxicating feminine musk that spoke of her need for him. Why wouldn't she ever acknowledge it?

"You promised to stay out of my life." Still looking up at him, she searched his eyes for his true motivations.

"I lied." He reached over and ran one large hand through the silky strands of her hair as he had wanted to earlier. She pulled away, a frightened, hunted look in her eyes. Tyson kept his face neutral, but inside, he swore angrily to himself. Damn it, he had pushed her too far again . . .

"Well, well, right on time. I must beg your pardon for being just a touch late myself. Business with the Chancellor, you know, most pressing. Well, come in." The Minister came bustling up, oblivious to the tension between them, presented one wide gray iris to the optical scanner, and mumbled a complicated series of code words. Ty couldn't make out more than one in ten. Then the huge, arching white barrier melted and they were inside the private port.

Scarlet real-wool carpeting ran along a luxuriously deco- rated corridor hung with holo-prints of the rich and famous. Because he'd been to the private port before, investigating a homicide, Ty knew that the discreet pearl buttons to the left of each print would start a bio-spiel. The narrator told the listener everything interesting about that particular celebrity, plus some juicy lesser-known facts as well. He wished for Shaina's sake that they could take a little more time to explore, but at the rate Minister Waynos was going, they both had to practically run to keep up with him. For such a portly little man, he could certainly move, and Tyson wondered if he had had a dose of symbiotes himself.

Once at the shuttle bay, the Minister stopped them and introduced a distinguished-looking gray-haired gentleman who looked to be in his early forties. In one hand, he was holding a flat case with a locking mechanism on it that Ty had never seen before.

"I'm Dr. Dulupe. Nice to meet you." He extended a hand for them to shake and smiled pleasantly all the while, showing white, even teeth.

"This is the neurobiologist I told you about. Also happens to be the Chief of Staff at the largest private hospital on planet and the Chancellor's private physician." Minister Waynos introduced them proudly. "And this, Dr. Dulupe, are Officers Mc-Cullough and Tyson, both very experienced in undercover operations. They are going to Syrus Six to try and rescue our Paul."

"Ah, yes, of course. So they are." The doctor continued to smile pleasantly.

"The symbiotes, Doctor, if you please. Time is of the essence." Waynos waved impatiently. The doctor nodded and raised the small, locked case up to eye level. Ty now realized it was chained to his wrist with a length of titanium wire. He stared fixedly at the lock for a moment, as though thinking very hard about something, and suddenly, with a small pop, the case opened. Inside, lying on a cushion of black crushed velvet like precious jewels, were two perfectly huge hypodermic syringes.

Tyson heard Shaina draw in a nervous breath and he didn't blame her. He didn't like the look of the long, sleek, wicked-looking silver barrels any more than she did.

"I apologize for the old-fashioned needles instead of a nasal spray but the symbiotes have to be given as an intramuscular injection. Roll up your sleeves, please," the doctor ordered in a no-nonsense tone that said he wasn't used to being disobeyed. He pulled one of the monstrous syringes out of the case and adjusted a minute knob on its side until he appeared satisfied. "All right, who's first?"

"Wait a minute, I'm still not completely sure about this." Tyson frowned and put himself between the large needle and Shaina. "Are you absolutely certain there are no adverse effects? How exactly do the symbiotes work?"

"My dear Officer Tyson, we really have no time for this . . ." Minister Waynos began, but the smiling doctor held up one hand and shook his head.

"No, Minister, I don't mind answering. Briefly, young man," he said, addressing himself to Tyson, "the symbiotes I am about to inject each of you with were bred from the same colony of neurobacteria. Once injected into your body, they will migrate to the speech and thought centers of your brain. Because the symbiotes are from the same bacterial colony and are always in communication with each other, they will enable you to form a neural net, a link, if you will, with your partner. This link will make thought transmission possible from a distance of up to one standard mile. The symbiotes, as I'm sure our good Minister has already told you, will also keep you healthy and give you increased regenerative abilities. And there are absolutely no contraindications or harmful side effects. I've been injected with symbiotes myself and you can see for yourself how healthy I am." He nodded at his fit body and smiled that blindingly white smile once more. Tyson wondered who would want a neural link with this guy.

"Are there any other questions or can we get on with this? You only have thirty minutes to make your launch window." Minister Waynos seemed more agitated all the time. Reluctantly, Tyson rolled up the flexible arm of his black pleather jumpsuit and allowed Dr. Dulupe to skewer him with what felt like a harpoon. Shaina did the same, wincing only a little at the bite of the huge needle. Tyson waited to feel something or to hear Shaina's thoughts, but there were no strange sensations at all.

"I don't feel any different," he said, rolling down his sleeve.

"No, you won't for a while. It takes the symbiotes a while to migrate into your bloodstream and cross the blood-brain barrier," the doctor explained. "They will become active in your bodies sometime in the next twenty-four to forty-eight hours. Of course, you'll be in hypersleep by then, so really, you won't notice the effects until you wake up in orbit around Syrus Six. Don't worry, no pain is involved; you'll simply start to sense your partner's thoughts." This wasn't exactly what Waynos had promised but before Tyson could point it out, Shaina spoke up.

"But, then . . . how do we turn them off or tune them out or whatever?" Ty thought she sounded a little panicky. Was she really that nervous about having him inside her head? Or was she worried about being inside his?

"Faron will tell you everything and help you master the symbiotes without fail. And now, you must go. The launch window is closing even as we speak." The Minister pushed them toward a small, recessed door that led to the private shuttle.

"Wait a minute . . ." Ty started to say but the door hushed closed and he found himself in a small, oval space with four comfortable-looking chairs that had multiple straps hanging from them. The entire shuttle was a uniform pale lavender, even the carpet and walls, and there were no windows. Only the strangely shaped air ducts set high on the walls provided relief from the monochrome effect; they glowed a dull silver. A low, female voice could be heard saying, "Will all passengers please be seated and secure your safety harnesses. We are due for lift-off in three minutes. Will all passengers please . . ."

"Well, guess we're on our way," Tyson remarked, glancing at Shaina, who was already sitting down in one of the plush lavender seats and trying to figure out the complicated tangle of buckles and straps. "This your first trip off-world?"

"Yeah," she grinned shyly at him. "I'm a little scared, you know?"

She should have thought of that before volunteering for this crazy mission, Ty thought but aloud he only said, "Me too, McCullough. Me too."

5

"Welcome, welcome, Master, Mistress. I thank the Goddess you have arrived safely." The clear tenor voice greeted them even before they had disembarked the small, functional shuttle and come aboard the ship. As Shaina rounded the corner and stepped through the air lock, she saw the person the voice belonged to.

"You must be Faron." She tried not to stare.

"I have the honor of being so called," he replied, still in that clear, rather beautiful voice. "You may look at me if it pleases you, Mistress. It will not distress me," he added, perhaps sensing Shaina's curiosity. That was another thing about Glamerons, she remembered; they possessed low-level empathic telepathy so that they were easily able to sense their masters' moods and thoughts. Just another trait that made them the perfect pleasure slaves. She gave in to her curiosity and stared, since Faron didn't seem to mind.

The being in front of them was so beautiful he was almost mesmerizing, although she could hardly say why. Dressed in a flowing gray robe, the Glameron had a slim, androgynous body about five standard feet, six inches tall, and wide, luminous eyes whose color seemed to shift continuously. His shoulder-length hair looked black to her, as black as Ty's, but when he shifted minutely, it turned a brilliant copper-red hue. A full, red mouth framing white teeth, high cheekbones, and hawklike facial features made him even more attractive—at least, Shaina thought so. His skin changed like the rest of him. One minute she was sure it was the same even, golden tan of Ty's and the next it looked creamy and pale.

"You look like someone I know," Tyson spoke behind her.

"I was just thinking the same thing. You look . . . familiar somehow. I've never met you before, though; I'm sure I'd remember it."

"Forgive me, Master, Mistress, but this is a reaction that most humans have to me. I look familiar to you because I resemble the person you each most desire. I am shaped by your psyches. I differ with every Master or Mistress I serve."

"But what if the person you are serving desires *you* most?" Shaina asked, trying not to think about the way the Glameron appeared to her and what it might mean.

Faron turned great, jewellike eyes that melted slowly between amber and ocean-green in her direction. "Alas, I have been long away from my home world, where anyone desired me for myself. I fear I have forgotten my true form." The Glameron bowed his head briefly as though acknowledging an ancient pain and then looked up again. "But there is no time to speak about me. Soon the ship will move into hyperdrive and we must all be safely tucked into our sleep chambers before that happens. I have less than an hour to show you around your quarters. When you wake, I will have but a day to instruct you before you must disembark to Syrus Six.

"I understood that we were going to have more time to get adjusted before we moved into hyperdrive and more time after we woke up to learn to use the symbiotes." Tyson sounded disgruntled and Shaina couldn't blame him. Minister Waynos had given them a very different understanding of the amount of time they would have before attempting this mission. Faron only shrugged, a beautifully fluid motion that looked like a dance step.

"Come."

He turned and swept before them, leading the two officers through a gilded real-wood archway and into the most luxurious room Shaina had ever seen. There was another real-wood floor done in a parquet pattern and real-wood furniture and carvings everywhere she looked. Expensive-looking one-of-a-kind holo-prints and even some genuine, antique-looking oil paintings hung on the round walls, which were covered in a soft, gray moss about a half an inch long that seemed to caress her hand when she ventured to reach out and touch it.

Faron showed them around to several more small but luxurious rooms: a food prep and dining area, several personal chambers, the fresher room where the sonic shower and necessary areas were kept. Each one led into the next in a kind of circular floor plan until they found themselves back where they had started in the central chamber.

"The hypersleep chamber is in the center of the craft. If you wish, you may take off your outer attire and put on the sleep robes provided for your comfort." The Glameron made a delicate one-handed gesture as he spoke and an opening appeared in the curving surface of the wall without a sound. The opening led into a dimly lit chamber where four empty hypersleep tubes stood in a row. Shaina looked at them mistrustfully; they reminded her of the syringes the symbiotes had been in, silver-sleek and utterly foreign looking. Each tube had a rounded front access flap, which was currently standing open, and one small window at eye level for its occupant to look out of.

"Is it time already?" she asked. Instead of answering, Faron handed her a short, plush robe, made of high quality synthi-cotton, that tied at the waist with a sash. He handed a similar if somewhat larger one to Ty, who immediately started stripping out of his pleather jumpsuit to put it on. Shaina tried not to watch as her partner's broad, golden-tan shoulders were revealed, along with his smooth, muscular chest and flat abdomen, corded with muscle. When Tyson pulled the jumpsuit casually down past his slim hips to show the silky trail of black hair that ran from his navel into the low-slung waistband of his snug black briefs, Shaina heard herself make a soft sound, deep in her throat. Ty must have heard the noise too, because he looked up from pulling the jumpsuit down, frowning slightly.

"See something blue, McCullough?" he asked, pulling the jumpsuit the rest of the way off and standing tall to stretch his firm arms over his head. The movement caused all the muscles in his abdomen to stretch and twitch in an absolutely mesmerizing manner and Shaina became suddenly aware that she had been staring at him for nearly a full minute. He had never looked so wild and untamed, so D'Lonian. Her breath was coming a little fast as she answered him.

"No, just thinking. It's my first trip in hyperspace, you know. Will we . . . are there any effects I should know about?"

"It has never been scientifically proven, but many people claim to have a dramatically increased libido after a hypersleep experience," Faron remarked, coming up behind her.

Great, she thought, as though being around Ty wasn't disturbing enough already. Her annoying partner only looked amused at the Glameron's words.

"Aren't you going to put on your robe?" He grinned a little, amber eyes flashing. Blushing furiously, Shaina turned her back to him and began stripping off the black pleather jumpsuit with quick, jerky motions. She could feel Ty's eyes on her back the whole time as she struggled with the sleeves, which seemed to want to cling to her arms.

"Wait, Mistress. Stop, please. You require assistance." The

Glameron's soft voice soothed her somehow and Shaina stopped struggling with the aggravating sleeves and just stood quietly for a moment. "A good slave will notice when his Mistress is in distress and act to help her before she asks," Faron went on in a lecturing tone. "The essence of being the perfect slave is anticipation. You will know what your Mistress needs or desires before she knows it herself. Come, help your Mistress, Tyson."

"What? But I thought you were going to . . ." Shaina protested.

"I don't think I should . . ." Ty said at the same time.

"The lesson begins here." Faron cut them both off in a tone that was almost sharp. "I sense that subservience does not come easily to you, Master Tyson. And allowing yourself to be served comes even less easily and naturally to you, Mistress McCullough," he said, turning toward Shaina, who still stood with her back to Ty. "But you must overcome these inhibitions and allow yourselves to serve and be served. Any falseness between you will be sensed immediately on Syrus Six and the result will be death, both for you and for my beloved Master Paul. So you *must* learn."

"Now, help your Mistress to disrobe, Master Tyson. Gently," he added. Shaina felt the large, warm hands caress her shoulders a bit hesitantly as Ty helped her slip the offending jumpsuit's sleeves off her arms. She stood with her arms crossed over her breasts, feeling glad that she had worn her best matching emerald green bra and panties set, as Ty pulled the suit down her waist and legs.

"Here, Shaina, hold on to me," he instructed in a low voice, as he knelt in front of her and pulled the suit's legs over first one foot and then the other. Wordlessly, she did as he asked, bracing herself with both hands on his warm, golden shoulders to keep her balance while he undressed her like she was a child. The warmth of his body radiating against her legs made Shaina feel weak in the knees and she was very glad the symbiotes weren't working yet. She would've hated for Ty to pick up her thoughts at this particular moment.

When she was standing shivering in only her green underwear, Ty stood behind her and, like a butler, held out the robe for her to slip both arms into the sleeves. Shaina did so and then shivered again as he pulled her against him and reached in front of her to tie the sash at her waist. His warm, masculine scent and the long line of heat from his mostly naked body pressing against her back lit a fire in her lower belly and made her squeeze her thighs together tightly. Goddess . . . she wasn't sure she could stand it.

"Very good, Tyson." Faron's voice seemed to break some kind of a spell and Shaina felt Ty move reluctantly away from her; she missed his warmth immediately. "But you must learn to call her only Mistress. The first name is never an appropriate address for a slave to use for his master or mistress. We will speak more of it later, but for now, our hypersleep tubes await."

The Glameron saw them both comfortably settled in side-by-side tubes and then took the tube on the end for his own. As Shaina looked out of the small window at the front of her tube, she hoped that she was up to this challenge. Not of infiltrating Syrus Six and rescuing the Chancellor's son but of having Ty serve her; she just wasn't sure she could take it.

6

"*Ty, please . . . I need you.*" *Her slender form moved beneath him, all cream and gold in the soft light. She looked so beautiful, like a creature made of moonlight. Her high, generous breasts were tipped with pale pink nipples, and the soft mound of red-dish curls between her slightly parted legs glimmered faintly like spun rubies.*

"What do you need, sweetheart?" he whispered gently, run-ning one hand down her smooth, creamy flank, loving the way she shivered and arched like a cat under his touch.

"Need you inside me, filling me up." She parted her thighs wider and he could see the pouting pink lips of her tender pussy spread wide for him, inviting him in. She was so wet for him, needed him so much. His cock was a throbbing bar of iron, urg-ing him to do what she asked. Urging him to fill her completely and fuck her thoroughly. To Bond with her and make her his forever.

"Fuck me, Ty . . ." she begged, writhing beneath him want-only. He found that he was closer now, the head of his cock rub-

bing along that sweet, slippery flesh. She was hot inside, burning with need for him. "Fuck me," she begged him again. "Fuck me and fill me up. Make me yours . . . always and only yours." With a groan he felt himself giving in, pressing the head of his cock into her slick entrance, feeling her warm wetness envelop him completely as he buried himself to the hilt in her sweet, tight cunt . . .

One dream merged into another. Hypersleep seemed to last forever.

Ty woke up from a strangely familiar dream about his aunt Pinky. He was twelve again and it was about the time she had given him a real live gerbil in its own habitat.

"It's really alive? Not just a 'bot with synthi-fur?" he asked excitedly and Aunt Pinky had nodded her cotton-candy swirl of hair and smiled.

"Got it on sale at the port, honey. The man selling them was going out of business. Look, I got you the food and everything." She held out a box full of green pellets that looked like food re-placements but smelled gross.

"Yuck! He likes to eat this stuff?"

"Sure does. That's choco-dogs and carbo-chug to him." Choco-dogs were his favorite. Aunt Pinky always knew.

"Can I hold him?"

"Sure can. Here . . ." She reached into the tiny square habitat and cupped the squirming bundle of fur in her elegant, long-nailed hand.

"Oh, he's so light and warm! Nothing like a 'bot. I'm gonna call him Mr. Wiggles."

"That's right, honey. Now if you sit on the floor and hold Mr. Wiggles in your skirt, he'll feel safe and get to know you."

"Okay . . ." He sat on the floor of his room and spread out the pale green striped synthi-cotton skirt, which had been an-other birthday present . . .

* * *

No, wait a minute . . . this wasn't right.

Tyson opened his eyes at last in time to see the beveled front of his sleep tube sliding open. The robe he wore was slightly damp with perspiration. Hypersleep raised your body temperature a few degrees and it felt a little like having a fever when you first woke up, he remembered. With a shrug of his broad shoulders, he peeled the robe off.

He tried to piece the rapidly deteriorating dream together . . . something about a gerbil and his aunt Pinky? But he had never had a gerbil or an aunt named Pinky. Choco-dogs made him queasy. And he had certainly never owned or worn a pale green striped skirt. . . .

"*I know you didn't. I did. Loved that skirt . . . gerbil chewed a hole in it and I caught blue holy hell from my mom.*" It took Ty a minute to realize the voice was coming from inside his head. He turned to see the sleep tube next to him slide open and watched as Shaina slowly opened her still-dreamy ocean-green eyes.

"Did you just talk inside my head?" he asked carefully, feeling distinctly strange about asking such a question. It seemed like something you would ask someone in a dream. He remembered some of the dreams he'd been having before the one about Mr. Wiggles and looked closely at Shaina. Was he still dreaming?

"I don't know. Did I?" Her face was still relaxed from the utter oblivion of hypersleep.

"I think you did," Ty told her, beginning to feel a bit more awake himself. Her creamy skin was flushed, he noticed, and wisps of her fiery red hair had begun to curl into tiny love-tendrils around her pointed, kittenish face. The white synthi-cotton robe she wore was damp and nearly transparent. He could clearly see the full curves of her breasts outlined in the emerald green of her bra. Her nipples were erect and pressing tantalizingly against the fabric. Suddenly, his cock felt like a bar of lead inside his briefs. *Take it easy. Just the aftereffects of hypersleep,* he thought, and this time he was reasonably sure the voice in his head was just his own internal monologue.

"What aftereffects?" Shaina looked at him and Tyson shook his head mutely. Had she caught his thought? "I had the strangest dream . . ." she whispered, still seemingly half to herself. "I was back in Second School and there was this girl in my class . . . Treena Tist, who I really liked. Only everybody called her . . ."

"Treena Tits because she had the biggest . . . wait a minute. That's my memory, not yours."

Tyson felt fully awake now and more than a little disturbed. What was going on?

"Ah, I see the symbiotes are becoming active. You have been sharing dreams." The Glameron's soft voice broke into Tyson's agitated thoughts.

"Wait a minute, when we agreed to be injected with these things, nobody said anything about sharing dreams," Ty pointed out.

"I can see why you liked Treena. She was really pretty."

"Could you please stop that for a minute?" he snapped irritably, looking at Shaina. Her eyes were still half-lidded and he guessed that she was having a difficult time shaking off the hypersleep. To make matters worse, he was still fiercely aroused and seeing Shaina leaning against the side of her sleep tube with that dreamy expression on her face, like a woman who'd just woken up after a night of hard loving, didn't help any. God, he just wanted to kiss her, just once. He wanted to taste those soft, pink lips . . .

"Why don't you?" she whispered in his mind. She thought she was still dreaming, Ty realized, but he couldn't help himself. Just one kiss . . . He stepped forward and pulled her unresisting body into his arms. She was soft and warm and smelled of that feminine musk that drove him crazy with need. He low-

ered his head and took her mouth the way he'd wanted to from the first time he saw her, burying his large hands in her glorious tumble of flame-colored hair and tilting her face up so that he could explore her lips thoroughly, claim her completely.

"Mmmm," Ty heard her purr through the symbi-link. She wanted this as much as he did, he suddenly understood. She felt the same fire, the same need whenever they touched. He crushed her against him. She felt so fragile and soft in his arms. He wanted to own her . . . to possess her completely. Wanted to Bond with her. He knew it was the dominant D'Lonian in him coming out, but he couldn't help it. Inside his head, he could hear Shaina hoping that this dream would never end.

"It's no dream, Shaina. It's real. I want you. I've always wanted you. I've always known you should belong to me . . ." His cock throbbed demandingly and he suddenly wanted to rip open her robe, peel down that flimsy little bra, and suck her ripe pink nipples until she screamed. Wanted to take her here and now, to spread her legs, mount her, fill her, fuck her until she moaned and begged for more . . . until she belonged to him completely and forever.

"Wait a minute . . . Not a dream?" Shaina suddenly stiffened in his arms and Ty felt a current of fear like a jolt of electricity through their link. Her eyes widened as she came fully awake. She slid out of his arms, although he didn't want to let her go, and backed carefully away from him, her frightened green eyes never leaving his face. Tyson realized with an inward wince that she must have heard his last thought.

"Oh my Goddess . . . can't believe . . ." Shaina's thoughts were nearly inarticulate and the air in the small sleep chamber was suddenly charged with nervous tension.

"I . . . uh, didn't mean that the way it sounded." He approached her carefully as she continued to back away. "Look, McCullough, I'm sorry."

She shook her head mutely. She was thinking that he looked

like some kind of a wild animal with his hair sticking up all over the place and his eyes like molten gold in his dark face. His teeth were so white and sharp . . . she had heard rumors about D'Lonian men and she wondered if they were true.

"*What rumors? That we bite our women's heads off during mating?*" Ty thought at her, fiercely sarcastic. He had never pegged Shaina as being racist.

"I'm *not* racist! *Just scared . . .*" she finished to herself but Ty heard it. Of course he did. He heard everything and so did Shaina . . .

"You," he roared, turning to the Glameron, who was standing quietly by and watching them as though he was viewing a particularly engrossing vid. "A little help here, damn it!"

"Certainly." Faron stepped forward calmly and turned first to Shaina. "Mistress McCullough, Master Tyson is enamored of you and has been from the first moment he met you. His caring and deep concern for your safety are what causes him to treat you in a less than civil manner sometimes."

"Master Tyson,"—he turned back to Ty—"Mistress McCullough both desires and fears you. Her fear stems from both inexperience and the somewhat exaggerated rumors she has heard about the extreme sexual appetites of D'Lonians, which I understand makes up a large part of your heritage. Were she not a virgin . . ."

"That's not exactly what I meant," Tyson growled, cutting off the Glameron's calm speech. "What I meant was how do we turn it off?" Across the room, Shaina was rapidly reciting prime numbers inside her head to keep from thinking any embarrassing thoughts he might overhear, but her face was red with mortification at Faron's blunt revelations. Ty wondered if she really was a virgin . . .

"Yes, I bloody well am. Does that make you feel happy? Or is it more like smugly superior? Just one more thing that you're good at that I'm *not*," Shaina yelled at him, her face crumpling into tears of embarrassment. Damn it all to hell, now he had made her cry when hurting her was the last thing Ty ever wanted to do.

"How do we turn it off?" he demanded, feeling ready to strangle somebody, preferably Minister Waynos, who had talked them into this in the first place. But the fat little bastard was light-years away at this point. Through the symbi-link he could hear Shaina thinking much the same thing. *Well, great minds think alike,* he thought, *although they don't usually have to hear each other do it.* He sighed.

"I am afraid, Master Tyson, that there is no way to 'turn it off,' as you put it, but there are techniques for controlling what messages you send through your link." The Glameron still spoke as mildly and calmly as if they were standing around discussing the weather instead of wallowing in each other's most embarrassing private thoughts.

"Okay, so gimme a technique. In case you didn't notice, we're having kind of a rough time over here. And so far you're not helping it any." Tyson's voice was tense.

"As you desire, so I shall serve. Come, place your hands in mine and try to clear your minds." Not knowing what else to do, Tyson seized the Glameron's hand angrily and squeezed, probably harder than necessary; Faron winced slightly but said nothing. Feeling slightly ashamed of himself, Ty eased up. They stood there, waiting for Shaina, who was still pressed against the far wall of the room looking at them mistrustfully, with tears drying on her cheeks.

The wall of the sleep chamber was covered with the same, pale gray moss as the other walls of the ship. Ty saw her turn her cheek against the soft touch of the moss as though for comfort. The gesture tore at his heart; he had never wanted to hurt or scare her, it was just that his need for this woman was so damn strong . . .

"*Shaina . . .*" he thought and then tried again out loud. "I'm sorry, McCullough. Please . . ." He didn't know what else to

say. Obviously he had scared her to death with his strong emotions and his desire to possess her. "It was just the aftereffects
of the hypersleep talking, Shaina. I'm sorry if I scared you," he
said desperately, although it was untrue. She obviously wasn't
ready to reciprocate his emotions, and until she was, he would
just have to keep them under wraps. If these damned symbiotes
would let him, that was.

"Come, dear one." Faron's voice was soft and coaxing. "It is
difficult to have another in your head for the first time. Let me
help you."

Shaina straightened and wiped the tears from her cheeks in
quick, jerky motions. "I don't feel like I can trust you now,
Faron," she said quietly. "After what you told Tyson about
me . . ."

"Child, I am sorry that I revealed your secret, but you must
understand that it was not a secret you could be allowed to
keep."

"I don't see why not. It's no one's business but mine." She
raised her chin defiantly and stared at the constantly changing,
jewellike eyes of the Glameron, which swirled green and amber
alternately. Faron stared calmly back.

"Have you really so little understanding of what will be expected of you on Syrus Six?" he asked sternly. "You cannot ab-
stain there and expect to be believed. If your innocence is
suspected, your lie will be exposed and you will be found out
and killed. Better for your partner to know now than have to
guess later at some critical time when both your lives and the
life of young Master Paul hang in the balance. Do you see?"

"I . . . I guess so. But that doesn't mean I have to like it."
Shaina frowned and took a deep breath. Ty could see her gathering herself for the ordeal ahead. "Can you really help us control this?"

"It is a certainty. Come, take my hand." Reluctantly, Shaina
did so. Inwardly, Tyson breathed a sigh of relief.

"Now," the Glameron said. They stood in a loose circle, both holding hands with Faron, although Ty made sure not to touch Shaina and he noticed she was equally careful not to touch him. "Close your eyes and clear your minds of everything but what I tell you. I want you to picture a blank white wall. Nothing has ever been written there. It is smooth and clean as an eggshell curving in the void of your minds . . ."

Tyson began to see the wall that the Glameron spoke of. It curved across his mind looking like the huge white barrier between the regular and private port sector back home.

"Good, Master Tyson, a very apt analogy," Faron murmured. "Now behind this wall is where you will keep your private thoughts. When you want to send a thought to one another, I want you to picture what you are saying being written in bold black lettering on the wall. The script that you see is all that you will send through your link. Master Tyson, you will attempt this first."

"I . . . don't know if I should." Ty had never felt so uncertain of himself before. He only knew he didn't want to hurt Shaina any worse than he already had. The Glameron didn't answer him in words but only squeezed his hand slightly. Ty found the gesture oddly reassuring. Hesitantly, he began to picture a black marking tube writing words on the vast, curving expanse of the blank white wall in his mind.

"Shaina, I don't know what to say." He concentrated fiercely on only sending the words and not the emotions he felt for her. After a moment, he heard her answer.

"I don't either."

Now that he was calmly concentrating, Ty noticed that her mental voice left a very distinctive flavor on the back of his tongue, sweet and a little salty. It was the way he had always imagined her soft little cunt would taste. He was very careful to keep this particular thought behind the white wall. *"You taste good inside my head, sweet."*

"You taste spicy." Unexpectedly, he felt her soft, cool hand slip into his. Ty dared to open his eyes and look at her. Her hair was tousled and her eyes were still a little puffy from crying. Her full lips were swollen from the passionate kiss they had shared earlier. God, she was beautiful.

"Thank you."

Hastily Ty closed his eyes and concentrated on the wall.

At last Faron declared himself satisfied with their progress. "Master, Mistress, I shall prepare nourishment for you if it would please you both to step into the fresher and cleanse yourselves. I will provide appropriate clothing for both of you after we eat and your real lessons will begin. I warn you, however, that mastering the mannerisms and society of Syrus Six will not be quite as easy as mastering the symbiotes."

Tyson groaned as he stumbled off to the fresher to take a much needed shower. If the second lesson was harder than the first one, he wasn't sure he could take it. Already he felt wrung out emotionally and physically and all he'd done for the past hour and a half was hold hands with Shaina and think really hard.

_____

7

Lunch—Shaina assumed it was lunchtime, that was what her body clock told her anyway—was a silent meal. She didn't know about Tyson, but she was concentrating fiercely on keeping her private thoughts behind the big white wall. To her it looked like something out of an educational vid she'd once seen in Second School about the atmosphere domes the first spacers had erected on the Earth's moon.

Mostly, she wanted desperately to examine the emotions she'd felt coming from Ty during the searing kiss they had shared. The passion and intensity she'd felt coming from him, the desire to possess her utterly, was both frightening and intriguing. But, she reminded herself, everything he had said and felt was just an aftereffect of the hypersleep—he'd said so himself. She knew *she* had certainly woken up feeling frisky, which was how she ended up in a lip-lock with her aggravating partner in the first place. Still, it was hard to also discount what Faron had told them both . . . There were stories about D'Lonian males—that they mated for life, that they were the most dominant and relentless lovers . . . but Shaina wasn't quite sure if she believed all that . . .

"Not quite sure you believe what?" Ty was looking curiously at her from across the small table covered with containers holding small quantities of high-energy food supplements, and Shaina realized she'd been projecting through the link again. Oh Goddess, would she ever get used to these bloody, doubledamned symbiotes?

"Nothing. Just . . . nothing."

"In the second personal chamber you will find appropriate clothing for your role as a Mistress and slave owner on Syrus Six. Please put it on and return to the ship's central chamber," Faron said. "Master Tyson and I will meet you there."

"Fine." Shaina left the food prep area quickly and went to find her costume. It was, as the Glameron had promised, laid out on a plush mattress that was furred with the same soft, comforting gray moss that lined the walls. Faron had explained that the moss was a mood sensor, genetically engineered to detect the emotions of the person touching it and produce the necessary endorphins to promote a sense of peaceful calm. Shaina wished she could lie on the mattress and let it soothe and comfort her until she felt composed but she knew there was no time. They only had the rest of this day period to learn their roles. By the next time cycle they would be orbiting Syrus Six and their deception would begin. Reluctantly, she picked up her costume and started putting it on.

A half-cup gold- and jewel-encrusted bustier was first. Looking at it lying on the bed, Shaina estimated that it was easily worth more than she made as a Peace Control Officer in an entire solar year. When she wiggled into it, she was dismayed to realize that the jeweled cups didn't actually cover her breasts at all. Instead, they acted as a type of support to present them for public display, thrusting them up and out in a way that was almost obscene. Wearing it, Shaina felt like her breasts were some sort of exotic fruit, jiggling on a tray.

Luckily, a short, tight jacket made of shimmering golden cloth was also included in the costume. Shaina put it on and looked for a way to fasten it but there were no buttons or zippers or magno strips to be found, nothing but a thin, gold chain to connect one lapel to the other. It was just as well, she reflected unhappily; the jacket wouldn't completely close over her breasts anyway. The best she could do was to hook the chain and try to be careful how she moved her arms. The slightest motion in any direction caused the jacket to gape and presented a full view of her nipples, which were rubbed erect by the scratchy golden fabric barely covering them.

Time to put on the bottom half of this mess now. At least, Shaina reflected, it couldn't be much worse than the top.

She was wrong.

At first it didn't look so bad. There was a pair of bikini-cut golden jewel-encrusted panties that matched the bustier, which Shaina thought had to be the most uncomfortable thing she had ever put on. When she did pull them up, she noticed there was a long split running along the front of the panties. For further display or easy access, she wondered uneasily. Or maybe for both? Well, at least they weren't *completely* crotchless.

She was relieved to see that a long golden skirt, made of the same material as the jacket, was provided to go over the peekaboo panties. Her relief was short-lived, because she soon discovered that a long slit ran from hem to waist in the very front of the skirt as well. The skirt had a low waist that showed off her midriff and what looked like the biggest genuine diamond she had ever seen was provided as a belly jewel. The skirt flared out from her hips and had a long, flowing train that would drag on the floor behind her. Shaina wondered briefly if Ty was supposed to walk behind her and hold it up, like the universe's largest flower girl at a joining ceremony. The thought made her suppress a smile. Maybe she would just let the train drag. She would just have to remember to keep her legs crossed at all times lest she flash anyone who happened to be looking at her.

Next, came golden high-heeled, calf-length boots that felt like they were made of the hide of some exotic animal. The boots hugged her legs lovingly, actually massaging her calves like a lover's hands, Shaina realized after a moment. They were easily the softest and most comfortable thing she had on and they almost made the rest of this get-up worth it. Almost.

Surveying herself in the full-length holo-viewer, Shaina realized that this gold, jewel-encrusted monstrosity made her happy hooker outfit of a few nights back look as prim as a First School girl's uniform. There were a few golden hair pins with rubies and diamonds as big as the end of her thumb left over and she decided to try an updo to complete her look.

Struggling with her hair, her arms raised over her head and her breasts completely exposed, it took her a while to notice that Ty had entered her room and was standing directly behind her, watching her do battle with her wayward tresses.

"Ty! What are you doing here?" She lowered her arms so fast that the golden bustier pinched her. "Ouch! You made me hurt myself!" she scolded nervously.

"I'm in considerable pain myself. You look gorgeous," he answered inside her head, giving her that feral grin that showed his sharp, white teeth. Shaina wished he wouldn't do that until it became absolutely necessary. There was a kind of intimacy in thought communication that was lacking in its verbal counterpart. It was much harder to lie, for one thing.

"Lie about what?" At least he was talking out loud.

"Nothing." She turned to face him, making sure to keep her arms down and her thighs together. At this rate, she'd be walking like a 'bot the entire time she wore this outfit, trying to hide herself.

"Don't hide anything. Not from me." He stepped forward

and pulled the edges of her golden jacket apart, revealing her flushed breasts and nipples rubbed erect by the scratchy fabric. She felt frozen in place, unable to move. "Beautiful." Ty leaned down to plant soft kisses on the top of each breast before letting the jacket fall back into place.

"Ty . . . you can't just . . ." She was at a loss for words but he understood her meaning anyway.

"Sorry, sweetheart, but it's D'Lonian custom to acknowledge beauty when we see it. And I can't take my eyes off you in that outfit."

"Well, it's the most uncomfortable thing I've ever . . ." she began, backing away from him. Then she caught sight of Ty's costume and the problems she was having with her own were driven right out of her head.

The top of his outfit consisted of two wide black leather straps that crisscrossed his broad, muscular chest diagonally and were joined with a round platinum ring in the center. Attached to the ring was a long leather strap that hung down, brushing Ty's corded abdominal muscles as he breathed and moved. There was a small loop at the end of this strap. Shaina stared at it blankly for a moment.

"*It's a leash,*" Ty whispered through the symbi-link and she tasted a little of his outrage at having to wear such a ridiculous thing. "*It was either the leash or the pain collar and I absolutely refused to wear that.*"

"Afraid I might have to discipline you to keep you in line?" She couldn't resist taunting him a little, trying to take the edge off the tension that was building between them in the small room.

"Not in the least. I just didn't like the way it felt. Choked me."

The bottom part of his outfit, Shaina saw, was just a simple pair of black leather pants cut low enough to show his hipbones in front and tight enough to make his firm ass look truly spectacular. There was an enormous bulge in the front of the pants that she tried hard not to stare at. Was that due to her outfit? He had said D'Lonians acknowledged beauty . . . She tried not to think about it and noticed instead the soft-looking black leather boots that completed his outfit.

"I . . . ah . . . like yours better than mine. Despite the leash." Actually, Shaina rather liked the leash. At least it gave her the illusion of control. *Wonder what it would feel like to wear that?* She saw Tyson's amber eyes flash as he caught her thought.

"This is pretty tame, actually. Faron tells me that I may have to wear a kind of . . . uh, harness once we get topside. It didn't sound too pleasant." He frowned and dark brows shadowed the hot golden eyes.

"I'm sorry." Shaina suddenly felt terribly guilty. "I got you into this. You're only here because of me."

"Yes."

"I mean, these outfits . . . they're crazy, completely insane. But being dressed like this is making it all seem so real. When I volunteered for this in the first place I don't think I really realized what would be expected of me . . . of us, I mean."

"You still don't," Tyson said grimly. "Come into the central chamber. Faron is going to brief us and then maybe you'll have more of an idea."

Goddess . . . Shaina took a deep breath and willed the tears that were suddenly right behind her eyes to recede. What had she done?

"Hey." With a softer tone, Ty turned back towards her and took her awkwardly in his arms. "It's okay, McCullough. Whatever happens, it's going to be okay."

8

"From the moment you step foot on Syrus Six, you must attend your Mistress at all times. You will obey her every command, you will anticipate her every wish, you will serve her in any way that she requires and you will *take pleasure* in it." Faron's voice was as close to harsh as Tyson had ever heard it. The Glameron was standing in the center of the round central chamber and lecturing them both. Shaina sat in one of the comfortable real-wood chairs, but Ty was kneeling on the real-wood floor at Shaina's feet—the only proper position for a slave, Faron insisted—and his knees were beginning to ache.

"Look." Holding on to his temper with both hands, he shifted to try and get into a more comfortable position. "I know we have to be convincing, but is it really necessary for me to act so ... I don't know ..."

"*Slavishly* devoted to me?" Shaina finished for him, holding one slim hand over her mouth. He knew she was trying to suppress a smile.

"*You're enjoying this entirely too much,*" he shot at her through their symbi-link. She didn't answer, only widened her green eyes and pressed her fingertips to her chest in a "who, me?" gesture. Ty grinned and shook his head.

"Master Tyson, it is absolutely essential that you are utterly and completely devoted to your mistress. You must give your-self to her body and soul without reservation and it must be ob-vious to anyone watching you." Faron's tone was emphatic. "It *must* be obvious because you have elected to present yourself as a Love slave."

"A what?" This got Ty's attention, and Shaina looked inter-ested, too.

"A Love slave. You have refused to wear the pain-inducing collar most Masters employ to keep their slaves in check. Only a very trustworthy and loved slave, one who has proven his loyalty and worth many times over, can be trusted without the collar. A Love slave."

"Love slave, hmm. That has definite possibilities." Ty grinned at Shaina, who blushed and looked down at her hands

"It is no laughing matter." The Glameron's tone was sharp. "Please be serious, both of you. You must begin acting as Mis-tress and slave. Tyson, you will follow your Mistress every-where unless she dismisses you. You will keep your eyes down and you will not speak unless spoken to. You will help her bathe and dress with careful attention to detail. You will eat on the floor at her feet and you will sleep in her chamber at the foot of her bed unless she requires your services."

"Goddess . . ." This from Shaina, who was now nearly scar-let with embarrassment.

"Mistress McCullough," Faron rounded on her. "This will never do! You must get over your embarrassment *now*. Tyson will be acting as your pleasure slave and as such he will service you sexually both in private and in public. Do you under-stand?"

"I . . . yes. I understand. But do they really . . . in public, I mean?"

"Child," Faron's voice was weary and infinitely gentle. "Yes. The Executor's Palace is dedicated entirely to sensual and sexual pleasure. In every room, no matter the activity in progress— eating, gaming, sleeping—there is always the pursuit of sexual pleasure as well. Everyone you see will be engaged in these activities; and if you and Tyson do not, then you will appear suspicious. I understand that you want to preserve your innocence, but preserving your life and the lives of your partner, and Master Paul when you find him, *must* take precedence."

Shaina bowed her head, taking the lecture in silence, and Tyson felt sorry for her suddenly. True, he wanted her, had wanted her from the first moment he laid eyes on her, but not like this . . .

"I don't want your pity." Her green eyes flashed at him and he sighed.

"Fine. I just don't like the idea of something like this being forced on you. Maybe we can try and fake at least some of it."

"Really? Do you think that's possible?" Her eyes were softer now, filled with a tentative hope. She really was afraid of him, Tyson realized, at least in *that* way. He wished privately that he could make her understand that despite his D'Lonian heritage he wasn't just some sexual animal that wanted to ravage and rape, that he would never do anything to hurt her.

"We'll try."

"All right." Faron had waited patiently throughout their symbi-link exchange and Ty reverted to verbal conversation. "I understand the public display thing, but why did you say I would have to . . . uh . . . service McCullough in public *and* in private?" They both looked at Faron expectantly. The Glameron sighed and shook his head.

"Goddess give me strength. Because, Master, Mistress, no place *is* private at the Executor's Pleasure Palace. There are surveillance devices everywhere. Why else would the Chancellor go to the trouble and expense of having you both injected with symbiotes? No matter how private your chamber may appear, be assured that your every move is being recorded. In fact, the most entertaining displays are shown in the viewing room on a continuous holo-loop. Do you begin to see?"

"I think we get the picture," Ty answered for both of them.

"And can you do this? Goddess knows I would go myself if my face were not already known and entered in the memory loops there. My children"—Faron's voice grew softer—"I understand how difficult this is for you both. When a dominant and submissive change roles in a relationship, it always makes for a difficult time."

"Wait a minute. Who said anything about Shaina and me being dominant or submissive?" He shifted on the floor once again. Damn, it was really hard, but he guessed he'd better get used to it.

Faron laughed gently. "Would you say to me, Master Tyson, that you would rather wear the leash than hold it?"

"Well no, but who would?" Ty looked bewildered.

"Mistress McCullough would," the Glameron answered softly, looking at Shaina with his endlessly swirling eyes. "She would wear the leash and submit to you. It would be far more suited to her emotional needs than it is to yours. If your roles could be reversed in this, then you might be a good deal more convincing. Then again, if you played your true roles in such a setting, for even a short period of time, I wonder if you would ever be able to relinquish them."

"Ty may be dominant but I'm *not* a submissive." Shaina turned red all over again and shifted in her seat, voice forceful.

"*Say that through the link,*" Tyson dared her, looking up from his seat on the floor to challenge her with his eyes.

"I . . . I don't want to."

"*You can't. You're the one who noticed how hard it is to lie this way.*"

"*Get back to the business at hand.*"

Shaina shifted in her seat uncomfortably again, the long, golden split skirt rustling as she moved. Tyson noticed that throughout their conversation she had been especially careful to keep her legs together and her arms down. He remembered how beautiful and full her creamy breasts had looked pushed up on display in the golden bustier, and his leather pants began to get uncomfortably tight as he wished he had sucked her nipples instead of just kissing the tops of her breasts. "Gladly, Mistress." He scooted closer to her chair so that he could take her booted feet in his lap. Slowly, he began to ease the soft golden boots down her legs.

"Tyson!" she protested, trying to pull her legs away.

"No, Mistress McCullough, allow your slave to service you. His touch on your body must become as natural to you as your own," Faron said sternly, watching their performance with a critical eye. "In fact, I perceive that the two of you are not nearly as comfortable with each other as you should be to play these roles believably. Stand at once, both of you."

Shaina stood immediately. Giving the Glameron an unfriendly glare, Tyson did as well. He didn't like being ordered around.

"Well?" he said when he and Shaina were standing side by side, looking expectantly at their instructor.

"Face each other," Faron said. "Now, Tyson, touch your Mistress."

Uncertain of what he was supposed to do, Tyson laid a hand on one slight shoulder. He felt Shaina trembling with tension beneath his touch, thrumming under his hand like a plucked string. Again he became aware of her fear and trepidation about getting too close to him, of letting herself be too vulnerable.

"Shaina, I would never hurt you, I swear." He touched her other shoulder as well, wanting to ease her anxiety.

"I . . . I'm not afraid of you, Ty." He could taste her desper-

ate desire to make both him and herself believe it. Faron's voice broke into their intense concentration.

"Touch her not as a stranger, Tyson," the Glameron instructed sternly. "Touch her as a lover, as a part of your own body, for that is what she must become to you."

"All right." Tyson frowned briefly at Faron and then turned his attention back to his partner. *"Sorry, McCullough."*

"That's okay. Just . . . just do what you have to do." She squeezed her eyes tightly shut and bit her lip as though trying to prepare herself for some savage sexual attack. The look on her face, the outright fear, squeezed Tyson's heart. Instead of groping her body or fondling her breasts as she so clearly expected, he cradled her beautiful face in his hands and leaned in to give her a gentle kiss on the lips.

"What . . . ?" Shaina's eyes flew open at the tender touch and Ty stroked along the smooth white column of her neck, letting his fingers trail over her collarbones and shoulders in a leisurely fashion.

"Just following orders, sweetheart." Smiling, he looked down into her ocean-green eyes. He ran his hands lower, grazing over the gold jacket she wore, feeling the hard little nubs of her nipples under the thin, scratchy fabric. Again she shivered beneath his touch but this time he knew the shiver, though still half fear, was also half pleasure. Still lower his hands traveled until he was stroking the stiff cloth of her outer skirt. Parting it at the center slit, he moved his hands inside.

"Ty . . ." She bit her lip again as his palm caressed the soft skin of her thighs, his thumbs brushing perilously close to the golden panties.

"Want me to stop?" She didn't answer—couldn't answer, he realized, and he took her silence for assent. Gently, he rested one large palm against the front panel of her panties, feeling the opening in the fabric and the soft, damp mound of curls that it

revealed. Warm, wet heat pulsed beneath his hand and he couldn't help letting one finger slide gently along her slit, dipping inward to caress her slippery flesh, gliding over her tender clitoris, making her jerk against him and cry out in helpless pleasure. God, her skin was so sweet and moist. He ached to drop to his knees before her, spread the pink outer lips of her pussy wide and tongue her warm, wet folds. To kiss her and suck her and lick her until she couldn't stand the pleasure and begged him to take her, to make her his. He wanted to Bond with her so damn badly, to make her belong to him . . .

"Bond how? I don't understand." Eyes wide, her pupils dilated with fear and desire, and a look of confusion came over her face. Ty realized she must have caught his last thought.

"Nothing." He abruptly dropped his hand and stepped back a little.

"That was excellent, Tyson," Ty jumped Faron's voice. He had forgotten the Glameron was even there. When he was touching Shaina, the whole universe narrowed down to just the two of them, to her warmth against him and their need for each other. A need she still stubbornly refused to acknowledge.

"It is Mistress McCullough's turn now," Faron said. Tyson watched his partner closely as she blushed almost as red as her hair.

"All right." Tentatively, she reached out with one slender hand and caressed his dark hair back from his forehead. It was a timid touch and it made him impatient.

"I won't bite, McCullough."

"Don't rush me! Close your eyes; this is too hard with you watching me."

"Fine." He did as she asked and after a moment he felt her hand return. She was more sure of herself this time. Shaina traced over his heavy brows and dark lashes with feather-light strokes that sent a chill of anticipation down his spine. She explored the bridge of his sharp nose and his high cheekbones

and then he felt one curious finger tracing his lips. Ty opened his mouth and sucked the inquisitive digit inside, stroking it with his tongue and licking gently, hearing a long, low sigh fall out of her as he did.

"Want to lick you all over, sweetheart." He opened his eyes at last to see her watching him, fascination and need written all over her sweet face.

"Ty . . ." Withdrawing her finger, she moved her hands down to caress his neck and shoulders, to feel the tense muscles under her palms. He had to close his eyes again as her fingers slid over his chest and nipples, flicking the flat, coppery disks lightly before continuing down his abdomen to the straining bulge in his tight leather pants.

"Go on, Mistress McCullough. He is your property. Every part of him belongs to you," Ty heard Faron's voice encouraging her. Still he felt her hesitate.

"Go on, Shaina." He made his mental tone as gentle as he could although his nerves were in overdrive. *"Touch me if you want to. Don't be afraid."*

"I'm not afraid!" She rose to the bait as Ty had known she would and he felt her slim fingers tracing his shaft and then grasping him fully through the tight leather. He had to hold himself back forcibly as she stroked him, wishing he could make the leather between them disappear so he could feel her cool hand encircle his naked cock. He could hear her wondering if he was really *that* big. He was about to answer through their link when Faron interrupted them.

"That will do, my children." At the Glameron's voice, Shaina's hand fell away, leaving Ty aching with need and frustration. "You are more familiar with each other now. Remember this lesson. Now you must make ready to go. Syrus Six is fast approaching."

They stepped apart awkwardly and Shaina wouldn't meet Ty's eyes.

"What do you think, McCullough? Are we ready to go?" He tried to keep the mood light despite the rigid ache in his pants.

"Absolutely." She risked a glance at his face. "Maybe... maybe owning a pleasure slave won't be so bad after all."

Privately, Tyson thought that *being* a pleasure slave might not be so bad if it meant getting to touch Shaina all the time and feeling her hands on his body as well.

9

"Everything you need has already been transported to the Palace. Master Tyson, you have the idol of Master Paul?" They were standing outside the entrance to the *She-Creature*'s lavender shuttle, about to be taken to the surface of Syrus Six, but Faron seemed anxious to give them one more going-over before they left.

"Gave it to Shai...I mean, my Mistress. No pockets in these things." Tyson indicated the skintight black leather slave pants with a shrug.

"I have it here," Shaina, dressed in her "rich Mistress" outfit, dug in her velour backpack, which she had refused to relinquish, and pulled out a tiny figure barely three inches high. It looked like an action figure of a young man with a pleasant, if ordinary-looking, face and bright, jewellike eyes.

"And you remember the password?" the Glameron asked anxiously.

"Zibathorpe." Shaina had to quickly set the figure down on the floor outside the shuttle before it grew rapidly to look exactly like the man it was made to resemble. The figure looked extremely lifelike except that it didn't move or talk—the perfect decoy. It reminded Shaina of the figures in an old-fashioned wax museum she had gone to on a First School class field trip.

"Remember, if Paul is in the vicinity, the idol will begin to glow. It is impregnated with his DNA and will respond to his proximity. It need not be life-size to indicate his presence, however," Faron assured them.

"Good, because if everyone is watching all the time . . ." Tyson gestured at the life-size figure. "Blowing him up like that could get awkward."

"No kidding." Aloud she said, "Eprohtabiz" and the idol once more shrank to the size of an action figure. She picked it up and put it back into her knapsack.

"The idol will also act as a communication device with the *She-Creature,* but you must use it sparingly. Every time you contact me, you risk being found out. If you find Paul, the easiest way to proceed is to make an offer for him and try to buy him. The Chancellor has provided you with an established line of credit that ought to allow you to purchase him at any price." Shaina rubbed her newly credited right thumbprint with her index finger as Faron spoke. The matter of changing her thumbprint to match the new identity she had been provided with had been surprisingly simple and excruciatingly painful. Her thumb still throbbed a little every time she flexed it.

"What if whoever has him won't sell?" Ty turned to Faron.

Faron looked grim. "Then you must do your best to steal him, although it may not be easy. The Palace is heavily guarded at all times and the penalty for stealing another Master's pleasure slave is instant death. If you play your parts well, however, no one will have cause to suspect you. And now you must go. I will be in constant readiness and keep the ship in the closest orbit around Syrus Six that can be managed. I will pray hourly to the Goddess for your success and safety. Farewell."

As he spoke, Faron was herding them both into the shuttle

and seeing them safely buckled in. The door whooshed shut and Shaina found herself once more in the plush, monochrome lavender shuttle hurtling towards an uncertain destination.

Trying to distract her mind, she wondered briefly about the color design of the shuttle. Who would want to make everything the exact same shade of lavender? Nervously she closed her eyes and tried to relax for the short journey, listening to the hiss of air through the strangely shaped silver ventilation ducts above her head on the lavender walls. Finally, though, the silence got to her and she had to talk.

"Well, we're on our way." She opened her eyes with a sigh and looked at Ty. "Remember your story?"

"I was born on D'Lonia of a human mother and a D'Lonian father. When my parents died, my father's family disowned me as a half-breed." Ty's eyes flickered briefly, as though with some internal pain, and then he sighed and continued. "I was sold into slavery and trained as a bodyguard and pleasure slave. I was sold to your family at the age of sixteen solar years and I have belonged to you ever since your thirteenth solar birth year when I became your personal slave. Oh, and my name is Tyber," Ty recited rapidly. "What about you? Ready to act the part?"

"Absolutely." Shaina tossed her head and put what she hoped was a bored, rich-girl expression on her face. "I'm Meshandra Sender of the Second House Senders of Rigel Five. We made all our money mining the asteroid belts and this is my first trip to the Pleasure Planet. It's my coming-of-age gift." She was quiet for a moment and then, because it was already beginning to seem easier to say difficult things mind to mind. *"Ty, I'm scared."*

"You can do this, Shaina. You've been undercover before." Aloud he added, "You made a damn fine hooker and I'm sure you'll make a damn fine Mistress."

"I was *supposed* to be a university student."

"Well, you could have fooled me. Certainly fooled that Centaurian." He grinned at her, that feral, D'Lonian grin that had always made her so uncomfortable. But Shaina found that she wasn't quite so unnerved by it as she had been in the past. The low, female voice of the shuttle suddenly spoke aloud.

"Arrival on Syrus Six is complete. Repeat, arrival on Syrus Six is complete."

"Here we go." She unbuckled the tangle of belts that held her in place and turned a bit awkwardly to take Ty's leash as they stood.

"Yes, Mistress," he said, blandly as the shuttle door whooshed open.

The first thing that met Shaina's eyes was an impossibly long marble corridor stretching straight out from the shuttle door and as far as she could see to the left and right as well. The marble was jet black with veins of what appeared to be pure platinum and viridian running through it. Recessed lighting in the form of iridescent glows shimmered faintly at the corners of the massive area, which was completely undecorated. But the glow-light picked out the veins of precious metals and minerals in the marble, causing everything to shimmer ever so slightly at the edges of her vision. Shaina shook her head and blinked, and noticed Tyson doing the same.

"Weird effect. Like being inside someone else's dream."

"Well, we both know what that's like." Stepping carefully out of the shuttle, she spoke aloud for the benefit of any listening devices. "Come, Tyber. You know I hate it when you drag behind me like that."

"Yes, Mistress." Shaina had the feeling he was about to add something else, no doubt sarcastic, via their symbi-link when a voice almost at her elbow startled her so much she dropped Ty's leash.

"That's a very fine specimen you have there, Mistress. Not

many are brave enough to take a D'Lonian to slave," the deep voice said.

"Oh!" Shaina let out a little shriek of fear as part of the marble wall seemed to move and come towards them. Instantly, Ty was between her and the speaker, crouched in a fighter's stance, his amber eyes narrowed, his muscles bunched and twitching with readiness.

"Well, he *is* dangerous, isn't he? And no pain collar, I see. A Love slave then. Are you sure that is wise, little Mistress?" the voice continued very mildly. Now Shaina could see that the person speaking to them wasn't part of the wall at all, but merely a tall, thin humanoid who was the exact same color as the black marble walls and floors. The humanoid's skin even shimmered slightly in the light of the iridescent glows as he (or she) walked slowly toward them. He was stone bald and only his eyes, glowing a mild red, were a different color than the glow surrounding them.

"Who . . . who are you?" She hoped her voice didn't sound too squeaky. So much for her bored, jaded rich-girl façade. She hadn't been on Syrus Six for two minutes and already she was acting like a rube from downplanet.

"Ah, it must be your first visit to our lovely world or I would not have shocked you so." The tall, thin being bowed gracefully. "Forgive me, little Mistress. I am T'lar and I will be your concierge during what we hope will be a most delightful stay here in the Executor's Palace. You can safely call off your slave now. I assure you, I mean you no harm."

"I've never seen anyone like you before." She wished she could take the words back at once. How was she going to appear rich and well-traveled if she kept making statements like that?

"No," the tall humanoid said smoothly, taking her remark in stride. "If you have never been to Syrus Six before then you would not have. I am a Kandalar, a native to this planet. We are unable to leave due to our reliance on a gas that is found only in the atmosphere here on Syrus Six and so we do not travel. But such was our desire to meet and mingle with other races that we made our home world a resort that is renowned the known universe over and so we have visitors from distant galaxies always and are quite content. But I *must* ask you again to call off your slave."

Shaina could see why the Kandalar was nervous. Ty still stood in a half crouch between her and the tall, thin humanoid and looked ready to attack if he made a wrong move. The Kandalar had an inch or two in height on her partner, but Tyson was far more massive. Wearing the primitive, black leather harness and pants, and with his unruly black hair shadowing molten-gold eyes, he looked completely untamed, a huge feline tensed to pounce. Wordlessly, she caught Ty's leash and pulled him closer to her side, where he continued to glower at T'lar.

"Easy, big boy."

"Just playing the part," he growled through their link, but Shaina wasn't so sure. The coiled tension she tasted in Ty's mental voice made her certain that if the Kandalar had seemed just a little more threatening, Ty might have gone for his throat.

The tall, thin humanoid seemed to think the same thing. "He seems very aggressive. Are you quite sure a collar is not in order?" T'lar asked, still looking uneasily at Ty. "I am thinking of the safety of all our guests when I ask this. D'Lonians, as I'm sure you're aware, can be quite savage."

"I'm not wearing the collar!"

"Don't worry. Leave it to me." Shaina gathered herself to her full height, helped considerably by the high-heeled golden boots, and answered as haughtily as she could. "I assure you, T'lar, that Tyber here is only dangerous to anyone who threatens me. He is trained as a bodyguard as well as a pleasure slave.

I am sure you will agree that a girl can't be too careful these days. It's a dangerous universe."

"Ah, well, I suppose not, Mistress . . . ?"

"Meshandra Sender of the Second House of Senders of Rigel Five. You will, of course, have heard of my father, Lord Sender." There was no such person, but they were betting that no one on Syrus Six would dig too deeply into their fabricated past, especially after seeing Shaina's impressive line of credit.

"Of course, of course. You should feel right at home here, little Mistress, as our chef is well versed in Rigelian cuisine," T'lar said smoothly, as she had hoped he would. "Well, owing to your status, I will not insist on a pain collar for your slave, but I hope you understand that in order to enter the Palace he must be properly attired."

"What's wrong with the outfit he has on now? I picked it out myself," she said, trying to sound haughtily offended. They were walking along the endless marble corridor now, Shaina keeping pace with the Kandalar's long strides with some difficulty and Tyson trailing behind them on the leash.

"And I am sure you have excellent taste, little Mistress, but here in the Palace we have a very strict dress code for slaves. I'm sure you'll understand and be more than willing to comply, as I am being lenient in the matter of the collar. It's absolutely non-negotiable, I'm afraid." The Kandalar sounded both firm and apologetic.

"Well, I expect that will be all right. Just tell me how to dress him and I'll do my best to meet your code." Shaina pouted a little but couldn't see a way around it; apparently Ty was going to lose his clothing, what little there was of it.

"Sorry, Ty, I tried."

"That's okay. Faron warned me I might have to change." Tyson's mental voice didn't sound too happy about it, but he seemed resigned.

"Oh, we're happy to provide the proper attire for your slave. I'll take you to a fitting room directly. It's just here, on the right." As he spoke, T'lar reached one long, cadaverously thin black hand out to a wall they had been walking beside and casually brushed its surface. For a moment, it seemed as though his hand melted into the wall. Then, with a quiet sigh, an opening appeared in the black marble and he led them inside a small, plush room that was as solidly turquoise as the outside corridor had been black. Shaina happened to be looking directly at the Kandalar as they walked into the room and she gave a little gasp when she saw the color of his skin flow effortlessly from the black of the marble hall to the turquoise of the room they were entering.

T'lar noticed her reaction and answered the unspoken question. "Ah yes, it is the trait of the Kandalar to match our surroundings. At one time it was a survival mechanism; now it is simply our own little oddity." He made a graceful, self-deprecating gesture and pulled his long face into a droll little smile that Shaina didn't quite trust. "You will find, as you explore the Palace, that most of our chambers are decorated in a single color. It's so *uncomfortable* to be too many colors at once."

"Certainly," Shaina answered. She was glad that the Kandalar at least had on a long robe or she wouldn't have been able to see him at all in the monochromatic room, which reminded her of the *She-Creature*'s shuttle a little. The robe appeared to be all colors and no color at once. It reflected the startling shade of turquoise the room was decorated in, but didn't quite mirror it. Shaina guessed it must be made of some special material that didn't force the Kandalar into being any one color, but simply allowed him to flow with the surrounding environment.

Looking around the room, she could see several low, flat platforms that she thought must be the Kandalars' version of couches. The walls, carpeting, and couches were all the same vivid turquoise, making the outlines of the furniture hard to see.

"Well, now, if you'll just have your slave remove his leggings." T'lar gestured dismissively at the tight black leather pants Ty had on. "And kneel up on one of our fitting platforms, please."

"Certainly," Shaina said again. "Tyber, do as he says." She gestured at her partner, who had a resigned expression on his face, and resolutely faced the other direction. From the rustling and creak of leather behind her, she was certain that Ty was following instructions but she was damned if she was going to watch. Despite a nagging little tickle of curiosity . . .

T'lar was standing by a recessed panel in the turquoise wall that had a keypad made of semi-precious gems. "Now, if you'll be so kind as to give me your slave's measurements so that I can order the correct size . . ."

"His measurements?" What was Ty? About a thirty-inch waist? He was certainly very broad in the shoulders . . .

"Uh, McCullough . . . I don't think that's what he's talking about." Ty's mental voice sounded half amused and half dismayed.

"Erect, of course," T'lar said, as though this would clarify her confusion. His long, thin hand still hovered over the jeweled keypad and he was waiting expectantly.

"Erect? Oh . . . *erect.*" Suddenly it sank in and Shaina had to fight to keep her face from turning scarlet. "I . . . uh . . . well, he's about . . ." She held her hands up, trying to guess how far apart to hold them.

"Surely you know the measurements of your own slave." The Kandalar looked at her skeptically.

"Well, of course I do, he's . . ."

"Ten and a half standard inches," Ty supplied in his driest mental voice.

"Ten and a half standard inches," Shaina finished weakly. *"My Goddess, are you really?"* she couldn't help sending, fighting the urge to turn around and see for herself.

"Well, actually it's more like ten inches, but I don't like the idea of anything too tight-fitting down there, if you know what I mean." Shaina didn't know how to answer that, so she said nothing.

While they held the quick, nonverbal communication, T'lar had been busy with the keyboard. With a small but audible pop, the door to the recessed panel slid open. He reached inside and pulled out what looked like a large, filigreed phallus made of dull copper-colored metal, with thin leather straps and a small mesh bag hanging beneath it.

"What's that?" Shaina couldn't stop herself from asking. The Kandalar looked slightly offended.

"Why, it's a sheath, of course, little Mistress. We like to ensure that the slaves in the Palace are properly covered and ornamented unless they are in use. Would you like to put it on your pet D'Lonian or shall I?"

"If he even comes near me with that thing . . ." Ty's mental voice was definitely threatening.

"Ty, I . . ." Shaina turned around at last and completely forgot what she had been about to say. Her mind was entirely taken up with focusing on what she saw and all the speech centers in her brain seemed to decide to take a vacation at once. She had thought before that Tyson looked spectacular in the tight black leather pants but the sight that greeted her now was absolutely mouthwatering.

Tyson was kneeling, legs spread, on one of the firm turquoise platforms, which were evidently made for this purpose. His broad back was ramrod straight and his fingers were laced behind his head, muscular arms out to either side, not moving an inch. The corded muscles in his torso and thighs were twitching ever so slightly with the effort of holding the demanding pose, but the look on his face was calm, even bored. The only thing that gave away a hint of his anxiety was the slight sheen of sweat on his golden-tan skin and the blazing fire in his amber eyes. Shaina tried hard but she couldn't keep her eyes from wandering over his magnificent body, past the silky trail of hair that led down his lower abdomen and coming to rest between his thighs where his thick cock was already semierect. He was every bit as big as he had said—as he had felt when she had touched him through the leather pants.

"Goddess, you weren't kidding," she thought, and then flushed bright red with embarrassment.

"Nope." Ty's mental voice was matter-of-fact. *"Guess not all the rumors you've heard about D'Lonian men are false, huh, sweetheart?"* He gave her the barest hint of his old, feral grin, showing just the tips of those sharp white teeth, and Shaina turned quickly away.

"Mistress? Mistress Sender?" T'lar's voice was anxious and Shaina had the feeling he'd been trying to get her attention for some time.

"Yes?" she said, snapping back to reality and trying to put the sight of Ty, naked and glistening, out of her mind.

"I said would you like to put the sheath on your slave or shall I?"

"Why . . ." Shaina had to stop and clear her throat before she could continue. "Why can't he put it on himself? He's quite . . . um . . . capable, I'm sure." Keeping her back resolutely to her very naked partner wasn't easy. She could feel her body wanting to turn around and catch another glimpse of him kneeling proudly, wearing nothing but the leather straps across his broad chest, the leash dangling down like an arrow pointing to his thick erection.

"It's not a question of whether he is capable, little Mistress." The Kandalar sounded utterly shocked. "Surely you know that pleasure slaves are not permitted to touch themselves? Their only release comes at the hands of the Master or Mistress to whom they belong. Forgive me for saying so, Mistress Sender, but you do not seem to me to be a very experienced slave owner."

"*McCullough, I think he's getting suspicious.*"

"*Don't worry, I'll handle it,*" Shaina answered fiercely through the symbi-link.

"Nonsense." She used the most imperious voice she could manage. "It is only that our customs are different on Rigel Four." Shaina did her best to look down her nose at the Kandalar, no easy feat since he was easily a standard foot taller than her.

"I thought you said your family was from Rigel Five, Mistress Sender," T'lar said mildly.

Damn and double damn it all to bloody hell! Shaina thought fast. "So I did and so they are. But I was schooled on Rigel Four and the customs there regarding pleasure slaves are quite different."

The Kandalar's eyes, which Shaina noticed were the only part of his body that did not change color to suit his surroundings, now glowed a steady, even red and narrowed to slits in his long, thin face. "What quadrant did you say the Rigel system is in, Mistress Sender?" he asked, frowning a little.

"This small talk is growing most tiresome, T'lar. I came to Syrus Six to have fun and celebrate my coming of age by spending an obscene amount of my father's credit, not to chitchat with the locals, however charming they may be. Can we get on with this please?" Shaina flipped her hair and rolled her eyes impatiently as though his question bored her.

"Most certainly, Mistress. My apologies if my questions offended you." With the mention of the credit she had to spend, the Kandalar became obsequious once more. Mentally, Shaina breathed a sigh of relief.

"*Don't get too relieved, sweetheart. Somebody's still got to put that contraption on me and if tall, dark, and turquoise over there lays a hand on me he'll draw back a nub."* Ty's mental tone was tense and Shaina knew he meant it. Fine, she had known going in that this mission would involve some embarrassing situations. She could take it in stride.

"Hand me the sheath, please." Holding out her hand, she felt like a surgeon in a hospital-drama vid asking for an instrument. Nurse, hand me the scalpel, the forceps, the penis sheath . . . Goddess, what a mess! T'lar handed her the sheath and she turned to face her partner once more. Okay, the goal was to get this thing on Ty as quickly as possible without touching his . . . touching him too much, she told herself.

"Hold still, Tyber," she said, unnecessarily. Ty was still rock solid in his kneeling position. Oh dear, she wished her mind hadn't put it quite that way . . . Never mind, how could she get this apparatus on him?

"Wait," the Kandalar said, just as she was about to fit the sheath over Ty's still semi-erect shaft, using only her fingertips. Shaina looked back at him in exasperation; couldn't he see that this was hard enough as it was? "Will you place the sheath on him without lubricating him first?" T'lar asked mildly. "You can, of course, do so if you wish but the chafing will be most painful. It is not usually done unless you are displeased with your slave and wish to punish him, and it may render him unable to service you for several days."

"Well, we can't have that." Ty's tone was definitely sarcastic. *"Guess you'll have to lube me up, McCullough."*

"Shut up! You're not making this any easier."

"Maybe I had better see to the fitting of the sheath. I wouldn't like any damage to come to your valuable property," T'lar said tactfully, advancing on them. Shaina heard Ty make a noise something like a growl deep in the back of his throat and she hastily blocked the Kandalar's path to her partner.

"No, he is my exclusive property and no one but me is to lay a hand on him. Give . . ." She cleared her throat. "Give me the lubricant." Wordlessly, the tall Kandalar handed her a small vial that was full of an opaque red viscous fluid. Stalling for time, Shaina opened the vial and poured a very little bit of the oily substance on her fingertips. It smelled faintly spicy, like cinnamon and cloves. "What's in this?" she asked, turning to T'lar. "Will it hurt my slave?"

"Most certainly not, Mistress Sender. It is simply a lubricant of our own concoction here at the Pleasure Palace. What you smell is essence of tare root, a mild stimulant that will keep your slave in readiness for hours. Be sure to rub it in well over the entire genital region to realize its full effect."

Goddess, it just got worse and worse. Shaina had been planning to just pour the stuff over Ty and now the Kandalar was watching and telling her she had to rub it in. She looked at her partner threateningly. *"So help me, if you say anything . . ."*

"Hey, don't look at me. We both knew there was going to be some groping going on. We just thought I'd be the one doing it, not you."

"You said we'd be able to fake it."

"I said we'd try. Some things you just can't fake. Look, I'll close my eyes if it'll make things easier for you."

Strangely, it did. Taking a deep breath to calm herself, Shaina studied her partner's face. The golden-amber eyes were closed and his dark lashes lay like black crescents on his cheeks. The stern, hawklike features were composed and there wasn't even a hint of his annoying grin. This was just business to him, Shaina realized, just another undercover mission to be completed like a vice sting back home. If Ty could kneel there so quietly and submit to having himself oiled and fitted with this ridiculous ornamental sheath, then she could certainly be as calm and professional about doing the oiling and fitting.

Calm and professional, she repeated to herself, as she poured a palmful of the viscous oil, trying not to think about it. *Calm and professional.*

"Mistress Sender, I understood you were in a hurry." T'lar sounded ever so slightly impatient. He was probably thinking that a sheath fitting had never taken so long before, Shaina thought.

"Quiet," she snapped. "I am warming the oil before I apply it. My slave is sensitive."

"*Got that right.*" Ty stirred minutely and Shaina could see the little tremors running along the long muscles of his thighs as he held rigidly still in the awkward position. "*Look, can we get on with this? My legs are killing me, McCullough.*"

Shaina didn't answer. Instead, she took a step closer to Ty, whose posture on the platform put his pelvis within easy reach. Uncertain of how to begin, Shaina held her palmful of oil between his legs and carefully cupped his heavy testicles. They felt warm and ripe in her hand as she traced them lightly, massaging the scented oil into the most sensitive and vulnerable part of him.

"God!" She felt Ty tremble, almost vibrate beneath her hand, and a low groan that sounded like pain came from deep in his throat.

"*Am I hurting you?*"

"*No, God, no. Just . . . finish.*" His eyes were tightly shut, his head turned away from her, his face pressed against one shoulder as he struggled to hold still under her light touch. She sensed that he was shielding most of his thoughts from her; there was an unyielding wall of white silence between them.

"*Okay.*" Shaina poured more oil into the palm of her hand and turned her attention to Ty's cock. It was fully erect now, straining up from between his legs and looking achingly rigid. She could sense the tension thrumming just under his golden skin as she spread the thick liquid along his shaft, holding his firmness in her hand. The texture was like silk over steel and the skin of the large, plum-shaped head was as velvety soft as a rose petal. She tried to encircle his thickness with her fingers and found that she couldn't—he was too big. Goddess, how could he even use such a thing? How would it ever fit? How would it feel? Shaina couldn't help imagining herself straddling Ty and feeling that delicious, straining thickness sliding inside of her, opening her up, filling her . . .

"Shaina, don't—you're driving me insane as it is!" His amber eyes opened and locked with hers. Shaina found she couldn't look away from the liquid gold depths blazing with desire.

Shame stained her cheeks a dark crimson as she realized that Tyson had caught at least part and maybe all of her last thought. The embarrassment brought her back to herself and she realized that she was stroking slowly along the length of his shaft and that Ty was thrusting into her hand, his back arching, his golden skin glistening with sweat. Pearly drops of liquid were beading at the head of his cock and his chest was heaving rapidly.

"Shaina, stop! You're going to make me lose it!" The cords in Ty's neck were standing out and his mental voice sounded hoarse and strained. She knew she should take her hand away but part of her wanted to see him lose control. Wanted to push him over that edge and feel him throbbing in her hand as he came in hot spurts . . .

"Mistress Sender, I fail to understand why you are pleasuring your slave when he has done nothing to deserve it." T'lar's voice was filled with mild reproof and Shaina gasped. She had been so engrossed in spreading the oil on Ty that she had completely forgotten the tall Kandalar was there. She pulled her hand away guiltily, as though she had been burned, and Ty uttered a low groan of pain or pleasure, she couldn't tell which. "I would never presume to rush you, but there is a banquet in the Red Pleasure Hall very soon and you will be expected to attend."

"Oh, uh, certainly. Here . . ." Fumbling with the leather straps, Shaina finally managed to fit the awkward filigreed sheath onto her partner. The little mesh bag that hung down from the bottom of it turned out to be for his testicles and Tyson hissed sharply as the cold metal touched his hot flesh.

"Sorry! Is it too tight?"

"Just cold." Shaina was grateful that he didn't seem inclined to want to discuss how the lubrication had gotten out of hand, no pun intended. She concentrated on getting all the straps that held the sheath in place buckled, which wasn't easy since her fingers were slick with oil. When she was finally finished and T'lar told her the straps were right, she thought Ty looked like some ancient and terrible fertility god with the copper sheath thrusting rudely from between his muscular thighs. It should have looked ridiculous, but instead, the gleaming filigreed metal made her think of the delicious thickness of his cock inside it and remember how achingly hard it had felt in her hand. Shaina shivered and tried to push the thought away, hoping Ty hadn't heard it.

"Can you walk in that thing?" she asked anxiously as T'lar pronounced himself satisfied with the fit and proceeded to lead them out of the turquoise fitting room and back into the silver-flecked black marble hallway.

"Barely. I'll get the hang of it."

"I guess it's to keep you from, uh, touching yourself."

"That and it's a lovely conversation piece."

Shaina was glad to hear that touch of sarcasm in Tyson's voice. He had been quiet and mostly uncommunicative while she'd adjusted the straps. She was afraid he might be angry at her.

"Angry isn't the word, sweetheart. Anger doesn't begin *to cover it."*

"Ty, I'm so sorry . . . I don't know what got into me. I just got . . . carried away."

"Forget it. We'll discuss it later."

Which was exactly what Shaina was afraid of.

10

Tyson really would have liked to go to their rooms first, but when he prompted Shaina to ask, T'lar claimed they had no time, and so they were on their way to the feast. All Ty wanted was a little time alone. Surveillance devices or no surveillance devices, he needed to take care of the severe problem Shaina had given him. God! He kept his head down and tried to look submissive, ignoring the other Masters and Mistresses with their pleasure slaves in tow as they wound their way through the sinuous monochromatic tunnels of the Pleasure Palace. Being a slave, Faron had warned him, was never putting your own pleasure first, waiting on your Mistress for everything, food, sleep, sexual release . . . And Ty had nodded his head and pretended to understand. Now he knew he had had no idea. His body was on fire and there was nothing he could do about it.

Ty shook his head and tried to forget the look in Shaina's eyes, deep green and heavy-lidded with desire as she stroked him. Though he tried not to, he remembered the tip of her pink tongue wetting her lush mouth as her small, soft hand drove him to distraction. Even worse had been the thoughts she had been unconsciously projecting through their symbi-link. Those vivid images of her straddling him, spreading her legs, and fitting the thick head of his cock into her warm, wet entrance had made him crazy. Shaina had been wondering what it would feel like to have him buried to the hilt inside her and Ty could almost feel the sensation of her sweet, virginal cunt opening up for him as he pressed deeper and deeper into her hot, slippery depths. He ached to be there, thrusting inside her, pounding up into her heat until he filled her and claimed her in the most primitive and savage way ...

He wondered if she had any idea of how she had affected him. Of how close he had come to lunging off that damned turquoise platform and pulling her to the ground. All of his D'Lonian blood demanded that he do it ... demanded that he spread her long, gorgeous legs and bury himself in her tight, wet pussy. His vision had gone completely red while she stroked him. Everything but her face had been obscured by Fuck lust and it was only by the barest thread that he was able to hold himself back. And then she had the nerve to say she had been simply carried away. *Carried away* ... His cock still throbbed in rigid protest beneath the ornate copper sheath. The stimulant in the lubricating oil she had spread on him was making it worse, making him so hard and needy that he wasn't sure he could be responsible for his actions if he didn't get some relief soon.

"And here we are, the Red Pleasure Hall. I will find you after the banquet, Mistress Sender, and lead you to your rooms without fail, but for now I have other guests to attend to. I bid you farewell." And with a last, thoughtful look from his softly glowing eyes, the Kandalar disappeared, literally melting into the background.

"Guess we'd better find a seat."

"Yeah, guess so." Tyson didn't trust himself to say much to

her right now; he was too busy rigidly shielding out his own ravenous thoughts. If she had any idea how close he was to just taking her here and now she would run screaming from the room. *What a joke*, he thought, *a Mistress who doesn't want pleasure from her pleasure slave . . .*

Trying to shake off his dark mood, Ty lifted his head for the first time and looked around the room. It was easy to see why it was called the Red Pleasure Hall. The walls and ceiling of the vast chamber were all a bright crimson. It looked like someone had painted the place with a bucket of fresh human blood. A long, low real-wood table ran the entire length of the hall and there were scattered high-backed cushions at intervals along it, most of them already occupied.

"I see a free spot over at the far end. Keep an eye out for the Chancellor's son." She looked at him a little uneasily and then seemed to remember she was playing the role of a wealthy Mistress.

"Come, Tyber." Giving a little jerk on the leash, she made her way down the crowded table to the empty spot.

Ty was well aware that she was simply playing a part, but he was already sick of being led around like a pet. At least all the other pleasure slaves he saw scattered around the great hall, mostly kneeling docilely at the feet of their Masters and Mistresses, got to enjoy the benefits of being a slave once in a while. Tyson was fairly sure he could look forward to nothing but more teasing and he wasn't sure he could take it. The ornate filigreed copper jutting out from between his thighs reminded him of his painful predicament and he was sure the metal sheath couldn't be any harder than the flesh it encased.

"Here we are." Stopping only a place away from the head of the table, she sank down onto a plush, high-backed maroon cushion, being careful to keep her legs together and her arms at her sides to avoid flashing.

Ty was minimally relieved to see that a few things in the hall were other colors besides the fresh-blood red. Being inside a room that was completely one shade gave him the strange sensation of having suddenly gone color-blind. He sank at Shaina's feet onto the scarlet carpet embroidered with burgundy snakes and began looking carefully around to see how the other slaves were behaving.

"Oh . . ." Shaina's mental voice was faint. *"They really do . . . in public."*

"What did you expect? Faron warned us, you know."

"I know, it's just . . ." Shaina's voice died away and Tyson watched her eyes getting bigger and bigger as she looked around and really took in the activities going on all around them. It would be an exaggeration to say that every person seated at the long real-wood table was engaged in some form of sexual activity. It was probably more like one in three. There were by far more Masters than Mistresses, he noted, and many of them had more than one slave.

"I don't see Paul, but the idol is glowing. He must be somewhere in the Palace," Shaina sent. She was pretending to dig in her knapsack for something important but was actually checking the status of the little figurine Faron had given them. Tyson didn't answer her; he was too busy scanning the length of the table as unobtrusively as he could. None of the slaves that he could see bore even a slight resemblance to the Chancellor's son.

Across the wide table from them, a man with bright orange hair and steel teeth was being serviced by two slaves at once, a male and a female who looked alike enough to be twins. Beside him sat an older woman with red lips and improbably large and bulbous breasts. She was smoking an adji-stick with one hand and idly stroking the erect shaft of a slave who looked young enough to be her teenaged grandson with the other. From the tense look on the young man's face, Ty thought he must not be enjoying the experience too much. A quick glance at his crotch revealed why: a tight silver cock ring encircled the base of the young slave's penis, keeping him hard, but unable to achieve release.

What kind of sick bastards were these? Ty continued to look around as unobtrusively as he could. To their left sat a fairly normal-looking middle-aged Mistress dressed in a flowing bright blue caftan, with a tower of pale brown hair piled atop her head. With her was a plump little blond slave girl whose own hair had been worked into an alarming display of curly ringlets held in place by pink sateen ribbons. To their right sat a corpulent humanoid whose faintly green-tinged skin and vestigial neck gills hinted of a Tenibran background. He was leaning back on his deep red cushion, being fellated by a beautiful naked slave girl with exotic violet eyes and long, dark hair that was rooted far down her back like a mane. Tyson caught sight of the eyes only in passing as her head bobbed rapidly over her fat Master's crotch.

"The teeth, girl, mind the teeth!" the Master yelled abruptly. His voice sounded bubbly, as though he were talking underwater, and the vestigial gills flexed in agitation. The girl pulled quickly away from his pudgy erection, slicked with her saliva, and began to pound her forehead against the floor at his feet. Despite the real-wool carpet, Ty thought, it had to hurt.

"Sweet Master, forgive me! I will do better . . ." the girl babbled. Suddenly she arched upward and back, her spine jackknifing into an impossible backward curve so her long hair almost brushed the soles of her feet. With slender fingers she clawed at a golden collar set with jewels, which had been hidden earlier by her mane. Ty noticed that her Master had a thick golden bangle on his wrist with several buttons on it. He was pressing one now, obviously controlling the pain collar that his slave girl wore. Her beautiful face contorted with agony, her purple eyes bulging with fear as her Master twisted a small knob on the side of the bangle and pressed another button with an angry jab of his pudgy finger.

"*Sonofabitch!*" Ty was getting to his feet without thinking, ready to lunge at the fat man's throat, when he felt a sharp yank on his leash.

"*Ty, no! You'll blow our cover!*"

"*Damn it, Shaina, we can't just sit here and watch while he kills her!*"

"*I'll distract him. Just hold on to your temper.*" Shaina was turning to the corpulent Master, obviously trying desperately to think of something to say, when the slave girl abruptly stopped convulsing and collapsed in a sweaty heap at his feet, taking great, gasping breaths as she tried to get enough air to weep.

"Such a damn nuisance breaking in a new slave," the Master said, speaking to Shaina in a conversational tone and paying not the least attention to Ty, who was still more than half inclined to rip the bastard's throat out.

He was, in Tyson's estimation, the worst kind of man, one who beats and abuses the helpless woman in his care because he can—because it makes him feel important. He knew Shaina had never understood why he spent most of his career as a Peace Officer in the Domestic Abuse department back home. But now, seeing this obese Master with soulless black eyes that looked like raisins pushed into fat lumps of dough, she had her answer. Ty lived to bust assholes like this. Back home, he would never have tolerated such a display, but here he was powerless to stop it.

"Most tedious." Ty came back to himself to hear Shaina agreeing with the fat Master in a small, sick voice. The man was casually stuffing his wilted erection back into his roomy silver pants and Ty could hear her thinking that she *so* didn't want to see that. "I mean they're so . . ." She was groping for words and finding nothing. The sadistic display of pain had unnerved her as well but at least she had kept her head. For the first time, Tyson was glad she was playing the Mistress and he was playing the slave instead of the other way around. Luckily, the fat man was happy to keep up both ends of the conversation.

"You pay good credits for what you think is a good product and what do you get?" he bubbled, in his underwater voice. "Look at her." He nudged the slave girl at his feet, who was sobbing as quietly and unobtrusively as she could. "When I purchased her from that no-good scum of a trader, he swore to me that her specialty was cocksucking. Should have insisted on trying the goods, but I was in a hurry. Got her back to my needle and found out the truth. She gives the worst head in the known universe. Worthless slut," he grunted angrily and ran one pudgy hand through his balding, greenish-brown hair. "I tell you the truth," he confided to Shaina. "I've been giving serious consideration to just having all her teeth pulled. Sometimes it's the only way."

"Oh, no!" Shaina gasped, obviously horrified by the suggestion. "I mean . . . think of her resale value," she added weakly, clearly seeing the puzzled expression on the Master's face.

"True," he said after a moment, appearing to consider her words carefully. "I don't think I want to be stuck with this one for too much longer. Maybe I should just cut my losses and sell her. She'll never be any good."

"Maybe you should." Shaina sounded relieved and Ty could hear her thinking that no matter who the girl got sold to, she couldn't have a worse life than she did right now with this fat, sadistic, self-absorbed monster.

"There's a brothel in my home sector and I know they'd pay top credit . . . Say, that's a fine specimen you have there," he interrupted himself, obviously noticing Tyson for the first time. Ty looked fixedly down at the floor, afraid that if he looked at the Master while the man was talking, the rage in his eyes would give him away. "Golden tint to the skin, black hair, powerful build. D'Lonian, right?"

"Half." Shaina took a firmer grip on the leash.

"You know, sometimes the male slaves give better head than the females. They have the equipment and know how to work it." He gave a coarse, bubbly laugh. "You interested in selling him?" he asked, giving Ty an appraising glance that filled him with a sick rush of rage.

"I couldn't possibly. I've had him since I was thirteen. He's a Love slave. I'd . . . I'd never find another one like him. Very loyal."

"So I see." The fat Master still eyed him with interest and Tyson heard a low rumbling growl and realized it was coming from his own throat. "Myself," the man continued, oblivious to his danger. "I always use the collar—it's simple and effective. Nothing like a little negative reinforcement to keep a slave in their place."

"Yes, well . . ." Shaina's voice sounded faint.

"You know, we never exchanged names. I'm Marso Jlle. I live in the Tenibrian sector, have a bit of a slave-trading business out there. Mostly just slaves I get tired of though. They never seem to last very long." He nudged his slave girl again with one fat foot and laughed hugely at his own joke, then held out one pudgy hand to shake—the same one, Ty noted, that he had used to stuff his prick back into his pants earlier.

"I'm, uh, Meshandra Sender of Rigel Five." Ty could hear Shaina thinking how much she didn't want to shake hands with the fat Marso but she made herself do it anyway. Afterward, he saw her wipe her palm on the golden material of her skirt as unobtrusively as possible.

"Well, if you change your mind about selling that D'Lonian, just let me know. I've got more than half a mind to try out that mouth of his." He made as if to reach out a fat hand and stroke Tyson's face and Shaina jerked hard on the leash, hastily putting herself between Ty and the corpulent Master.

"I assure you, he's not for sale," she said as firmly as she could.

"Let me know if you change your mind." Marso Jlle repeated. "In my experience, Mistress Sender, everything has a price." Giving Ty one last, appraising stare out of his flat, black eyes, he turned back to his quietly sobbing slave girl and began to reprimand her again.

"Is it your first trip to the Pleasure Palace, my dear?" The soft, kindly voice was coming from the middle-aged Mistress on their other side. Her pale brown hair was piled in a high, wispy pouf, rising a good two feet above her head, and she was swathed in a voluminous peacock-blue caftan made of some silky material. She stroked the plump blond slave girl at her side kindly if absently as she spoke. "I only ask because you look a trifle mystified by all this." She waved her hand at the banquet hall, indicating all the varied sexual acts still going on around them.

Mystified? Sick to her stomach was more like it, Tyson thought, looking up at his partner.

"Well, it is all rather . . . dazzling," Shaina replied. Ty snorted. *"Dazzling?"*

"Shut up! What am I supposed to say?" At that moment, the sharp, sweet sound of a thousand bells of all sizes and tones ringing all together startled them both. It was a deafening sound and Shaina jumped, nearly dropping Ty's leash. But the smiling Mistress beside them perked up a little.

"Ah good, that will be the Executor. I thought she'd never arrive. My sweet little L'Mera here is starving to death, aren't you, my pet?" She stroked the beribboned mass of corkscrewing curls on the blond slave girl's head and the slave nuzzled her palm affectionately. Tyson noticed that she was one of the few slaves besides himself that wore no pain collar. "My dear," the Mistress continued, talking to Shaina in the kindly tones of a benevolent older aunt, "since you're new to the Palace, let me give you some advice. It's considered rather bad manners to let your slave service you during the feast."

"Oh?" Shaina arched one eyebrow and Tyson thought he detected a note of relief in her voice.

"Yes," The Mistress nodded wisely. "Save it for after the banquet, so you'll be fresh for the Mandatory Pleasuring."

"Mandatory . . . ?" Shaina couldn't seem to get the words out of her mouth.

"Yes, my dear. We are all enjoying the exclusive privilege of staying at the Executor's Palace. All she asks of us, besides the very nominal ten-thousand-credit-a-night room fee, of course, is that we all put on a little show nightly after the banquet. It lets her know that we're enjoying her hospitality. Ah, here she is now." She turned eagerly toward the head of the table, where a most unusual figure was taking her place on a gold-embroidered crimson satin cushion.

"Didn't know the Executor was female." Ty watched with interest as the tall figure settled herself at the head of the table.

"Sexist porcine. Why shouldn't she be? Males don't rule the universe anymore."

"They do here. Look around, sweetheart. Besides you and the lady beside you, how many Mistresses do you see?"

"Looks like only . . . hmmm, fifteen out of more than a hundred, give or take. Still, the Executor more than makes up for the lack of other females all by herself."

"Yeah, she's . . . colorful, isn't she?"

The being currently seated at the head of the table made "colorful" a considerable understatement. She was tall and thin almost to the point of emaciation, with long, platinum blond hair, softly glowing red eyes, and a patrician nose. Her features were stern, more handsome than beautiful. More immediately eye-catching was her clothing. A long, tight-fitting sheath of a gown made of some kind of leather clung to the meager curves of the Executor's body and Tyson was sure that every possible color in the known spectrum had been employed in its manufacture. Starting with the palest imaginable pastels at the high neck, the gown gradually shaded to deeper, more vivid colors in the bodice and hips. The colors grew deeper and darker toward the bottom of the gown and the hem brushing her long, thin, bare feet, was a midnight blue so dark it was almost black.

The gown was startling enough, but staring closely at her exposed face and arms, Ty realized that the Executor herself was constantly changing her skin color to match all the many different shades in her dress. Beginning with the pale, frosty pink at the neck and running down to the midnight blue of the hem, her complexion ran the gamut through each shade and then repeated, never more than one color at a time but each color lasting only a fraction of a second. It was like watching a living, breathing rainbow.

"Isn't she a Kandalar? I thought the reason all the rooms in this Goddess-forsaken place were just one color was because they found it uncomfortable otherwise," Shaina stared in awe at the Executor. *"That's what T'lar said, anyway."*

"I don't know. Why don't you ask your fat friend?" Ty indicated Marso Jlle with a small nod of his head. *"You know, if I get a chance to catch that son of a bitch alone . . ."*

"You won't lay a finger on him because there are surveillance devices everywhere," she reminded him sternly. *"But I think I will ask the lady beside us what she knows. She seems to like to talk."*

The food was starting to arrive now, being served by unobtrusive Kandalar waiters who literally blended into the background. Tyson heard Shaina thinking how disconcerting it was to be sitting quietly at the table and have a serving dish suddenly seem to appear out of thin air right in front of you, held by a nearly invisible, perfectly camouflaged hand. He himself had no such experience because the slaves were not served anything. His stomach rumbled angrily, it had been a long time since their final meal before leaving the *She-Creature* and he wondered what he was supposed to eat. His question was soon answered.

Looking around, Ty noticed that the other Masters and Mistresses were filling large plates for themselves first and then putting a few morsels for their slaves on smaller, side plates which they then placed on the ground. Apparently, slaves weren't allowed to eat at the table, or eat very much at all for that matter. Tyson's stomach growled again as he watched the food being served. It wasn't just the usual supplements. Instead of the small mounds of reconstituted food, there were large plates of fresh vegetables and heaping platters of meat dripping tantalizing juices. He supposed for ten thousand credits a night, you had a right to expect a gourmet feast.

"Here you are, you can stop drooling now." Shaina's mental voice sounded amused and she was already handing him a plate full of vegetables and meat and even some fruit. Tyson noted that she had filled the large plate for him and kept the smaller one for herself. *"Sorry you can't eat at the table, but it might attract suspicion, even if you are my Love slave."*

"At this point, I'm happy to eat anywhere. Don't you want more than that?" He eyed the small portions she had placed on her plate.

"No, I kind of lost my appetite." She nodded at the fat slave trader, Jlle, who was eating with plenty of gusto, if not many manners. His slablike cheeks were already shining with a thin, oily film of meat juice and the front of his satin shirt was stained with splotches of grease. He was chewing loudly, smacking his lips, and belching appreciatively between bites. Meanwhile, his slave was crouched at his feet nibbling a single piece of fruit, not a very large one either, Ty noted.

Perhaps sensing their eyes upon him, Marso Jlle turned and said around a mouthful of food, "I see you feed your slave very well. Don't you find it makes him too complacent to be of much use afterward?" He looked disapprovingly at the large plate of food in front of Ty as he spoke.

"Tyber is never complacent," Shaina answered haughtily. "I feed him enough to keep his energy up so that he may tend to my needs. Aren't you worried your slave might starve on such short rations?" The slave girl looked up briefly, a haunted, hungry look in her violet eyes, before quickly returning to her single piece of fruit, which she had nibbled in tiny bites almost down to the core.

"I just don't let 'em get fat. Not much call for a fat slave." The corpulent Master seemed to be completely unaware of the irony in his statement. "Still," he continued, "not much call for terribly skinny ones either." He wiped one pudgy hand on the front of his shirt and tossed a half-gnawed bone with some meat still clinging to it onto his slave's plate with a clatter. "Eat up, pet. I think I'm going to want to sell you and it won't do if you're all skin and bones. And teeth," he added as an afterthought and roared with bubbling, underwater laughter, his vestigial gills flexing in amusement.

Tyson saw Shaina push her almost untouched plate away. Apparently she had lost her appetite completely.

"I wonder," she said in a low voice, turning to the Mistress beside her and pointedly ignoring Jlle, "if you know why the Executor is so . . . so multicolored when all the other Kandalar appear to want to stay one color at a time."

"Oh certainly. It is, for a fact, an interesting tale." The middle-aged Mistress appeared to have eaten her fill, although her plump slave was still eating daintily from her small plate, and was now disposed to talk while the other diners finished at a more leisurely pace. Ty kept his eyes on his plate but listened as the Mistress spoke.

"My name is Cassandra Shybolt of the Io Shybolts, by the way, but everyone just calls me Mistress Shy."

"Meshandra Sender of Rigel Five." The middle-aged Mistress nodded pleasantly. Formalities out of the way, they could now begin to gossip.

"So, Meshandra, I can only tell you what I've heard but fortunately I keep my ear to the ground around here." Shaina nodded for her to continue, which she seemed only too happy to do. "The Executor's true name in the Kandalarian tongue is T'Sinatia T'Solera, which means 'she who is as many colored as the sun.' But it can also mean"—she lowered her voice and leaned in toward Shaina—" 'She who is driven mad by color.' "

"You see, the story goes that once the Executor was like all the other Kandalar, desiring only one color at a time. Changing colors causes them discomfort bordering on pain, don't you know? At that time, in her youth, she had a Love slave that pleased her above all others. He was a Glameron of surpassing beauty and she loved him so much that she freed him to be her consort, which, quite frankly my dear, is just unheard of." Mistress Shy nodded her head sagely and continued her tale.

"The story goes that they lived in perfect bliss for one solar year and one solar day and then a handsome young slave trader with beautiful, colorful clothes came to stay at the Palace. He sat by the Executor and her consort every night for a week and by the end of that time her Glameron had fallen hopelessly and helplessly in love with him. She knew it was so because her consort's appearance changed. He stopped being all one color at a time, the way she desired, and began to resemble the slave trader's idea of beauty.

"Well, when she confronted her consort with his betrayal he confessed that it was true, he had fallen in love with the slave trader and he wanted to leave her. The Executor begged him to reconsider but he would have none of it. He was determined to go. So, heartbroken but unwilling to keep him against his will, she let her Glameron go with the slave trader. But she promised them before they left that someday she would have revenge. Of course the trader didn't listen. He and the Glameron were too much in love to worry about the future. They left the Palace and were never seen again."

"That's a fascinating story, but what does it have to do with the Executor's color fetish?" Shaina kept her voice low.

"Why, my dear, after her consort left, the Executor went a little mad." Shy was almost whispering now. "She convinced herself that her Glameron had fallen in love with the slave trader because of his beautiful clothes and she vowed to be as colorful and beautiful as he was in case her consort ever came back. That's the reason behind the dress that constantly forces her to change color. It's a sort of masochism, you know, quite painful for her. A great many Kandalar had to die to make that garment, and it's not the only one she has by a long stretch."

"You mean . . . her gown is made of the skin of other Kandalar?" Shaina sounded almost faint.

"Oh, certainly, my dear. You see, whatever color a Kandalar is at the time of death, that is the color the skin stays. So when someone displeases her, she has them put in a cubicle in the exact shade that she wants and starves them to death. That way the skin is nice and loose when they die. The cubicles are called the 'colored chambers' and you have only to *mention* them to the Kandalar attending you if you are displeased to see an instant improvement in your service. Scares them half to death, poor things, although I'd never really report any of them. L'Mera and I are quite content to live quietly and leave well enough alone, aren't we, my pet?" She stroked the pink cheek of her blond slave girl, who promptly kissed her hand. "Yes, it frightens them even more than being sent off-planet where the gas they breathe is not available because that, at least, is an instant death, not a slow and lingering torture." Her slave girl became quite bold at this point and reached up to plant a hungry kiss on her Mistress's cheek near the corner of her mouth.

"Ah, L'Mera, you naughty girl! Wait until the meal is over, I have just been telling this nice young Mistress by my side here how rude it is to allow service in the middle of the banquet, although it *is* getting on toward dessert, I suppose." Turning to Shaina she added, "She is so eager to please . . . but it seems your D'Lonian is quite eager to service you as well."

"*You have no idea.*" Ty had finished eating some time ago and now nudged his way between Shaina's legs and rubbed his rough cheek against one tender thigh, acting the part of the affectionate Love slave to the hilt, much to her apparent discomfort.

"*Ty, stop it!*" Shaina blushed and tried to push him away but Ty wasn't going anywhere. Up until now, she had been keeping her thighs together and her legs closed, but now he forced her to spread them to accommodate his broad shoulders and large body. Ty thought he could see just a hint of red curls through the slit in the golden material of her panties, and the musky, feminine scent that was purely Shaina was already invading his senses and firing his D'Lonian blood.

"Ah, how sweet. I think I heard you tell Marso over there that you have owned him since your thirteenth birth year?" the mistress inquired, watching with interest as Tyson continued to press his body between Shaina's legs.

"Yes . . ." She was still trying to push Tyson away and he was resisting her efforts and continuing to rub his face against her smooth, creamy thighs.

"Oh, let him be, my dear. The Mandatory Pleasuring is about to start at any moment anyway. He can't hurt anything." The Mistress nodded her high pouf of light brown hair knowingly. "I suppose your parents must have given him to you as a love tutor, then?"

"A . . . a what?" Tyson was planting hot, open-mouthed kisses against the inside of her knees and calves. God, how he wanted to taste her sweet, creamy pussy, but he would take what he could get at the moment. He could feel her uncertainty and nervousness at the touch of his searing mouth on her bare flesh and it was only making him hotter.

"A love tutor, dear. Where I come from on Io, that's what we call a slave trained in the art of breaking in virgins. I suppose he must have been very good with you your first time for you to have formed such an attachment to him."

"He's . . . ah . . . very attentive," Shaina gasped, as Ty licked a long, slow, hot trail from her calf to her inner thigh. "A very good tutor," she added, seemingly not quite aware of what she was saying.

"Yes, he seems the type, although you wouldn't think it of a D'Lonian. I suppose he has his wild side, though?" The Mistress was still watching with interest as Tyson continued to kiss and lick along Shaina's thighs, gradually getting closer and closer to the split in the golden panties.

"Yes . . . wild . . ." Shaina panted, trying unsuccessfully to close her thighs. "I can't . . . sometimes I can barely control him. Like now," she added, pressing her palms against his broad shoulders in an effort to hold him away from her.

"Ty, what the bloody hell are you doing? Stop it right now!" Ty thought her demand sounded a little weak, a little hesitant.

"I'm acting the part of your Love slave." He tried to make his mental voice businesslike, as though he was only interested in playing the role he had been assigned. *"Relax, Shaina. You're supposed to be enjoying this, remember?"*

"Well, I'm not!" But if she wasn't enjoying it, why was her body trembling ever so slightly under his large hands? Why was her breath coming in short little pants as he got closer and closer to the sweet vee between her legs? Tyson thought she

was lying to herself as well as him. But he didn't intend to let her lie much longer.

Suddenly, the loud sound of a thousand discordant bells sounded once again, startling them.

"Ah, the Mandatory Pleasuring has begun. Be quite sure your slave does a good job, my dear. Sitting so close to the Executor, one doesn't want to risk offending," the middle-aged Mistress whispered. "L'Mera, my darling, we can begin now," she cooed, turning her attention to the eager, plump little blonde.

"You heard her, Shaina. Can't risk offending the Executor." Ty pressed even closer between her legs.

"Ty, please! You said we could fake it!" Shaina sent, her hands still placed firmly on his shoulders as she tried to hold him back. It was like pushing against a brick wall, he heard her think.

"Too risky with the Executor sitting right there." Ty nodded briefly at the multicolored being looking fixedly around the table where every Master, Mistress, and slave was now engaged in some form of sexual activity. Putting his large, warm palms on Shaina's smooth inner thighs, he pressed her backward into a recumbent position on the cushion and spread her legs at the same time. He wasn't going to hurt her but he wasn't going to be denied either. Beneath the ornate copper sheath his cock was like a bar of lead and if he couldn't sink it to the hilt in his beautiful redheaded partner, Ty at least meant to thoroughly taste her sweet pussy.

"Ty . . ."

"Relax, Mistress, and let me pleasure you," Tyson said aloud, still pressing her legs apart. He could feel the tension quivering in the long muscles of her thighs and see the smaller ones in her abdomen fluttering with fear.

"It's just a part, McCullough," he told her, making his men-

tal voice stern and disinterested. *"You're undercover and you have to act the part. Don't let it rattle you. Relax."*

"A part, right. Just a part." Ty felt her thigh muscles relax, just a little, under his palms. He bent his head, laid a gentle, open-mouthed kiss on the soft reddish fur that the slit in the golden panties revealed, and felt Shaina tremble beneath him.

"That's all it is, just a part." Nuzzling between her thighs he bathed in the warm, female scent of her. If it helped her to think that he was only doing this as a part of their cover, then fine. Ty knew the truth, that he had wanted to claim her this way from the first minute he laid eyes on her, when the wild, D'Lonian side of him had spoken up and said, "mine." Something about Shaina McCullough called to his blood and he had to have her.

"All right. I ... I'll try to relax. You ... you won't hurt me, will you?" Her voice was small and fearful, yet full of desire. Tyson realized she didn't even understand her own deep need herself.

"Never," he whispered in her mind. Despite the D'Lonian blood in his veins that demanded he take her here and now, he wanted to make this good for her. Wanted to be her .... what had the other Mistress called it? Oh, yes, her love tutor. Tyson put one large, warm hand on her taut belly and pressed her back into the cushions.

"Relax," he said again, in a low, commanding voice. "I'm going to taste you now, Mistress. Close your eyes and let yourself feel."

"Goddess ..." Shaina moaned out loud, squeezing her eyes tightly closed and finally letting her body fall back fully into the cushions. Tyson felt the resistance in her thighs loosen and he leaned forward and spread the golden panties completely apart to reveal her sweet cleft.

She was already wet with desire. He could see the moisture shining on the plump inner lips, so softly pink and swollen with need. Ty couldn't wait any longer. Carefully, using his thumbs to spread her open, he let his tongue travel from the entrance of her hot little cunt to the top of her slit where her clitoris was throbbing with longing. He swirled the tip of his tongue around and around the tiny kernel of desire, causing her to gasp and buck her hips upwards to meet his mouth.

"Oh, Goddess...Ty..." He heard her moan inside his head and felt her pleasure almost as intensely as he would his own. Savoring the sweet, salty taste of her and wanting more, he put his mouth more fully against her, sucking and licking her clit with greater intensity, kissing her cunt the way he would kiss her mouth.

Shaina was almost delirious with pleasure now. Sobbing and gasping, she buried her small hands in his hair and pulled him towards her, riding his mouth shamelessly as he tasted her the way he had always wanted to.

"Goddess, Ty, inside me ... please!"

Her heat was setting him on fire. Putting both large hands beneath her and grasping her firm little ass, Ty pulled her to him as though her small pelvis was a bowl of water and he was dying of thirst. In a way, he was. Pressing his mouth against her hot, slippery folds, he plunged his tongue into her entrance, loving the taste of her need and feeling her approaching orgasm as he sucked her and spread her, working her open.

"Ty ... Oh, I'm going to ... Oh ..." Shaina was panting and gasping, unable to get a deep enough breath as the pleasure overwhelmed her body. As her orgasm built inside her, Tyson could feel it build in him as well. He didn't know if it was the symbi-link or simply the sheer intensity of his need for her, but he suddenly understood that when she came, he was going to come with her. His one regret was that he couldn't be buried inside her when it happened.

"Come, Shaina. Want to feel you come for me, sweetheart. Want to taste your sweet pussy coming all over my tongue ..."

"Ty!" she cried out loud, pressing her body up to him, giving herself without reservation as the orgasm overtook her at last. Ty felt her body grow rigid with the release of tension, tasted the fresh wetness of her pleasure on his tongue as she cried out his name in a broken voice, her fingers tight in his hair and scratching his shoulders as she bucked against his mouth.

"Oh God, Shaina, you're so sweet! Love to taste you, love to make you come..." Ty felt his own pleasure reach a peak as well. His achingly hard cock throbbed with release as his balls tightened and he spent himself in the cold copper sheath in hot, uneven spurts before he collapsed against her thighs, gasping raggedly.

11

Shaina just lay there for a moment, floating on the aftermath of pleasure and feeling Ty pant, his shoulders heaving against her legs, his hot breath still blowing over her thighs. She had had orgasms before, of course she had, although only with her own hand. But having Ty's tongue on her . . . in her was a whole new experience. The connection between them at the moment of climax had been incredible. She knew he had only been playing a part, the role of her Love slave, but she couldn't help wishing, just a little, that it could be for real.

Stop it, Shaina, she scolded herself. *Ty is what he's always been to you, just a coworker. It doesn't mean a thing.* Although damned if he wasn't amazingly good at what he did. Absently, Shaina ran both hands through his thick, soft hair and contemplated getting up. But Ty seemed so comfortable, like a lazy cat curled up with his head resting against her thigh, that she hated to disturb him.

"Stupid whore!" A thick, bubbling voice broke into her inner monologue and reminded Shaina that there were more people in the world than just Tyson and herself. Lots more, in fact, and she was lolling around half naked in front of all of them, having just enjoyed the best orgasm of her life.

"*Really, the* best?" Double damn him, how did he always catch her most embarrassing thoughts? Shaina wondered. She would really have to work on her shielding.

"*Don't start, Ty.*" Blushing, she struggled to get back into a sitting position.

"*Why would I start when we just finished?*" That self-satisfied, feral D'Lonian grin was back on his face as she pushed him away. The knowing look of shared intimacy in his liquid gold eyes made Shaina feel suddenly shy and self-conscious.

"*Help me sit up, you big lug! Something's going on over there.*"

Abruptly, Tyson did as she asked, pulling her up and turning his attention back to the obese Master, Marso Jlle, beside them. Shaina knew how much Tyson loathed and despised the man already. She could taste it in the back of her throat like iron filings whenever Ty thought about the fat merchant. Quickly, she grabbed Ty's dangling leash, as though it would do any good if he decided to go for Jlle. At least she could remind him again that they were undercover. She just hoped that the fat Master wouldn't use the pain collar on his trembling slave again.

"You stupid little bitch, how am I to pay proper respect to Her Excellency if you don't pleasure me correctly?"

As unobtrusively as she could while still holding tightly to the leash, Shaina leaned over just a little and craned her neck. The slave girl with the long, dark hair and exotic purple eyes was kneeling before her Master, knocking her head against the floor again.

"Master, forgive me! I tried . . . I will try harder . . ."

"*What's the problem this time? Teeth again?*" Ty looked ready to interfere if Jlle started using the pain collar.

"*No, I don't think so . . .*" Still looking out of the corner of her eye, she answered. *"I think the problem is that he can't . . . you know, get it up."*

"Serves the asshole right," Ty growled in her head.

"Oh, dearie me." The racket and commotion that the corpulent Marso Jlle was causing had gotten the attention of both Mistress Shy and her slave, L'Mera, who were apparently finished with their own display of pleasure for the Executor. The middle-aged Mistress leaned in toward Shaina and whispered, "I can't quite make it out from here. Is he unable to achieve . . . completion?"

"I think so," Shaina whispered back, still keeping one eye on Ty as she talked. "He seems kind of . . . well, limp."

"Oh my. I know you've never been here before, so you can't understand, but that is considered a grave insult, my dear. If he were Kandalar, he'd be in one of the colored chambers before you could blink." Shy's kindly face was concerned, although Shaina privately thought that a few weeks in a small room without food might do Jlle a world of good. She heard a short bark of laughter from Ty as he caught her thought and agreed with her.

"Stupid, worthless little whore!" Jlle was still screaming at his cringing slave. The Executor was looking on quietly, her sharp red eyes trained on the fat Master, her long face expressionless. He pulled back his grease-stained sleeve revealing the golden bangle and Shaina felt Ty tense beside her. "I'll show you what happens to slaves who can't fulfill their duties!" he bellowed in his strange underwater voice, his skin flushing an ugly mottled greenish-red.

"Stop." The Executor spoke for the first time, rising from her seat on the gold-embroidered red satin cushion and bringing herself to her full height, her skin flickering through colors so fast she seemed to blur around the edges. Her voice was not loud, but deep and commanding, and in it were all the bells they had heard earlier, modulated by the rich timbre of her tone. Shaina thought she had never heard a sound so surpassingly sweet and terrible at the same time.

"Your Excellency, I am so sorry. This worthless slave..." Jlle began, sounding a little panicky and trying to cover his wilted organ with a spare crimson table napkin, which made it look like he had a lapful of blood.

"The slave is not to be punished at this time. You are interrupting others in the act of pleasure. This must not be. You may send her away and deal with her later. We will tolerate no further disturbance." The deep, melodic voice vibrated throughout the hall and Shaina realized that everyone had stopped whatever they were doing to stare at the red-faced merchant. Jlle evidently realized it as well because he motioned angrily at the cringing slave girl and spoke in a self-conscious half-whisper. "Well, don't just sit there sniveling, you whore's git. Get yourself to the common slave quarters and don't dare to show your face to me again before I come for you. You should be grateful for the Executor's mercy. I would just as soon kill you here and now."

Giving one wide-eyed, terrified glance over her slim shoulder, the slave girl scuttled from the hall. As she left, another huge clanging of bells could be heard and Shaina saw the Masters, Mistresses, and slaves all along the long table getting up and gathering their things. The Mandatory Pleasuring was apparently over.

"Ah, poor child, she did not deserve to be so disgraced. The common slave quarters, such a shame." Shy shook her pouf of brown hair sadly.

"Is that bad?" Shaina inquired.

"Bad? My dear Meshandra, the only thing worse is a public flogging! Which the poor dear may yet receive as well. That is the usual way of things."

"So only slaves who are being punished stay in the common

quarters?" How was Ty ever going to search the male slave quarters now?

"Certainly. It's almost the same as putting them up for auction. Other Masters and Mistresses may go there and try them out . . . Oh no, the thought is quite horrid. My poor dear L'Mera, do not look so. I would cut off my right hand before sending you to the common quarters." She spoke soothingly to the blond slave at her feet, whose large blue eyes had filled with tears at the thought.

Shaina exchanged a glance with Tyson and then looked back at Mistress Shy.

"So the slaves who weren't present tonight would have to be there? I mean, there's no place else to leave your slave?" she asked carefully.

"My dear, how you do talk! Leave your slave, whatever for? Without one's slave, how is one to sleep or dress or bathe or do anything properly, really? No, I find my L'Mera quite indispensable." She patted her slave's cheek once more and then motioned for the girl to help her up. "And now, if you'll excuse me, I must go to bed. It has been such a trying day. It was lovely to meet you, and for a novice, I thought your display of pleasure was quite good. I shouldn't even be surprised to see it again tomorrow." She gave Shaina a swift, dry peck on one cheek, ruffled Tyson's hair, which Shaina could tell annoyed him greatly, and swept out of the great hall in a swirl of peacock-blue fabric.

"*Well, so much for searching the slave quarters tonight,*" Shaina stated with a mental sigh of aggravation. "*Wherever Paul is, we'll have to try and find him tomorrow.*" The Pleasure Palace was a strange and repellant place, so much so that she had been hoping to get in and out on the same day. Now she saw clearly that it wasn't going to be quite so simple to complete their mission.

"*Never mind. We'll figure something out tomorrow. For*

now, we might as well enjoy at least one night in a ten-thousand-credit-a-night room. We're not likely to get the chance again."

"Unless we get Paul out of here safely and earn the five million credits apiece," Shaina pointed out, standing up from the cushion and arranging her clothing. Ty's words had reminded her that they were going to be sharing a room tonight, and after what had just happened between them, the thought made her nervous.

"Don't know about you, sweetheart, but I'll have better ways to spend the money than renting a room at the universe's biggest freak show." Tyson's mental laughter made her smile, just the tiniest bit. At least she wasn't alone in this crazy place.

"Gotta agree with you there. This place gives me the creeps." Shaina took his leash and began filing out of the room with the other Masters and Mistresses, nodding and smiling as she went. Tyson kept his head down, playing the part of the submissive slave to the hilt. *"Now where is our room?"*

As though summoned by her thought, T'lar suddenly appeared by her elbow, startling her almost as much as he had the first time. The tall Kandalar's skin was completely red but he slid into the silver-flecked black of the hallway instantly as they crossed the threshold of the Red Pleasure Hall.

"Mistress Sender, how did you enjoy the banquet?" he inquired in his deep, oily voice, folding his long, thin hands beneath his chin—in an earnest gesture of interest, Shaina supposed.

"Oh we, I mean *I* enjoyed it very much. The food was excellent and the Executor was a feast for the eyes. Her gown was quite beyond compare. Tell me, T'lar, would it be possible for one to purchase such a garment?" If a being who was the exact same color as his immediate environment can be said to pale, T'lar did, fading from true black to almost gray at her question.

"I am afraid such, ah, garments are constructed for Her Excellency the Executor's use only. Now if you will follow me, I will show you to your room." The rest of the trip was made in a frosty silence, which was exactly what Shaina had hoped for. In her estimation, the less she talked to the lanky Kandalar, the better. She didn't care to have a repeat of their earlier conversation when she had almost blown their cover through sheer nervousness.

Sooner than she would have thought possible, they found themselves outside a pair of huge, arching double real-wood doors with elaborate designs carved around the edges. T'lar turned to her, one thin hand hovering just above the wooden surface of the righthand door.

"This is to be your chamber while you stay at the Palace, Mistress Sender," he said, bowing briefly and formally so that his bald head gleamed in the overhead glows. "You have been assigned the suite of the Starving Nun."

"The what?"

"The Starving Nun," T'lar repeated, patiently in his deep, somber voice. "It is a small bit of local history here at the Palace. Perhaps you would care to hear it?"

"I have a feeling I'll be sorry but go ahead." Shaina risked a quick glace at her partner to see that Ty was interested as well.

"Very well. Over twenty standard years ago, a nun of the order of the Sisters of Spotless Purity came to stay at the Palace. She announced that her order had heard of the God- and Goddessless doings practiced on a daily and nightly basis here. They had worked tirelessly for years to raise the sum of credit necessary for her to stay as long as it took to change the shocking habits of the Palace. Or so they thought.

"On her first night here, the nun stood up before everyone assembled at the nightly feast and announced that she was going on a hunger strike and as long as even one being in the Palace continued to practice such abhorrent behavior, she would not let a morsel pass her lips."

"Really?" Shaina was fascinated despite herself. "And what happened?"

"After a week or so, she became too weak and had to retire to her chamber." T'lar motioned at the large double doors. "This chamber."

"Oh . . ." Shaina said faintly. "And did . . . did she die?" She really didn't want to stay in a room where she knew for a fact someone had died.

"I think old T'lar's getting you back for asking to buy a dress made out of his hide," Tyson sent, his amusement coming through the symbi-link loud and clear.

"Shut up, Ty." Shaina was still looking anxiously at T'lar, who was apparently savoring the discomfort he had caused her. "Did the nun die?" she asked again.

"Well, as it happens, little Mistress, no. The ending to my tale is quite romantic. You see, a handsome young slave trader was here at the time that the Sister's credits ran out. She was young and beautiful, although considerably thinner than when she had first arrived. When she failed to pay her bill, her freedom became forfeit. So he bought her and took her away."

"Bought her?" Shaina gasped. "You mean they sold her like a . . ."

"A pleasure slave—yes, Mistress Sender. Whereupon, of course, she was enabled to experience the very activities she had come here to protest. I am sure it was most instructive for her." There was a satisfied smirk on the long face that Shaina was beginning to dislike more and more. She wondered briefly if all the Kandalar were such pains in the ass or if T'lar was going for some kind of a record.

"At this point, may I draw you attention to the print-pad located to the right of your chamber door?" T'lar motioned gracefully to a small gray pad embedded in the black wall. "Each night before you retire, you will be required to pay for the day's pleasure. As you came late this evening, you will only be charged for half a day's stay tonight. Please do not fail to settle your account every night. The consequences of ignoring this necessity are, as I am sure you can guess, most regrettable. Good night, Mistress, and pleasant dreams." He bowed formally once more and swept away, leaving Shaina staring after him.

"Well, that was an interesting little story," Ty remarked as Shaina pressed a slightly trembling thumb against the print-pad and sighed with relief as the credit indicator light turned green at her touch. *"I'm guessing not many people default on their accounts here."*

"Not if they know what's good for them." Shaina pushed the huge double doors open and walked through a short hall that opened into the chamber of the Starving Nun. *"Wow, this is plush. At least they use more than one color in the guest rooms."*

Ty snorted. *"Yeah, they really went all out and splurged. There are at least* two *colors in here."*

In fact, Shaina counted three, although two of them were shades of green and the third color was a deep, royal blue. The first thing she saw was a huge, canopied bed covered in a shimmering emerald green satin coverlet. A profusion of pillows was heaped at the head of the bed, and ornately carved realwood bedposts held up the lighter green canopy, which was worked with elaborately embroidered designs in royal blue. At the foot of the bed was a small round pillow and a synthi-cotton throw folded neatly into a rectangle.

"Guess that's where I'll be sleeping." Tyson apparently also noticed the slave sleeping arrangements.

"Tough luck, Ty." Shaina smiled a little, covering her mouth with one hand. Actually, if he had to sleep in the same bed with her, maybe this was the best way. It was . . . safer somehow. She touched the soft coverlet with one hand, wondering how such a rich fabric would feel against her skin.

"Looks like our luggage got here all right." Ty began rummaging in the huge trunk sitting out of the way to one side of the bed. *"Good, I can't wait to get out of this thing."* He indi-

cated the copper sheath and Shaina could taste the disgust in his mental voice.

"*Ty, should you? Remember what Faron said about them watching all the time . . .*"

"*To hell with that. Not even these damned kinky Kandalar can expect a slave to wear this all the time. At least not inside the room, anyway. I'm going to get out of this thing and take a super hot anti-bac shower and then I promise I'll come back and play the dutiful slave to the hilt. See you in a few.*"

"*Okay.*" For the benefit of any surveillance devices she added out loud, "Tyber, if you wish to refresh yourself you may do so now." Tyson bowed briefly and disappeared through another real-wood door that presumably led to the bathroom and Shaina wandered over to the trunk to see what other outfits she had been provided with. She found a startling array of gowns, most of them more elaborate than the one she had on, much to her dismay. The golden bustier had been pinching her unmercifully all evening but she knew better than to complain. Compared to what Ty had to wear, her Mistress costume was a piece of cake.

She had just found one relatively simple-looking black gown that was scooped low in the front, lower in the back and had the obligatory split in its skirt when she heard Ty come back into the bedchamber.

"*That was quick.*" She turned around and noticed that he had put back on the skintight leather pants but remained shirtless.

"*A dutiful slave must never keep his Mistress waiting.*" He had a mocking little grin on his face and a gleam in his eye that made Shaina nervous for some reason.

"I trust you are refreshed now, Tyber." She let her face fall into the haughty, bored look of a spoiled rich girl. "It certainly took you long enough."

"My apologies, Mistress." Ty bowed low before her, that

mocking, D'Lonian grin still playing around his full lips. "I should have been quicker. But I have taken the liberty of drawing my Mistress a bath to ease the ache of her long journey. Will it please you to accompany me?"

"A full-immersion bath? Nobody has baths anymore. They're a terrible waste of resources."

"Not here, apparently. Come on, I'll show you." Tyson turned and led her to the bathroom and before she could stop herself, Shaina gasped.

"Oh my Goddess, it's huge!"

"Nah, just ten standard inches. Oh, wait, you meant the tub." Ty was giving her that grin again and Shaina took a moment to frown at him severely before turning her attention back to the huge black tub that dominated the room. It was raised on a platform with three steps leading up to it and she wasn't sure what stone it was made out of but its highly polished surface gleamed softly in the light of the overhead glows. A faucet in the improbable shape of an ornately carved animal's head projected from one side and pink, foaming, scented water was gushing out of its gaping mouth. The tub was almost full of frothy water and it looked quite big enough to accommodate several people, which she supposed, might be the idea.

"Goddess, that's enough water for fifty showers." Walking forward, she dipped her hand into the pink, sudsy water. It was the perfect temperature, she thought, just this side of too hot, and she wondered how Tyson knew she liked that. *"Did you already take one?"* she sent, looking back at Ty, who was busy igniting some light tapers that sat on a long counter made of the same black stone as the tub.

"Of course not. A lowly slave take a bath in there? Don't think so. There's a sonic shower around the corner." He gestured towards a far corner of the huge room. *"I cleaned up in there."* Then, with a low bow, he said out loud, "If my Mistress is ready for her bath, I would be pleased to assist her." He came

around the corner of the huge tub and stood in front of Shaina, looking down at her with those hot, molten-gold eyes, and the hunger in that look made her heart skip a beat. Slowly, he reached for the fastening of the chain that kept her short golden jacket together and released the clasp so that it gaped open momentarily revealing her breasts. Shaina felt her nipples peak immediately as the humid air of the bathroom caressed them.

"Oh no you don't, Ty." She snatched the sides of the jacket together, covering her breasts and took a step back.

"Oh yes I do, Mistress." Tyson emphasized. *"Or have you forgotten that we're probably being watched?"* He walked to the glow control and turned it down low so that most of the light in the room came from the tapers flickering on the counter top. "Allow me to help you undress, Mistress. Your bath will grow cold," he said firmly, coming to stand before her again and placing both hands on the sleeves of her jacket.

"Ty . . ." Shaina felt the same helpless nervousness that she had felt at the mandatory pleasuring. She knew it was probably silly to be shy about being nude in front of Ty after all that had happened between them earlier, but she just couldn't help it.

"It's just a part, McCullough. A role you have to play," Ty reminded her as before. *"I'm your slave and you're my Mistress. It'll look wrong if I just leave the room and don't at least help you undress. Come on, you can do this."* His mental tone was patient, almost bored. Only the fire in his amber eyes made Shaina think he had anything more than a professional interest in undressing her. Reluctantly, she forced herself to let go of the sides of her jacket and allowed Ty to remove it.

Once again her breasts were bared, pushed up for display by the golden bustier, and though Shaina wanted desperately to cover herself with her hands, she realized that it wouldn't look right at all. Instead, she turned her back to Tyson and let him work the long row of tiny fastenings along her back that held the bustier together. Putting it on by herself had been quite a chore and she had to admit it was nice to have help getting out of it. She breathed a sigh of relief when the tight, pinching garment was finally removed, since it was the first time she'd been able to get a deep breath the whole day.

Silently, Tyson worked the clasp on her skirt and removed that as well before coming back around to face her and kneel in front of her. "If my Mistress will allow me?" Reaching up he hooked his fingers into the waistband of the golden bikini-cut panties and pulled them slowly down her legs. He helped her remove her boots and then Shaina was completely naked in front of him as he knelt before her. She caught a brief thought from him, that she looked beautiful, all pale cream and auburn fire in the flickering taper light. There was something in his amber eyes, a look she couldn't quite read, but it sent a sudden flurry of chillbumps down her spine anyway. She shivered in the humid air, wrapping her arms around her body and trembling.

"Forgive me, Mistress, you are cold. Allow me to assist you into the tub."

"Yes, that would be . . . acceptable," Shaina said, feeling slightly surreal. She allowed Ty to take her hand and lead her up the three steps to the raised tub and then held onto him as she carefully sank down into the delicious warmth of the bath. "Oh . . ."

"Is it too hot?" His voice sounded a little more normal Ty and less devoted slave, which Shaina found comforting.

"Almost, but that's the way I like it." Realizing that as her slave he would already know how she liked her bath, she added, "You have done well, Tyber, as usual."

"Thank you, Mistress. Allow me to tend you." Before she could ask what he meant, Shaina felt him pulling the jeweled hairpins out of her hair, letting it fall in a warm waterfall down her back. "Lean your head back, Mistress, that I might tend your hair," he murmured. Shaina closed her eyes and did as he commanded, relishing the feel of warm water pouring over her hair and Ty's strong fingers massaging a shampoo scented like exotic flowers into her scalp.

"That's lovely, Tyber." She relaxed despite the awkward situation. Once again, it might only be a role he was playing but Ty was marvelously good at it. No one had washed her hair for her since she was a very little girl and she found the sensation of Ty's large, competent hands rubbing her scalp wonderfully soothing.

"My Mistress has beautiful hair." His voice was low and quiet; she felt his breath warm against her ear. "It is a pleasure to serve you so, Mistress."

"Indeed . . ." Shaina didn't quite know what else to say and decided to just relax and enjoy the lovely pampering. By the time Ty rinsed her hair carefully, making sure not to get any water in her eyes, she was half asleep in the huge black tub.

"Sit up now, Mistress. It is time to bathe you." Ty's voice brought her back from a semi-doze and before she knew it, Shaina was sitting up in the tub.

"I'm probably clean enough now, Tyber," she said, thinking she should get out of the bath before she fell entirely asleep.

"How can you be, Mistress, when I haven't scrubbed you yet?" Hearing that low, seductive growl in his voice, Shaina suddenly felt much more awake.

"Scrubbed me?" She began to lose the lovely relaxed feeling.

"Certainly. It is a great pity that the Kandalar appear to have forgotten to provide us with bathing sponges. But for tonight, at least, I will simply have to use my hands. There is plenty of cleansing foam, at least." Shaina watched mutely as Ty gathered large handfuls of pink bath foam from another, smaller faucet and leaned towards her. "Hold out your arm, Mistress," he commanded, and without waiting for her to comply, he took her by the hand and began rubbing the pink foam along the length of her right arm in long, caressing strokes. The left arm was next, and then he scrubbed her back, being careful not to get the foam in her newly washed hair. Ty then had her put each leg out of the water in turn for a thorough coating of pink foam.

Shaina was beginning to feel relaxed again—Ty's large, warm hands on her body felt wonderfully good, like an all-over massage—when he pulled her against the back of the tub and whispered in a low, intimate voice in her ear, "Now for your breasts, Mistress."

"Oh, Tyber, really I think I am clean enough." Shaina fought to keep her voice level but it went all high and squeaky at the end of the sentence anyway.

"Nonsense, Mistress. Just relax and let me tend you." He was sitting behind her on the steps leading up to the tub and she felt those large, warm hands, slick with soap, slipping around the sides of her body to cup her naked breasts as she lay, half floating in the hot water.

"Goddess . . ." she whispered weakly as she felt him caress her breasts, felt her nipples harden in his palms as he rubbed her gently but firmly.

"Does it please you, Mistress?"

"Very . . . very much, Tyber." Shaina bit back a moan as he began to pinch her nipples lightly, rolling them between his fingers and thumbs and causing electric sparks of pleasure to shoot from her breasts to the sensitive area between her legs.

"Shall I wash lower?" he asked, one large hand traveling from her chest to her abdomen and dipping suggestively just an inch or two into the water that covered her there. It seemed that Shaina had lost the ability to think, she could only feel. And what she wanted to feel right now were Ty's large, strong hands all over her body.

"Do as you think best," she whispered, not trusting herself to say anything else.

"Yes, Mistress." She felt his hand dip lower into the water, spreading her legs and parting the slick folds of her sex as he tenderly caressed the sensitive bud of her clitoris with one gentle finger.

"Oh . . . that feels . . . feels so good," she gasped, and closed her eyes tightly while thrusting her pelvis up to his stroking hand. She felt one long finger slide a little way into her tight, virginal pussy and moaned at the sensation, biting her lip to keep from crying out.

"You're so tight tonight, Mistress, almost like the first time. Do you remember the first we made love?" Tyson whispered, still stroking her gently as he talked, driving her crazy with his gentle, insistent touch.

"The . . . the first time?" Shaina wondered at first what he was talking about. Then she realized that he must be detailing their bogus past together for the benefit of the surveillance devices. "Oh yes, the first time. It was . . ." She couldn't continue. Ty's hand on her, his fingers inside her were making it too hard to think.

"I remember you were frightened, Mistress. Afraid I might hurt you. But I love you with my whole heart and I tried to make you understand that I wanted only your pleasure. Remember?"

"I remember," Shaina whispered. His mouth was on her now, his hot tongue licking the sensitive spot just under her ear and sucking the tender area between her neck and shoulder.

"I remember how it felt the first time I slid into your body and felt your soft, wet heat around my shaft," Tyson breathed in her ear. "I remember the way you opened for me, the way you cried out under me when I began to move. To thrust inside you."

"Yes . . ." She could feel her orgasm building now, could vividly picture the things Ty was telling her. His words, as much as his hand, were driving her to distraction. Shaina found she was moving rhythmically in time to his fingers stroking over her clit and into her passage—although not nearly as deep or as hard as she found she wanted him to go.

"I remember the way you wrapped your legs around my waist and matched me stroke for stroke. The way you scratched my back and called my name and begged me to fuck you harder, Mistress. I remember holding you close as we came together, filling your sweet, hot cunt with my seed as you trembled and sobbed beneath me. It felt so good to take you that way, so right. As though we belonged together for ever and always. As though we would never be parted. Do you remember?"

"Oh Ty, how could I forget?" Shaina moaned, thrusting against his hand shamelessly, giving in to the pleasure that was so close to tearing her apart. But just as her orgasm was about to reach its crest, Ty abruptly stopped his motions and pulled away.

"I am glad the memory lives on in your heart as well, Mistress. But now it is time to rinse the foam from your body. I wouldn't like your beautiful, creamy skin to dry out from overexposure to the soap."

"Time to *what*?" Half turning, she faced him to see if he was serious. *"Ty, what are you doing?"* She wondered if he had any idea at all how close she had been, teetering on the very brink of release.

"Just giving you a taste of your own medicine, McCullough," he sent back, flashing her that wicked D'Lonian grin. *"Don't worry, we've got all night."* And with that disquieting statement, he helped her to her rather unsteady feet and proceeded to pour rivers of warm water over her body and breasts, using a golden container with a spout that looked as though it had been made for that exact purpose.

"I think I am sufficiently rinsed now, Tyber," Shaina said crossly after the fourth or fifth gallon of pink, sudsy water had poured over her. She didn't have to put up with his teasing, she thought. She could simply go to bed and guess who would be sleeping down at the foot? That's right, Mr. Time To Rinse himself.

"Not quite, Mistress. There is one area that I have neglected to rinse and since I spend such a long time soaping it, I think some rinsing is a definite necessity."

"Oh, you mean . . ." Shaina faltered.

"Yes, Mistress. Be so kind as to spread your legs for me that I might attend you." Ty turned her so that she was facing him and spread her thighs apart with his strong hands. Feeling like her legs were made of flavor-gel, Shaina let him. "Hold on to my shoulders, Mistress, if you are unsteady." Tyson kneeled before her with the watering spout in one hand.

"All right." Shaina placed both small, trembling hands on Ty's broad golden shoulders as he carefully spread the tender, swollen lips of her sex and poured a thin rivulet of warm water over her sensitive clit. She was still throbbing from the gentle stroking of his fingers. The water soothed and tormented at once, tickling and tingling over her enflamed flesh, and Shaina couldn't stop herself from gasping out loud. She grabbed Ty's shoulders hard as he poured.

"There now, I think you are quite well rinsed. Would you agree, Mistress?" There was a mischievous light burning in his hot, amber eyes but Shaina could do nothing but grit her teeth and agree.

"Yes . . . yes, Tyber. I think you're right."

"Step out of the tub and allow me to dry you, Mistress." He helped her out of the deep tub to stand on the topmost step. Standing one step below her, he was only a little taller than she, and for a moment, Shaina found herself close enough to look deeply into his eyes. They flickered golden-amber in the taper light and his hawklike features were half obscured by darkness. It made him look like a man divided in half by light and shadow. For a moment, Shaina saw her partner clearly for the first time. *This is what he is,* a voice in her head whispered. *Half human and half D'Lonian. Half man and half beast.* The thought frightened and excited her at the same time and her body was strung tight as a wire. She searched his eyes, looking for his true nature. If they were to make love tonight, would Ty be gentle and slow or would he ravage her, claim her body with rough kisses and hot, savage thrusts into her tight, virgin cunt? Shaina wasn't sure she had the courage to find out.

The moment ended when Ty leaned forward and gave her a slow, teasing kiss. Parting her lips, he explored her mouth with his tongue until she sighed with pleasure. His mouth tasted slightly spicy and wild and the warm, masculine scent of him filled her head. He eased away slowly and began patting her down with a plush synthi-cotton towel. He rubbed her arms and legs and back dry and when he got to the soft triangle of reddish hair between her thighs, Shaina spread her legs without having to be told.

"I'm trying to dry you off, Mistress, but you're still so wet." With the towel, he gently patted her throbbing sex.

"Can you recommend a remedy for that?" Shaina asked softly, not sure if she was playing along or being serious.

"I'm sure I can come up with something." Tyson grinned at her and Shaina noticed the huge bulge in his tight leather pants. She remembered rubbing the lubricating oil onto his hard cock earlier that evening and wondering how that thick shaft would feel inside her. She was desperate to find out and yet . . . she was still so afraid. If only he wasn't so *big*.

"I think it's past your bedtime, Mistress." Ty gave her a smoldering look, and without warning, swept her into his arms and carried her into the bedroom. Shaina gasped and wrapped her arms around his neck, feeling the smooth, powerfully muscled skin of his bare chest rub against her naked body as he walked. Depositing her gently in the middle of the huge four-poster bed, he climbed onto it beside her.

Shaina lay on her back on the bed and felt small as Tyson

loomed over her. He had dimmed the glows in the bedroom as well. He looked huge . . . almost animalistic with his thick black hair wild around his head and his eyes glittering like topaz in the half-light. She wanted him, knew the whole night had been leading up to this in one way or another, but now that she came to the actual act, she found herself freezing up and losing her nerve. Sensing her reluctance, he leaned back a little and looked into her eyes.

"*What's wrong, sweetheart?*" His mental tone was as close to tender as Shaina had ever heard it and it calmed her somewhat.

"*I don't know, Ty. I'm just . . . scared. I wonder if . . . I mean, would you mind . . .*" She hesitated, biting her lip nervously.

"*We don't have to actually do this tonight, Shaina.*" Ty's voice was still gentle, not angry or upset as she had been afraid he would be. "*We agreed to fake it as much as possible. I'm sure I can give a good enough performance of 'servicing' you that no one will ever know the difference.*"

"*And . . . you don't mind?*" Shaina apprehensively ran one hand over his muscular bicep.

"*Shaina, please try to understand this once and for all: I'm not interested in hurting you or doing anything that makes you uncomfortable unless we really can't avoid it. Come on, get under the covers with me and we'll give a performance they'll never forget.*"

He was stripping off his leather pants as he sent this thought through their symbi-link. Shaina caught a glimpse of his thick, hard cock only briefly before he slid under the covers and pulled her close to him.

"Mmm, you feel so good in my arms." Large hands rubbed over her slender body and he dipped his head to kiss her mouth slowly and lingeringly. She could feel his thick length along her belly, hot and throbbing for her and she whispered in his ear, "Service me, Tyber. Just as you did the first time."

"Spread your legs for me, Mistress," he answered, maneuvering so that he was on top of her, leaning over her in the gloom of the bedroom. "It will be my pleasure to do as you command."

Shaina felt him parting her thighs and she gasped a little, feeling panicky.

"Ty, you said we wouldn't really . . ."

"Relax, Shaina. I'm just making it look more realistic. I'm going to rub against you, that's all. Okay?" As though to prove his point, the length of his shaft rubbed against her lower abdomen as she cupped him between her legs.

"Okay." She trembled as she felt his hard, hot flesh brush against her. Despite his promise that they wouldn't actually have sex tonight, she still felt completely open and vulnerable in this position.

"Fine, pretend I'm putting it in now." He made a small, thrusting motion with his hips, pressing against her more forcefully and Shaina drew in her breath in a small gasp.

"Oh!"

"Oh? Come on, sweetheart, you can do better than that. If we're going to fake this, you have to help me. Let's do this right. I'm putting my cock inside you now, can you feel it?"

Ty made another small gesture with his hips and Shaina wiggled beneath him, moaning a little as she moved.

"Better?" Anxiously, she searched his eyes as he loomed above her.

"A little, but not much. Here."

"What . . . what are you doing?" Ty had reached between them and was parting the folds of her wet sex with his large, blunt fingertips, spreading her open completely, making her utterly vulnerable to him.

"I promise I'm not going to fuck you tonight, Shaina, but you need to feel this to fake it. I'm just going to be rubbing against you here. *Can you feel me?"*

Shaina gasped as the flared head and thick shaft of his rigid cock rubbed firmly over her sensitive, swollen clit. Tyson's eyes burned hot gold in the dim room as he pressed against her and thrust again, not into her but gliding over her, wetting his shaft with her moisture as he spread her tender pussy lips apart with his cock and the cleft of her cunt cradled his thickness.

"Goddess . . ." she moaned out loud, spreading her legs wider to better feel the sweet pressure between her thighs.

"*That's more like it, sweetheart. Keep it up. I'm fucking you now. Can you feel it? Can you feel my cock inside you, fucking deep inside your sweet little pussy?*" Ty's voice in her head was white-hot as he leaned over her, thrusting against her cunt.

"I can feel it!" He rubbed against her again, harder this time. "I can feel you, Oh, Ty!"

"Yes, Mistress," he grated, thrusting harder. "*Do you feel me, Shaina? Do you feel me filling you up? Stretching your cunt with my cock? Shoving it all the way inside you?*"

The hot, dirty words in her head and the delicious friction of his thick shaft against her wet, open sex was too much. Shaina felt herself building towards orgasm again and she knew that this time nothing could stop her. She thrust up, matching her partner stroke for stroke as he moved against her, wrapping her legs around his waist and clawing his broad back with her nails. Goddess how she wanted him inside her . . .

"*Ty . . . think I'm going to come . . .*" His response was immediate.

"*Good, come for me, sweetheart. Wanna feel you coming all over me, all over my cock. Wanna fuck you till you scream and fill you up with my cum.*" The words pushed her over the edge, and Shaina felt herself let go, exploding in slow motion like a star in deep space going nova. At the same time, she heard Tyson's hoarse shout and felt a wet warmth against her belly. His pleasure, which she felt through their link, was as intense as her own, and the connection between them seemed to grow stronger and more solid. For a split second, Shaina felt that she could find the answer to any question she wanted in his mind. And then the pleasure ebbed and the moment was gone.

"*Oh . . .*" she whispered through the link after a long, panting moment. "*How do you do that to me, Ty? When you talk like that while you're touching me . . .*"

"My Mistress is satisfied?" He did not answer her question.

"More than satisfied." She wanted to talk further about it, to ask him if he felt the same strong connection between them when they shared the intense pleasure of orgasm, but he was already getting out of bed and fetching a towel to wipe her clean. Afterwards he climbed back into bed, not beside her, but at the foot of the huge four-poster, in a slave's proper position

"Good night, Mistress." Ty's voice in the darkness was deep and soft. Shaina wished very much that he was lying beside her instead of way down at the foot of the huge bed, but she understood it wouldn't look right.

"*Ty?*"

"*Hmm?*" His mental voice was heavy with sleep and Shaina felt bad for disturbing him. Though she wanted to ask him to hold her, she realized how silly it would sound. Just as he had been earlier in the banquet hall, Ty was playing a part. That was all. The thought should have been comforting. She had nothing to worry about, nothing to fear from him; he was only doing his job and he didn't really want her for anything more than a coworker, after all. But instead, Shaina found that it depressed her greatly. She lay on the bed, her face buried in the satin pillow cover, listening to Ty's deep, even breathing and trying not to cry, until she fell asleep.

12

Tyson was having a dream about the first time he'd ever tried touching himself *there*. Some of the older girls in First School had been talking about it in the girls' room and he had overheard them and couldn't wait to try it. *Sneaking in the front door, careful, make sure nobody's around. Then up to my room, shut the door, this is private. Pull up my skirt and push down my favorite panties, blue like the sky, to touch just* there. *Mmmm . . . feels tingly and good. Sort of naughty too . . .*

Ty woke up with a groan and rolled on his side to look at the still-sleeping Shaina. Wasn't it hard enough for him to be around her, wanting her the way he did, without having to share her erotic dreams too? Last night had been pure torture and it had taken all the self-control he possessed to keep from taking her savagely instead of just pretending. His D'Lonian blood had been boiling in his veins, insisting that Shaina belonged to him and he should claim her fully, forging a Bond between them. But he had held off. When they did make love he wanted it to be on her terms. Otherwise he'd lose any chance he ever had of keeping her forever. But damn it, it was so hard to stop.

Shaina began to stir, her dream breaking up into fragments, and Tyson prepared to play the dutiful slave for another long day. And under that role was another one, the disinterested coworker. He was determined that Shaina would not guess his true emotions until she was ready to reciprocate them. Until then, he would have to shield his thoughts carefully; he knew Shaina was still picking up his random thoughts from time to time and he certainly was getting a lot from her. He knew, for instance, that she had wanted him to hold her last night after their "performance" and he had wanted to do it so badly. But he just couldn't trust himself. Even after their mutual orgasm, he'd still wanted her so much . . .

"*Good morning, sleepyhead,*" he voiced through the link, seeing Shaina's eyelids flutter open at last, revealing sleepy deep green eyes that reminded him of the ocean on a calm day.

"Good morning, Tyber," Shaina responded out loud. A little more shyly, she sent, "*Morning Ty. What's the plan for today?*"

"*Basically, I think we'd better spend the day exploring this place. Spread some of the Chancellor's credit around and look like you're having the time of your life. We can stop by the common slave quarters and see if Paul's there. If he is, you can make an offer and maybe we can be out of this freak show by tonight.*"

"*Won't they think it's suspicious, only staying one night?*" Shaina sat up in the bed and stretched, careful to keep the satin sheet above her breasts.

"*Nah, you can make up a story about your credit running out. Maybe Papa Sender didn't know you were taking this little vacation and he's pissed off, so you have to go home. Something like that.*"

"*Sounds reasonable. After all, I am a spoiled brat.*" She tossed her head so that her silky red hair fanned over her bare shoulders like living flame. Tyson thought how beautiful she was.

"*Yeah. Well, it's time to get up now, brat. Time's wasting.*

"*I'm with you. Let's find Paul and get the hell out of this bloody place.*"

"*Such language, Mistress. I was beginning to think you were enjoying yourself.*" Ty stood up and stretched, giving her a sardonic look as he did so. Shaina dropped her eyes and blushed, trying not to look at his naked body.

"*Don't tease, Ty. You know we're only doing what we have to do.*"

"*I know. Sorry.*" He sighed and reached for the discarded leather pants. There it was again, Shaina's unwillingness to admit there was anything between them but a working relationship. Would it ever change?

"Tyber, what are you doing?" she asked, in her Mistress voice as he squirmed his way into the skintight leather.

"Dressing so that I might attend you, Mistress." He spoke through gritted teeth, trying to button the too-small fly.

"Have you forgotten the proper dress for a slave in the Executor's Palace?" She nodded at the copper sheath he had been so glad to get out of the night before, lying on the small table near the doors. Damn, he hated to put it back on.

"I will, of course, dress as befits a slave when we leave our chamber, Mistress. If my Mistress will be so kind as to prepare me?" He picked up a small vial of the viscous red oil, which had been left in a small basket with some fruit and flowers on the table. Shaina paled and her green eyes widened.

"On second thought, I am sure it will not be necessary to replace your sheath until just before we leave. I have a mind to take a shower this morning to help me wake up. Be so kind as to fetch me a robe, Tyber." Her tone was haughty.

Tyson went to the huge trunk of clothes and pretended to search inside it.

"Doubtless I should be beaten for it, Mistress, but it seems I have forgotten to pack your robe." He turned a bland face to Shaina as she sat up in the huge bed and clutched the sheet to her breasts. *"What's the big deal, McCullough? I saw it all last night, you know."*

"I know, but that was in the dark and now it's broad solar-light." She indicated the pale blue light coming in through the embroidered drapes hanging at the large double windows across from the bed.

It was the first natural light Ty had seen on this planet and it lifted his spirits considerably, even if it was weak as water and barely there. Syrus Six was a good distance from the blue giant star it orbited. He grinned at Shaina and pulled back the drapes so that even more light shone in.

"Tough, sweetheart, but don't forget we're being watched. I'm going to have to dress you, so I'll see you in the altogether no matter how bright or dark it is. Besides, if I can wear that damn contraption"—he indicated the sheath—*"then you can walk around in the buff a little bit. It won't kill you."*

"Fine." Shaina lifted her head defiantly and threw back the covers, rising to the challenge as Tyson had known she would. She flushed from head to toe as she walked slowly to the bathing room, but she never faltered even as she felt his eyes on her body.

"You're beautiful, you know," Ty couldn't help thinking. He admired the regal tilt of her head, and her slender body was firm and rounded in all the right places. Her full breasts were tipped with pale pink nipples, just made to be sucked, and that sweet, downy patch of reddish curls between her legs . . . He could feel himself rising to attention in the uncomfortably tight leather pants just watching her. Shaina turned to him and tossed her hair again in that defiant little flip, causing it to cascade down around her creamy shoulders.

"I am most seriously displeased, Tyber. We will see to the matter of my robe at a later time, but for now I am anxious to explore the Palace. Have my outfit for today laid out for me when I get out of the shower. I will wear the black gown." And with that, she turned her shapely backside to him and sashayed into the bathing room, closing the door behind her.

Tyson breathed a sigh of relief as they finally shut the doors of the Starving Nun's chamber behind them. Getting Shaina dressed in her current outfit, a long, black gown that was cut low everywhere and clung to her slender body like a jealous lover, had been hard enough. He kept wanting to touch her creamy skin more than was absolutely necessary, wanting to kiss her and take her back to the bed to finish what they had started the night before. But allowing her to oil him and replace the copper sheath had been pure, unadulterated torture. The gentle touch of her small, soft hand on his cock as she oiled him lingeringly was enough to make Tyson ache for release and there wasn't a damn thing he could do about it. The D'Lonian blood in his veins howled that he had to have her right now, that she was his, damn it, and Tyson had to ignore it. But he didn't know how much longer he could go on doing that . . .

"Good morningtime, little Mistress. I trust you slept well?" It was T'lar, of course. He slid smoothly up to them as though he had been waiting for them all night—as, Ty reflected, maybe he had.

"Well, if it isn't my favorite Kandalar." Shaina gave the tall, thin humanoid an arch smile. "I am in search of some breakfast at this moment. If you don't mind, T'lar, can you direct me to some food?"

"Most certainly, Mistress Sender. In fact, might I suggest that you break your fast in the viewing room? There may be something of interest for you to see there."

"Lead the way by all means, T'lar." Shaina waved her hand imperiously, and with a low, graceful bow, the tall Kandalar preceded them down the long, black hallway, his bald head gleaming in the light of the overhead glows.

"Wonder what he wants you to see?" Ty tagged along at Shaina's heels and kept his eyes down like an obedient slave.

"In this place, who know? Probably some perverted display that would make a whore blush back home." Shaina's mental voice was grim and the set of her slender shoulders was tight. She really didn't like it here. Not that Ty could blame her.

"Take it easy, sweetheart. We'll be out of here soon."

"From your mouth to the Goddess's ear."

They stopped outside a large, golden saloon, in which one entire wall was covered with paper-thin viewers. In the center of the room was a holo-grid. It was inactive at the moment, but from the scenes flashing across the viewers, mostly sexual in nature, Ty thought he could guess what would pop out of the grid eventually. Small round tables for one or two occupants were scattered around the golden wood floors, and the walls were decorated with darker gold etchings and designs. Tyson saw the fat merchant, Marso Jlle, sitting by himself in one corner, for once with no slave at his feet. Jlle was digging into what looked like a huge pile of entrails, thick ropes of glistening purplish tissue that he slurped down with relish. Disgusting, Ty thought and hoped that Shaina hadn't noticed. She had barely eaten anything the night before and he was sure watching Jlle eat his grotesque breakfast wouldn't do anything for her appetite.

"Here you may acquire food for yourself and your slave. I wish you a good meal and I will find you after you finish to see if you require anything further." T'lar melted away into the black hallway as Shaina made her way to a small table in the corner and pointedly put her back to both the wall full of viewers and the holo-grid. Ty settled on the floor at her feet, keeping an eye on the viewers and the grid just in case.

A thin, golden-skinned Kandalar with a waterfall of pale hair came almost immediately to their table. She had the biggest tray that Ty had ever seen and it was completely covered with steaming delicacies on thin, golden plates.

"Do you see anything that pleases you here, Mistress?" the Kandalar asked in a soft, low voice. "If not, I can easily send to the kitchens for something else."

"That won't be necessary." Looking over the tray, she pretended to take her time choosing among the dishes. *"What are you in the mood for, Ty?"*

"I'm not picky. Anything with plenty of meat."

"Fine." Shaina selected several plates from the tray, keeping one for herself and setting the other on the floor for Tyson. The Kandalar bowed and left.

"At least the food is good here; you have to give them that," she sent reflectively, digging into something that looked like an omelet with flecks of unfamiliar vegetables in it.

"It might taste better if I didn't have to eat it off the floor," Ty replied while balancing his plate on his knees and taking a bite of his breakfast.

"Oh, poor baby, my heart bleeds for you." She nudged him under the table with her foot and Tyson reached out and captured her slim ankle in one large hand. The black gown gaped open momentarily and he caught a glimpse of the matching black silk panties that peaked from between her creamy thighs. He remembered pulling them up her long legs where they covered the triangle of crisp red curls and hoped he would get a chance to pull them down again later.

"Ty, honestly . . ." Shaina complained, pulling her ankle away. Tyson grinned at her and was about to go back to his meal when suddenly the holo-grid behind her popped into life with a small, electric sizzle. The bite he had been about to eat froze halfway to his mouth.

"Uh, McCullough, I think you might want to see this."

"What is it showing? More sick bastards performing twisted

sexual perversions? No thanks." Shaina took another bite of her omelet and kept her back resolutely to the holo-grid.

"*Suit yourself. It's just that the 'sick bastards performing twisted sexual perversions' happen to be us.*"

"*What?*" Shaina dropped her eating utensil with a clatter and turned abruptly to face the holo-grid. There on its rectangular six-by-six-standard-foot surface was a very convincing reproduction of both of them during the Mandatory Pleasuring at last night's banquet.

Tyson watched Shaina gasp in undisguised horror as she saw the holo-Ty spread the holo-Shaina's thighs and begin to taste her. The holo-Shaina moaned and buried her fingers in his hair to pull him closer as he tenderly parted the lips of her sex and kissed and sucked her swollen pink clit while she writhed beneath his mouth.

"*Oh, my merciful Goddess!*" Shaina moaned through the link, flushing red with embarrassment. "*How can they show this at breakfast?*"

"*So you object based solely on the fact that they're showing it at breakfast?*" Ty choked back a laugh. "*You think this is more of a dinner show?*"

"*Ty! How can you laugh at this? It's humiliating!*"

Actually, Tyson thought it was hot. The night before, he been completely involved in tasting his beautiful red-haired partner and hadn't been able to watch the look in her eyes or the expression on her face while he did so. Now he was able to really study her, to watch the way her body moved under his tongue, to see the way her fingers tugged at his hair and scratched across his back as she rode his mouth. The look on her face alone, her eyes squeezed tightly shut and her pink mouth open slightly, panting with pleasure, was enough to have him hard and throbbing inside the copper sheath as he watched.

"*I . . . I can't believe I really look like that when you . . . when we . . .*" Shaina seemed unable to finish her sentence.

"*Look like what? Beautiful, hot, wanton, wild?*" Ty watched their holo-images writhe on the grid.

"*Try slutty, cheap, disgusting, and perverted.*" Her mental tone was grim. She threw down her gold linen table napkin and stood up abruptly, grabbing his leash. "*Come on, Ty, we're going.*"

"*What about breakfast?*" Ty demanded, rising to his feet to follow her.

"*I just lost my appetite.*" Shaina stalked out of the viewing room, keeping her eyes down and trying to avoid the looks of the other Masters, Mistresses, Kandalar, and slaves as they passed. They were almost to the door when suddenly, Marso Jlle was blocking their path.

"Good morning, Mistress Sender. That was quite an impressive display last night." He nodded at their images still writhing on the holo-grid, leering so widely that his fat cheeks almost swallowed his tiny raisin eyes. "Seeing you ride your D'Lonian's mouth so eagerly has given me an even greater appreciation of his . . . ah, oral abilities. I've still a mind to try that mouth for myself when you change your mind about selling." His vestigial gills flexed with amusement and his flat black eyes glittered greedily.

Ty felt a growl curling up from his throat, but Shaina held him in check with a sharp tug on the leash and a brief look. "I've told you before that Tyber is *not* for sale," she said in her frostiest tone, looking down her nose disdainfully at Jlle. "And frankly, Master Jlle, I'm surprised you had time to notice anything my slave and I were doing last night. As I recall, you were most preoccupied with your own performance, or lack thereof."

The Tenibrian merchant's face turned a mottled red-green color and he clenched his fat hands into fists. "You dare . . ." he said thickly, his undersea voice bubbling unpleasantly in his thick chest. He took a step forward and Tyson pulled the leash out of Shaina's hand getting between them. Jlle took one look at his fierce amber eyes and bared white teeth and stepped back as quickly as he had stepped forward. The message Ty was sending was clear: *Touch my Mistress and pay the consequences.* The growl in his throat was building to a snarl.

"Animal like that ought to have on a collar," Jlle muttered angrily.

"I don't need a collar to control my slaves." Voice sugarsweet, Shaina stepped around so that she was standing beside Tyson and took his leash as unobtrusively as she could.

"*Easy, Ty.*" She wrapped leather around her hand.

"Now if you'll excuse me, Master Jlle, I have important matters to attend to." She stepped around the portly Tenibran but Jlle wasn't done yet.

"You'd better hope your credit never runs out, Mistress Sender," he spat. "Because if it does, I'll buy you myself and teach you to use that pretty mouth for better things than insults."

Shaina didn't even bother to turn around. "That is a pleasure I fear you'll never have, Master Jlle." She gave him a last icy glance and swept out into the black, silver-flecked hallway without looking back.

Tyson did look back. As the red rage cleared from his vision, he saw that Jlle had left the doorway, but he could still catch a glimpse of their holo-images writhing on the grid in the center of the viewing room. By the set of Shaina's shoulders, she was still hideously embarrassed, although Ty thought she had handled the situation with the fat Tenibran very well, much better than he probably would've.

"*You know, it just occurred to me that this was what that Mistress beside you meant when she said she wouldn't be surprised to see our performance again.*" Ty tried to get her to lighten up.

"To think that . . . that animal had the nerve to say those things . . ." Shaina's mental voice was choked with loathing and disgust. *"And to think that everyone in there is watching us . . . do what we did, over and over . . ."*

"Oh come on, McCullough, get over it. After all, it's old news to these people."

"I guess maybe they have seen it all before," Shaina sent, reluctantly, but Tyson could see she was still burning with embarrassment; her creamy skin flushed a rosy pink.

"They certainly have. Don't forget we did that last night in front of all of them. The holo is nothing compared with the real thing."

"Goddess, did you have to remind me? Of all the awful things to do, showing us acting like that right in the middle of the room . . ."

"But we did act like that in the middle of the room."

"I said don't remind me!"

"I trust you enjoyed your breakfast, Mistress Sender?" T'lar's unctuous voice slid smoothly over Tyson's ears as the tall Kandalar appeared out of nowhere as always.

"I most certainly did not," Shaina fumed, marching down the hall and refusing to stop for anything. The Kandalar had to hurry to catch up to her rapid strides.

"But, whatever can be the matter, little Mistress? Were you not pleased with the food?

"The food was fine," Shaina snarled, suddenly rounding on the worried humanoid. "It was the entertainment that ruined my appetite."

"But . . ." T'lar look of utter confusion was marred only slightly by a sly smile. "Did you not enjoy watching yourself as you ate? It is a great honor to be chosen for display on the holo-grid, especially for a novice to the Palace such as yourself."

"I have never . . . *never* been so deeply humiliated in all my life!" Shaina spat, poking T'lar in his narrow chest. "To think that you have the nerve . . ."

"*Easy, sweetheart. Remember that this is part of the package deal when you come here. He's going to get suspicious.*"

". . . that you have the nerve to record my bad side like that," Shaina finished somewhat weakly, withdrawing her finger and attempting to look more composed.

"But Mistress, the holographic image is three-dimensional. What 'bad side' do you speak of?" T'lar protested.

"Never mind, T'lar. I am sick of the viewing room. For now, take me to the common slave quarters. I have half a mind to buy a new slave to take my mind off that display."

"Certainly, Mistress Sender. Do you wish to view the male or female quarters?" T'lar asked, instantly accommodating, as always whenever credit was mentioned.

"The female quarters first, I think. And if I don't see anything that I like there, we can visit the male quarters." Shaina tossed her head and flashed her eyes in Ty's direction. "This D'Lonian of mine is getting a bit tiring and a change of flavor might be nice."

"*Oh, you wound me, McCullough.*"

"*Watch it, Ty.*" Shaina's back was to him as they marched along the corridors and he couldn't tell if she was kidding or not. He sighed. It was shaping up to be a long day.

13

Shaina didn't know when she'd been more humiliated. Even the time in Second School when the magno tabs on her skirt had failed and her entire third-period bio class had seen her panties didn't begin to come close. She had known when she accepted this mission that some awkwardness was inevitable, and Faron had told them that everything they did would be recorded, but somehow it hadn't really sunk in until just now in the viewing room when she'd had to watch herself being pleasured by Ty over and over. Had to watch herself writhe under his mouth and scratch at his shoulders as he made her cry and moan and beg and come in front of everyone.

Ty was acting like it was no big deal because it *was* no big deal to him. He was just her coworker—who happened to give her mind-blowing orgasms as part of the job they were doing together. It didn't matter to him. But damn it, it mattered to her! It mattered because sex was supposed to mean something.

Sex is a gift, honey. Shaina could almost hear her mom's voice inside her head. *If you go giving it away to just anyone, it loses all its value. Wait until you find the right one to give it to. You'll know when you meet him.*

Shaina wasn't still a virgin because she was prudish or uninterested in sex. Far from it. She was still a virgin because she was waiting for the right one. The way she'd felt the night before, after Ty had bathed her so tenderly and stroked against her until she'd exploded in his arms, had made her wonder, just a little, if he might be the one. There had always been a strong attraction between them, which was why she had been so uncomfortable working with him back home. But Shaina had let her fear of his D'Lonian side hold her back and denied even to herself that there was anything there.

Now she wondered if Ty would ever feel the same way about her that she was beginning to feel about him. Or would he just go on being smirkingly sarcastic and coldly professional in turns throughout the mission?

"Mistress, may I present to you the female common slave quarters?" T'lar's oily voice interrupted Shaina's musings and she made an effort to pull herself together. She needed to stop concentrating on her private life and get back to the business at hand. The life of the Chancellor's son hung in the balance and she had been hired to save him. Her own needs and emotions had to be put on the back burner until this situation was resolved, she told herself sternly.

"Excellent. Let us see if anything catches my fancy," Shaina replied in her most imperious voice and followed the tall Kandalar past a set of gold-leaf double doors and into a room decorated entirely in shades of deep rose pink.

Shaina scanned up and down the room, which was set up rather like a stable, with a row of long, narrow stalls along each wall.

"Wow, slaves on the hoof," Ty commented but she didn't answer. Instead, she paced slowly up and down the rows of stalls,

pretending to examine the various slave girls for sale. There was something for every taste, Shaina noted. She saw girls of all races and body types. Here was a Solarian mix—her bright green skin clashed terribly with the rose-colored room. Her long, thin, snakelike body was curled on a golden blanket and her deep green patch of pubic hair stood on end and hissed when Shaina approached her stall. Across from her was a plump Rhomboid with frizzy purple hair and a double vagina.

"This one is particularly good for a couple to share," T'lar remarked, seeing Shaina's interest in the Rhomboid girl. "Rhomboids are so accommodating, you know."

"Are all the slaves in here for sale then?" she asked, passing the Rhomboid's stall and pretending interest in a skinny brunette in the next stall instead.

"Most are, Mistress Sender. Some are here only for punishment; they are in disgrace and will eventually return to their various Masters and Mistresses. If you have any questions, you have only to ask. I know which are for sale and which are not."

Shaina nodded and continued down the row of stalls until she came to something new. It was a human-looking slave girl wearing a harness of a type Shaina had never seen before. The girl, who looked only a little younger than herself, with hair a magnificent shade of strawberry blond, was mounted on a platform that looked very like the ones in the turquoise fitting room where Ty had acquired his sheath.

The platform was waist high and rose pink, of course, instead of turquoise. The girl was kneeling on it on her hands and knees, presenting her backside to the stall entrance. She was forced into a kind of crouch by the cruel-looking leather straps that ran between her wrists and ankles, which were bound tightly together with golden links. Golden poles that were thin but looked immensely strong were fixed between her thighs, holding them widely open. But what drew the eye and held it was her sex.

When she noticed what had been done to the girl's vagina,

Shaina gave a little gasp of mingled horror and fascination. Between her widely spread thighs was another device made of thin gold bands in the shape of a capital V. It had been fixed inside the slave girl in such a way that the apex of the V was at the top near her little pink clitoris and the arms of it spread out and held her tender lips apart, baring her sex completely for anyone to see. The soft, rose-colored inner flesh of her cunt glistened with moisture, looking swollen and throbbing with need, and her tight little entrance was easily accessible to anyone who walked into her stall.

"Even for this place, that seems extreme," Ty sent through the symbi-link, his amber eyes wide.

"Goddess, yes, poor thing! How can she stand to be so . . . open?"

"Doesn't look like she's got much choice. And I thought this damned sheath was bad."

Shaina couldn't stop staring at the exposed slave girl, her whole body quivering with tension as she knelt in the humiliating position. Shaina's cheeks flushed red and she found herself wondering what it would feel like to be put display like that, open for anyone to touch or see. How would the cool leather straps of the harness feel on her naked skin and how would the cunning little V-shaped device feel inside her pussy, spreading her wide and wet and open?

As though feeling Shaina's eyes upon her, the slave girl turned her head as well as she could and looked at her out of pleading sky-blue eyes. Her features were shockingly lovely, the kind of face, Shaina thought, that you saw on the vid screen back home.

"Ah now, this is Trebekka. As you can see, she is being punished," T'lar explained casually, nodding in the slave's direction. "She was a naughty slave and refused to pleasure her Master properly, so he has set her up here for all to try until she has learned her lesson."

Shaina gasped. "You mean just anyone could come in here and . . . and try her out?"

"Oh, certainly, Mistress. It's a common practice among those wishing to sell slaves. If you let the buyer get a taste of the goods, he is more likely to buy. Any good slave should give proven satisfaction before credit exchanges hands. In fact, in most of the auction houses on the other side of the planet, the merchants refuse to sell their slaves untried. It reduces the number of complaints and returns, you see."

"How . . . how so?" Shaina choked, unable to drag her eyes from the harnessed slave girl.

"Why, I would think it would be obvious, little Mistress. If the potential buyer publicly puts the slave he wishes to purchase to the test and finds him or her acceptable, they are less likely to be able to claim dissatisfaction later."

"Publicly?" Shaina's eyes widened in horror. "You mean they . . . try them out right up there on the . . . on the auction block?"

"Oh, certainly—the more witnesses the better," T'lar said casually. "In fact, the auction houses often employ people just for that purpose, to make sure a buyer gets satisfaction before he signs the contract. Would you like to try Trebekka out? Allow me to demonstrate her sensitivity."

And before Shaina could protest, the tall Kandalar had taken a long wand with what looked like a feather attached to its end off the wall of Trebekka's stall and used it to stroke along the slave girl's swollen pink clitoris, eliciting a tortured moan from her slender throat.

"Oh, no, stop! Please don't . . . don't hurt her," Shaina begged, grabbing T'lar's rose-pink arm and stopping him from repeating the action.

"Hurt her?" He gave her a mystified look. "It doesn't hurt her, Mistress Sender, except to increase her sexual need. You see, her inner tissues have been liberally coated with the same lubricating agent that I provided you to use with your D'Lonian's sheath. It increases sexual arousal to a fever pitch and keeps it there for hours. It is a form of torture, you might say, but a very mild one, as no actual pain is involved." As if to prove his point, the slave girl wiggled and arched her back as well as she could, presenting her hot little sex as if begging for another stroke from the feather wand.

"No actual pain, huh?" Ty's voice in her head was full of sarcasm and Shaina turned to look at him with surprise.

"It hurts? Why didn't you tell me?" she demanded, feeling awful that her partner had been in pain this whole time and she hadn't had any idea. She put her hand up and stroked his face, pretending to stroke the hair out of his golden eyes as they communicated. His skin was smooth and warm, and as her hand passed over his cheek, he turned his face and placed a lingering kiss in her palm that sent a tingle throughout her entire body.

"To be hard for hours at a time? Hell, yes, it hurts, sweetheart. But it's more of an ache after a while. Don't worry, I can stand it. As for why I didn't tell you, there was nothing you could do about it, so why bring it up?"

"We could have avoided using that bloody oil," Shaina pointed out, angrily, trying to keep her face smooth and unperturbed, just a Mistress tending to her slave

"And let the damn sheath rub against me with no lubrication? No thanks! It's painful, but I'm used to it. I'm always hard when I'm around you anyway." He gave her his familiar feral grin, a white slice in his dark golden face. Shaina tried not to blush and dropped her hand abruptly.

"Don't tease, Ty."

"I'm not. Think you'd better pay attention to your friend T'lar. He's looking restless." Shaina shook her head and turned back to T'lar, who was indeed exhibiting signs of impatience.

"My slave appeared to have something in his eye," she remarked, offhandedly.

"Are you interested in Trebekka or not, Mistress Sender?" T'lar asked, hanging the feather wand back on the wall of her stall. "She will be on display as you see her for the rest of the day."

"I don't know, T'lar. I want to look around some more before I make a decision and I haven't even seen the male quarters yet. Maybe I can come and have another look at her after the banquet tonight."

"Ah, but I am afraid that will be quite impossible. You see, the quarters are closed at night. The way we see it, the Masters and Mistresses have all day to play with them, and to be at their best, even slaves need to rest. We here at the Palace are not barbarians, you know."

Shaina had an entirely different opinion of the Palace personnel and from the sound of Tyson's mental snort, he did as well. Rather than commenting, however, she motioned for T'lar to lead the way through the remaining stalls.

As they came to the end of the long row, Shaina saw a familiar figure bending over the last stall. It was Cassandra Shybolt, the friendly Mistress from the night before with her tower of pale brown hair. Sitting quietly at her feet was her plump blond slave girl, L'Mera.

"Ah, Meshandra, my dear, how are you?" Mistress Shy asked, looking up from the last stall with a radiant smile. "You're looking very well today," she went on, without waiting for an answer. "And your tame D'Lonian, delightful. I understand you were privileged to be featured on the holo-grid in the viewing room today and I was not a bit surprised to hear it. Such a lovely display of pleasure you made last night."

"A star is born."

"Shut up, Ty." Shaina didn't need to look at her partner to know he was grinning. She could feel her face glowing red with

embarrassment; all she wanted to do was change the subject as quickly as possible.

"Yes . . . well," she said uneasily. "Are you interested in buying a new slave, Mistress Shy?"

"Well, I *had* thought about it, you know. L'Mera gets lonesome sometimes and might like to have a companion. Would you not, my sweet?" The middle-aged Mistress turned to her slave girl, whose hair was fixed today, Shaina saw, in what looked like thousands of long, thin tight braids, each one tied at the end with a bit of purple silk. A jeweled anti-grav collar around her neck caused the braids to float suspended in midair around her head like a lot of blond snakes. She nodded vigorously at her Mistress's question, causing the snakes to bob and wiggle alarmingly.

"And which one have you picked out?" The way Mistress Shy put it, it sounded rather like buying a pet for your pet. Pretending interest, she peered into the last stall. Inside was huddled a thin girl with long black mane and exotic purple eyes, whom she instantly recognized as Jlle's slave from the previous night's banquet.

"If I may be so bold," T'lar interjected, stepping forward and peering into the stall as well, "as to remark that you have very eclectic tastes, Mistress Shybolt. This slave could scarcely be more different from your favorite here." He indicated L'Mera with a wave of one long, thin hand. The slave girl made a face and snatched at the hand waving near her, nearly succeeding in sinking her teeth into one skeletal digit. T'lar drew back his hand quickly with a hiss of disapproval.

"L'Mera, my darling, no," Mistress Shy cooed reprovingly. "That was very naughty, but it just so happens that I agree with you completely." She turned to face the tall Kandalar. "You may leave us until we are finished talking, T'lar," she said in the coldest voice Shaina had yet heard her use. "You can wait for Mistress Sender outside the quarters."

T'lar bowed low, his thin face displaying no emotion whatsoever, and left, walking smoothly but rapidly.

"He's no good, that one. Too oily, if you ask me, and not to be trusted. But then, none of them are." Mistress Shy sighed and shook her head at the Kandalar's retreating back. "Now, where were we? Ah yes. I think this little slave will make a delightful companion for my darling L'Mera and Jlle is willing to let me have her for a pittance."

"I'm glad you're buying her." Shaina truly meant what she said. "I think she'll make a fine addition to your, uh . . ." Her mind went blank. What did one call a collection of slaves? A gaggle? A flock? "Your harem," she finished rather weakly.

"You're right, my dear Meshandra," Mistress Shy said affectionately. "Come here, darling." She motioned to the thin slave, who crawled tentatively on hands and knees to the front of her stall. "Would you like to join our happy family, my sweet?" she asked, stroking one pale, thin cheek gently. The slave nodded her head vigorously and leaned into the caress eagerly to emphasize her agreement. "And what is your name, my pet?" Mistress Shy continued in the same, gentle voice.

"Sha . . . Shazzer," the slave whispered in a husky alto voice.

"Why, that's a lovely name, darling. I think we'll get along just famously. Oh, Meshandra, are you leaving so soon?"

"I wish to look at the male slave quarters as well." Shaina shrugged casually. "Nothing here caught my fancy."

"Ah, well, I've already been there today, so I'll leave you to it and see you at the banquet tonight."

"Until then." Shaina turned to go but the middle-aged Mistress called her back once more.

"My dear Meshandra, I had almost forgotten to warn you. You seem to have a kindly heart despite your privileged background. You feel for the less fortunate slaves, do you not?" She nodded at Shazzer, who was currently making friends with L'Mera in one corner of her stall.

"Yes, I suppose," Shaina answered, wondering where this was going. Through the symbi-link, she could hear Ty silently wondering the same thing

"Well, I just thought I should mention that there is a slave boy, the second to last stall at the far end of the quarters—he has fair hair and the most beautiful eyes, but he's rather sickly looking. You'll know him when you see him, I'm sure."

"Yes?" Shaina asked again, trying to be polite. What was this woman going on about now? Her gossip had been useful the night before, but now it was simply holding them up.

"Well, knowing your kind heart, I'm sure you'll be tempted to take him, but my advice to you is *don't*. I have it on very good authority that he has an incurably bad attitude. You'll want to try and save him, but I'm afraid it's *quite hopeless*. Don't even think about trying. Do you understand?" She stared fixedly at Shaina and then directed her gaze to Tyson as well.

"All right." Shaina looked at her oddly.

"What is she talking about?"

"I have no idea. I think she's about three carbo-chugs shy of a six-pack," Ty sent back.

"Mistress Sender, I am sorry to interrupt, but do you wish to view the male slave quarters or not?" T'lar was suddenly at her elbow, giving Mistress Shy a wary look and staying well clear of L'Mera's teeth.

"I said I did, didn't I? I'll come right now if you're so impatient," Shaina said, haughtily, secretly glad for the Kandalar's interruption. "I'll see you tonight, Mistress Shy." She tossed her hair and turned to go. "Come, Tyber."

She gave a tug on Ty's leash, eliciting a dark look from him and a sullen "Yes, Mistress."

"Goodbye, dear. Please remember my advice. And T'lar?"

"Yes, Mistress Shybolt?" The Kandalar inclined his head warily.

"That's a lovely color on you. I don't believe I saw this particular shade of pink in Her Excellency's gown last night." She smiled sweetly at him and turned back to her new slave.

T'lar tightened his thin lips until they nearly disappeared in his rose-pink face but he made no reply except a deep bow. "Come, Mistress," he said to Shaina. "Let me show you to the male quarters. They are just down the passageway from here."

Shaina and Tyson followed the Kandalar down a short stretch of hall to a long room that was the exact mirror of the female slave quarters except that it was shaded a brilliant true orange. They walked slowly down the rows, stopping now and again to examine several slave boys, who came eagerly to greet them. Shaina was beginning to give up hope when at last she saw him.

At the far end of the quarters in the second to last stall was Paul, the Chancellor's son.

14

"*That's him! I'm sure it is,*" Shaina sent excitedly, but Tyson was relieved to see that she still wore the same perpetually bored expression that was part of her Mistress Sender persona.

"*That's him all right. Don't act too eager, but see if he's for sale. If we're lucky, we could be off Freak Planet in time for dinner.*"

Shaina approached the Chancellor's son casually and Ty followed on his leash. Paul was crouched in the far corner of his stall, wearing a diamond-studded sheath and collar. Aside from looking a little paler and a great deal thinner than the idol Faron had given them, he seemed completely unharmed. He had a mild, unremarkably handsome face and light brown hair with blond streaks. In fact, his eyes were the only feature in his face that was anything but nondescript. They were wide and beautiful, almost too large for his face, and Ty couldn't quite make out their color, no matter how long he looked, because they seemed to shift constantly, slipping from deep blue to ocean green to chocolate brown to glowing gold as he watched. In their gorgeous, jewellike depths there was nothing but unruffled serenity, and his thin body appeared unmarked. Of course, Tyson thought grimly, who knew what kind of psychological and emotional torture the poor kid had been through? Those kinds of scars wouldn't show on the surface.

"What about this one. Why is he here?" he heard Shaina asking. "What's his name?"

"That one has no name. He is the Executor's special favorite."

"If he's such a favorite, why is he here in the common quarters?" Shaina looped the leash around her wrist and pulled Ty closer, as though she were signaling a pet dog to heel. Tyson obediently crouched on the orange flooring beside her, which allowed him an eye-level view inside the stall.

"It is unclear if he had done anything to displease her. Perhaps she simply likes to offer him to her guests." T'lar shrugged his rack-thin shoulders with chilling indifference. "He's been here ever since he came to the Palace almost, let me see . . . two solar months now. I'm not certain of his planet of origin. Her Excellency takes him to her room now and again, but not above once a week or so, I should say. Other than that he is free for common use. Would you like to try him?"

"I don't know. . . . Let me see him closer. Come here, boy," Shaina commanded imperiously, holding out one hand. Immediately, Paul got to his hands and knees and crawled over to her. He rubbed one cheek mechanically against her open palm and gave her a look of abject devotion that was utterly devoid of intelligence. Ty looked again to be sure he was seeing correctly, but the beautiful, glowing eyes of the Chancellor's son were completely empty.

"Goddess, what's been done to him?" Shaina's mental voice was horrified.

"Don't know. Lights are on but nobody's home."

"He seems, uh, most compliant. More so than most of the other slaves I've seen," Shaina remarked, withdrawing her hand from Paul's cheek with a slight shudder. It seemed to take a minute for this to register with Paul, but when it did, he simply sat down where he was at her feet and looked up at her with an adoringly vacant expression.

"Ah, that will be the influence of the love collar," T'lar said, nodding his bald, orange head sagely.

"Love collar? What's that?" Shaina made a show of bending down to study the diamond-encrusted collar encircling Paul's neck.

"Possibly the technology has not reached your home-world yet, Mistress Sender but it is a much more subtle way to control slaves than a pain collar. You see, it acts on the pleasure centers of the brain to render the slave wearing it utterly compliant. No matter what you do to him or her, the slave derives only pleasure from the act. Beat him or pet him, it is all the same. Watch." The Kandalar drew back one thin hand and slapped Paul hard across the face. Shaina gasped and Ty had to hold himself back. He thought grimly that before they left the planet he would like to have just a few minutes alone with T'lar—that was all he would need.

Paul was the only one who seemed unaffected by the slap.

Instead of cringing or cowering back in the far corner of his stall, Paul leaned against the tall, thin Kandalar's legs. He rubbed himself like a cat against T'lar and pressed his cheek, on which an elongated red handprint was still visible, against the hand that had slapped him. If anything, his eyes glowed brighter, shifting colors more rapidly with what Ty could only assume was pleasure.

"You see?" T'lar asked, motioning to Paul, who had turned his gorgeous, vacant eyes up to him. "Pain or pleasure, it makes no difference. Of course, some masters still prefer the pain collar for obvious reasons, but the love collar is, in my humble opinion, much more effective in controlling an insubordinate slave."

"But there's no locking device that I can see on it." Shaina bent forward to examine the collar again, although Tyson could see she was actually checking to make sure Paul's face was all right. "What keeps him from simply taking it off?"

"But that is the beauty of the love collar, little Mistress. Once you put it on, the slave wearing it would never dream of taking it off. Observe." He leaned down to address Paul, putting one thin finger under the boy's chin to tilt his face up. "Slave, would you like to remove your collar?"

"Take off my lovely collar? By no means, Master." Paul's speech was slow and dreamy, but very definite. Ty thought he sounded like a man flying on a very large dose of Nonnie, the street name for a designer drug back home that went by the name of Nonchalance and caused the user to forget all his anxieties and inhibitions. Nonnie users were frequently also inadvertent suicides because they forgot their fear of death and lost all concept of their own mortality. Ty had once seen a Nonnie freak walk in front of a speed-loader with perfect indifference. The man had been crushed to death with a smile on his face.

"You see?" T'lar turned to them triumphantly. "You can do anything you like to him and he remains perfectly safe. Would you like to try him?"

"I don't know," Shaina hedged. "What if I try him and like him, then what? Is he for sale?"

"Oh, I am afraid not, Mistress Sender. He is, as I told you, the exclusive property of Her Excellency the Executor. She will never let him go for any price." He shook his bald orange head decisively.

"So much for home in time for dinner. Guess it'll have to be plan B.

"What's plan B?"

"Grab him tonight and run like hell."

"*Oh, for some reason I thought you had a more detailed plan.*" Shaina was definitely being sarcastic, but Tyson ignored it.

"*Don't worry, sweetheart. I've got something in mind.*"

"I don't wish to acquire a taste for something I cannot own." Shaina turned to the gaunt Kandalar and put on her most petulant expression. "I think I prefer to retire to my own rooms. This fruitless excursion has tired me considerably and I feel in need of a nap. You may have lunch sent to me there."

"Very well, Mistress." T'lar's low bow was unable to conceal his irritation at the lost sale; his lips were thin and his eyes glowed the ruby red of hot coals. He turned and swept before them out of the male common quarters, shifting colors as he did so to match the black hall. Shaina had to almost trot to keep up with him.

"*So what's your plan?*" She strode purposefully after T'lar and made disdainful eye contact with the other Masters and Mistresses they met in the hall. "*We can't get him away in the state he's in now. He's like a Nonnie freak on the nod.*"

"*That's just what I was thinking, but once we get the collar off, it should be simple enough to convince him to run. After all, the poor guy has been used and abused by all comers for the last two standard months. I don't think he has much to hang around for.*"

Shaina shivered ever so slightly. Tyson could see the ripple under her long black gown. "*It's too horrible. Can you even imagine the life he's been living? If you can call it living.*"

"*Yes, I can.*" Ty focused on the floor, trying to look like an obedient slave. "*But I don't want to. Shaina, we've got to get him and us out of here as soon as possible. Now here's what we're going to do . . .*"

15

"That's enough, Tyber. Leave me be. Truly, your performance tonight is beyond bad," Shaina shoved Tyson from between her legs, although it was the last thing she wanted to do. His hot mouth felt so delicious against the skin of her inner thighs and the way his tongue slid over her aching cleft made her want to pull him closer, not push him away.

"My apologies, Mistress. Truly, it is raining in the garden of my heart." Ty bowed low and knocked his forehead against the royal blue carpet of the Blue Pleasure Hall, where the nightly banquet was being held.

"More. Make a scene, McCullough. Everybody here has to believe you're really pissed at me."

"I am very displeased!" Shaina ramped up her performance with a raised voice and a petulant expression. "You have shamed me in front of everyone here. Have you nothing to say for yourself?" People were starting to stare, the Masters and Mistresses looking up from the business of the Mandatory Pleasuring to see what the commotion was about. *Good,* thought Shaina.

"Mistress, I cannot apologize enough. Allow me to try again to please you, I beg." Ty attempted to insinuate his face between her thighs once more and again Shaina pushed him away. From his spot three places down the table, Marso Jlle looked up from the new slave girl he had purchased, the snakelike Solarian, whose forked green tongue was currently wrapped three times around his shaft. Shaina tossed her hair angrily when she noticed his attention.

"No! I've had enough of your lackluster performance. In fact, I think you need to be taught a lesson. I am sending you to the common slave quarters for the night. Maybe a night on the hard floor of a stall instead of the soft foot of my bed will teach you something."

"No, Mistress, I beg you . . . Every moment away from you is agony." Ty was really hamming it up and Shaina felt nervous laughter bubbling up inside, but managed to contain herself.

"Leave my sight!" She put as much forcefulness into her voice as she could, pointing one finger in the direction of the huge, double real-wood doors. "If you are very lucky, I will come to see you in the morning to learn if your night away from me has done you good. Now go."

Through the link she added, *"Good luck, partner."* Tyson slunk out of the banquet room looking like a kicked dog.

"If we do this right we won't need luck. Just be ready."

"Got it." With as much dignity as she could, Shaina rose from her blue silk cushion and excused herself, leaving just before the end of the banquet.

"Mistress Sender, I trust you enjoyed the banquet. But where is your charming D'Lonian?" T'lar managed to sound both distressed and surprised at the same time, though Shaina knew perfectly well he was neither.

"I am sure you have already heard that I was forced to send him to the common slave quarters. His performance at the

Mandatory Pleasuring tonight was simply dreadful." She swept along the wide corridor to her room, not bothering to see if T'lar was following.

"But of course, Mistress. The slave quarters are closed for the night, but do you wish him displayed tomorrow morning? I would be happy to see to it myself." Shaina spared a brief glance back at the Kandalar; T'lar's red eyes glowed with anticipation.

Just bet you would, she thought. Briefly she pictured Tyson confined in one of those terrible gold chain and leather harnesses and shuddered.

"I think not," she replied after what she hoped looked like careful consideration. "Possibly he is simply feeling out of sorts. I will check on him tomorrow morning and see if his attitude is improved."

"Very well, Mistress." There was definite disappointment in the oily voice. They had reached the double doors leading to the chamber of the Starving Nun and Shaina made a show of placing her thumb on the payment keypad and watching the indicator light turn green while T'lar spoke. "And will you require me to send you another slave to fulfill your needs?"

"I . . . ah . . ." Here was a complication she hadn't anticipated. "I think not, T'lar. I am tired and cross right now. I want only to go to bed and relax and not be bothered by anyone. Is that clear?"

"Perfectly, Mistress. Pleasant dreams." The tall Kandalar faded away and Shaina was left to herself at last. Sighing, she pushed the double doors firmly shut and looked around the empty room. It seemed strange to be here all by herself without Ty playing the dutiful slave on the outside while making sarcastic remarks inside her head. She decided to run a bubble bath in the hugely wasteful tub and try to relax. If everything went according to plan, it would be her last chance at a real, full-immersion bath.

Shedding her uncomfortable Mistress outfit as she went and dropping everything on the floor the way a spoiled rich girl would, Shaina went into the bathroom and ran herself a bath. As she settled into the steaming water, she found herself wishing that Ty was there to scrub her as he had the night before. Remembering his large, capable hands on her body, soaping her breasts and stroking between her legs, made her shiver despite the hot water she was sitting in. Oh, she would be so glad once they were out of this place, but she had to admit she'd miss having an excuse to let Ty touch her . . . that way. If only he were here right now . . .

Shaina let her head rest on the curving black surface of the huge tub and spread her legs, enjoying the warm rush as the heat from the foamy water washed over her pussy. It seemed to make her clit so sensitive, almost throbbing with the need to be touched, to be stroked. Idly, she ran one small hand over her full breasts, caressing pink nipples hard with the need to be fondled and sucked, and wished she could feel Ty's hands and mouth on her there.

Goddess, what was wrong with her? Had she already gotten so addicted to her partner's touch that her own didn't satisfy her anymore? Shaina didn't know but suddenly, it seemed as though every part of her body was crying out for him, wanting him, needing him . . . She brushed her fingertips over her ripe nipples again and groaned out loud.

"Am I interrupting something?" The voice in her head was totally unexpected and Shaina sat frozen in the bath for a moment before jerking her hand away from her breasts as though she had been burned. As though Ty could actually see her.

"I can't see, but I can imagine." His voice through the link was a little fainter. Maybe they were stretching the limits of the symbiotes' range, but she could still hear him clearly. His tone was low and dark and Shaina could taste his desire, could roll it on the back of her tongue like cinnamon candy.

"*I was just taking a bath to relax,*" she sent defensively and then wished she hadn't. Now Tyson would be imagining her naked in the huge black bathtub.

"*I don't have to imagine. I already saw you that way last night, remember? You were beautiful.*"

"*Ty, honestly,*" Shaina could feel a red-hot blush creeping up her cheeks. "*Did you contact me for a reason or just to embarrass me? Are we still a go for tonight?*"

He sighed deeply. "*No, unfortunately. Paul is gone. Apparently this is one of the few nights that the Executor wanted to use him. The slave beside me says he won't be returned until sometime next morning.*"

"*Oh, no! Don't tell me we have to go through another day on this wacked-out planet.*" Shaina sank lower into the bubbles, her forehead creased with frustration.

"*Hey, at least you get to spend it in the lap of luxury. I'm lying on the floor in a stall and it's hard. But the worst thing is that I don't get to tend you tonight,* Mistress." His tone was teasing but Shaina could taste the truth behind his words. Ty really was sorry that he wasn't there with her. "*But maybe I can help you tend yourself,*" he added in that seductive tone. Shaina could almost see his amber eyes blazing at her when he spoke that way.

"*Ty, please. You're embarrassing me.*" She could feel the blush spreading to encompass her whole body in a hot, red rush and she sank even lower in the bubbles until pink, foamy water splashed over the sides of the tub.

"*Why, because I caught you touching yourself? Why should that embarrass you, Shaina? Because nice girls don't do that?*"

"*No, because nice girls don't . . . do that, as you put it, with someone else listening in.*" Shaina's tone was prim.

"*Who said I only want to listen? If I can't be there to touch you in person, I can at least help out a little.*"

"How . . . how do you plan to help?" Shaina felt her breath coming a little shorter.

"Put your hand on your breast again." Tyson's mental voice was so masterful and stern that Shaina followed his orders without even thinking about it. She cupped one breast in her hand, feeling the nipple harden against her palm.

"I . . . I'm doing it."

"I know you are, sweetheart. I can feel your pleasure through our link. Do you know what I'd be doing if I were there right now?"

"Tell me." Shaina closed her eyes tightly. She could almost see Ty at the other end of their link, lying on the floor of the slave quarters with the hard, copper sheath jutting from between his muscular thighs.

"I'd be sucking your nipples. I haven't gotten to do that yet, you know, and I want to. Want to taste your sweet skin and feel those sweet pink nipples of yours get hot and tight inside my mouth while I lick you."

"Mmm, Ty . . ."

"Pinch your nipples, just a little. Pinch them for me, Shaina." Again that deep, commanding tone that Shaina felt helpless to disobey. *Faron was right,* she thought distractedly as she twisted her hard pink nubs between her fingertips. *Ty should have been the Master.*

"I'm pinching them, Ty. Oh . . . it feels so good."

"Where does it feel good, Shaina? Not just in your breasts. Where else does it make you feel good?"

Shaina squirmed with embarrassment but found once again that she couldn't lie through their link. *"It feels good all over. It seems to send sparks of pleasure all through my body. Especially . . . between my legs."*

"Your pussy, sweetheart. That's where it feels good, doesn't it?"

"*Yes.*" Shaina moaned breathlessly as she pinched her nipples harder, twisting a little to feel the sparks of pleasure course through her.

"*Put your hand between your legs now, Shaina. Don't touch yourself yet, just put your hand between your thighs.*"

"*Okay.*" Shaina allowed one hand to dip beneath the surface of the foamy water and rested it on the mound of soft, springy curls between her legs.

"*Do you know how much I love your pussy, sweetheart? It's the sweetest little part of you, so soft and pink and delicate. I love the way you get so wet for me when I touch you and taste you. The way your sweet little cunt opens up for me. The way your body understands what it needs from me even if you don't.*"

"*Oh, Goddess, Ty!*" Just holding her hand between her legs wasn't enough. Shaina wanted badly to touch herself, but she couldn't just yet—because Tyson hadn't told her to.

"*Just wait, sweetheart. I'll let you know when.*" His whisper was like rough velvet rubbing the inside of her skull. "*I love to spread your tender pussy lips and lick you. Love to put my tongue inside you and make you beg for more while I eat you. Do you want to touch yourself now?*"

"*Yes, Ty . . . you know I do.*" More water sloshed over the side of the tub as Shaina shifted anxiously.

"*Then open your thighs, sweetheart. I want you to spread open those sweet pink lips for me, spread yourself wide, Shaina. I want your pussy wide open and hot. Are you open?*"

"*Yes . . . Oh!*" Shaina spread herself as he told her to and the hot foamy water caressed and invaded her at once, making her gasp and cry out.

"*That's good. Now gently, with just one finger, I want you to stroke yourself. How does it feel? Are you wet, sweetheart? Is your sweet little pussy all creamy and hot for me?*"

"*Goddess, yes! Oh, Ty, I wish you were here!*" Shaina moaned as the pad of one delicate finger traced over her throbbing clit, which felt swollen and hot with need.

"I wish I was too, Shaina, but maybe it's a good thing I'm not." His tone was grim.

"Why not?" Shaina couldn't imagine a single reason why Tyson shouldn't be here with her, touching her as she was touching herself, stroking her . . . tasting her . . .

"Because I'd want to fuck you, sweetheart." Ty's mental voice was rough with need and unfulfilled desire. *"You don't know how hard it is for me to hold back with you when everything I have in me is telling me to take you and to make you mine."*

"It's . . . it's the part of you that's D'Lonian, isn't it?" Shaina still stroked over her hot clit as they talked. The idea of belonging to Ty sexually used to scare her, but now she found the thought deeply compelling. To have that thick cock shoved all the way inside her . . . stretching her . . . filling her to the limit . . .

"Yes, Shaina, it is. I'm sorry if it scares you, but when I'm with you I want to possess you completely. I want to spread your legs and press the head of my cock inside you. Want to watch while my shaft opens you up and listen to you moan and beg until I'm all the way into your sweet, hot cunt. Do you want to feel me filling you up, sweetheart? If I were there right now would you spread your legs for me and let me fuck up into your tight little pussy?"

"Oh Ty . . . I don't know. You know I want to. I'm just scared."

"Don't be scared, sweetheart. Just say yes. Say you want to feel me filling you up."

"I . . . yes, Ty. I do," Shaina found herself admitting and she knew it was the truth. More than anything, she wanted to give herself to her partner, to feel his thick shaft opening her, filling her as he described.

"Are you still touching yourself, Shaina? Are you close, sweetheart?"

"Yes, so close . . ." She closed her eyes tighter and gasped as her finger stroked over and over the hot, engorged bud of her clit.

"I want to be there with you and watch you come," Ty told her. *"I love the way you gasp and moan when you finally let go. I want to feel your sweet cunt quivering around me, want to feel you crying and begging beneath me while I fuck you."*

"Oh, Ty . . . I'm almost there. Don't stop!"

"I want to feel you come, feel your pussy trembling while I shove my cock deep inside you. And I want to fill you up with my cum, Shaina. Want to fuck you hard until I come inside you. Is that what you want?"

"Oh, Ty, you know I do."

"Then come for me now, sweetheart. Make yourself come. I want to feel your pleasure through our link." His voice was deep and commanding inside her head, and Shaina could see those molten gold eyes flashing as he ordered her to come.

"Yes! Oh, Goddess, Ty . . . I'm there, I'm coming . . ." Shaina gasped as she felt her orgasm sweep over her, sudden and sharp and sweet. It felt so good to let go when he ordered her to, so good to submit to him and do exactly as he said.

"I can feel you, sweetheart. I can feel your heat . . ." Ty's mental voice faded out for a moment and Shaina could imagine him, his thick cock throbbing inside the ornate copper sheath as he joined her in their shared pleasure.

"Did you . . . too?" she asked hesitantly after a moment, when she had crested down from the sharp pinnacle of orgasm and could think again.

"Hell, yes, like a rocket. God, wish I was there with you right now to hold you." Shaina heard the wistful tone in his mental voice and suddenly felt almost like she might cry from loneliness.

"I wish you were too, Ty. I know it's silly but this place is so weird. I don't feel safe without you in the room with me."

"Don't worry, honey, you're safe enough as long as the Chancellor's credit holds out." Shaina grinned a little. Ty was trying to cheer her up. *"If it makes you feel better, put that canister of emotion spray I know you have in your purse under your pillow. If anybody comes near you, a squirt of that stuff will stop them in a hurry. We'll be together again tomorrow when you come to check on your 'disobedient' slave. Tonight just try and get some sleep."*

"I'll try. Good night, Ty."

"Night, sweetheart. I lo . . . I'll see you in the morning." Ty's voice cut off abruptly, leaving Shaina to wonder what exactly he had almost said.

It was funny but she felt closer to him now that he was in another part of the huge Palace than she had when he was in the room with her. Sighing, she climbed out of the tub and toweled off. Slipping into a sheer silk nightgown, she decided to take Ty's advice and pulled the small silver canister of spray out of her velour knapsack. It was silly, she knew, but once it was tucked under her fluffy, deep green pillow she felt better, more secure.

Course I'll never have to use it . . . was her last thought before drifting off to sleep.

As it turned out, she was wrong.

16

Shaina woke up suddenly and completely out of a sound sleep with the knowledge that something was terribly wrong. She reached out automatically for Ty with her mind but found nothing, only empty space where he had been. Had the link been broken?

"*Ty? Ty?*" she sent, urgently into the darkness. At last she heard a faint sound on the other end of the link, more of a mental groan than a reply, but it was at least enough to let her know he wasn't dead. Unless he was wounded or dying . . . Oh, Goddess . . .

Shaina sat up and swung her legs over the side of the immense bed. She had to go to him, she had to . . .

A slight noise in the far corner of her room let her know she wasn't alone.

"Hello?" Shaina called, hating the quaver in her voice and feeling powerless to stop it. With numb fingers, she felt under her pillow, the palm of her hand brushing over the heavy, smooth texture of the satin sheets until she felt the cool metal canister of emotion spray. She grasped it tightly in one fist, her eyes wide in the darkness of the cavernous space, trying to see who or what was in the room with her.

Another slight noise, a slow, brushing scrape like a soft-soled shoe over thick carpet, made her jerk her head to the left. It was coming. It was right beside the bed now. Shaina stared into the darkness, feeling blind and helpless. Suddenly she saw two points of red moving towards her, glowing like hot coals in the pitch black.

Without stopping to think, Shaina pointed the nozzle of the small metal canister in her hand at the intruder and pressed the trigger with all her might. The glowing red lights were abruptly extinguished and she heard a high, unearthly howling coming from the direction of the floor. Standing on the bed and leaning far over, Shaina scrabbled along the wall until she found the dimmer switch to light the room. She smacked the switch hard with the palm of her hand and blinked rapidly, half-blinded herself by the sudden radiance that poured down from the overhead glows.

"My eyes! Mistress, why did you . . . Ah, S'landra, Goddess of all that is goodness and light, why did my mother never love me?" It was T'lar, curled into a fetal position on the deep green carpet and sobbing like an infant as the emotion spray took full effect.

"T'lar? What are you doing skulking around my room in the middle of the night?" Shaina asked in exasperation, getting off the bed and going to kneel by the gaunt frame on the floor. Then, remembering her Mistress persona, she added, "Answer me at once!"

"I . . . Oh Mistress, forgive me . . . I am a terrible person. Truly I am the lowest of the low . . ."

Shaina sighed. He was only to the guilt stage and it could take all night to get him sober enough to answer questions—like what was wrong with Ty.

She went to the bathroom and brought him back a wet synthi-cotton hand towel. "Here, wipe your eyes." Fumblingly, T'lar took the towel and wiped at his red, streaming eyes, his face and hand changing from the green of the carpet to the white of the towel as he did so.

"Forgive me, Mistress . . ." he mumbled again and Shaina shook her head impatiently.

"What are you doing here? What's wrong?" she asked in a tightly controlled voice. It took every bit of self-control she had not to yell, "What's wrong with Ty? Where is he?" But she managed to hold it back and simply stared piercingly at the tall Kandalar, who had managed to compose himself enough to at least sit up instead of sprawling on the floor weeping.

"I beg your pardon if I startled you, Mistress Sender . . ." he began, his deep voice wobbling between registers as he struggled to keep his emotions in check. "I know I am not worthy to lick your esteemed toes . . ."

"Never mind about my toes. *What* is going on?" Shaina demanded.

"I came to tell you that there has been a disturbance in the slave quarters," T'lar blurted out, obviously trying hard to stick to the facts.

"What kind of disturbance?" Shaina wanted to strangle him. Had Paul been returned and had he and Ty been captured trying to escape? But Ty certainly would have notified her through their symbi-link . . . unless he couldn't wake her up . . . Goddess! What a mess!

"A person, a Master, entered the male slave quarters tonight and there was a . . . problem with your slave. Ah, how it grieves me to be the bearer of this dreadful news!" T'lar broke into a fresh spate of sobbing and Shaina began to feel panicky. Tyson could be dying or dead and here was this idiot sobbing on her floor. She hauled back and slapped the weeping Kandalar across the face, surprising him enough, at least, to stop his crying, and leaving a pale handprint on his thin green cheek.

"What happened to Ty . . . I mean my slave? Is he all right?" she demanded.

"Oh yes, he is merely sedated right now. The Master who entered the quarters tried to use him, but apparently your D'Lonian objected rather strenuously. No one is seriously hurt, of course . . ."

"Thank the Goddess! Why didn't you say so in the first place instead of sneaking up on me like that and frightening the life out of me?"

T'lar sniffled loudly, wiping his long nose on one sleeve of his flowing no-color robe. "I didn't want to startle you with bad news too suddenly, Mistress," he said sullenly. Then his thin face crumpled again and he wailed, "Oh, Goddess, I wish I had never been hatched!" He broke down weeping again.

Shaina grabbed an outfit from her trunk and changed in the bathing room while she waited for the morose Kandalar to recover himself.

"T'lar, I insist on being taken to see my slave this instant." Her demand was made while emerging from the bathroom. She had dressed in record time.

"But Mistress Sender, no one is allowed in the slave quarters at night . . ." T'lar dried his eyes on his sodden robe and stood shakily to his feet. "It is the rule."

"What?" Shaina didn't have to fake her outrage. "How dare you speak to me of rules? Obviously the Master who bothered my slave had no compunction about breaking them. You will take me or I will go myself."

"Yes, Mistress Sender." The sullen tone was back in T'lar's voice. It occurred to Shaina that the Kandalar would probably never forgive her the squirt of emotion spray and its embarrassing consequences, but she didn't give a damn. Goddess knew she had been publicly embarrassed more than once on this benighted planet and she thought T'lar would survive his shame.

With T'lar leading the way and Shaina hot on his heels, they at last came to the male common slave quarters. Upon entering the bright orange room, she saw a small cluster of tall, thin Kandalar, all clothed in flowing no-color robes and all the exact same shade as the room, bending over a huddled shape on the floor.

"Ty!" Shaina cried, pushing through the crowd of emaciated humanoids to find him lying unconscious on the ground. Tyson's bare, muscular limbs were splayed out and his head lolled to one side. His thick black hair was in his face and when Shaina knelt beside him and brushed it off his forehead, she could see the whites of his eyes glistening sickly in the overhead glows beneath the thick fringe of lashes.

"Oh, Ty," she whispered, taking his head in her lap and holding him tightly. At least he was still breathing. "Is there a doctor here? I demand medical attention at once!" she shouted, looking up into the ring of long, orange alien faces surrounding them.

"I am a healer, little Mistress, and there is no need to shout." One of the Kandalar detached himself from the others and stepped forward. "Your slave is merely sedated and in no immediate danger; I beg you will not concern yourself."

"Yes, I bloody well *will* concern myself." She found she was smoothing Ty's hair compulsively away from his face and made herself stop with an effort. "What happened here? Why was my slave sedated? Who dared to tamper with him without my permission?"

"It was Master Jlle," one of the other Kandalar said uncomfortably. "He slipped past the Eye at the doors and came into the quarters. He said he wished to try a slave. I tried to explain that the quarters were closed and that the slave he wished to try was not for public sampling, but he would not hear me. I think he was intoxicated. He came to the stall of the D'Lonian slave and required that the slave service him."

"And what did Ty . . . Tyber do?" Shaina asked, feeling sick.

"I fear he reacted in a most disturbing fashion, Mistress."
The Kandalar bowed subserviently. "Not only did he refuse to
service Master Jlle, he threatened to knock his 'teeth down his
fat throat,' I believe is how he put it. But Jlle would not hear; he
demanded service. I saw that the D'Lonian slave was about to
do him bodily harm and I was forced to tranquilize him since
he wore no collar." In illustration, he raised a small, wicked-
looking silver dart gun that he still held in one hand. "By the
time I had tranquilized the slave, others were here to help me
restrain Master Jlle."

"Did Jlle hurt my slave in any way?" Shaina asked angrily.
"If he so much as harmed a hair on my Tyber's head . . ."

"No, no, Mistress. I swear by S'landra that he never so much
as touched your slave," the guard protested.

"Your oaths mean nothing to me," Shaina said coldly. "You
would do better to save your breath for praying that when my
slave regains consciousness he tells the same tale you do. In the
meantime, I want him taken to my rooms at once that I may
tend him." There were mutters of apprehension from the gathered Kandalar but no one moved to obey her orders. "Well?"
Shaina demanded imperiously, looking from one long orange
face to another.

"Mistress, your slave will not be released to you until after
his flogging tomorrow." It was T'lar speaking; Shaina recognized him by his bald head, the only thing that differentiated
him from the other tall, thin Kandalar. He stepped forward, apparently completely recovered from the emotion spray, although his red eyes still watered a little.

"Flogging? What are you talking about?" Shaina demanded,
holding her partner tightly.

"*McCullough?*" she heard faintly, through the link. She
spared a quick glance down and saw to her relief that Ty's eyelids were fluttering and the amber eyes were beginning to focus
on her face. "*What happened?*"

"*Never mind. Just rest for now.*" Shaina looked up at the tall Kandalar hovering over her and swore she could detect a slight smirk on T'lar's long face.

"A slave who offers harm to a Master or Mistress is treated like an untrustworthy animal, Mistress Sender," he explained, his tone silky smooth. "A punishment must be administered or the cur will never learn his lesson."

"But he never even touched Jlle!" Shaina protested, hugging Ty protectively to her chest.

"*Ouch, McCullough, not so tight.*"

"*Shut up, I'm trying to save your ass!*"

"It is true that Master Jlle was not harmed, and you can be grateful to B'ler,"—he nodded to the Kandalar holding the dart gun—"for tranquilizing your D'Lonian when he did. A slave who offers harm to a Master or Mistress, unless he does so while defending his own Master or Mistress, must be flogged. A slave that actually *inflicts* harm must be instantly destroyed by order of Her Excellency, the Executor."

"But Tyber was provoked! I refuse to stand by and watch while my slave is punished needlessly while the bastard responsible for this fracas goes free. Where is Jlle, anyway? What is being done to him?" Shaina felt her face growing red with emotion and she was trembling as she fired questions at the watching Kandalar.

"Master Jlle is being dealt with as befits his status," T'lar said, smoothly. "And I am afraid there is no appeal you can make that will change the fate of your slave. Her Excellency's policies, once enacted, cannot be changed. Really, Mistress Sender, you are being most overprotective and acting more like your D'Lonian's lover than his Mistress. The flogging is nothing to be upset about, really. It is a simple matter of forty lashes with an agony whip, no more."

"Forty lashes?" Shaina heard her voice rising. "I will never agree to this, I . . ."

"Let it go, sweetheart." Ty had closed his eyes again, but he reached up and squeezed her hand, warningly.

"Let it go? How can you say that, Ty? Do you understand what they're talking about here?"

"I understand—but look at the way they're looking at you. The more you protest, the more suspicious they get. This is just another one of the things they consider normal here."

"But Ty . . . forty lashes with an agony whip!" Shaina felt her eyes filling up with tears and tried to hold them back. She waved at the waiting Kandalar and managed to choke out, "Give me a moment to consider this." The circle of alien faces backed up somewhat and she was able to concentrate on Tyson.

"I'll live through it, Shaina. It's pain by nerve induction. It'll hurt like hell, but it won't do any permanent damage."

"Permanent damage? Ty, are you listening to what you're saying? We can't let them do this."

"We can and we will." Tyson's voice was like steel inside her head. *"It's the only way, Shaina."* He opened his eyes again and brilliant green warred with intense amber for a moment before Shaina squeezed her eyes closed in defeat. He was right, she knew he was, and yet everything inside her was screaming that it was wrong, that she couldn't let them do this. But Ty was staring at her, a look of certainty on his hawklike features.

"All right, but if I ever get a chance at Jlle alone . . ."

"You'll have to take a place in line behind me," Ty's mental tone was grim. *"I'll rip the fat bastard's head off if I ever get another chance at him while these damn Kandalar aren't watching. But we have to be careful now, more than ever. Let go of me and get back to the room. We'll work something out later."* Stiffly, he pushed away from her lap and sat up, wincing as he worked out the tension in his muscles. Immediately the watching circle of Kandalar drew back with low murmurs of apprehension, as though Ty were a rabid canine that might bite without provocation.

"Tell them to take me, that I won't be any trouble. Go on," Tyson urged her. *"Do it, McCullough, I don't want them to think they have to give me another shot of tranquilizer. My head already feels like it's been used as a shard ball."*

"You . . . you may take my slave," Shaina heard herself saying, very much against her will. "He won't harm anyone. He was simply trying to keep himself for me. He has . . ." She swallowed hard. "He had not been accustomed to any touch but mine. That is why Jlle upset him with his . . . his demands." The words left a bad taste in her mouth, and she promised herself again that she would make Jlle pay if she got half a chance. "When . . . when will the flogging be scheduled?"

"Floggings are always held after the evening banquet, Mistress Sender. I realize that is a long time to be without a slave, and one will, of course, be provided for your needs in the meantime if you so desire."

"No." Shaina got shakily to her feet and stood over the still-sitting Ty. She rested one hand on his head, letting her fingers comb through the unruly dark hair. Ty sighed audibly and leaned his head back against her thigh, letting his eyes close in exhaustion. "I want no one but him." She realized as she spoke that the words were true. "I will leave my slave in your care, but he had better not be harmed in any way or I swear . . ." She let the sentence dangle, being unable to think of a threat that was bad enough.

"No harm will come to him, little Mistress," T'lar said smoothly, stepping forward from the bunch of milling Kandalar. "You may have him back after the flogging tomorrow night. In the meantime, we will keep him in a stasis chamber. That way, he won't even fret about his fate. We are, as you see, eminently civilized about such things."

"Yes, you're the soul of compassion," Shaina muttered sourly.

"*Ty, I'm so sorry...*" She reached down to caress one golden cheek.

"*Not your fault, sweetheart.*" He turned his head into her touch, accepting the caress and laying a tender kiss in the center of her palm. "*We'll work something out tomorrow night after the fl... after the banquet. Okay?*"

"*Yes.*" Shaina didn't trust herself to say anything else.

"*In the meantime try to keep a low profile. Don't do anything suspicious. I won't be able to talk to you from the stasis chamber, but I promise we'll have one hell of a planning session after I get out.*"

Then they were taking him away. Two whip-thin Kandalar had flanked Tyson while they talked and he was being led by the leather leash from the long, deep-orange room. He looked over one golden-tan shoulder to meet her eyes as he walked.

"Ty..." Shaina whispered aloud and she couldn't quite keep the tears from coming, although she stared straight ahead and tried not to let them fall.

"*Keep your chin up, McCullough.*" Winking at her, he gave just a hint of that old, savage D'Lonian grin. "*Everything's gonna turn out. You'll see.*"

"Ty..."

"*Bye, sweetheart. See you in a few.*" And he was gone.

17

Tyson emerged from the stasis chamber with the exact same thought he had gone into it with: *This is going to hurt*. It wasn't that he was a coward, hell, no. But he had seen the marks left by an agony whip. They were illegal in most solar systems and he knew what he was in for. He had told Shaina that there would be no permanent harm and he supposed that statement was true, as long as you didn't count deep red welts that stung and burned for days as the nerves affected by the whip slowly regenerated, as permanent harm.

Anyway, there was nothing to do about it now but endure it. And after it was over, they had to make serious plans to get off this hell-world. They would snatch Paul—Ty already had a few plans on that account—then signal Faron to get into position and get out of here on the shuttle. When he was back home, with Shaina safely in hand, he would figure out how to spend the rest of his life—hopefully with her by his side. After what had happened between them the other night, Ty was fairly certain she would be ready to accept his feeling for her soon . . .

"It is time, D'Lonian. Prepare yourself." Tyson looked up

from his musings to see T'lar and another Kandalar standing over him, motioning for him to follow. It amazed him that they were so used to treating slaves like cattle that they simply expected him to follow them to what was certain to be a very painful punishment. If he had been there on his own it would've been a different story. But there was Shaina to think about.

He saw her sitting on a cushion at the center of the long table beside the kindly Mistress Shy and her face looked as though she had been crying. The banquet hall was a purple one this time, walls, carpets, cushions and napkins all the deep, vivid color of a fresh bruise. The Kandalar standing unobtrusively around the room matched it exactly, all except the Executor, who was as silent and multicolored as ever sitting at the head of the table.

Ty saw that Shaina had dark circles under her bloodshot eyes as they led him to the center of the room. A gilded metal rack was waiting, with golden chains that had manacles attached. To one side, a hulking Norsoth lounged indolently, a coiled, many-tongued whip dangling from one huge, pawlike hand, its ends spitting and crackling with blue flame as it swayed slowly back and forth.

Oh, this is going to be fun, Tyson thought sourly, seeing the bulging muscles ripple under the Norsoth's pale blue-gray hide. He could feel a slow clenching begin in the pit of his stomach. As T'lar and the other Kandalar manacled his hands in place, he had a moment to be glad that his back would be facing the Masters and Mistresses sitting at the long table. He didn't want Shaina to see his face during the flogging. He was fairly sure he could keep from crying out, but as for controlling his facial expressions . . . of that he couldn't be certain.

"Ty, I tried everything. I appealed to the Executor herself and I couldn't . . . they wouldn't . . ." Shaina's mental tone was thick with distress, and once again, Tyson was glad she couldn't see him.

"*It's okay, sweetheart. Everything's going to be o ...*" At that minute he heard a hush drop over the huge room and felt the coiled tension build to a pitch behind his back. For a moment there was dead silence broken only by the wicked hiss of the whip. Then there was a sudden crack.

And then there was only pain.

18

Shaina didn't understand how Ty could bear it. Aside from an occasional muffled grunt of pain, he gave no verbal indication that the flogging was hurting him at all. But Shaina could see the convulsive jerk of his body each time the whip bit into his smooth golden-tan back. Could feel the hideous waves of nerve-induced agony through the symbi-link as the crackling pain-inducers at the ends of the whip's tails licked around his muscular flanks, until Ty abruptly slammed up a white wall of silence between them, cutting her off.

She watched in helpless horror, her hands clenched into trembling fists, as the whip cracked again and again against his flesh, and all she could think was that this was all her fault. She had gotten him into this. If it wasn't for her stubborn insistence on taking a dangerous mission to prove that she was every bit as good an officer and as competent in difficult situations as Ty, he would never have been here in the first place.

The huge Norsoth grunted with effort as he swung the whip, and red welts began to crisscross Tyson's broad, golden back. Shaina could see the muscles bunching and flexing under his skin every time the lash fell, creating another stripe to mar that smooth perfection. T'lar had assured her again and again that the skin would not be broken, that if even a drop of her slave's blood was shed she would be eligible for damages. *As though he were a piece of valuable property that could be used roughly as long as he wasn't permanently broken,* Shaina thought bitterly.

Across the table and three places down sat a sullen Marso Jlle. Shaina had shot the fat trader a venomous, hate-filled glance, which he returned with interest, when she first sat down, and then had done her best to ignore him the rest of the banquet. She had barely picked at her food, unable to get the picture of Ty bound to the golden whipping post that was displayed prominently in the center of the room, promising entertainment to come, out of her head.

From the somewhat subdued Mistress Shy at her side, Shaina had learned that Jlle's punishment in the whole affair was the loss of his slave-quarter privileges for the remainder of his stay at the Palace, which accounted for the surly look on his fat face. It was a punishment hardly adequate in Shaina's opinion. Her fingertips itched for a sonar-knife to push into Jlle's fat gut.

Shaina's feelings went beyond outrage and horror as the whip fell again and again. She had lost count of the lashes and she longed to close her eyes, but if Ty was strong enough to endure the beating, the least she could do was watch his agony and not turn away. The Norsoth raised his arm again for what seemed like the thousandth time, but this time, Shaina saw something different. Trickling between Tyson's broad, red-welted shoulders was a tiny rivulet of crimson.

"Stop!" Shaina was on her feet, shouting, not caring that everyone in the room was looking at her.

"There have been only twenty-six strokes, Mistress Sender . . ." T'lar began, stepping towards her but Shaina ignored him.

"Look what you've done to my slave!" she demanded, striding around the table to stand beside Ty and pointing to his back. "I was promised that not a drop of his blood would be shed," she pointed at the tiny trickle of blood, so small it was difficult to see among the angry red marks on his back. "Your clumsy Norsoth has damaged him. I demand that the flogging be halted at once."

"Whip him 'til he bleeds! It's no more than that animal deserves!" The unpleasant, gurgling undersea voice of Marso Jlle rang out in the cavernous room as he got ponderously to his feet. "He tried to attack me, would've torn out my throat if the guard hadn't tranquilized him. He ought to be destroyed."

"He didn't want you touching him, you fat tub of guts," Shaina heard herself shouting back. "Goddess knows, I'm sure nobody you don't own can stand to be near you!"

"You little bitch . . ." Jlle's face was mottled with rage and he took a step towards her, his hands clenched into fists. Suddenly there were several Kandalar standing between them, and the muttering of the other Masters and Mistresses escalated to a dull roar as people started standing up from the long, low table to argue one side or the other.

"Jlle is right. A slave who threatens a Master or Mistress deserves what he gets." The man with bright orange hair and steel teeth Shaina remembered from their first banquet was shouting.

"And who ever heard of a D'Lonian slave without a pain collar? They're so savage and unpredictable . . ." an effeminate Master with waist-length cobalt blue hair and thickly made-up eyes said, casting a mistrustful look at Tyson's manacled hands.

"Jlle shouldn't have been in the quarters after hours trying to obtain service from a slave who was clearly off-limits in the first place." This was from Mistress Shy, who was glaring angrily at the fat trader, now being tactfully restrained with some difficulty by two whip-thin Kandalar.

"Enough!" The deep, bell-like tone of the Executor rang out above the pandemonium, and an abrupt silence fell over the entire room. It was so quiet that Shaina could hear Tyson's labored breathing and the minute rattle of the fine golden chains that held his manacles in place. She turned to face the Executor, who was dressed in another of her multicolored outfits, this one with a long, flowing cape that must have taken the hides of hundreds of Kandalar to make.

"Your Excellency," T'lar began nervously, licking his thin lips with a purple tongue.

"Silence. Never has there been such a disturbance. It must not be." Her face was impassive but her skin flickered rapidly through every shade in the cape and her eyes blazed ruby red with annoyance. "Mistress," she inclined her head to Shaina, who had the presence of mind to bow deeply. "Our apologies for any damage to your slave. T'lar will see that he gets medical attention directly and then he will be returned to your rooms." She snapped two long, skeletal fingers and T'lar quickly unshackled Tyson, who slumped for a moment before straightening with what looked like a very painful effort and shambling after the tall Kandalar.

"*Ty.*" He was rigidly maintaining the wall of silence between them, keeping her out or keeping his pain in, she couldn't tell which. He left the hall, giving her one unreadable look from his amber eyes as he followed T'lar.

"Master Jlle," continued the Executor. "You will refrain from shouting comments in the hall. It is most disturbing to us and we dislike it excessively."

"Forgive me, Your Excellency," Jlle said sullenly. "But I don't think it's right to have such a dangerous slave with no collar to control him. Mistress Sender endangers us all."

"Be that as it may, it is not your place to say such things. You will retire to your rooms for the night and if another such occurrence comes to our attention, you shall be asked to leave the Palace. Do you understand?"

"Yes, Excellency," Jlle muttered. He turned to go, giving Shaina a glance filled with the purest malice as he left the hall.

"Mistress Sender, you are new to us and perhaps unaware of the consternation your uncollared slave has caused," the Executor continued, looking at Shaina again. "We have no choice but to order your D'Lonian be fitted with a pain collar to curb him during your stay with us. His neurons will be mapped tomorrow when he has recovered somewhat from his flogging."

"He is a Love slave, Your Excellency," Shaina protested. "I have never had problems with him before Master Jlle interfered with him."

"We have spoken. We do not intend to speak further on this subject." The Executor turned and swept from the room with a rustle of her rainbow-colored cape. Numbly, Shaina followed after a safe interval of time had gone by. The other Masters and Mistresses, along with their slaves, were also crowding from the room. A low murmur of concerned talk filled the air and Shaina was given several angry glances, none of which she paid the slightest attention to. Ty was the main thing now, getting to him and making sure he was all right . . .

Shaina wandered the corridors numbly for a while before finding herself in front of the double doors that led to the chamber of the Starving Nun. Would Ty already be back in the room? And, more importantly, would he talk to her?

Almost reluctantly, Shaina keyed the print-pad and pushed open the double doors. Tyson was lying on his stomach at the foot of the bed as befitted a proper slave. He looked up briefly as she opened the door and then laid his head back on his arms. His entire back was covered in a thin, semitransparent microskin that adhered snugly to every contour. Shaina could faintly make out the red welts crisscrossing his back through the healing membrane and the sight made her feel almost sick with anger and guilt.

"Tyber, are you well?" she asked out loud. *"Please, Ty, talk to me. Don't shut me out!"* she pleaded through the link. She crossed hesitantly to the side of the bed and just looked at him. Her hands itched to caress the unruly black hair from his forehead and look deep into those amber eyes, but she was afraid of what she might see there.

"I am well, my Mistress." His voiced reply formal, he sat up with a small wince and turned towards her. *"It's okay, McCullough. Stop looking like you lost your last friend."*

"I thought I had." Shaina sat carefully beside him on the bed and he scooted over a little to make room for her. She studied his back again, one small hand hovering just over his red-welted shoulder, not quite daring to touch. *"Does it ... does it hurt very much?"*

"Not right now. The healer slathered me with numb cream before putting on the microskin. He says he'll check it again tomorrow."

Shaina shifted uneasily on the bed. *"That's not the only thing they want to check. After T'lar took you out, the Executor ordered me to have your neurons mapped. Ty, they want to fit you for a pain collar tomorrow. We have to get out of here!"*

"Damn! Let me think a minute!" Ty's golden eyes closed briefly and then he opened them and sighed. *"It'll have to be tonight. Once they get a pain collar on me, our hands will be tied. Literally and figuratively."*

"Ty, I hate to say this, but I don't see how we're going to get Paul out of here ..."

"We're not leaving him." Ty's response was immediate and definite. He turned to face Shaina more fully, his golden eyes full of fire. *"Everything we've been through in the past couple*

of days, he's been going through for months. I wouldn't leave a canine I liked here, let alone another humanoid."

"Take it easy. I'm not suggesting we leave him—I just have no idea how we're going to get him out."

"Leave that to me. I'll think of something." He sighed and closed his eyes wearily.

"Ty . . ." Shaina could barely look at him, she felt so bad. "I just want to say that I'm so sorry. I know that's totally inadequate . . ."

"Sorry? What do you have to be sorry for, McCullough?" Ty opened his eyes and looked at her in surprise.

"What don't I have to be sorry for? All the pain and humiliation you've gone through." She gestured at his shoulders. "Your back . . . This is all my fault. I got us into this. You never would've come if it wasn't for me."

She turned her head away, unable to look at him, hugging herself tight with both arms. She had begun to think that Brent Tyson was the one, the man she had been waiting for, but she had screwed everything up. Now he would tell her she was right, that she was to blame for everything. Maybe he even hated her . . .

"Hey, look at me." A large, warm hand turned her face towards him and raised her chin until she was forced to look into those amber eyes and Shaina realized he had caught the last part of her thought. "I don't blame you and I don't hate you, Shaina," he sent, his mental voice soft and low. "I could never hate you."

"But it's my fault. I took this mission because I wanted to prove I was as good an officer as you. I wanted to show you that I didn't need you." Shaina's eyes blurred with tears and she wanted to turn her face away, but Ty's hand on her chin kept her from doing it.

"Doesn't matter if you need me or not, sweetheart," he whispered in her mind. "I *followed you on this mission because* I *need* you. *Understand?*"

"No . . ." Shaina shook her head. "*I don't understand any-thing.*"

"*That's all right. We'll figure it out together.*" And then he was kissing her, tenderly taking her mouth with his own, cupping her cheek in one large, capable hand as he explored her. Making her understand.

19

Ty kissed her, trying to show her how he felt without scaring her. But *God,* the guilty thoughts she was projecting were tearing him up. He wanted so much to tell Shaina how he felt—that he loved her, that he wanted this to be forever. But saying it out loud might ruin everything.

Her mouth tasted sweet, like the dessert wine she must have been sipping at the banquet, and he wove his fingers through her hair, loving the silky texture of the long, red strands. Before Ty knew it, she was in his arms and returning the kiss with passion. He could hear her wondering through their link if he was up to anything other than kissing.

"I'm still a little stiff." Flexing his shoulders experimentally, he winced at the mild discomfort his action produced. *"But the numb cream took care of most of the pain. Are you interested in putting on a farewell performance for the surveillance devices?"* He kissed a slow, hot trail down her neck, taking time to savor the uniquely salty-sweet flavor of her skin. He stopped to lick and bite gently at the tender curve where her shoulder met her throat. Ty felt Shaina shiver under his mouth and restrained his

natural D'Lonian urge to bite harder, to mark her more permanently.

"Are . . . are you sure you want to?" She gasped at his touch and tilted her head to one side, baring her throat more fully for him, offering herself, her ocean-green eyes tightly closed.

"You have to ask?" Tyson could feel himself growing painfully hard inside the carved copper sheath. *"I always want to with you, sweetheart."* He caressed her arms and back slowly as he sucked at her neck. She was wearing another of those provocative Mistress outfits that drove him wild. This one was a deep green, one shade darker than her eyes, and it was cut low enough in front that Ty could see the curving swells of her breasts when he looked down. Her nipples were a delicate rose and looked achingly hard. He reached down, cupped a full breast through the material of the gown, and rubbed the sweet pink nub with his thumb. Shaina made a hungry little noise and pushed forward, thrusting her breast more fully into his palm. He wanted to peel the top of gown down and suck them until she moaned.

"Why don't you, then?" She made a shrugging motion with her shoulders and the gown came sliding down on first one side and then the other. *"Damn thing's been trying to come off all day anyway,"* she murmured through their link, obviously feeling his mild amusement at the ease of her disrobing. Her ripe breasts were completely bared for him and Tyson took a moment to appreciate their full, symmetrical beauty before pressing her down against the firm mattress of the big bed and tracing one erect pink nipple slowly with his tongue.

"Please, don't tease me . . ."

"Is this what you want?" Abruptly, he sucked her ripe nipple into his mouth, making her moan and arch her back, offering her breasts to him without reservation. Ty nipped lightly, making her gasp and wiggle beneath him. He loved the way she was so responsive to his touch and knew she would be wet and

ready for him, her soft little pussy lips pouting and slick with need. As if hearing his thought, Shaina parted her thighs and made a slight thrusting motion with her pelvis.

"Ty please, I need you . . ."

"Hang on." Sitting up, he unbuckled the rigid sheath, setting it aside with a sigh of relief. Shaina sat up beside him and looked at his lap. His cock was hard and throbbing with need. It jutted out from between his thighs, gleaming slightly in the dim glowlight with the excess sheath lubrication.

"Can I . . . could I touch you?" One small, shapely hand hovered uncertainly over his shaft.

"Go ahead, sweetheart." It was Tyson's turn to gasp as she took him in her hand and slowly caressed the rigid, aching length of him. Her small, soft hand drove him crazy and it wasn't lost on him that this time she was touching him because she wanted to, not just to lubricate him for the sheath.

"I always wanted to. I was just afraid."

"You never have to be afraid of me, Shaina. I would never hurt you."

"I know . . ." Her hand was making him ache with need, and he gently pulled away and leaned closer to capture her mouth once more.

"Well, this is going to be our last performance here on Freak Planet, so let's make it a good one, okay?" He started to lower her back to the bed, but she stopped him, her hands on his shoulders, her green eyes wide.

"Ty, I don't want to . . . I mean, this time I don't want to pretend. I don't want to fake it. Do you understand?"

"Shaina, you don't mean that." Ty looked into her eyes and she looked back, a little scared but determined.

"Yes, I do." She tossed her hair with that little defiant flip that always squeezed his heart and gave him a serious look. *"I want you, Ty. Want to feel you inside me, filling me up."* She reached up and tangled one hand in his hair, pulling him in for

a luscious kiss. Tyson could feel her warm tongue pressing between his lips in wanton invitation. He broke the kiss abruptly and pulled back, looking down at her flushed face and heavy, half-lidded eyes. He could feel her desire through their link and knew she meant what she said but . . . could he really let her give him her innocence?

"*Shaina, I lo . . . I mean I want you too, but I don't want to take your virginity from you.*"

"*But I want you to. I want . . . I want to give myself to you. Goddess, that sounds so corny.*" Shaina sighed and shook her head.

"*No, it doesn't. It sounds hot and I want you . . . God, you have no idea how much I want you, Shaina, but are you sure?*" Ty looked into her eyes, wanting to be certain.

"*Yes. I think I've wanted this for a long time. I just couldn't admit it to myself. I've just been scared . . .*"

"*Because I'm half D'Lonian?*" Ty tilted her chin to look her more fully in the eyes.

"*I guess that sounds foolish, doesn't it? I mean, you can't believe everything you hear . . . right?*"

"*I won't lie to you, Shaina. Some of the things you've probably heard are true.*" Tyson stroked her hair gently. "*I would never hurt you. I have control over my D'Lonian urges, not the other way around, but I can't deny that half of myself. It makes me dominant, makes me want to possess you. Do you understand me, sweetheart? I'm trying to be straight with you.*"

"*I . . . I understand.*" Shaina looked a little frightened but still determined. "*I want you, Ty. Please, don't make me wait any longer.*" Her ocean-green eyes pleaded as she stood. Very deliberately she pushed the gown down to the floor and stepped out of it. She stood before him naked, all creamy skin and flame-bright hair, and Tyson knew he was lost. Possessing Shaina had been the only thing he wanted from the first minute he had laid eyes on her. He pulled her in for another long, luscious kiss and then pressed her gently back on the bed and began kissing a trail between her breasts and down her softly rounded belly.

"*Ty?*"

"*Relax, sweetheart. I'm just making sure you're wet enough to take me. And I want to taste your sweet pussy again before I make love to you.*"

"*Goddess, Ty, when you talk like that it makes me crazy!*" He was spreading her thighs now and kneeling between her legs. He placed a hot kiss on one creamy thigh, causing her to shudder beneath him.

"*I have better ways to make you crazy.*" He parted her sweet, plump lips, swollen with desire, and placed a soft, open-mouthed kiss on the aching pink bud of her clitoris. "*Love the way you taste, Shaina . . .*"

Her small hands crept up and buried themselves in his hair, urging him closer, begging him not to stop. Tyson leaned forward and pressed his tongue into her hot channel, loving the taste of her cunt on his lips and in his mouth as he spread her thighs wider to get better access to her body.

"*Don't stop. I'm close!*" He could feel her shaking apart under him already, could feel her pussy trembling and clenching around his tongue, and he pushed her over the edge and beyond. Soon, he would feel her tremble that way around his cock. He couldn't wait to fill her completely, to possess her utterly . . .

He shut his eyes, frowning to himself. No, not quite completely. That would have to come later, but for tonight he would take her farther than she had ever gone before.

"Ty . . ." she gasped out loud. Bucking her hips up to meet him, she finished her orgasm, as he wrung the last, sweet spasms from her hot, wet pussy.

At last, Tyson looked up at her. Her face was flushed a rosy red and her beautiful hair was wild, spread over the pillow. Her green eyes were full of need.

"Please, Ty. I want you now . . . in me." She lay there, wet and naked and open just for him and asked for what he wanted desperately to give her—but Tyson knew he had to be careful. A part of him, the D'Lonian part that wanted only to claim and possess, wanted to spread her thighs wide and fuck roughly into her until he filled her with cum, marking her as his forever. Red began to seep into his vision, the Fuck lust threatening to overcome him. Ty fought savagely to suppress the desire. He wanted to be gentle, wanted Shaina to always remember her first time as something special, something tender. He couldn't do that in their current position.

"Come here, sweetheart." He moved so that he was leaning back on the pile of soft pillows and motioned Shaina to straddle him.

"What about your back?" She sat up and moved over to him.

"It's fine, I promise. It might be a different story when the numb cream wears off, but for now I don't feel anything but a little itching and tingling. Now come here and sit on my legs. Let's get a little closer." He put a note of command into his mental tone and Shaina crawled obediently forward and sat carefully almost in his lap, her legs spread wide to straddle his muscular thighs. Tyson could see her pussy lips spread open as well, wet, pink and inviting, and it took all of his self-control not to pull her forward and ram into her immediately.

"Is this right?" Shaina asked innocently, positioning her soft, open sex just over the head of his cock, her slippery folds barely brushing his aching flesh.

Ty gritted his teeth in an effort to hold back. *"Yes, that's right, sweetheart."*

She hesitated for just an instant, biting her full, pink, lower lip, a troubled look in her green eyes. *"Ty, there's just one thing before we ... before we do this. When we were talking the other night about this while I was ... was touching myself, you talked about, um, coming inside me."* Her cheeks flushed deep red with embarrassment and she could barely meet his eyes for a minute. *"But the thing is, I think I forgot to get my required hormone injection before we left home. I'm not completely sure I'm safe right now. I'm really sorry, I know how careless that must sound considering the mission we're on. I was going to tell you if it came up,"* she rushed on, still keeping her eyes down. *"But do you think you could not ..."* Shaina broke off, unable to finish the sentence.

"Don't worry, sweetheart, I have enough control to pull out at the right moment," Tyson assured her. Privately, he reflected that if she had expected him to do anything else, she had absolutely no clue about D'Lonian culture and physiology. Despite all of his hot words to her the night she had been touching herself in the tub, Ty had never had any intention of coming inside her until they reached a clearer understanding about their relationship, whether her government-mandated birth control was up to date or not. The act of ejaculating inside a female would cause a permanent biochemical bond to form between her and her D'Lonian lover. D'Lonians called it a Soul-Bond and it was utterly unbreakable. It would tie them together forever, hence the rumors that D'Lonians mated for life—they did. Ty would never risk that with Shaina unless he knew she felt the same way about him that he did about her. But there was no time to go into that now with her straddling his cock and waiting to feel him inside her.

"Just lower yourself down until you feel me start to slip inside you," he whispered soothingly into her mind.

"Like this?" Following his directions, she lowered herself until the head of his cock was lodged just inside the entrance of her pussy. Again, Tyson fought the urge to thrust into her tight, virginal channel.

"That's right. Now just relax and let me slide into you. It may hurt a little at first, but once I get all the way in, it'll feel better." He hoped that was true. He had never been with a virgin before and he was determined to make Shaina's first time good.

Shaina tried to follow his instructions, but it was difficult because of her inexperience and his large size. She lowered herself until nearly half of his shaft was buried in her tight, slippery sex and then stopped.

"Ty, I can't . . . can't go any further. You're so big and I'm just too tight . . . I'm sorry." Tears of effort and frustration stood in her beautiful eyes, making her look vulnerable and hurt, making him want to hold and comfort her.

"It's all right, sweetheart. Don't be upset. Do you want to stop?" He looked anxiously into her brimming eyes.

Shaina's response was immediate and definite. *"No, I want to do this. I want you inside me, but I can't do it on my own. Ty, I think you're just going to have to . . . just do it. I don't care if it hurts. I need you in me now, please!"* She was bracing herself for the inevitable pain, her eyes squeezed into slits, her lips parted slightly, panting with longing and need.

Tyson didn't want to hurt her, but he found he couldn't deny her either. She looked so beautiful, flushed and naked in his lap with half of his hard shaft buried in her soft, tight cunt. He could feel her throbbing around him, could see the way her wet pussy lips stretched to receive him, to take him as deeply into herself as she could. But as she said, she couldn't manage it all on her own. He would have to finish the job.

Trying not to think about it too much, Ty took Shaina's hips firmly in his hands. Taking a tight grip on her, he thrust up quickly, breaching her thin barrier and pressing his cock deeply inside her until he felt the end of her tight channel press against the head of his shaft.

"Oh Goddess!" Shaina gasped out loud and he could feel

the sharp bolt of pain that lanced through her as he fucked into her pussy, filling her completely for the first time.

"Are you okay, sweetheart?" Her eyes had overflowed briefly with the sudden pain. *"Am I hurting you?"*

"Not now. Just . . . just wait a minute. I have to get used to this. To having you in me." She blinked and brushed her fingers against her eyes, brushing away unwanted tears, which Ty longed to kiss away. He was nearly overwhelmed by her beauty and her bravery. The way she had opened for him, had accepted him into her body despite the hurt it caused her awed him.

"God, Shaina, you are so beautiful." He loved the sight of her straddling him. Her cheeks were flushed with exertion, her eyes bright and soft, and her breasts tipped with ripe, rosy nipples that jutted out at him defiantly despite her pain.

"I . . . I think I'm ready now." Bracing her small hands on his chest, she leaned forward experimentally so that just about an inch of his hard shaft slid out of her wet sex, keeping his penetration shallow. *"But go slow, all right?"*

"Of course." Once again Tyson rigidly held his D'Lonian urges in check and moved slowly but gently inside her tight pussy, pulling nearly all the way out before pressing inside again to bury himself in her body as deeply as he could.

"Oh, Ty . . . that feels so . . . oh . . ." Shaina gasped and placed both her hands over his, which were still planted firmly on her hips. She looked down, watching as he moved her body, fucking her in a slow, delicious, deliberate rhythm. He knew she could see his thick shaft sliding in and out of her sweet entrance, could feel her pleasure building through their link, and knew she was ready to go further and deeper.

"Sit back, sweetheart, and let me get really deep into you."

"Will . . . will it hurt?" Green eyes filled with fear.

"It shouldn't. Shaina, if you want to do this, then we've got to do it right. Lean back and let me really fuck you." He put the commanding tone in his voice again, the one she seemed to re-

spond to so well. Shaina did as he told her at once, sitting back so that he could completely fill her sweet, creamy pussy with his aching shaft. They gasped simultaneously with the sudden increase of sensation and then Ty tightened his grip on her hips and got ready to move.

"What now?" She was panting with pleasure.

"Now I'm going to ride your sweet little pussy hard." He pressed in deeply, making sure she could feel every inch of his thick shaft stretching her open. *"Is this what you want, Shaina?"*

"You know it is. Do it, please, Ty. Fuck me!"

Her hot words in his head were all it took to drive him over the edge. Holding her tightly, Ty began to move inside her sweet, slick tightness, pressing himself deep inside her grasping pussy. Her face flushed with pleasure as she gave herself up to him completely, gave herself up to being fucked. God, she was beautiful! He loved to watch her breasts bounce in time to their rhythm and her flame-red hair sway around her shoulders as he thrust into her again and again.

"Oh, Goddess . . . Oh, Ty . . . Don't stop!" Her voice was little more than a breathy moan as she leaned back and surrendered herself to him. Surrendered to the sensations of his body in hers, his thick cock sheathed in her tight cunt. He loved that sound in her voice, loved the way she called his name when she was close. It was beyond erotic to hear her beg for more while she trembled around him. Impaled by his thickness, she submitted to him completely as he gave her what they had both needed for so damn long.

"Ty . . . think I'm going to . . ." Through their link, Tyson could feel her orgasm approaching, sharp and sweet and utterly overwhelming. He continued to work, thrusting steadily into her, pressing hard against her swollen pink clitoris with every deep thrust of his cock in her body, giving her what she needed to reach it.

"Work for it, Shaina. Come on sweetheart, you deserve it.

Wanna feel you come around me." He gripped her hips even tighter and quickened his pace.

"*Almost . . . almost there . . . Can't quite . . .*" Shaina's head was thrown back, her eyes tightly shut, and her face was a mask of intense, pleasurable concentration. Her small hands gripped convulsively at his forearms and then at his thighs as she leaned back even further, widening her stance to get even more of his shaft inside her. She was reaching for release, but wasn't quite able to get there. Suddenly, he understood what she needed.

"Come for me, sweetheart," he commanded her aloud, thrusting into her as deeply as he could. "Come for me *now.*"

"Oh, Ty!" She wailed and he felt her soft pussy begin to shudder around his shaft. "Oh!" She sobbed and her hands flexed into fists as she came, drenching him in a new wave of soft, wet heat.

The feel of her pussy spasming around his hard flesh was almost too much for Ty. Every instinct he possessed was shouting at him to clamp down on Shaina's hips and fill her with his seed. To come inside her and forge the Soul-Bond. To make her his forever. But he had promised to pull out and now was not the time to Bond. Grimly, he rode out the waves of her orgasm, barely trusting himself to move as she shuttered and quaked around him. At last, she stuttered to a stop and Ty forced himself to pull out of her, lifting her off him, though he had never wanted to do anything less. Only when his hard shaft was completely clear of her sweet, sucking pussy did he allow himself to explode, spurting wave after wave of hot, sticky seed between their bellies until he was done.

"*Wow . . .*" Shaina murmured in his mind, obviously surprised by the amount of cum he had produced. Ty could have told her that it was a D'Lonian trait. The more seed ejaculated into a female's sex, the stronger the Bond it produced. He wanted Shaina Bonded to him forever and his body had responded to his want and need for her.

"Sorry." Ruefully he wished, despite his better judgment, that his cum was filling her belly instead of making them both sticky. *"I'll get something to clean us up."* He rolled out from beneath her and went to the bathroom to get some damp towels before she could protest.

Tyson wiped himself up carefully and returned to the bedroom, holding a warm, damp towel before him, only to find Shaina curled in a small ball on her side sobbing as if her heart would break.

"Shaina?" Dropping the towel and he eased into the bed beside her, almost afraid to touch her. *"Did I hurt you? I'm so sorry, sweetheart . . ."*

"No, I'm okay, really . . ." Shaina rolled over to face him, her eyes red from crying. *"It was just . . . intense. That's all. More . . . more than I ever expected it to be. Sorry to get all emotional and girly on you."*

"Don't worry about it. Get as emotional as you want." Ty pulled her to him and cradled her gently in his arms. Leaning down, he kissed her eyelids softly and deliberately kissed the tears away. Shaina gave a long, low, shuddering sigh and cuddled closer to him, letting her head rest on his shoulder. He wished again, fiercely, that he could tell her how very much he loved her, how much he needed her in his life forever.

"That was wonderful Ty. I just wish that . . ."

"That what?" He tilted her chin to make her look at him, but her face suddenly took on a closed, secretive expression that he couldn't interpret and she shook her head slightly.

"Nothing. I mean, I just wish that it could have been someplace other than here, in a way. I never though my first time would be recorded on surveillance devices. I hope we don't end up on a porno-loop somewhere in this freaky palace."

Tyson had the distinct feeling that she had been about to say something else, but he decided to let it slide. Shaina was already upset enough as it was.

"Well, I hope not too, but at least if we do, we won't be around to see it. Listen, I think I know how we can get out of here and take Paul with us."

"Really? Oh, Ty that's wonderful! You have no idea how much I want to get off this hellhole of a planet."

"Bet I do." He sat up and experimentally flexed his shoulders and back a little. However, he still only felt a slight, annoying, itching sensation. Whatever was in that numb cream, it really worked. *"Let's get you cleaned up and I'll tell you."* He rolled off the bed and collected the now cold towel. *"I'll just be a minute, I need to get a fresh towel."* He headed for the bathroom.

"Your back. Ty, your back!" The concern in Shaina's mental voice caused Tyson to turn back around and face her.

"What about it? Is the microskin coming off?" He tried unsuccessfully to turn his head far enough to see over his own broad shoulder but he couldn't quite manage it.

"No. Ty, your back is almost healed!"

20

Shaina could scarcely believe what she was seeing. Beneath the semi-transparent microskin that covered Ty's back, the red welts from the flogging appeared to be healing almost magically. When she had first come into the room and looked at him, the welts had appeared angry and swollen. She had cringed inwardly, thinking of the weeks of painful healing Ty had ahead of him. Now, barely an hour later, the wounds were, if not completely healed, at least so close to it as to make almost no difference. The smooth golden perfection of Tyson's broad back was barely marked, with only a few pink lines to show where the whip had cut him, and even as Shaina watched they began to disappear.

"What do you mean it's almost healed?" Ty tried again to get a look at his own back, but, of course, he couldn't.

"Come on, I'll show you." Shaina slid off the bed a little stiffly, feeling a deep, not entirely unpleasant ache between her thighs, and tried not to wobble as she grabbed one muscular arm and herded Tyson into the bathroom. She thought it likely

she would be walking with some difficulty for a while, but the soreness seemed to be wearing off.

"*Look.*" She placed Ty's back to the mirror that covered one wall by the imposing black stone sink and half turned him so that he could get a look at his nearly healed back.

"God . . ." The pink lines were being swallowed by the normal golden-tan of his regular skin color even as they watched. "*That numb cream is something else. These welts should have lasted for weeks, even months.*"

Numb cream? Shaina had a sudden realization. "*Ty, come back in the room* now*!*" She tugged urgently at his arm, pulling him back through the bathroom door and pushing him down on the bed. Tyson was so startled by her insistent tone that he allowed her to do it, a bemused look on his face. "*Lie on your back again.*" Shaina arranged him so that he was pressed firmly against the pillows and his nearly healed back was concealed.

"*Okay, okay, what?*"

"*Don't you see? A minute ago I was really sore between my legs from our . . . from what we did, but now I feel perfectly fine. You were flogged not two hours ago and now there's hardly any evidence of it. It's not the numb cream that's healing your back so quickly—it's the Goddess-damned symbiotes!*"

"*You're right!*" Ty surged upright on the bed and then remembered himself and lay back against the pillows quickly. "*This is bad, sweetheart, really bad.*" His heavy, dark eyebrows lowered like a thundercloud on his high forehead and shadowed his amber eyes. "*I mean,* really *bad. If they didn't suspect us before, they sure as hell will now.*"

"*I know. Who goes to the trouble and expense of injecting their slave, even a Love slave, with symbiotes? It would be like lining your waste disposal chute with platinum and diamonds. No offense, Ty.*"

"*None taken. Because you're right. Okay, we're not going to panic. We know we're being recorded, but I don't think the images from the surveillance devices are necessarily being watched every single minute. Otherwise, there would already be a hoard of Kandalar knocking down the chamber door. This just gives us one more reason to get out of here tonight."*

Shaina saw the intense look of concentration on his face and knew he was considering what to do. She crossed her arms over her breasts, suddenly cold and scared. The motion caused her to remember she was still naked and rather sticky.

"Um, I know we're in a critical situation here, but do you think there's time for me to take a quick shower?"

"That's a good idea. Take a shower and take the idol Faron gave us with you."

"In the shower? I'm not sure if it's moisture-resistant." Nevertheless, she fished around in her velour knapsack until she found the small, glowing idol of the Chancellor's son Faron had given them.

"That's okay. You don't have to actually take it in the shower with you. Just turn up the water and stand right next to it while you contact Faron. With luck, the noise of the water will screw with the surveillance devices. Hurry, Shaina. Tell him to be in position no less than an hour from now. When we go, we're going to be moving very quickly."

"Got it. In the meantime I guess you'll just have to lie on the bed and look pitiful." She tried to grin at him, despite her fear, and he grinned back, confidently.

"Yeah, poor me. To have such a cruel Mistress, who insists I service her even after such a brutal flogging."

"Don't remind me." Shaina shut her eyes briefly, remembering how hard it had been to just sit there and watch her partner being beaten so cruelly. It had been the worst experience of her life.

"Sorry." Ty's expression softened as he saw the pain cross her face. *"Don't worry about it, Shaina; there was nothing you*

could do. Now why don't you hit the showers? We're leaving
Freak Planet in no more than an hour and a half."

"I can't wait!" Shaina threw one more glance over her
shoulder. She went into the bathroom and closed the door.

Only when she was in the bathroom alone with the water
running to block out the noise did she finally allow herself to
collapse. Leaning against the black stone wall by the small, hidden shower alcove, she let the tears flow that had been threatening to come back ever since she had made herself stop crying
in front of Ty.

"Goddess . . ." Hiding her eyes with one arm, she leaned
into the cloud of steam curling from behind the sliding shower
door. The reaction was completely unexpected, and yet she
guessed she shouldn't be so surprised. It wasn't the dangerous
situation they found themselves in that bothered her. Tyson
said he had a plan to get them all out safely and Shaina trusted
him implicitly. He had never let her down before. What was
twisting her guts and making her feel like her heart was lying
naked on the cold bathroom floor was the aftereffects of sex
with Ty.

Shaina had known her first time would be an emotional experience. She had waited so long for it that it couldn't be anything less. What she hadn't counted on was the rush of feelings
for her partner while they had made love. The sheer intensity
had overcome her as he brought her so gently, so sweetly, helping her ride the crest of pleasure and bringing her to a shattering climax that left her feeling devastated. Leaving her open and
utterly vulnerable to him. Before he had made love to her,
Shaina had thought he might be the one, the man she wanted to
giver herself to and stay with forever. Now she was absolutely
certain.

Brent Tyson was the only man in the universe for her—but
he didn't know it.

She had come close to telling him, too damn close, when he was holding her and kissing her tears away so tenderly. Could any man touch you that way and not have more than friendly feelings for you? Not love you? Shaina didn't know, and she had been dying to ask him how he felt. But then, he had calmly accepted the explanation for her tears and gone on to talk about other, more pressing matters, and Shaina knew the experience was over for him. What she had felt as mind-blowing, emotionally intense sex, Tyson had seen as just another duty. Just another part of the mission. It meant nothing to him, less than nothing, and she had better get over it, Shaina lectured herself.

Still, a part of her couldn't help wishing she could turn back around, go into the bedroom, and tell him how much it had meant to her. How she had let him into her heart when she let him into her body. She pushed that part down and away from herself. They had a mission to complete and Ty was right to get on with business, no matter how much it hurt her. Sighing, she thumbed the idol in her hand and held it close to her face.

"Hello, Faron?" she whispered softly.

"All set." She emerged from the shower wrapped in a fluffy white sythi-cotton towel. *"Faron's in position now and he says he'll be waiting in the shuttle for us when we make the break."*

Ty frowned from his place on the bed. *"That's not really necessary. I'm sure we can manage the shuttle on our own; we did on the way down here."*

Shaina shrugged and began digging through her trunk to find a suitable outfit. *"I think he just wants to be here. He seems to genuinely care for Paul. I guess the Chancellor and his family are more than just employers for him.*

"I guess. Listen, I think you'd better put that damned sheath on me one more time." He grimaced as he looked at the copper contraption Shaina knew he had come to loathe.

"Don't worry, Ty. Just think, it'll be the last time you have to wear the bloody thing." Her tone was sympathetic.

And it would be the last time she had an excuse to touch him so intimately, she thought, pouring a handful of the viscous red lubricating oil that smelled like cinnamon and cloves. But she pushed that thought away resolutely. *"So tell me, partner, how are we going to get out of here?"*

"I demand a slave to service me for the night!" Shaina said in her most imperious, pissed-off Mistress tone. She was standing in front of the Kandalar guarding the main entrance to the male slave quarters and making as much fuss as she possibly could, drawing all eyes, and, she hoped, all the attention of the surveillance devices to herself.

The difficult part of the plan had been getting rid of the everpresent T'lar, who had been, predictably, lurking around their chamber door. However, Shaina had set him off to the kitchens with a request for some rare and complicated Rigelian delicacy, which she had to make up on the spot, having no idea what anyone ate on Rigel Five. She had poutingly told the tall Kandalar she was hungry for a midnight snack and he had gone, giving her a sullen look from his glowing red eyes as he left.

As soon as they were certain he was gone, Shaina and Tyson had walked briskly down the mostly deserted corridor to the slave quarters, where Shaina was being as difficult as she possibly could. While she distracted the guard and the surveillance, Ty was creeping quietly around the smaller service entrance, which he had noticed while spending his one fateful night in the quarters. The plan was to grab Paul and leave the life-size idol in his place. As soon as he had Paul's collar off and had a head start down the corridor that led to the shuttle bay, he would send Shaina a thought. She, in turn, would wind up her rant and appear to relent in her demands and stalk off, ostensibly back to her quarters, but actually to the bay as well. With a little luck, they would be into the shuttle and well on their way to the *She-Creature* before anyone noticed the idol wasn't Paul.

"What if they notice the idol before we get to the shuttle?" Shaina asked anxiously when Ty explained the plan.

"Then we run like hell, sweetheart." Ty's tone was grim. It wasn't the most elegant plan, more down and dirty than the stylish spy vids Shaina had loved as a little girl, but they were running out of time and she thought it would work.

"I said, I insist upon having a slave for the night. Did you hear me, guard?" She resisted the urge to look in the direction of the service entrance. *"How's it going?"* Aware that Ty was already inside the quarters, she was getting anxious.

"Pretty good. He's asleep, I'm going to get the collar off before I wake him. Say a prayer that he wakes up in his right mind and this thing hasn't fried his brain."

"Don't forget the password to expand the idol is Zibathorpe."

"Got it."

"But Mistress, the slave quarters are closed at this time, as you must surely know." The Kandalar guard demurred, clearly unhappy and uncertain of what to do.

"It was *your* ham-fisted Norsoth that injured my slave so that he couldn't properly service me and now *you* will provide me with another slave until he is well. I was promised compensation and every possible courtesy by Her Excellency the Executor herself." Shaina was really getting into the role.

"While I am sorry for your inconvenience . . ." The Kandalar guard began reciting reasons why he couldn't open up the slave quarters for her personal perusal after hours and Shaina let him ramble on, pasting a furious expression on her face as she tapped one slipper-clad foot and concentrated on Ty.

"Got the collar off now and he's coming around. . . . Seems to be okay, although the poor kid is scared to death." Another rather lengthy silence, in which Shaina assumed Tyson was

talking to Paul and getting him reoriented to the world without a love collar. It must be an ugly shock, she thought, to find yourself in the middle of such a situation with little or no memory of how it had happened to you in the first place. *"All right, the idol's in place and we're moving out. Keep all of the guard's attention on you. It'll only take a minute for us to get past and then we're home free down the hall to the bay. Follow us as soon as you reasonably can. We'll be waiting."*

"Got it." Turning to the guard, she poked one angry finger in his long, thin chest and snarled, "I don't want to hear any more of your excuses! You will open the slave quarters for me this instant so that I may select another slave to serve me or I will see you sent off-planet or better yet, to the colored chambers, before this night is through!" This statement got all of the guard's attention and he paled considerably, turning a shade of dirty gray that no longer matched the black hallway and which, Shaina reflected, wouldn't have looked at all nice in any of the Executor's rainbow-colored Kandalar-skin gowns.

"Mistress, please be reasonable," he pleaded and Shaina thought she heard a definite quaver in his voice as he begged. Out of the corner of her eye, she saw Ty and a shellshocked-looking Paul scuttle past the guard, hunched over and moving quickly as they made their way down the corridor leading to the shuttle bay. She let the Kandalar guard blather on nervously for another minute or two before holding up her hand to stop him.

"It occurs to me that arguing with you and listening to your foolishness is a waste of my valuable time and energy." She affected a yawn as she spoke. "I will take this up with one of your superiors tomorrow. For now, I am going to bed."

"As you wish, Mistress. I am certain someone can be of assistance to you tomorrow." The guard was clearly relieved that she was willing to let the matter drop, at least for now. He made a low bow, his bony forehead nearly brushing the black floor, and Shaina tossed her hair and swept away from him, not bothering to acknowledge his parting gesture.

"We're almost to the shuttle. No problems so far." She heard Ty's voice inside her head as she walked slowly and deliberately down the long, polished hall as if she had every right to be there. Dimly, she could make out two pale figures far down at the end, which must be Ty and Paul. *"Do you want me to wait for you?"*

"Keep going; I'm right behind you. The sooner you get into the shuttle the better. Two slaves running free attracts a lot more attention than one Mistress wandering the halls. If someone stops me, I can always say I'm lost."

It was then that she felt a firm, cold grip on her upper arm and a familiar voice whispered in her ear. "Mistress Sender, I regret to inform you that the kitchens are completely out of Rigelian lamb loin with ecru bitter berry glaze. In fact"—he turned Shaina around by force and she found herself facing T'lar's glowing red eyes in the dim hall—"it just so happens that our head chef is an off-worlder who studied exclusively at the Rigel Five Institute of Universal Good Taste. Surely you've heard of it. I understand all the better families on Rigel Five get their personal chefs from among its esteemed classes. No?" He drew closer, his burning gaze boring its way into her skull, and Shaina found that her tongue had turned to a lump of lead in her mouth and she couldn't think of a thing to say. Dumbly, she shook her head.

"Well, that is a great pity, although not as much of a surprise as it once might have been." T'lar continued, pulling her still closer. He grinned angrily, baring long yellow teeth. "You see, our very fine chef also informed me that there is no such delicacy as Rigelian lamb loin with ecru bitter berry glaze, as all Rigelian cuisine is fungus-based, because the entire population lives entirely underground. Does this surprise you?"

"Of course not," Shaina finally found her voice. "What surprises me is that you have the nerve to advertise authentic Rigelian cuisine while your head chef is obviously an incompetent moron who wouldn't know a true delicacy if it bit him in the backside!" She was getting back into the part and playing it well, she thought. "Now I suggest you take your filthy hands off me this instant, T'lar, before I decide to lodge a complaint. If I decide to tell my father about this . . ."

"You have no father and no family on Rigel Four or Five. I checked." T'lar hissed, squeezing her arm so tightly Shaina thought she would surely have a bruise the next day. "I knew something wasn't quite right about you from the first minute you set foot in the palace. But now it all makes sense."

"Shaina? We're to the door now. Where are you?" Dimly, like a speck on the horizon, Shaina could make out Ty's figure at the end of the long, dim hall. She just hoped that T'lar, whose whole attention was bent on her, wouldn't notice.

"On my way." She turned her attention back to the irate Kandalar gripping her arm. "I don't know what you're talking about. My father is a very important person and he'll see you skinned alive for this." Voice cold, she tried to turn so that they would be facing the other direction and Ty wouldn't be in their line of vision.

"You're a Slave Finder, admit it!" T'lar spat and Shaina felt the ugly snub nose of a disintegrator suddenly sticking into her side. "And you just happen to be wandering along the hall leading to the shuttle bay to check that your shuttle is ready for your grand escape. Let's go check it together, shall we?" He turned her firmly back towards the end of the long hall and began pulling her rapidly along as his smooth, inhumanly long strides ate up the ground remaining between them and the *She-Creature's* shuttle. Shaina dug in her feet as well as she could and tried to resist despite the threat of the disintegrator, but the soft-soled Mistress slippers that went with her outfit simply slid along the highly polished floor with aggravating ease.

"I've been watching you from the first, *Mistress*." T'lar hissed, still looking at Shaina even as he dragged her down the hall. "I should have known when I saw what you had brought as your slave. No one enslaves a D'Lonian without a collar—savage beasts!" He continued his tirade. At least, Shaina thought, he kept his attention fixed on her and not the end of the corridor, and T'lar's voice was low enough that no one but herself could hear it.

"Shaina?" It was Ty again and he sounded puzzled. *"What's taking you so long? Is anything wrong?"*

Shaina realized that at this distance, T'lar's Kandalar camouflage allowed him to blend in perfectly with the black hall and all Tyson could see was her own pale figure coming down the hall. She also realized that if Ty understood what was really going on, he would come back for her and they would both be caught and killed. T'lar believed she was planning on stealing a slave, but he seemed to have no idea that she was actually in the process of doing it right that minute. If they were discovered in the act, it would mean certain death for both of them and eternal slavery for Paul. She couldn't let it happen.

"I'm fine. Get in the shuttle. I'll be there in a minute." Maybe if she could get T'lar close enough to the tunnel, Ty could surprise and disarm him, but she didn't want to risk having her partner run all the way down the hall, away from the safety of the shuttle and possibly into a lethal disintegrator blast. When she got just a little closer she would warn him. Just a little closer, she told herself. With relief, she saw the two small figures at the end of the hall disappear into a piece of the wall. They were safe inside the shuttle. Now if only they would stay there . . .

She had been shielding her thoughts as tightly as she could but apparently some of that last thought leaked through.

"Shaina, I can tell something's wrong. I'm coming back."

"No! Stay in the shuttle!"

"Why? What's going on?"

She saw the door in the wall slide open and saw Ty's large, broad-shouldered frame outlined in the pale lavender light from the *She-Creature*'s monochrome shuttle. It was so close and yet so far. Shaina thought she could even hear the hissing of the shuttle's strange air vents in the still hall. T'lar must have heard the telltale hissing as well, because he turned his attention from Shaina and saw the shuttle's entrance as well.

Behind Ty, half hidden by his body but still visible, was Paul.

"No . . ." T'lar breathed, shaking his bald head in disbelief. "You wouldn't dare . . ." Suddenly, he lifted his head and gave a strangely nasal howl. To Shaina, it sounded as though he was trying to pull his guts out of his aristocratically long, pointed nose, but the strange sound had a most unwelcome effect. Immediately to their left and right, sections of the long hall began to slide open and the long, thin shapes of Kandalar began to pour out. There were ten, then twenty, then too many to count and all of them were eerily quiet as they converged around T'lar and herself.

"Stop him! They are Slave Finders!" T'lar roared into the silent mob. He pointed one long, thin arm at Tyson's shape at the end of the hall, and what seemed like hundreds of pairs of glowing red eyes followed his gesture.

"Ty, go!" Shaina screamed out loud, forgetting to use the link as T'lar dragged her with him, charging down the long hall at the head of the mob of Kandalar that were running, still whisper-quiet, toward the open shuttle door.

"I won't leave you!"

Shaina's heart sank as she watched him beginning to step outside the safety of the shuttle into the melee in the hall. They were close enough now that she could see the anguished expression on his face.

"Then we'll both die right here and now! Go on, get in the

shuttle and take off!" Tone urgent, she willed him to stop being so stupidly stubborn.

"No! Not without you!" He suddenly had something in his hand and one of the Kandalar to her right made a bubbling scream and fell, gasping with an exploded throat. In response, a burning beam of harsh yellow brilliance knifed through the air and part of the wall beside the shuttle's entrance collapsed in a heap of dust. Obviously T'lar wasn't the only one armed with a disintegrator.

"Alive, you idiots! Curse the eggs that hatched you, we want them alive!" T'lar screamed as a second blast took out another section of wall, this one much closer to the shuttle. Shaina saw Ty duck as the blast went past his head, but he still wasn't leaving. Another Kandalar dropped, clutching his chest, and a third fell, a twist of purplish guts spilling from his ruined abdomen. Still, what seemed to Shaina like hundreds more still raced to the end of the hall.

"Ty, I'm begging you to leave." Shaina could feel tears of anger and frustration welling up in her eyes even as she was dragged along, breathless and panting. They were getting closer to the shuttle all the time. Soon it would be too late.

"And I'm telling you I'm not going anywhere without you, sweetheart," he sent back grimly, his amber eyes flashing and his face etched in lines of determination and anger.

"Take him, take him and the slave they have stolen!" T'lar was screaming. Long, thin alien arms were reaching out and more than one of them held a dart gun that Shaina knew would only stun, not kill. But a blast from a disintegrator would be a merciful death compared to what Ty would wake up to when the dart's poison wore off. It was almost too late.

"Ty, if you care about me at all, then go!" she tried, one last time. She was close enough to see him shake his head in rigid negation.

"I told you I'm not . . ." But his voice cut off abruptly inside

her head, like a vid screen being clicked to mute, and Shaina watched in horror as another section of wall just above the doorway collapsed, sending a cloud of dust into the air. When it cleared briefly, she could see Tyson's large frame lying in an awkward posture on the floor, half in and half out of the shuttle. Suddenly the familiar, graceful figure of Faron appeared behind him and dragged him into the pale lavender light. The door shut almost in their faces.

"*Ty?*" Shaina tried sending through their link, but she got no response, just empty space where he had been.

Ty was gone.

21

"Is he well?"

"He's coming around, Faron. It took long enough though. Eight standard hours, didn't you say?" A disapproving sound, like someone "tsking," could be heard in the blackness. "How much of that stuff did you give him?"

"Not so much, Mistress Shybolt, but one of the Kandalar's darts hit him as well. It is a dose not many could withstand. Without his strong D'Lonian constitution, we might have lost him as well as Mistress McCullough. It is a pity about her." The voice was soft and detached. Faron's. Tyson's head felt like someone had used it to crush rocks for ore in the asteroid belt and he didn't dare open his eyes as he listened groggily to the conversation going on over his head.

"A pity indeed! You have only yourselves to blame if you lost people back there. Sending in amateurs to do a job like that!" The voice was thick with disgust and Ty began to think he recognized it. Of course, the brown-haired middle-aged Mistress who had sat beside them at the first banquet. But what was she doing here aboard the *She-Creature*? And where was Shaina?

"As I recall, the job was offered to you and your partner, not once but twice. You refused it both times." Faron's voice was soft and still courteous, but, Ty thought, lightly mocking. It was coming closer . . . *Wait for it,* he told himself.

"Because it was a suicide mission and you know it. L'Mera and I are willing to help anyone with the credit to pay and we even do some pro bono work on occasion, but walking into a trap like this . . . It was a fool's mission. You're lucky you got even one of your operatives back alive." Mistress Shy's tone was angry and abrupt.

"We have recovered Paul, which was the main objective all along. I consider this mission a success." Faron's voice was directly above him now. Ty pistoned one hand up and out, caught the Glameron by his slender, beautiful throat, and squeezed hard. He opened his eyes at last to see the elegant face turning an alarming shade of reddish-purple. He pulled until Faron's head was level with his own aching one and asked the only question that mattered.

"Where's Shaina?" he grated, looking into the gorgeous, swirling eyes. "Where is she?"

"Master Tyson, please!" Faron gasped in a choked voice, his delicate hands scrabbling at Ty's fingers to no avail. His eyes were swirling ocean-green and his face was turning quite blue, a color scheme Ty thought suited him, although the Glameron obviously had other ideas.

"Turn Faron loose at once, Tyson." The commanding voice came from Mistress Shybolt, looking a full fifteen years younger with her pale brown hair hanging free around her shoulders and wearing more formfitting clothes than one of her usual billowy caftans.

"Things have changed, *Mistress,*" Ty sneered, still keeping a firm hold on the Glameron's throat although he did loosen his grip enough for Faron to get a thin, wheezing breath. "You see, I'm not really a slave."

"Of course you're not," Shy said calmly. "You're no more a slave than L'Mera here." She gestured and the familiar form of her blond slave girl came into view, also dressed in more normal clothes. Her hair, Ty noticed, was pulled into a simple, no-nonsense bun at the back of her neck instead of one of the startling updos she had affected in the Palace.

"Nice to meet you in a more normal setting," the blonde said, holding out one small, shapely hand and smiling so that her friendly snub-nosed face crinkled engagingly.

"Nice, uh . . ." Tyson realized he would have to let go of Faron's throat to shake her hand and he did so very reluctantly. "Nice to meet you too," he said formally, taking her hand while the Glameron slumped to the floor of the deck and gasped for breath.

"What are you doing here? And where's Shaina?" he asked, after he had finished shaking hands with the blonde and with Mistress Shy as well.

"You do seem to keep coming back to that, don't you? Bit of a one-track mind," Shy remarked with an unreadable smile.

"I love her," Ty said simply and realized that he was saying it out loud for the first time.

"I can tell. A visit to Syrus Six often changes relationships that way." She nodded to L'Mera, who smiled back at her and stepped closer to give the older woman a warm embrace. "We were only coworkers before our first mission. Now we're partners in every sense of the word." L'Mera nodded and gave her a kiss on the cheek.

"How nice for you," Tyson said dryly. "But it doesn't really answer my question. Where is Shaina? Don't tell me we left her back on that hellhole of a world?"

"I am afraid we were unable to bring her with us." Faron remarked, rising unsteadily from the floor and making sure to keep far out of Ty's reach while he talked. "But you will be happy to learn that you will receive her share of the credits as well as your own for a mission well accomplished."

Tyson rounded on the Glameron, feeling his features distort with a rage so great he could barely keep himself in check. "I don't give a good goddamn about the fucking credits, Faron," he said in a low, carefully controlled voice. "All that matters to me is finding Shaina and bringing her back safely. Now I don't know where in this solar system we are, but we're going to turn this bucket of bolts around and we're going to find her. *Now*. Am I making myself perfectly clear?"

"But I am afraid that will be quite impossible. You have been unconscious for quite a while and by this time I am afraid that Mistress McCullough will be . . . deceased." Faron finished in a whisper, watching the agitated Tyson uneasily.

"What?" Ty exploded. He could feel his hands working convulsively, and his vision was turning a deep, bloody red. The D'Lonian blood in his veins boiled with rage and disbelief.

"The penalty for stealing a slave is death, and the Executor is rarely lenient or anything less than severely expeditious when carrying out her sentences. I am afraid your partner would have been executed almost as soon as we left the planet and they discovered the theft of Master Paul. I'm so sorry," Faron added unconvincingly, backing slowly away.

"No, I can't believe it! I won't accept this. There must be a way . . ." Ty shook his head. Suddenly, all the strength ran out of his legs and he sank to the floor of the deck. Shaina dead? Gone forever beyond his reach, when he had never gotten to tell her how he truly felt, how much he loved and needed her? Tyson cupped his head in his hands, feeling a black despair that threatened to engulf him. The whole reason he had come on this mission in the first place was to protect the woman he loved and he had failed. Failed utterly and lost her forever.

"There *is* a way, which is what I came to tell your beautiful, bone-headed friend there in the first place." Mistress Shy gestured at Faron, who was still staying well out of reach across the cabin, and then knelt on the floor beside Tyson, placing a gentle hand on his shoulder. "Your partner's not dead, or at least she wasn't as of a few standard hours ago when L'Mera and I left Syrus Six. It's a long shot, but there's a possibility you could still get her back alive."

Tyson lifted his head and looked into her kind brown eyes. "Just tell me what I have to do."

22

Later, Shaina thought it all seemed like the most vivid nightmare. She was dragged before the Executor herself in a lavish suite of rooms that were a multicolored blur around her. A thorough search of the slave quarters had been conducted and the theft of Paul had been discovered when the idol left in his place didn't respond to the Kandalar guard's questions and slaps. The Executor's voice was like a clanging alarm bell reverberating inside her head, asking her questions she must not answer, until Shaina felt she might go mad. One thought kept replaying in her head over and over again: Ty was gone. He was probably dead and she had never told him how she felt.

The strangest thing was, although the Executor kept firing questions, pacing from one side of the huge room to the other, her skeletal frame flickering through different shades of color so fast she seemed to blur around the edges, she seemed already to know the answers she was demanding. At first, when Shaina was dragged before her she seemed quite pleased, but when T'lar admitted that Shaina's "slave" had escaped and when it came to light that Paul had been taken as well, she became furious. But she seemed less interested in the details of the escape than if finding out if anyone else had been involved.

"We are particularly interested to know if there was a Glameron involved," she told T'lar, glowering at the cringing Kandalar. "A Glameron of surpassing beauty it would be, slender and graceful as the moonrise over Bethuna." Her glowing red eyes seemed, to Shaina to look almost dreamy for a moment but they flashed angrily again almost immediately. "Well?" she snapped at T'lar, who was standing beside Shaina, who had been forced to kneel on the hard floor at the Executor's feet.

"I . . . It is possible, Your Excellency." T'lar stuttered nervously. "We attempted to apprehend them, but they were already into the shuttle by the time we came down the corridor."

"And so you let them escape? All but this one, who is useless to me?" The Executor's voice rose as she spoke, reverberating throughout the rooms in agitation. "Have you any idea the lengths and expenses we went to in laying the trap which you have just sprung prematurely, T'lar?" she bellowed.

"Excellency, please! I had no knowledge of any trap. I simply suspected this woman and her companion of being Slave Finders and so I acted accordingly." T'lar knelt before the long, thin feet, which tapped impatiently on the pale marble floor veined with every imaginable color. His own skin was also changing color, although not at the alarming pace of the Executor's, and he winced, seemingly in pain, from time to time. Shaina thought the color changes must hurt him, but she couldn't spare her former personal Kandalar much of her attention. Her mind kept covering the same territory over and over again. She and Ty had walked into a trap. He might be dead already, and she would certainly be dead soon.

"Enough! I will hear no more of this foolishness. T'lar, we are most seriously displeased with your incompetence. We are inclined to believe that your usefulness to us is at an end. Also, we've a mind for a new pair of gloves to take our mind off this aggravation." Her voice had grown softer, but it was colder than ice as she eyed her trembling servant.

"Your Excellency, no! No, I beg you most humbly to give me another chance . . . Had I but known of your plan . . ." T'lar gabbled frantically, knocking his bald head against the marble floor, the colors flowing over his skin more rapidly.

"Our mind is made up. Guards." The Executor clapped her cadaverous hands once, sharply, and a matching pair of Kandalar dressed in flowing black robes came forward and dragged T'lar to his feet. "Note the color of his skin as he stands on the magenta vein of marble." She nodded at the color on the marble floor that pleased her. "Take him to the colored chambers and be sure the shade is an exact match. It would be a pity if he disappointed in death as he has in life. His hide should be ready for tanning in one standard month, maybe a little more. Go and do not fail me."

The two Kandalar guards dragged the wailing T'lar out of the chambers. The Executor turned her attention to Shaina, who was still kneeling before her. Shaina wondered dully if her fate would also entail being turned into a stylish new item of apparel. She had no doubt whatsoever that she would die in some horrible way—she only hoped it would be quick. She tried to be interested in her fate but nothing seemed to matter anymore now that Ty was gone. She tried to remember her home world and her mother and her job as a Peace Control Officer, tried to make herself feel something, anything. But she was just numb.

"Now for you, little one." The Executor eyed her appraisingly, her eyes glowing red with concentration, her rich, bell-like voice thick with malice.

"How will you kill me?" Shaina was a little shocked to hear herself asking. "Think I'd make a nice pair of boots to go with your new gloves?"

Get a grip, girl! she ordered herself. Mouthing off to the being who held your life in her hands wasn't going to help anything. Still, as Shaina saw it, it couldn't hurt too much at this point, either.

The Executor's already thin lips narrowed to a small, tight line in her face and she regarded Shaina with disapproval. "No, your hide remains the same boring color no matter where you are. It is a serious failing in your race. No . . ." She continued thoughtfully. "You and your D'Lonian have cost us enough credit already and we are inclined to get at least some of it back. Killing you, while most satisfactory, would accomplish nothing."

"What did you have in mind?" An icy layer of frost lay over her emotions, making it difficult to care.

"You have experienced our fine planet from a position of privilege and wealth." A cruel smile curled The Executor's thin lips. "But that is only half the experience we offer here on Syrus Six. Let us see how you enjoy a change in your position."

"What . . ." Shaina couldn't get anything else to come out of her mouth. The fine layer of frost was melting rapidly as she began to realize what the Executor was talking about.

"Guards!" The Executor clapped her hands a second time and a pair of Kandalar guards, identical in every detail to the first set, appeared out of nowhere. "There is a slave auction taking place on the far side of the planet tomorrow. Get her fitted for a pain collar and see that she is there."

"You can't mean it . . ." Shaina gasped. "Please, I'll do anything . . ."

"Oh, we mean it, my dear. And you are certainly correct— you will do anything your new Master or Mistress commands you to do. The pain collar will see to that. Tomorrow at noon, you will be sold to the highest bidder and then your new life will begin. As a pleasure slave." She nodded to the guards, who each caught Shaina under one arm and dragged her from the room. Shaina closed her eyes and struggled not to cry. It was, literally, a fate worse than death.

* * *

The next few hours were, if possible, even more nightmarish. Shaina was hauled off to a room that looked like a picture out of a mad scientist's wet dream and her neurons were mapped, using a painful and messy process that involved electrodes and a huge vat full of green gel. By the time the gel was washed off her naked, trembling body and she was dried, the pain collar was ready. It was a plain, dull silver band that closed tightly around her throat, making Shaina feel like she couldn't get enough air.

"Test it." The emotionless voice of the Kandalar technician spoke to her right and suddenly Kate felt as though every nerve in her body was on fire at the same time. She arched her back in a spasm of agony, all thought pushed from her mind by the sheer, overwhelming sensation.

As suddenly as it had started, the pain was gone. Shaina was left panting on her hands and knees, not caring anymore that she was naked, not caring about anything at all but getting breath into her lungs and not hurting anymore.

"Works fine," said another toneless voice to her left, and then a long, thin hand was clipping a leash onto the ring located at the front of the collar. Shaina was led like an animal down the halls where she had so recently walked as a Mistress, leading Ty in the same way. *Oh, Ty . . .* she thought. She wondered what he would say to see their positions reversed like this. The collar was hateful, but she thought she honestly might not mind the leash if only he were the Master holding the other end. No point thinking of that now—she had to concentrate on surviving.

"Where . . . where are you taking me now?" Shaina asked, stumbling to keep up with the long strides of her Kandalar handler as they walked rapidly down the black hall. A bolt of agony so brief she might almost have imagined it arched like a flicker of lightning through her body and was gone, leaving a dull ache behind.

"Slaves do not speak unless spoken to," the toneless voice droned. "However, I will answer you this once. You are to be taken to a transport with several other slaves Her Excellency has a mind to sell. You will be transported to the Syreen auction house on the far side of the planet and sold at auction tomorrow at noon. It is a small, exclusive house for pleasure slaves only, for which you may consider yourself most fortunate. If Her Excellency wished, she could have you sold at one of the common markets where you might be purchased for any number of uses. But Her Excellency believes you will fetch the most credit as a pleasure slave."

The emotionless way he spoke chilled Shaina to the bone and she wondered what other uses she might be sold for. What could be worse than being a pleasure slave?

"Well, what have we here?" The thick, unpleasant underwater voice broke into Shaina's miserable train of thought. "Had a bit of a credit problem, did we? Answer me, slave!" It was Marso Jlle, of course and Shaina had never felt more naked as his black, soulless eyes crawled over her flesh avidly like fat slugs. She glared back at him, refusing to say a word. Another bolt of agony flared through her body, leaving her panting with pain a moment later.

"You must answer every question directed at you by any Master or Mistress," her Kandalar handler said in that same toneless voice.

"You heard him, slave." Jlle grinned at her in a most unpleasant way, his fat cheeks bunching like raw dough and the vestigial gills in his neck flexing as he spoke. "Answer my question."

Shaina cleared her throat and raised her head defiantly. She might have a pain collar around her neck, but she would not be intimidated by this disgusting excuse for a humanoid. "My credit," she said clearly and distinctly, "is just fine."

"Then what . . . ?" Jlle began.

"Mistress Sender and her slave have been discovered to be

Slave Finders," Shaina's handler explained. "They stole a most valuable slave. As punishment, Mistress Sender is to be sold at auction tomorrow at noon."

"Sold, eh?" An unholy glee had come into Jlle's fat face and he actually rubbed his puffy hands together in anticipation. "The D'Lonian too?" he asked, eagerly.

"Unfortunately the D'Lonian posing as Mistress Sender's slave escaped," the handler said. Shaina only hoped he was right and that Ty was alive somewhere safe.

Jlle's face fell, and for a moment, his gills went quite limp. "Ah, a pity. They would have made a lovely matched set," he muttered in his muddy voice. "Still, one's better than none. Which house will the auction be held at?"

"Syreen," the handler told him.

"That's the far side of the planet!" Jlle exclaimed, outraged, and for a moment Shaina had a small hope that he would be too lazy to travel the distance. The handler merely shrugged.

"It is where Her Excellency sells all her pleasure slaves."

"Very well, it's a trip, but it's worth it. I'll be there," Jlle said and Shaina's heart sank. "Think of it, my beauty." Jlle leaned close and his underwater voice gurgled unpleasantly in her ear. "By tomorrow evening this time, you'll finally be putting that pretty mouth of yours to good use." He reached out and cupped Shaina's chin in one hand, running his pudgy thumb over her bottom lip. Acting purely on instinct, Shaina bit him as hard as she could.

Jlle howled and pulled his thumb away. The next minute, Shaina was stretched naked on the hard, black stone floor, writhing in pain. It was the longest jolt she had received yet from the pain collar, and she lost all track of time as her nerves screamed over and over that they were burning. That her whole body was on fire . . .

Abruptly the pain ceased and Shaina lay dazed on the floor, panting for breath. Jlle stood over her, looking down, gills flexing in amusement and a look of sadistic triumph plastered over his fat, greenish face. Shaina glared up at him. Despite the dull throbbing throughout her body, the pain had been worth it. She only wished she could have bitten the fat merchant's thumb all the way off.

"You'll be paying for that by this time tomorrow," Jlle promised her, still holding his thumb gingerly. "Before I had only half a mind to own you. Now I won't be outbid. You are as good as mine, *Mistress*."

He left without a backward glance and the handler dragged Shaina in the opposite direction down the hall to the transport and her unthinkable fate.

The large crossplanet transport was full of about fifty slaves, both male and female and of all races, sitting silently in rows. Shaina's handler clipped her leash to a locking mechanism above her head and left to join the other Kandalar at the front of the ship. A few minutes later the door whooshed shut, a muted mechanical grumbling began, and then the shuttle was moving.

The journey was a silent one. None of the slaves seemed inclined to talk and Shaina didn't blame them. She was more than willing to take a blast from the pain collar for a good cause, such as biting Jlle, but a casual conversation with another slave to pass the time didn't seem like a good enough reason to take a jolt. She fell asleep after a while from pure emotional exhaustion and woke up when the shuttle landed with a bump.

For a moment, Shaina was disoriented. Where was Ty and what was she doing sleeping sitting up instead of tucked into her plush bed in the suite of the Starving Nun?

Then everything came rushing back to her. Tyson was probably dead, and she was alone on this hideous planet and about to be sold to the highest bidder, who was most likely to be Jlle.

Goddess, how could things get any worse? She was about to find out.

"Come, lovie, we've only got an hour to prepare you for the auction." A small, prissy man with the distinctive triple-ringed iris that denoted an Ashantai heritage took her leash from the Kandalar handler. He led Shaina to a grooming room in the huge, black building the slaves had been herded into after landing. If this was one of the smaller auction houses, Shaina thought, she would hate to see a big one.

The room she found herself in had a grooming table and large tub, although nothing as huge as the black stone monstrosity in her suite at the Palace. Various pots, jars, and tubes of cosmetics lined one counter and a confusing variety of leather, metal devices and harnesses hung on the walls. With apprehension, Shaina thought of the way the slave girl in the female slave quarters had been shackled so that she was completely exposed to anyone and everyone. Surely she wouldn't be put through such an ordeal, would she?

"Into the tub, my dear," the little man said kindly. He helped Shaina into the warm water and began to wash her all over with a stiff sponge, in much the same way one would wash a pet. Bits of her hair were still stiff from the neuron-mapping gel of the night before, and the groom tsked loudly to himself as he washed it gently with a delicate, floral-scented shampoo.

"Lovely color," he murmured as he helped her out of the tub and dried her hair. "Natural, I'm sure. You must be pure human stock, so rare these days. I'm sure you'll fetch a handsome price. Now then, no tears, my sweet. You'll spoil those pretty eyes by making them all puffy," he continued, for despite her determination to be strong and think of survival, Shaina couldn't help crying. The man she loved was dead, she was naked, with a pain collar around her neck that kept her from escaping as effectively as though she were chained in place, and she was being groomed to go on the auction block to be sold to the highest bidder. She suddenly remembered what T'lar had said about prospective owners "trying out" the merchandise before they bought it and began to cry even harder.

"It's your first time on the auction block, isn't it, my dear?" her groom said kindly and Shaina nodded her head, afraid to speak. "Yes, I can always tell. But it's not all bad, lovie. Think of it, you might be bought by some kind Master who wants a Love slave. He'll take you to live in the lap of luxury and you'll never have to worry about anything again but how much cream you want on your redberries."

As he spoke, the groom was working quickly, piling Shaina's hair into a fashionable mass of loops and curls on top of her head and drying her tears so he could make up her face, which he did with the ease of long experience. To Shaina, who almost never wore any makeup, it felt strange to suddenly have a face full of it.

"There, aren't you lovely?" the groom exclaimed. He held a mirror briefly in front of her face and Shaina was startled to see a near stranger staring back at her. Her high cheekbones had been dusted with a soft gold blush and her wide green eyes had been dramatically enhanced with swooping lines of dark blue liner. Her full lips were now a pouting red in keeping with the rest of the makeup. She wondered what Ty would say if he could see her now; she looked a lot more like a whore than she had the night she was tracking the Red-Head Rapist. That night had only been a few short weeks ago, counting the time spent in hypersleep, but it seemed like ancient history now, she thought sadly.

"Face all done, time for your body." The little groom whisked the mirror away and got Shaina to kneel on the grooming platform with her hands behind her head. "Ah, this is a lovely little bush, my dear, but I'm afraid it will have to go," he remarked.

Before Shaina could even get the nerve to protest out loud, he had lathered and shaved her pubic hair, leaving her feeling even more naked than before. Her groom then proceeded to rub a sweet-smelling cream into her skin. It made her glisten with golden highlights all over her body, even the newly shaved lips of her sex. It was horribly difficult for Shaina to stand this intimate touch, even though the groom was completely impersonal.

"Ten minutes to auction!" A high-pitched voice came from outside the grooming room's door.

"Almost ready!" Shaina's groom called back. "Well, they certainly don't give me much time to work," he grumbled, getting Shaina to kneel on her hands and knees again and putting the last touches on her makeup. "Well, it's just lucky for me that you're such a beauty." He smiled and patted her cheek approvingly, and then began hastily searching among the leather straps and devices hung against the wall.

"Now, let me see . . ." he murmured, fingering a particularly frightening-looking leather harness as he spoke. "You've a nice slender build, yes, this one should do nicely. Oh, and we can't forget this . . ."

"Oh, Goddess, no! Not that, please, *please*. I'm begging you!" Shaina gasped, forgetting that she could be shocked into submission by the collar around her neck for daring to speak.

For in his other hand, the little groom held the familiar, golden V-shaped device she had seen on the slave girl at the Palace.

"Easy, my sweet." The groom approached her gently, like a man taming a nervous animal—which, Shaina realized, was all she was to him. "I'm sorry, lovie, but it's necessary. If it's any consolation, all the others will be wearing one too. Be reasonable now . . . how can your future Master see if he's getting what he wants if you don't wear a spreader?"

So that was what the horrid little device was called, Shaina thought wildly, a *spreader*. Shaking her head in negation, she nearly bolted from the room until she saw a small metal control box suddenly appear in the groom's hand.

"Now, I don't want to hurt you to make you behave, but we've less than ten minutes until auction and my girls are never late taking the block," he said sternly. "I'll make a bargain with you, my pet: we'll leave off the harness but I'm afraid the spreader is non-negotiable. All right?" He gestured at her, the control to her pain collar in one hand and the hateful golden device in the other and Shaina realized there was no escape. Shivering, she forced herself to hold still and spread her legs.

"Now there's a good girl," the groom crooned. Shaina felt him part her thighs and fit the spreader between her freshly shaved lips, spreading her sex wide open. The metal felt cold against her feverishly hot flesh and the slightly rounded end of the V cupped her clitoris, making it feel swollen and utterly vulnerable. Shaina bit her lip and squeezed her eyes closed. Surely, surely this was the final indignity. She could suffer no degradation worse than this.

But she was wrong.

"A last finishing touch, and then you're done, lovie," the groom said approvingly. Reaching back on the counter, he brought out a small pot of some viscous golden fluid. In his other hand he held a long-handled brush with soft bristles.

"What's that?" Shaina watched warily as he dipped the long-handled brush in the pot.

"Why, I call it my honeypot, for that's what it looks like, doesn't it?" he asked, smiling a little, and began brushing a little of the sticky substance onto her exposed nipples. Shaina shivered at the rasp of the brush over her bare nipples and noticed a curious heat along her flesh where the viscous substance touched her.

"Feels nice, doesn't it?" the groom murmured, still with that same little smile, as he moved around behind her and began brushing the substance over the widely spread lips of her sex and the tender pink flesh inside. Shaina noticed the heat growing and spreading throughout her body when the prickly bristles caressed her swollen clitoris, making her suddenly ache to rub herself.

"Yes . . . but what is it?" The brush actually penetrated her body and reached deep to paint the quivering walls of her cunt with heat.

"Just a little something to get you in the proper mood for the auction, my dear," her groom explained, dipping into the pot again and coating her agonizingly exposed flesh with another layer of the liquid. "Working already, is it?"

Working it certainly was. Shaina now felt as though every inch of her skin where the brush had touched was on fire with need. Her nipples felt hard and achy and her clit was swollen, hot, and suddenly incredibly wet with the desire to be licked and sucked. Her honeyed cunt felt horribly empty and she longed for a hard cock to fill her and fuck her. The sensations and her strange feelings scared her even through the fog of lust she was suddenly experiencing.

"What . . . what have you done to me?" Shaina was trembling and trying to rub her legs together to get a measure of relief. But the spreader inside her pussy lips wouldn't allow her to get any satisfaction. In fact, the more she moved, the worse the sensation of heat and lust got.

"Ah, yes, you're ready for the auction block now, all right." The groom smiled, looking very pleased and not bothering to answer her question. "Come, lovie, on your hands and knees now. The bidders like to see proper submission in their slaves." He clipped a leather leash to her collar and lowered the grooming table so that Shaina could crawl stiffly to the door.

The need was growing worse by the second and she felt

she'd go mad if she wasn't fucked soon. She couldn't go to the auction block in this state, she thought wildly. She would act like a common whore, like a female beast in rut . . .

"How long . . . how long will this last?" she gasped, sitting back on her haunches and refusing to go any further until he answered her questions.

"Why, as long as it needs to, my sweet, until your new Master claims you." Seeing her uncomprehending look, he added, "you'll feel the fire until you give the one who buys you satisfaction. The only antidote for my special honey is your Master's shaft inside you, lovie. When he claims you with his cock and spills his seed into that sweet little cunt of yours, then and only then will you find relief."

23

Tyson rubbed his sore and newly credited thumb. Looking carefully around the large, black-marble room, he stood in the back and waited for the auction to begin. His limit was a million credits, the most Faron had been able to get approval for, but it should be more than enough as long as he avoided getting into a bidding war. Before leaving, Shy had instructed him on how to behave and act and wished him the best of luck.

"You and your partner would make excellent Finders with a little practice," she had told Ty, giving him a fond kiss on the cheek before taking a shuttle back to her own ship. "Look me up if you both get out of this alive—and good luck." Then she had gone, the blond and smiling L'Mera in tow, wishing him the best of luck also.

Now Ty stood in the auction house Shy had directed him to and leaned back against one of the huge marble pillars that dominated the room, looking at the small stage at the far end and willing Shaina to appear. He had been afraid to try and contact her through their link lest he startle her into giving something away; but he was sure he could feel her here, somewhere near, and he couldn't wait to claim her from the block and whisk her back to the *She-Creature* and tell her how he really felt. That he loved her and needed her and wanted her in his life forever. No more procrastinating, he promised himself. He would tell her the minute they were safe in each other's arms aboard the ship and heading home.

Ty wore a long cloak of gray velvet, with a hood that shadowed his features, over normal-looking clothes and leather boots. He had thought the cloak was ridiculous at first, but Shy had assured him that many prospective buyers, who wished to remain anonymous for one reason or another, often dressed this way. And as Tyson was a wanted man on Syrus Six now, he most certainly did want to remain anonymous. Now, looking out among the crowd waiting for the auction to begin, he saw quite a few cloaks with hoods, as well as various headgear useful for shadowing buyers' features and more than one pair of dark glasses.

"Here for the bidding?" The thick, underwater voice was unmistakably familiar and Tyson had to catch himself quickly from turning to face the speaker head-on. "They always start these auctions late," the voice continued plaintively and Tyson looked carefully out of the corner of his eye to see the corpulent figure of Marso Jlle lounging beside him, dressed in a simple brown robe that was obviously tailored to hide his considerable gut. The fat Tenibrian merchant was by himself for once, without even one slave in attendance, and he obviously didn't recognize the former D'Lonian "slave" from his time at the Palace.

"Came all the way crossplanet to attend this auction," Jlle went on, rubbing his credit thumb importantly as though he was itching to buy. Tyson's own hands were itching but for an entirely different reason. He wanted in the worst way to punch the slimy bastard, but there was no way he could afford to cause a scene. He wished briefly for a disintegrator or even a sonic knife, but all such weapons were strictly forbidden inside the auction house and besides, stabbing Jlle or reducing him to a small pile of ashes, no matter how quietly he did it, was still sure to attract unwanted attention. The best Faron had been able to give him was a memory-stun patch. Undetectable to the weapons detectors at the door, it would knock out the average humanoid memory for twelve to fourteen standard hours.

"There's a slave here I've had my eye on for a while," Jlle continued, oblivious to his dangerous situation.

"That right?" Tyson murmured, fingering the small foil patch in his pocket and talking out of the corner of his mouth, still not looking at the Tenibrian.

"Little whore was posing as a Mistress while I was at the Palace," Jlle continued, obviously expecting his companion to be impressed at his casual mention of the opulent Pleasure Palace. Ty felt a cold finger pressing the base of his spine as he realized that Jlle must be talking about Shaina. "I'm a friend of the Executor and while I was there she and her 'slave' stole one of her Excellency's favorite pets. Now she's going to the block." He gave a short, gurgling laugh that sounded like someone barking underwater and nodded to himself. "I've got two million credits and time to spare. I intend to buy her and teach her a lesson she won't soon forget."

"Two million is a lot for one slave, isn't it?" Ty felt slightly panicked. If Jlle outbid him . . . He would have to do something to incapacitate the fat Tenibran before the auction started, he decided, fingering the patch in his pocket again and looking around apprehensively. Fortunately, no one was paying them any attention. Every eye was glued to the small platform with the auction block where the auctioneer, a large feline humanoid with a sleek purple pelt and a short, vestigial tail was testing his voice amplifier in preparation for the beginning of the auction.

"Two million's not too much for this little bitch. Saw her when they were taking her to auction and she nearly bit my thumb off when I tried to touch her." Jlle rubbed his sore digit—not his credit thumb, Ty noticed—and shook his head. Good for Shaina. It gave Tyson hope to think that she had still had enough spirit to fight back even as she was being taken away to be sold. That was the girl he knew and loved—she never gave up.

"Sounds like a bad deal, untamable," he remarked, still keeping his face hidden in the folds of the cloak.

Jlle grinned, a very unpleasant expression that showed teeth like an aquatic predator, sharp and stained with some unmentionable substance. "Don't expect to tame her," he said. "Not at all. But it's sure to be fun trying. My only regret is that her partner, the one posing as her slave, got away. He was D'Lonian, if you can believe that, and she was trying to pass him off as a Love slave!" He laughed his gurgling laugh again. "As though anyone would keep a D'Lonian as a Love slave, as savage and temperamental as they are!"

"Yes," Ty said, rounding on the fat merchant suddenly, unable to take any more. "Everyone knows that D'Lonians are uncontrollable beasts. They'd rip your head off soon as look at you."

"That's ri . . ." Jlle agreed before he got a good look inside the hood that had been covering Tyson's face. When he saw the distinctive amber-gold eyes glaring back at him, he jumped as though shocked, all three of his chins jiggling like a bowl of flavor-gel, and the soulless black piggy eyes got as big as Ty had ever seen them. "I . . . you're . . ." he stammered, trying to back away. But Tyson held him firmly by the high brown collar of his well-tailored robe.

"Yes, that's right, I'm the D'Lonian," Ty snarled fiercely in a low voice meant only for Marso Jlle's ears. "And this particular D'Lonian owes you one, Jlle." He pulled the high collar away from the back of Jlle's neck, causing it to tighten against the fat throat so that the Tenibrian choked and gasped. Then he jammed his other hand far down inside Jlle's robe and slapped the stun patch on his pudgy back, right between the shoulder blades where it would have the most effect.

"You . . ." Jlle gasped. "I . . . who am I?" he asked. A puzzled expression clouded his small black eyes as the patch's neuron blockers raced through his skin into the cerebrospinal fluid and from there to his brain in a matter of milliseconds.

"Don't worry about it. Just stand by the pillar and be quiet." Tyson was a little afraid that Jlle might protest, but the fat Tenibrian merchant went where he pointed and stood quietly, much to his relief. No one appeared to have noticed anything out of the ordinary and their little altercation had taken barely five minutes. Still, when he directed his attention to the platform at the front of the room again, he saw that the auction had finally started.

"Sold to the gentleman in front. Sir, if you would please come and offer proof of satisfaction and then we can proceed with the next slave up for bidding . . ." The auctioneer's voice rang out and Tyson had a moment of panic, thinking he had missed Shaina—but no, the slave on the block had dark brown skin and piercing blue eyes. He watched as the highest bidder strode up to the platform on the center of the stage and proceeded to . . .

Ty winced and shook his head. It appeared that claiming Shaina from the auction block might prove a bit more difficult and considerably more embarrassing than he had imagined.

"Come on, lovie, you're next." The prissy little groom nudged her towards the platform. Shaina was forced to crawl naked onto the stage and climb onto the platform as well as her trembling limbs would allow. At any other time, the fact that she was naked in a crowded room and about to be sold, probably to the most repulsive humanoid she had ever met, would have been uppermost in Shaina's mind as she made her way to the platform.

But not now.

Now she was only concerned with the throbbing need that burned through her body like a rogue star devouring a planet, consuming her utterly and completely with a heat that could not be denied. Her nipples felt hard and aching with the need to be sucked and caressed and her naked, vulnerable pussy, the soft lips spread wide by the golden device fixed inside them, was swollen and wet. Only one thought filled her mind as she climbed onto the waist-high auction block and posed herself in the correct position, on hands and knees with her breasts thrust out and her legs spread to give the audience a clear view of her slippery sex. Only one thought but it dominated her mind completely: She needed to be fucked. Needed it badly and needed it soon before the desire pushed her over the edge of sanity. Needed to feel a thick cock spreading her, filling her, possessing her completely ...

"We'll start the bidding at ten thousand," a voice to her left said, but it barely registered in Shaina's mind. There was no room left for anything but need.

Tyson saw her when she was put on the stage, but at first he barely recognized her. It wasn't just the fact that she was naked. He had seen her naked several times in the last few days and that didn't faze him, except to make him angry that Shaina should be put in such a degrading position in front of so many people. Nor was it the startling makeup that made her ocean-green eyes look even more exotic or the way her hair was piled in a beautifully messy swirl on top of her head, showing the graceful curve of her white neck, encircled with the dull silver of the pain collar.

No, what bothered Ty was the way she moved. The way her

bare body curved with a sensuous rhythm with no prompting whatsoever as she posed on the auction block, showing off her considerable assets and writhing as though to some elusive, erotic music that only she could hear. The way she was twisting her body, thrusting out her firm breasts and spreading her legs invitingly . . . it wasn't the Shaina he knew at all. Why was she acting this way? Had she been brainwashed?

The bids were flying fast and furious, and before Ty knew it, the sum was over a hundred thousand credits and climbing. He could well understand why every man in the room would want to own the exquisite creature on the auction block, but he intended to be the one to walk away with the prize. He didn't want to startle her into giving anything away, but he had to get her attention and make her stop acting like a . . . well the way she was acting. She was going out of his price range quickly.

"Three hundred thousand credits—do I hear four?" The auctioneer was shouting.

"*McCullough!*" He used the symbi-link for the first time since arriving back on the planet. "*Shaina, what are you doing?*" It was no use. She continued to writhe on the platform as though she hadn't heard him. Could the symbiotes be degrading already? Was it possible that Shaina couldn't hear him through their link?

"I hear six hundred thousand. Do I hear seven?" A man beside Tyson with blue hair and brown eyes raised one finger discreetly and the price jumped again. Damn it all to hell, what was wrong with her?

"*Shaina, stop it! You're pushing up the price and I've got a million-credit limit!*" He anxiously raised his hand to top the bidder beside him, and tried to catch her eyes as she posed on the block. The bidding was suddenly down to him and the blue-haired man beside him and Tyson was getting desperate.

As before, his pleas seemed to have no effect on her at all. "Nine hundred thousand for the redheaded beauty on the block. She's pure Earth stock, gentlemen. A rare find and well worth every credit! Do I hear one million credits?" the auctioneer urged. The blue-haired man beside Tyson made as if to raise his hand, but Ty turned on him suddenly and gave him such a menacing look from his blazing amber eyes that the man actually fell back a step in fear.

"She's *mine*," Ty growled so fiercely that the man put his hands behind his back.

"Fine, too rich for my blood anyway," he muttered sullenly, backing slowly away from the glowering D'Lonian.

"Nine hundred thousand going once, going twice . . . sold to the intense gentleman in the gray cloak," the auctioneer said, frowning at Ty as he spoke. "Sir, if you'll just come up to the platform and give proof of satisfaction you may claim this exotic little beauty and we'll proceed with the auction."

Ty approached the platform warily, not quite sure of how to proceed. Maybe he could just pretend he was in a hurry and get out of there quickly with Shaina in tow. Accordingly, he mounted the steps leading to the block and strode as purposefully as he could to the print-pad on the auctioneer's podium.

"Sir." The auctioneer stopped him just as Ty was about to place his thumb on the pad. "I'm afraid I can't let you do that until you offer proof of satisfaction."

"Look," Tyson tried to bluff his way through. "I'm a very busy man and I don't have time for any foolishness. I'd just as soon take the slave and go."

"Sorry, sir, house rules." The auctioneer appeared completely unruffled, not a hair of his sleek purple pelt out of place. "I cannot allow you to purchase this slave unless you provide proof of satisfaction."

"I'll sign anything you want." Tyson lowered his voice earnestly. "I'll swear in front of the whole room that I don't intend to return her . . ."

"Sir, I'm afraid if you don't intend to provide proof of satisfaction then I'll have to reopen the bidding." The auctioneer was beginning to look annoyed. "We have a number of slaves to get through here and we're already behind schedule. Do you want this slave or not?"

"Yes, all right, I want her," Ty answered shortly.

"Then claim her," the auctioneer advised, raising perfectly shaped purple eyebrows in Shaina's direction. Hesitantly, Ty approached her, not quite sure what to do first.

"Shaina?" He stepped to the black marble waist-high platform, which offered easy access to the slave being auctioned off. She made no reply, only continued her languid, erotic movements, posing and preening in slow motion, moving to music only she could hear. Now that he was close to her, Tyson noticed that her nipples were shiny wet and looked as though they had been coated in some sort of liquid or gloss. They were hard and aroused and he suddenly ached to suck one into his mouth and learn the delicious salty-sweet flavor of Shaina's skin all over again.

"Shaina, it's me. It's Tyson, sweetheart." He touched her hesitantly on one flank and she reacted. Not to his words, he realized, but to his light touch. Moaning, she turned around on the platform and nuzzled suddenly beneath his cloak, insinuating her smooth cheek against the magno tabs that held his pants together at the crotch.

"Shaina, what . . . ?" But she was already pulling the tabs apart, using only her teeth, and pressing her lips to his rapidly hardening shaft. The physical contact seemed to increase the sensitivity of their link, which Tyson had begun to believe was almost dead. He gasped out loud when her tongue found the head of his cock and his mind found hers at the same time. Shaina's consciousness was a burning wilderness of lust that scorched Ty when he touched it. And as she sucked him into her mouth, she sucked him into her psyche as well. She infected

him with her need like a ravenous virus seeking a host as she took as much of his shaft as she could down her soft, willing throat.

"*No! Oh God . . .*" Ty groaned out loud as she sucked determinedly, pulling back for a few, long delicate licks along the pulsing vein that ran the length of his cock before dipping her head to take him into her hot, wet mouth again. If she went on like this he would lose himself in her completely, would become a mindless creature of pure lust with no room for rational thought.

What had done this to her?

Forcing himself, Ty gripped her head in both hands and pulled her off him, although it was possibly one of the hardest things he'd ever done. Ignoring the glare from the auctioneer, he knelt on the platform so that his head was even with hers and looked deep into her eyes, although every instinct he had was screaming at him to turn her around and bury his cock to the hilt in her sweet, tight pussy.

"*Shaina.*" He stared into those frighteningly blank eyes, still the beautiful ocean-green but gone mindless with lust. "*Shaina, it's your partner, Ty. Brent Tyson. Do you remember me? Come back to me, Shaina, please!*"

For a moment, he was afraid that something had been done to permanently damage her mind. She was acting almost as strangely as Paul had when he wore the love collar. Ty's hands clenched into fists. If someone had done something to her to make her into nothing but a mindless sex-toy for the rest of her life . . . But then, to his immense relief, recognition flickered in her eyes.

"*Ty . . . ?*" Her mental voice was hesitant, but he could have shouted with joy. She would be all right, he could sense it. He kissed her red lips gently, tasting himself on her mouth and loving her so much he thought his heart might burst. "*Is it really you? I thought . . . thought you were dead. I saw you fall.*"

"*It's me, sweetheart. Told you I wouldn't leave without you.*"

"*Oh, Ty . . .*" But he was losing her again. He could almost feel her mind growing fuzzy and slipping away from him through their link. Her eyes were going blank and the burning lust was threatening to claim her once more. She leaned forward and captured his mouth with hers, thrusting her soft tongue between his lips for a long moment before pulling back.

"Fuck me." He had never heard her use this growlingly low, throaty voice before. Turning around on the small, square platform, she knelt on her hands and knees before him like a female beast in heat. She spread her thighs, presented her hot, wet sex to him, and she kneeled forward to wave her rounded ass in the air enticingly as she did so.

"Oh, God . . ." Tyson moaned aloud at the sight. He noticed, for the first time, her soft little pussy. Completely shaved, the tender lips were held wide apart by the same type of golden device they had first seen at the Palace. The pink inner lips and the opening of her sex had been coated with the same sticky substance that was painted on her hard nipples and she was obviously wet and swollen with need. The D'Lonian blood roared suddenly in his veins and Tyson ached to do as she had asked him. And yet . . .

"*Shaina, I don't want to do this with you when you're like this.*" He had to do it. The glaring auctioneer and the impatient audience of bidders left him no choice. But it just seemed fundamentally wrong when Shaina was out of her head this way. It would feel like making love to an animal instead of the woman he loved.

"*Ty, please!*" She came out of the lust-haze for a moment to communicate with him. "*You have to. I need you inside me now! Need you so bad . . .*"

"*You don't know what you're saying.*" He reached forward to caress the smooth, creamy white ass trembling in front of him—he couldn't help himself. His cock jutted out in front of him, aching to feel her sweet wet tightness around it.

"Yes, I do. It's just hard to think right now. He put ... the groom, he put honey on my ... on me." His touch caused her to wiggle her ass enticingly into the air and shiver.

"You mean this sticky stuff on your ... all over you?" Ty looked down at her wet, open sex.

"Yes! Makes me so ... Ty, please! I need you in me. I can't think of anything else. He said ... said I wouldn't have relief until my Master claimed me." Her whole body was trembling beneath his hands now and without quite knowing how it happened, Tyson found himself poised behind her. The head of his cock brushed against the slick, inviting entrance to her pussy. He thought her heat would burn him to ashes as she moaned and backed to meet him, trying to get his shaft inside her tight passage.

As he touched her, the chemical agents in the "honey" enflamed Tyson as well, and something inside him snapped as the D'Lonian part of him came to the forefront.

"I'll claim you ..." he growled out loud, and her hips were in his hands. He thrust forward, opened her tight little cunt, and claimed her for his own with one rough thrust after another as he stretched her wide to receive his thick cock.

Shaina threw back her head and howled—there was no other word for it—when he thrust inside her and rode her with a rough intensity she had never known before.

"Oh, Goddess. Fuck me, *fuck me!*" She screamed and arched her back. Her thighs spread wider to offer herself to him, naked and primal and hot. Hard nipples brushed the cold stone as she crouched beneath him. Accepting his sexual onslaught into her body, she submitted completely to him. "Fuck me, Master!" she moaned. "Harder. Oh! Come inside me, I need to feel you come!"

Some semblance of sanity tried to reassert itself in Tyson's brain. Shaina was begging him and his D'Lonian instincts were urging him to do the same thing. To drive hard and fast into her wet, tight pussy until he filled her completely with his seed. But there was a reason he should not do it. Only he couldn't think of it right now with Shaina thrusting back against him and begging him to fill her up with his cum.

"You don't mean that, Shaina . . ." He tried to overcome the Fuck lust that colored his vision crimson and think clearly for a moment.

"Need it . . . I need it so bad. He said it was the only way, only my Master's seed inside me could stop the burning, relieve the need . . . Please Ty. Please, Master, I beg you . . ." Tyson could feel the beginnings of her orgasm rolling to him through the symbi-link. She was shuddering and crying under him as he pounded into her, opening her soft, quivering body ruthlessly, skewering her on his cock again and again as he thrust into her sweet, tight pussy.

"Oh! Ah, Master . . . I'm . . ." As her orgasm took her, she moaned and begged, saying that she needed him. That she needed his cum inside her.

Do it. It was the voice of his D'Lonian blood. It pounded in his veins, roared in his ears, and drowned out the tiny voice of logic inside his head that was trying to remind him why he shouldn't.

Claim your mate, it urged. Ty struggled briefly with himself, but the thrumming in his blood, the pulsing need in his veins, and Shaina's cries in his ears were simply too much.

With a roar, he thrust as deeply as he could into her wet, welcoming cunt, pulsed into her, filled her with his cum, and forged the irrevocable Soul-Bond of a D'Lonian with his mate.

24

"*Ty . . . ?*" The voice in his head was hesitant but clear, as though Shaina was coming out of a dream—or perhaps a nightmare, Tyson thought grimly. He was still shaking with effort and emotion, still gripping her hips and feeling her body clench velvety tight around him. But now he too could think and the enormity of what he had just done came home to him.

Oh, God. He had forged the Soul-Bond and tied Shaina to him for life without asking her first, without even telling her how he felt and finding out if she had the same feelings for him. The Bond would degrade in time if they stayed away from each other, but that wasn't going to be easy. Separation between Bonded D'Lonian mates caused depression and deep yearning, an almost physically painful sensation that was hard to live with. Ty could already feel the changes in his own body, the way Shaina seemed to be an extension of himself. He had an almost overwhelming urge to take her somewhere private and safe and claim her again at a more leisurely pace to strengthen the Bond. He only hoped that Shaina wouldn't notice the immediate changes in herself as well.

"*Ty?*" Stronger this time, he could hear her wondering what was happening and feel her confusion, like a hazy cloud inside his own consciousness. "*Ty, where are we? What's going on? You feel . . . different inside my head.*" Great, she noticed. Tyson felt like kicking himself.

"*Later.*" Tone grim, he withdrew from her and fumbled to get his pants closed with suddenly clumsy fingers. "*Right now we've got to concentrate on getting out of here.*" He turned to the auctioneer, who was waiting expectantly behind his podium.

"Well? Is Sir quite satisfied with the merchandise?" One purple eyebrow was raised high and there was a sardonic glint in the auctioneer's eyes that was nearly an out-and-out smirk. Ty guessed the show he had just put on with Shaina was more passionate than the usual perfunctory performance required to prove satisfaction.

"I'll take her." He felt more than a little surreal as he pressed his thumb to the print-pad and watched the indicator turn green.

"So glad you're pleased, Sir," the auctioneer said courteously. He handed a small metal box to Ty, who stared at it blankly for a moment. "The control to her collar," the auctioneer explained. Tyson nodded, fumbled the box into his pocket, and mumbled a hurried thanks. Then he grabbed Shaina by the hand and hauled her to her feet and off the stage.

"*Ty, why are you so upset? And how do I know . . . why do I feel what you feel?*"

"*I'll explain everything later. Right now, every second we spend on this planet we're in danger. Come on!*" Tyson pulled her along behind him, still naked and trembling. He wanted to wrap her in his cloak but that would draw too much interest. A Master wouldn't treat his slave with such consideration. Shaina was weak and disoriented and he had to support her most of the way. Luckily, the auction house wasn't far from the port and he estimated they could be there in less than ten minutes.

He hustled her through the crowded outer area filled with cheaper auction houses and slavers selling everything from household slaves to skilled laborers. They were almost to the port when, checking over his shoulder briefly, Tyson was dismayed to see that they were being followed. Not by the auction house guards as he had feared but by Marso Jlle. The pudgy Tenibrian merchant still had a look of confusion pasted on his doughy face. When Tyson stopped abruptly, he stopped as well, a half step behind, looking aimlessly around, while crowds of people flowed around them.

"Jlle, what are you doing?" Exasperation tinged his voice. Still holding Shaina firmly in the crook of one arm to support and shelter her, he half turned to face the merchant.

"Following," Jlle said blankly. Tyson sighed. Having had his memory short-circuited by the patch, the Tenibrian had apparently fixated on Ty as his source of orientation.

"Well, don't . . ." Ty started to say when he was interrupted.

"Hey, Master, got any scrappers you wanna sell cheap?" The voice came from a ragged man to Tyson's left with a bright blue eye patch in the middle of his forehead. He was standing behind the counter of a small, ramshackle stall with a sash of bedraggled red bunting hanging limply from its top crosspiece.

"What?" Turning his attention from the blank-faced Jlle, he realized the man was talking to him.

"I'm buyin' scrappers—you know, throwaways. Slaves nobody wants no more," he explained. Leaning around Tyson, he peeled up the eye patch in the center of his forehead, revealing a milky, blind-looking orb about half again as big as his other eyes. "Ah, but I can see this one's no throwaway." He peered at Shaina intently before lowering the patch and nodding to himself. "She's prime stock, she is. Too bad. Only needed one more to fill me quota."

"Where do the slaves you buy go?" Tyson held Shaina protectively close. She was quiet now, not asking any questions, and he could feel a bone-deep weariness in her that twisted his heart. She didn't even react to the sight of Jlle, which must mean she was pretty much out of it.

"Well, most of 'em go to the radon mines or the asteroid belt. They don't last long there, I can tell you." The man laughed, a cracked, yellow sound that scratched the air between them. "But this lot here"—he gestured behind the stall to where Ty could see a small transport that was mostly full— "This lot's gonna have it easy. They'll be goin' to the waste-treatment moon as serves the Andromeda system."

"Sounds like a nasty job." Pulling Shaina closer, he wondered if they would be able to get to the port undetected.

"Oh, it is. It is," the ragged slave-buyer said, reflectively. "But at least they lives a good long time there. Sewage up to yer armpits, but you won't die right away like. Gives 'em lots of time to reflect, don't ya know."

"Yeah." Ty prepared to move on, but the man with the eye patch spoke again.

"What about that one then? He'd do," he said, nodding at Jlle, who was still following close behind them.

"What one?" Ty was honestly mystified. He had almost forgotten Jlle in his need to get Shaina out of this place.

"That one. The fat one. He belong to you?" Pointing a crooked brown finger, he indicated Jlle. Ty began to grin.

"Why, yes, he does, actually." Ty nodded.

"Why come he ain't got no collar then?" the man asked a bit skeptically.

"Well, he's been in my family a long time, wouldn't know what to do if he did get away, so we didn't bother with one. Unnecessary expense, you know," Tyson improvised rapidly. "But lately he's been more trouble than he's worth."

"Oh?" The slaver looked interested, perhaps scenting a possible sale.

"Yeah." Tyson gave a long-suffering sigh and shook his

head. "He's still strong, a good hard worker, and he does just about whatever you tell him, but he's getting a little soft up here." He tapped his temple with his free hand, still holding Shaina close with his other. "See, he gets these crazy ideas sometimes, delusions. Thinks he's a rich merchant who stays in the Pleasure Palace. Claims he's a personal friend of the Executor herself." Ty nodded his head and made a twirling motion with one finger beside his ear and the ragged slaver burst out laughing.

"Well, well, and aren't we grand, then?" he asked, peeling up the eye patch to look at Jlle, who simply nodded blankly and continued staring into space. "Well, he looks strong enough, though perhaps a mite flabby. A month on the waste-treatment moon would take care of that, though. Plenty of good hard work to keep a body busy up there." The slaver nodded sagely.

"Well . . ." Tyson pretended to think the matter over carefully, eyeing first Jlle and then the ragged slaver.

"What do you say, Sir? I'd be willing to give you forty credits though I don't usually like to take 'em without a collar." Obviously the man was eager to fill his quota.

"Here . . ." Tyson turned to Shaina and dug in the pocket of his cloak for the box the auctioneer had given him. Studying it carefully, he found the release button and pressed it. The cruel silver band gave a muted click and a small hissing noise as the catch released and he was able to take it off her neck.

"Ty . . . what?" Her mental voice was still confused and exhausted and Tyson risked pressing a soft kiss to her pale temple.

"Just relax, sweetheart. You'll never have to wear this again, I swear." Ty kissed her again and took his arm from around her briefly, making sure to keep her close. He turned to Jlle and fiddled with the collar in his hands until he found the adjuster. Even let out to its maximum setting, the collar was still a tight fit, but at last he had it cinched to his satisfaction around the Tenibrian's fat throat.

"It's not keyed to his neurons, but it'll still give him a jolt if he acts up," he told the slaver, handing him the control box. "He's quiet right now, but you'll probably have to use it if he starts having delusions again."

"Thank you, Sir. Since you threw in the collar, I'll up me price to fifty credits, only I don't do prints, for reasons I'm sure you'll understand." The slaver dug in one pocket, produced a fifty-cred chip, warped and cracked with age, and pressed it into Tyson's hand. Tyson pocketed it and smiled. By the time the memory patch wore off, Jlle would be up to his pudgy armpits in raw sewage and Ty couldn't think of a better place in the universe for him.

"Pleasure doing business with you," he told the slaver and turned to gather Shaina to him once more. A few minutes' brisk walk would get them to the port and the *She-Creature*'s shuttle waiting nearby.

The ragged slaver pulled up the eye patch once more, looked at Tyson and Shaina steadily and smiled. "Good-bye, Sir, and a pleasant trip to you and your lady." He made a low, somewhat rusty bow in Shaina's direction and then turned away to herd the unresisting Jlle into his transport.

On his way through the port, Ty dropped the warped fifty-cred chip in the Holy Sisters of Spotless Purity charity box. He considered it the best fifty credits he had ever spent.

25

The water pouring over her skin was soothingly warm and someone was scrubbing her gently all over with a soft sponge. She was half standing, half leaning in the shower, being supported from behind by someone's firm, muscular chest, a strong arm encircling her waist as the liquid sluiced over her naked body.

"What?" Shaina heard herself ask in a drowsy voice. "Where . . . ?"

"Back on the *She-Creature* and heading for home, sweetheart," said a deep voice in her ear as the sponge continued its gentle, relaxing movements.

Ty then. It was Ty and everything would be all right. It occurred to her that he was washing her the same way he had when he was pretending to be her slave at the Palace. But that couldn't be. Since he had bought her at the auction, he was the Master now, she thought drowsily. He had always been her Master. Well, if her Master wanted to wash her . . .

The auction! Suddenly everything came back to her in a horrible rush—having her neurons mapped, wearing the pain collar, the indignity of being prepared for public sale like an animal or a prime piece of property. Shaina gasped, her eyes opening wide, and put both hands to her throat, feeling for the cold silver band that had set her nerves on fire . . .

"It's all right, Shaina. I told you you'd never have to wear it again. You're safe now, I promise." The soothing voice and the fierce feelings of protectiveness and possession coming from Ty calmed her somewhat. She belonged to him, she thought in a hazy, contented way. He would take care of her now. He would take care of everything. It seemed as though there was something else about the auction that she should remember, something important, but nothing really seemed to matter as long as she was safe with Ty's strong arms wrapped around her.

She stretched, pressing back against him even more, loving the feel of his skin, slippery and wet and smooth as silk against hers. But though his large hands on her body were soothing, there was still something wrong, something that was making him worried and upset. Shaina could feel it with a clarity that hadn't been between them before. She wondered briefly if the symbi-link was getting stronger somehow.

"Ty, what's wrong?" She felt his body stiffen behind her. He turned the water off and his hands were on her shoulders, turning her around to face him. His naked body was luscious, rock hard, with streams of water dripping down his broad, golden-skinned chest and chiseled abdomen, but his face looked so grim that Shaina began to feel frightened. "What is it?"

"Shaina, I have something to tell you and you're not going to like it," he began when there was a discreet knock on the door.

"Master Tyson, Mistress McCullough, we have only ten minutes to enter hypersleep. I suggest you come out as quickly as possible." It was Faron's soft voice but there was a note of urgency in his tone.

"Damn," Tyson muttered under his breath but he grabbed a

synthi-cotton towel for himself, handed Shaina one as well, and began to dry off without saying another word.

"Ty, what were you going to tell me?" After she wrapped a sleep robe around herself and knotted it securely, they hurried out the door and into the *She-Creature*'s hypersleep chamber. Shaina saw that Faron and Paul were already sealed into two of the long, silver sleep tubes and Tyson was busy getting into a third.

"No time right now, just get in your tube." He motioned for Shaina to take the fourth tube in the row.

"But you can't just leave me hanging like this! What is it? What?" She settled into the tube but still hesitated to pull down its sleek silver hatch.

"Never mind; there'll be plenty of time to tell you later." With that cryptic statement, he pulled the hatch of his sleep tube closed and Shaina had to do the same.

26

He woke from a dream of being submerged naked in a vat of oily green gel, feeling like he was going to drown or go mad from the horrid, slimy sensation all over his skin . . .

"That was how they mapped my neurons for the collar." He sensed her distress at the horrible memory.

The sleep tubes were open now and all Tyson wanted to do was go to her, wrap his arms around her, and hold her. He wanted to wipe the distress and hurt out of her mind and make her understand that he would never let anything like that happen to her again.

Ty was halfway out of the tube when he remembered what he had done at the auction. He would have to tell her everything and then she would probably hate him. Shaina begging him to fuck her was no excuse. She had obviously been high on the weird lust-inducing drug that had been smeared on her body and Ty should have been strong enough to control his D'Lonian urges to bind her to him anyway. But damn it, she was his. She belonged with him, they belonged together. Every instinct he had insisted it was true and his body had acted on it even though his mind knew he shouldn't. Now he would have to pay the consequences.

As though sensing his emotions, Shaina stepped a bit unsteadily out of the tube and went to him. "What is it that you have to tell me?" Her expression was serious. "Because whatever it is, it's making you terribly upset. I can feel it. And that makes me upset."

She was going to be more upset in a moment, Ty thought grimly.

"Let's get dressed first, then we can talk." He knew they only had about an hour before they got home and he hoped it would be enough time to explain adequately and at least try to apologize. Shaina gave him a funny look but she reached for her clothes anyway. Tyson reached for his as well. He saw that what Faron had laid out for him was the black pleather jumpsuit he had worn to the ship in the first place, his Peace Officer uniform. When he zipped it up and turned around, he saw Shaina was wearing hers as well. The sight of his partner in that familiar uniform was like a punch in the gut that left him breathless and hurting. They were going back home to their normal routines and jobs, but nothing would ever be normal between them again. Maybe the sight of him in his uniform affected Shaina as well, because she whispered through their link, *"It's really over, isn't it?"*

"Yeah, sweetheart, it's over." He meant more than the mission. Once he told Shaina what he had done, he was pretty sure any chance he'd ever had of having her in his life on a permanent basis would be over too. She was a stubborn woman with a mind of her own. She wouldn't let the pain of a neglected Bond keep her from staying out of his life if she thought she was justified.

"Ty, just tell me . . . What is it?" The concerned look in her ocean-green eyes nearly undid him.

"Come into the main chamber." He left her to follow without looking back. He chose one of the comfortable real-wood chairs, although his first impulse was to sit on the floor at her feet. That was over now, though. He wasn't her Master and she wasn't his Mistress. *Time to move on and get it over with,* Ty told himself.

Shaina settled herself on a chair opposite him, looking unhappy and apprehensive; Ty could feel both emotions through the symbi-link as well as the D'Lonian Bond, a double dose of misery. And it was only going to get worse.

"I . . ." He started when Faron appeared in the doorway, beautiful and androgynous as always.

"We have achieved re-entry orbit and we will be in position to take the shuttle back to our home port very soon," he informed them. "The Chancellor sends his regards and his joy for the rescue of his son. He says to tell you he cannot wait to meet the two heroic officers who saved the child of his heart." He beamed at them for a moment before his face lost its beatific expression and grew extremely grave. "But I see I have interrupted at a most inopportune moment. Please forgive me. Paul and I will leave you alone." He disappeared from the doorway with a low bow, leaving Ty as tongue-tied as ever and with less time than he had thought to try and explain.

"For heaven's sake, just spit it out!" Shaina looked anxiously at his face, which was twisted into an unhappy frown.

"Fine," he snapped back. "Do you remember the first time we . . ." He wanted to say *made love* but it sounded too needy, even inside his head. "The first time we had sex?" The look on Shaina's face was hurt for a moment but she quickly smoothed her features.

"Yes, I remember." Her voice was quiet. "How could I forget, Ty? It was my first time." She colored a little as she spoke, her creamy cheeks flushing a clear, soft red, but she refused to drop her eyes. Ty closed his own eyes and shook his head. God, he had hurt her feelings already. How much worse was it going to be when he told her?

"*When you tell me what?*" She was exasperated and he realized he had been projecting his thoughts through the symbilink. Abruptly, he snapped up a white wall of silence between them. Shaina didn't need to be inside his head just now.

"The first time we . . . the first time, you asked me not to . . . You asked me to pull out, remember?"

"Yes, because my hormone injection wasn't up to date."

"Well, I don't know how much you remember about the auction . . ."

"Not a whole lot, actually," Shaina admitted. "That stuff they smeared on me pretty much gave me a one-track mind and I wasn't thinking about anything but . . ." She blushed again. "Well, I wasn't really thinking very clearly at all," she finished softly, looking down at her hands. Her hair fell in a soft, flame-colored halo around her face so that Ty couldn't see her eyes.

"I didn't think so. You seemed kind of out of it, way out of it, actually." He sighed heavily and forced himself to go on. "Well, I got caught up in the moment and you were asking me to . . . to . . . Anyway I didn't that time. Didn't pull out, I mean." God, could it get any more awkward?

"Oh, my Goddess . . ." Shaina looked really upset now and Ty thought grimly that things were going from bad to worse. "That means I might be . . . might be . . ." She couldn't finish the sentence.

"I know." Tyson tried to numb himself for what was to come. "And I want you to know I'll be responsible if . . . if you are. But that's not all, Shaina. I . . . there's something I should have told you a long time ago, but it's hard to explain." He went on to tell her, haltingly, of the Bond that had been forged between them in that moment on the auction block. He spoke quietly and mechanically, looking down at his hands, afraid of what he might see if he looked in her eyes. When he was finished, Shaina was quiet for a long time.

"So you're saying there's a Bond between us now, an actual biochemical Bond that can never be broken?"

"It's called a Soul-Bond and yes, it's pretty much permanent. But it *can* be weakened," Tyson earnestly tried to reassure her. "We'll just have to stay away from each other for a while and eventually it'll fade to a manageable level."

"Just stay away from each other? That's the way it is?" Her voice trembled slightly. Ty wanted desperately to know how she was feeling, what she was thinking, but now it was Shaina putting a wall between them.

"That's the way it is." He felt wretched. He had a sudden crazy impulse to get down on one knee and ask her to marry him. Beg her to stay in his life forever the way she ought to be. But she was so obviously upset at the idea of a Bond between them that he couldn't bring himself to do it. It was too late and he had ruined everything.

"Ahem . . ." It was Faron, announcing himself discreetly at the doorway. "I am sorry to interrupt, but we are now within shuttle range, although you may take as much time as you like, of course . . ."

"No," Shaina stood up, brushing automatically at the wrinkles in her pleather jumpsuit. "No, I think we're finished here." Her face was very pale and she was still maintaining a solid wall between them, but she moved quickly, getting to the shuttle before Ty could even get out of his chair.

The ride down was absolutely silent, except for the hissing of the strange vents and the low, feminine voice of the *She-Creature*'s shuttle advising them to buckle their safety harnesses before they touched down. Faron and Paul sat quietly in two of the chairs, perhaps sensing the tension in the air, and Shaina obviously was in no mood to talk, either. Tyson wanted desperately to say something but he didn't have the faintest idea of what to say. *Sorry I forged an unbreakable biochemical Bond without asking how you felt about it first? Not to mention that I might have accidentally gotten you pregnant. There ought to be a greeting card for either or both situations,* he thought sourly.

Before he knew it, they were disembarking from the *She-Creature*'s shuttle and walking out into the familiar home port. Waiting for them was Minister Waynos and a tall, handsome middle-aged man with piercing blue eyes and a distinguished touch of silver at his temples, who Tyson guessed must be the Chancellor himself. There was a discreet trio of burly guards around him, two women and one man, all of whom looked like they had stepped straight out of a soldier-of-fortune vid.

"Father!" Paul ran to the tall man, whose face broke into a wide smile as he wrapped the young man in a strong hug.

"Paul, I thought I'd never see you again," he murmured into his son's hair. "Are you . . . did they hurt you, son?"

Paul pulled back a little and there was a troubled look in his jewellike eyes, the only feature in his face that didn't resemble the Chancellor's. "I don't remember much," he said softly. "They put a collar on me that made me . . . I don't know. It's all kind of hazy now."

"Probably just as well," his father said under his breath. He turned to Faron and nodded his head. "Faron, it's good to have you home. I'm so glad you were able to bring Paul back." His voice was noticeably cooler and Tyson noticed that he kept one arm protectively around his son.

"I would not have come home without him," Faron answered, his eyes whirling with colors that were too vivid. Eyes like Paul's, Ty suddenly realized. "He is my son too, Lawrence," the Glameron continued, still looking at the Chancellor.

Tyson did a double take. What? He had been all set to confront the Chancellor with what he had learned from Mistress Shy and L'Mera, that he and Shaina had been sent into a situation that experienced, professional Slave Finders had considered a suicide mission. But Faron's statement took all the wind out of his sails and the words died on his lips. He looked at Shaina to see how she was taking this, but she had her head turned and her arms crossed tightly, obviously deep in her own thoughts.

"But . . . I thought you were both male," Ty couldn't stop himself from saying. Were Glamerons ambisexual or something? How else could it be possible for Paul to be the son of both the Chancellor and Faron? And yet he resembled both of them strongly.

"When you have enough money there are ways and means," the Chancellor said, never taking his eyes off Faron. "Paul owes half of his Y chromosomes to me and half to my lover, Faron. I thought at the time I paid the outrageous gene-splicing fee that a child would make my lover happy enough to stay with me. But I was wrong."

"Lawrence, I never dreamed she'd take him. I never thought . . ."

"No, you didn't, did you? You thought your little infidelity would affect no one but yourself. Did you think I didn't notice the way you remodeled the shuttle, the way you . . ."

"Please, don't!" It was Paul, looking from one parent to the other, a pleading look in his jewellike eyes. "I can't stand it. I'm home now and nothing else matters. Right?" He took the Chancellor's hand in one of his and reached out to take Faron's in the other. "Right?" he repeated, looking anxiously from one parent to another.

"We'll talk about it later," was all the Chancellor would say. Faron simply looked sad. Tyson was relieved that the family spat had been avoided. It had been about to become a very uncomfortable situation.

He looked over at Shaina again to see how she was taking the news about Paul's unusual family unit; but as before, she seemed preoccupied and when he tried to feel her through their link the white wall of silence was still firmly between them. Still, he could feel her emotions through the D'Lonian Bond. She was upset and he supposed he couldn't blame her.

Now that the family spat had been narrowly averted, Minister Waynos, who had been standing quietly by while the Chancellor spoke to Faron, seemed eager to change the subject. "Well, well, hail the conquering heroes," he said a little too heartily, stepping forward to wring first Tyson's hand and then Shaina's. "We are forever grateful for your timely rescue of young Master Paul. Are we not, Your Grace?" He turned pointedly to the Chancellor, who broke off his staring contest with Faron long enough to nod graciously and smile.

"Indeed, such bravery shall not go unrewarded," the Chancellor said, in a more formal tone than Ty had yet heard him use. "I am well aware of the danger you faced so bravely to bring my son home to me."

"It would have been nice if you had let us know exactly how dangerous this mission was going to be." Ty found his voice at last. "McCullough and I went through a lot of trauma on Syrus Six, not all of it physical. A lot of mistakes could have been avoided if we had been given a clearer picture of the situation we were walking into. Am I right, McCullough?" He turned to Shaina but she had suddenly gone so pale that Tyson thought he could almost see through her.

"Excuse me." She would not look at him. "I . . . I have to go. Right now."

"Shaina!" Ty called but it was too late. She was walking away, nearly running in fact, down the long, opulent corridor of the Private Sector Port. Disappearing in the crowd, her hair was a flash of scarlet rapidly getting smaller and more indistinct.

As he watched her go, as the distance between them widened, the Soul-Bond began to ache and all his D'Lonian instincts urged Tyson to go after her. They belonged together. It was wrong for her to leave. . . . Ty closed his eyes tightly and forced himself to ignore the urging of his blood. Shaina was gone and she wasn't coming back. No matter what his D'Lonian blood or the Soul-Bond told him, she didn't belong to him. She never had and she never would.

27

"Oh, Goddess . . ." The words came out brokenly. She sank down on her gel mattress and finally allowed herself to collapse now that she was safe at home. Mistakes that could have been avoided, he had said. *Like the mistake of letting herself fall in love, maybe,* she thought bitterly, although she knew that wasn't what Ty had been referring to. How could she have ever allowed herself to dream that he would feel the same way for her? To Brent Tyson she was just *McCullough,* a coworker and nothing more.

Inside her body, somewhere close to her heart, the Bond he had forged between them pulsed and throbbed as if to deny her thoughts. The Bond . . . the Soul-Bond he had called it. And he had apologized again and again for being so careless, for making such a huge, monumental *mistake.* . . . There it was again—the whole situation was nothing but a mistake. If she happened to be pregnant with his child, that would be a mistake too. Whoops, so sorry, McCullough, never meant to knock you up and I *certainly* didn't mean to tie you to me for life. *Didn't mean to tie himself to a woman he didn't really love is what he meant,* Shaina bitterly told herself.

And now he tells her that all they had to do was stay away from each other to weaken the Bond. Why not just come right out and say, "Hey, the mission's over and it's time to move on?" As if she needed a bigger hint.

Well, Shaina decided, if she and Ty were supposed to stay away from each other, it could certainly be arranged. She would hate moving away from her mother but her older brother Peter lived on Washington, the smaller of their two moons, and he had told her often enough how badly they needed Peace Control Officers. With her part of the money from the mission to Syrus Six, she would certainly be able to afford to relocate. If there was a baby, she would raise it herself. That would be easier on Washington, too, because there was no government-mandated Birth and Child Control Office. People there could have as many children as they wanted. Hell, Peter had three already. Yes, Washington would certainly be far enough away to suit even Ty.

Shaina sat up abruptly and wiped the tears off her cheeks with angry, jerky swipes of her fingers. She would set her plans in motion right now. She called up the holo-phone. "Work," she told the phone and while it automatically dialed the number, she cleared her throat and tried not to look as miserable as she felt. Already, just with the thought of so many millions of miles between herself and Tyson, the Soul-Bond was a throbbing ache, an empty place in her heart that hurt like a sonic knife between her ribs when she breathed. She hoped it would get better when she moved, but something told her no matter how many miles she put between herself and Ty, the ache would still be there.

"Hello, Be'tena?" she said brightly, when the familiar form of the station operator glowed into view before her. "It's Officer McCullough. Can I talk to the Chief?"

28

Shaina had been gone from work for a whole week and Tyson was beginning to wonder if she was ever coming back. Her empty desk was like a mute reminder that they had parted on bad terms, and he longed to call her up and apologize again but he knew it wouldn't do any good. *Get real, Tyson,* he told himself. What he really wanted to do was go to her and tell her how much he loved her. Hell, he wanted to *show* her. Show her that she belonged with him, that she belonged *to* him, his D'Lonian blood growled. But Shaina already thought he was an asshole. Being a possessive asshole wouldn't make things any better, so he had to stay away.

Even though the Soul-Bond throbbed and ached worse every day he spent without her.

His skin felt itchy and tight and his body was in a constant, uncomfortable state of arousal. Ty knew that the pain and discomfort he was experiencing was, in some ways, like the withdrawal a drug addict experienced when attempting to quit using. He knew Shaina had to be feeling the same. He *needed* her, damn it. And she needed him. If only there was a way to make her see . . .

"Hey, what's this?" Ty felt a hand on the top of his head, messing up his hair and kneading his scalp roughly. He looked up to see Tony from Vice looking down at him, grinning.

"Cut it out, Tony." He made a halfhearted attempt to dislodge his friend's hand from his head.

"Not 'til you guess. What is it?" Tony's fingers continued to knead.

Ty frowned. "I don't know. What is it?" Tony wouldn't quit until he asked.

"A Sonorian brain sucker." Tony said promptly. "And what's it doing?"

"I don't know, Tony. What *is* it doing?" Ty asked dutifully.

"Starving to death!" He cheerfully collapsed into the chair next to Ty. "Whew, sure am glad it's Friday."

"Yeah," Tyson said, trying to smile. "Me, too."

"Well, I don't know why. Judging by the look on your face you don't have any hot dates lined up. What's wrong with you, anyway, Tyson? Ever since you got back from Pleasure Planet you've been dragging around here, looking like last year's holo-ghost. What gives, can't get used to boring old New Brooklyn again after living the high life on Syrus Six?"

"No, nothing like that." Ty doodled with a rase-o-mark on the surface of his plasti-desk and then wiped the lines away with a magno-strip. "I'm just tired, I guess. Maybe I should have taken a week off to recoup like McCullough."

"A week off? What are you talking about?" Tony's pink eyes got wide and Tyson looked up at his friend with a small frown.

"Well, I assume that's what she's doing. McCullough loves this job; it's in her blood. I doubt she'd take more than a week off, no matter what."

"Ty, she's not just taking a week off," Tony said softly. He ran one hand through his white-blond hair nervously. "I . . . Man, I thought you knew. I thought of all people McCullough would have told you first."

"Told me what?" Ty asked irritably, a feeling of dread growing in the pit of his belly. "She hasn't quit or anything, has she?"

"She quit and she's moving to Washington. I thought you knew. I was going to ask you if you were coming to the port to see her off tonight."

"Tonight? You mean she's leaving tonight?" Tyson was on his feet, his amber eyes wide with agitation. "Tony, are you sure about this?"

"Hell, yes, I'm sure. Everybody knows but you. Everybody else from the whole station is going . . ." But Tony was talking to an empty space.

Tyson was already gone.

29

The entry chime rang and the door grid showed the last person Shaina had expected to see. Tyson was standing outside the entryway to her apartment, a look of grim determination on his hawklike features. As she watched, he ran one large hand through his hair, making it stand up in a dark cloud around his face. Her hand hesitated over the in-switch. Could seeing him now, just hours from her flight off-planet, really do anything but make matters worse? And what did he want anyway? He was the one who had said they needed to stay apart.

Ty jabbed the intercom button impatiently. "Open up, McCullough. I know you're in there."

She pressed the talk button. She knew he couldn't see her since the outside holo feed was broken. "What do you want?"

"To talk some sense into you." Ty sighed and ran both hands through his hair this time. "Oh, hell, that didn't come out right. Look, I just need to talk to you before you go. Please, Shaina."

Maybe it was his pleading tone or possibly it was his more intimate use of her first name, but Shaina found herself hitting the in-switch after all. "Have a seat in the living area. I'll be right down." She wondered if she was doing the right thing or not. Ty probably just wanted to know if she was pregnant and after she told him that he wasn't going to be a father he would leave her alone.

Shaina took a quick glance in the mirror before going down the lift, even though she hated herself for doing it. Why should she care how Ty saw her now? But she couldn't help checking. She had been in the process of getting ready for her flight, which was only hours away, and her hair and minimal makeup looked perfect. She hadn't gotten around to getting dressed yet, but she was wearing her favorite synthi-silk robe, which came to mid thigh and was just a shade darker than her hair. The deep crimson color made her skin glow a creamy peach and added to the luster of her eyes. Under the robe she had a matching synthi-silk gown and panties. The whole set had been a gift from an old boyfriend who had hoped to take her to bed. He had been disappointed, of course. Shaina had gotten rid of the boyfriend, but kept the sexy negligee set, which she rather liked.

Now, as she surveyed herself in the mirror, she reflected that although she felt like crap, at least she looked good. If Ty was expecting to see her dragging around, looking sad and defeated, then he was in for a surprise. Though the D'Lonian Soul-Bond had been pulling at her all week, making her itchy and restless and unaccountably aroused, she was determined not to show it. No, she would be cool and poised. She would tell him what he wanted to know and see him politely out the door and out of her life once and for all.

With a determined little toss of her head, Shaina stepped into the personal lift and punched the down button. Ty was going to see exactly how much she missed him, which was not a bit.

When she got to the entry level, she stepped off the lift to find him pacing back and forth in her living area like a caged feline. He stopped when he heard the lift and looked up as she stepped down, his amber eyes blazing with an intensity Shaina had never seen there before. She had planned to be cool to the point of rudeness, but she hadn't counted on that look in his eyes. Nor had she counted on the way the Soul-Bond would react when she saw Tyson in person again. An aching throb started just under her heart and traced its way down to the tender vee between her legs, catching her by surprise. Her nipples were instantly erect and she felt wet and swollen with a need she had been denying all week. The erotic sensations were impossible to fight, but Shaina tried to hide them anyway.

"Shaina." Ty stepped toward her and instantly took a step back as though he couldn't trust himself to get too near her. She could smell him in the climate-controlled air of her apartment, warm and musky and wild, the smell of a male animal on the prowl. The scent seemed to go straight to her brain and fog it so that she couldn't think of anything to say or how to act.

"I'm not pregnant," Shaina blurted out and was instantly annoyed with herself for letting Ty affect her so strongly. Trying to get some sense of control back and act as coolly uninterested in him as she had planned, she added, "So if that's what you came to find out you can go. You're free and clear, off the hook."

"I don't give a damn if you're pregnant or not." Large hands clenched and opened rhythmically as he growled and took a step toward her. Shaina found herself half scared by the look in his eyes and more than half aroused. As he got closer, the Bond between them seemed to tighten like a wire in her belly and the heat she felt in her breasts and between her legs intensified immensely. An involuntary look at the bulge in the crotch of his black pleather uniform plainly showed Ty was feeling the attraction between them as well. *Take it easy,* she told herself. *It's just a biochemical reaction caused by the Bond.* But her body didn't care what caused the reaction between them. Her body wanted him, now . . .

Shaina found herself remembering the way things had been

on Syrus Six. The way he had teased and tasted her until she reached such shattering climaxes. The way his cock had felt inside her, thick and hard and deep as he rode her until she begged and moaned . . . She shook her head to clear it.

"Why are you here, then?" she made herself ask and didn't like the way her voice trembled ever so slightly. Ty took another step toward her. Her first impulse was to step back but that would be admitting defeat. Defiantly, she raised her chin and looked him in the eye, although it was difficult to do. Naked lust, a need that matched her own, stared back from those amber depths. He wanted her every bit as much as she wanted him, even more if that was possible, Shaina realized.

"I'm here for this." With one more step he erased the distance between them and took her by the arms. He pulled her in for a rough, demanding kiss that took her breath away. His hands moved from her arms to caress her back in a long, sweeping motions. He pulled her closer, molding her body against his, and explored her mouth as though he had every right to.

Shaina found herself melting against him. Loving the crush of his big body against hers and the way he took without asking, she had to rely on his strength to hold her up as he bent her back against his arm. But despite the way her body responded to his, there was a part of her, a small corner of her mind, that insisted this wasn't right . . .

"Wait . . . stop!" she gasped, when he finally broke the kiss. "Stop, we . . . we shouldn't be doing this. You said we had to stay away from each other, Ty."

"Fuck what I said." He had her pressed up against the wall, kissing and nipping along the slender column of her throat. She moaned and bowed her head to one side to allow him better access, even though she knew she shouldn't. His large, warm hands molded her breasts through the thin synthi-silk robe, twisting her already swollen nipples between his blunt fingertips until she thought she would scream from frustration. Still, she couldn't completely let go, although her body desperately wanted to.

"You said we had to stay apart . . . to weaken the Bond." She loved the way his hands felt on her breasts, wished he would pull down the robe and gown and touch her bare flesh.

"That can be arranged, sweetheart." His answer through the symbi-link, to her thought rather than her words, startled her. They had been far apart, out of the range of the symbiotes, all week and now, to hear him speak inside her mind again, his tone hot and intimate . . . Shaina felt her legs might fold up under her as he peeled back the robe. With a low popping sound, the spaghetti straps of the gown gave way so that her aching breasts were bare for him. Her pink nipples thrust out, demanding attention. The gown fell to the floor, leaving her with only the open robe and small crimson panties to cover her. With a low groan, Ty leaned down and sucked as much of one breast as he could into his mouth. One hand cupped the other and he rolled the nipple between his thumb and forefinger as he ground against her. His cock branded her belly like a bar of steel.

She parted her legs so that one was wrapped around his lean hips and the other supported her rather shakily as she leaned back against the wall. Tyson's cock ground into her, pressing against the throbbing ache where she needed him most. He parted the plump, moist lips of her pussy through the silky red panties and rubbed against her swollen clit until she thought she would scream if she didn't come soon. Inside . . . she needed him inside her and damn the consequences. She scrabbled uselessly at the slick black pleather, seeking a way to make him naked, to crumble the barriers between them.

Obviously understanding her need, Ty reached between them with his free hand and unzipped his uniform in one sweeping motion, freeing his thick shaft to press against her. He reached down and pushed aside the thin strip of material covering her hot, needy sex. He took a moment to run blunt fingers over her slick folds and Shaina's hips bucked helplessly as he found her slippery clit and pressed with exactly the right amount of pressure, pushing her relentlessly toward the edge of the orgasm she needed so badly.

"God, sweetheart, you're so wet," he said roughly in her ear. Two thick fingers rubbed and slid into her, filling her, although not as much as she needed to be filled. "Can't wait to be inside you . . . need you so much . . ."

The head of his cock, already slippery with need, rubbed against her, pressed into her, crowning inside the slick entrance to her body. One quick thrust and he would be all the way into her, filling her, riding her, fucking her. Shaina couldn't wait, she needed this so desperately, craved it like a drug. The Soul-Bond twisted urgently, whispered that she had to have him in her, that she couldn't live without this . . .

The Bond!

Shaina's head cleared suddenly. All this, the urgent need to have him inside her and Ty's overwhelming drive to possess her, was only because of the Soul-Bond, not because he loved her or cared anything about her. It was a simple biochemical reaction to her nearness that was causing him to act this way and her to respond to his touch. Just the Bond and nothing more.

Shaina pushed against him suddenly, sending Ty stumbling back and away from her, off balance for a moment because he hadn't expected the move. Shaina backed away from him, panting and fumbling for the sides of her robe, trying to cover herself from those opaque golden eyes that held nothing but a feral hunger that she so badly wanted to respond to. But she wouldn't. Wouldn't become some object he used out of animal lust and then cast aside again.

"Ty, stop it," she panted, willing him to listen to her, to understand she meant what she said even though her body was now almost screaming for his. "You're not . . . you don't really love me or want me. It's just the Bond, the Soul-Bond that's making us both act this way."

"Fuck that." His eyes were angry and his chest was heaving. He started to step forward, but Shaina held out one hand, palm up to stop him.

"Please Ty, don't." Her voice was breaking and there was a lump in her throat that made talking difficult. "Don't," she repeated. "I won't let you do this to me again."

"Do what?" Holding his ground, all his muscles tensed as though he were about to spring if she said the wrong thing.

"Use me and throw me away when you're done," Shaina shot back. "I'm leaving here, Ty. Leaving tonight and there's nothing you can do to stop me. So get out of my house. Now."

"Shaina . . ." It was as though all the feral energy evaporated from him at once. The wild animal disappeared and left only Ty, looking sad and beaten, in front of her. "I'm sorry." He shook his head. "So sorry that's what you think of me." With a gesture of defeat, he zipped up his uniform, leaned against the wall, and closed his eyes tiredly.

"What else am I supposed to think?" Shaina tried to swallow past the tears that were threatening to blind her. She wrapped her arms tightly around herself, trying to keep the hurtful emotions inside. "I thought we meant something to each other on Syrus Six. When you touched me . . . held me. The way you made love to me . . . But it was nothing to you. Nothing at all." Blinking to hold back the tears, she turned away, not able to look at him anymore.

"It meant everything to me," he answered, his voice low and harsh behind her. "Shaina, *you* mean everything to me."

"You're just saying that because of the damn Soul-Bond. You'd say anything right now." She heard the accusation in her voice but she couldn't help it.

"You're right." Shaina thought his voice had gotten a little closer, but she refused to turn around and make sure. She didn't want Ty to see her crying. "But not about the Bond," he continued. Closer still, she thought, still hugging herself with both arms. "I'd say anything to get you to stay, anything to make you mine forever. Shaina McCullough, I've wanted you from the first time I laid eyes on you. But I was afraid to scare you off. Every time I tried to get close, you pushed me away and ran in the opposite direction." His breath was warm on the back of her neck, but Shaina still refused to turn around.

"I was afraid." She wanted badly to believe him. "Afraid of your D'Lonian side, of what you might do to me."

"When we were together on Syrus Six, did I ever give you reason to fear me?" Voice quiet, he slid gentle fingertips along the backs of her arms until she shivered.

"No," she breathed, remembering the tender way he had made love to her. Even on the auction block, when he had gotten a little rough, it had been only because she had urged him to, because she needed him to take her hard . . . Shaina shivered at the memory. Goddess, how much more did she need him now? But she couldn't . . .

"Why not?" He used the link. *"Why fight it, Shaina?"*

"Why did you tell me you were sorry for forging this Bond between us? Why did you say we had to stay apart?" she countered, wiping angrily at the tears that were rolling down her cheeks.

Tyson sighed heavily. "I thought you'd be upset that I forged an unbreakable Soul-Bond between us without asking you first. I meant to ask you. I had promised myself that the moment I had you safe on board the *She-Creature* and away from that freak show on Syrus Six that I would tell you how I felt. How I've always felt about you. Shaina, please . . ." He turned her around to face him, his hands on her shoulders gently insistent.

"What do you mean how you're always felt about me? I thought we were just coworkers." Unable to meet his eyes, she wiped nervously at her wet cheeks, wondering if he could possibly be for real.

"You know it's more than that, sweetheart. It's always been more than that. How can I explain this?" he mused for a moment. "Look, you know I'm half D'Lonian . . ." Shaina nodded for him to continue, Tyson didn't often speak about his heritage and she was curious. "Well," He sighed again and ran a hand through his hair. "My parents are dead now, died in a shuttle crash when I was nineteen. But it was my dad who was full-blooded D'Lonian.

"I remember he used to tell me how he knew the first time he met my mom that she was the one for him. He said that a voice inside him just spoke up and said, 'Mine.' It wasn't logical or politically correct. My mom's parents were blue-bloods, high society from Tengwar, and they completely disowned her when they found out she planned to marry a D'Lonian. But neither one of them cared because it was *right*."

Ty lifted her chin so that Shaina had no choice but to meet his eyes. "Shaina, that's how I feel about you, how I've felt from day one. From the first minute I saw you I knew you were the one for me, the only one. It wasn't love at first sight or any of that sentimental bullshit you see on the romance vids. It was a gut feeling that we belonged together. When I saw you, I felt like I'd found a piece of myself I didn't know I was missing."

"Why . . ." Shaina swallowed and tried to find her voice. "Why didn't you tell me any of this before?" Beginning to feel her barriers crumble, she just needed that last little bit of reassurance.

"I was afraid to scare you away. While I was training you, when we worked together, you always seemed frightened of me, not willing to open up or get close. I know now that was because you were a virgin and you'd heard all kinds of crazy rumors about D'Lonian men. It was so frustrating. I wanted you so badly, and yet I knew if I went too far, I'd scare you off forever. When you decided to take the mission to Syrus Six, I thought I saw an opportunity to get closer to you. Besides, there was no way I was letting you go into danger like that on your own."

His words rang true and Shaina could feel herself letting go, letting herself believe. It was the most wonderful feeling, as though a layer of frost around her heart was finally thawing. She felt the Soul-Bond throb strongly within her and she finally dared to speak. "Ty, while we were on Syrus Six I started to feel the same way. That we belonged together, I mean. I . . . I've been waiting for the right man all my life and when I got to really know you, I knew you had to be the one. But even though the . . ." she blushed, "the sex was amazing, you always acted so indifferent afterwards. I thought you thought of me only as a coworker."

Tyson gave a dry laugh and shook his head. "I was afraid of admitting my feelings too early. Afraid you'd run as far as you could in the opposite direction. And then, when I forged the Soul-Bond between us without even asking you . . . well, I thought I'd blown any chance I ever had of keeping you in my life. This past week without you has been hell, sweetheart, and not just because of the Bond." Pulling her close, he bent his head and nuzzled his face into the curve of her neck. She shivered as his warm breath blew over her skin. "Not that the Bond doesn't make it worse. I don't think there's been a single minute this whole week I haven't wanted you."

"I've felt it too," Shaina admitted in a low voice. "The wanting, I mean. Is this . . . I mean, I'd like to know what I can expect now that we're Bonded."

Tyson pulled back from her and grinned, that feral D'Lonian expression that used to frighten her so much. Now Shaina found it caused a shiver of desire throughout her entire body to have him look at her that way, as though he already owned her and knew exactly what to do to make her moan.

"That's right, all I told you about the Soul-Bond is how to weaken it." Ty gave a low, self-deprecating laugh. "What a fool I was! As if I could ever let you get away." He kissed her tenderly on the lips, claiming her gently but firmly. "We've got a lot of catching up to do, sweetheart."

"What . . . what do you mean?" Shaina asked, a little breathlessly, as Tyson's hands began to roam over her body once more.

"I mean that in D'Lonian culture, the first week after a couple Bond is the most important. Sort of like a honeymoon period."

"What happens during the first week?" She moaned as his hand reached beneath her robe again to tease her nipples with a light pinch.

"After the Bond is forged there's an urgent biological drive to strengthen it, to make sure it's solid." His hand moved slowly down her taut abdomen. "The longer that drive is ignored, the stronger the need becomes."

"And how . . . how do you strengthen the Soul-Bond?" Voice unsteady, she closed her eyes when Tyson slid one large, warm hand into her small crimson panties to cup her wet sex.

"How do you think, sweetheart?" Fingers parted the tender lips of her pussy and rubbed slowly along the side of her swollen clit. "The same way you forge it in the first place." He slid two long fingers into her, pressing hard until she cried out in wordless pleasure. "I need to *fuck* you now, Shaina." His voice was a low, possessive growl in his throat. "I need to fuck you to make you mine forever."

"Yes . . ." It was all she could do to get the words out; he was making her dizzy with need. "Bedroom . . ." she managed to gasp, pointing a shaky finger towards the lift.

"Fine." He picked her up in one quick motion and headed into the lift.

Shaina wasn't sure how they got from the lift to her gel mattress, but suddenly she was lying on her own bed. Ty loomed over her naked. He pinned her down and kissed her neck urgently as he coaxed her legs apart. Shaina spread her thighs willingly, feeling her love for Ty and the Bond between them throb in her chest and groin like another heartbeat. Tyson wasn't kidding when he said they had lost time to make up for. She could feel the need for his body within hers growing by the moment, a huge, all-consuming emotion that blotted out all rational thought.

"Need to be on top of you this time, sweetheart. Need to feel you under me." He reached between them and tore the thin red panties away, leaving her wet and naked and open before him. Shaina understood now that it was all about possession. Ty had to mark her, to claim her irrevocably as his own. He needed to be above her, the male-dominant position that enabled him to achieve maximum penetration and fuck her as deeply as possible. She felt deliciously submissive as she spread her thighs even wider, feeling the broad head of his cock rub her slick inner folds.

She welcomed him, waiting to be claimed and mastered. "I'm ready, Ty. Don't make me wait, please!"

With a low roar that might have been her name, Ty entered her at last with one rough thrust. Shaina cried out, loving the way his thick shaft stretched her open and filled her until she could take no more. He held still for a moment, the head of his cock pressed against the mouth of her womb, pinning her helplessly to the bed, spread wide and utterly vulnerable, before he pulled back and started to move.

"Oh, Ty . . . Oh!" Shaina heard herself crying as he pressed her thighs wider apart to give himself room to work her hard, to ride her sweet, unresisting pussy the way she needed him to. He started a slow, rough, deliberate rhythm that seemed designed to drive her completely crazy, and the slick friction between their bodies was exactly what she had been needing for so long. Shaina dug her nails into his shoulders, urging him wordlessly to go faster, deeper, harder . . .

"This the way you like it, sweetheart?" Pressing deeply inside her, he filled her to the limit with himself. "This the way you need to be fucked?"

"You know it is . . . Oh!" Deep inside she was beginning to feel the elusive stirrings of orgasm. The sensation swelled inside her with each fierce thrust of his cock as Ty ground against her, pressing again and again against her throbbing clit. Coming . . . she was going to come and she wanted to feel him come as well. Wanted to feel him fill her with his seed and forge the Bond all over again from the inside out. She was close . . . so close . . .

Tyson seemed to read the look on her face, because he pounded inside her even harder, making her cry helplessly with an overload of sensation. *"You're close, aren't you, sweetheart?"* he whispered through the symbi-link, his breath harsh in her ear.

"Yes . . . yes . . ." The need to come drove everything else out of her head.

"Gonna keep fucking you 'til you come, Shaina. Gonna fuck you deep and hard until I feel your sweet pussy squeeze around me. Then I'm gonna press inside you as deep as I can and come inside you, fill you up and make you mine. Understand?"

"I . . . ah! I understand . . ." Loving the way he pressed so deeply into her, Shaina sobbed. Each lunge seemed to catch somewhere under her heart, filling her with love and desire and the simple, primal urge to feel her man's seed inside her. To feel him filling her up as he promised he would. Claiming her forever.

"Then come for me, sweetheart," Ty commanded her in a forceful growl, and Shaina found her body responding as always to his command, to his utter mastery over her body.

"Goddess!" she wailed and felt herself slip over the edge of orgasm. Felt her body give way before his at his order. Felt her pussy clenching around his thick, invading shaft as she came helplessly, and gave herself to him utterly, mind, body, and soul.

Tyson must have felt her lose control because he roared and pressed inside her as deeply as he could. Burying his cock to the root in her wet, sucking sex, he filled her with a rush of throbbing warmth. As he did, Shaina felt the Bond pulse as the wire between them became a thick, unbreakable rope and she knew nothing but death would ever part them again.

30

He woke up from a dream about holding her favorite furry comfort-bot teddy bear to find Shaina cuddled in his arms instead. He had been sharing her dream. She felt so right as he pulled her tight against him that Ty never wanted to let her go. Then he remembered that he never had to. It was like being filled to the brim with liquid solarshine to know that the Soul-Bond was safely reinforced and Shaina McCullough was finally his forever.

"I'm yours, but would you mind not squeezing quite so hard?" Her mental voice was amused and she wiggled back against him in a way that made Ty instantly aroused. She was his, but the Bond could still use a little more reinforcing, he reasoned.

"You're insatiable." Shaina twisted around to lock eyes with him and gave him a teasing kiss on the nose. "Give a girl a chance to recover, though, will you? Oh . . ." This last was a sweet little moan and her eyelids fluttered shut as Tyson nuzzled beneath her jaw to plant a hungry kiss in the sensitive spot under her ear.

"You were saying?" Amused by her reaction, he pulled back reluctantly.

"I was saying that you're going to wear me out. Not that I mind so much," Shaina whispered, smiling. Tyson grinned back. A few more kisses and he knew he'd have her positively purring and more than ready for action, but first they needed to talk.

"I'll have plenty of time to wear you out after the joining ceremony." Shaina's eyes opened wide and she pushed away from him and propped herself up on one elbow.

"Joining ceremony?" Her words were tinged with disbelief. "What joining ceremony, Ty?"

"The one we're going to have as soon as possible. Oh, by the way, will you marry me?" he asked, still grinning. "You might as well, you know." His gaze ran over her and he thought how delectable she looked, all soft and naked after a night of hard loving. "I'm pretty sure you missed your flight to Washington."

"The flight! Oh my Goddess . . . Ty. Everyone from the station was going to be there. What must they think?" Shaina ran one hand distractedly through her tousled red hair. "It's a good thing I told my mom not to come; she'd be worried sick. And those were nonrefundable tickets."

Tyson snorted. "As if you couldn't afford it. And who cares what everyone from the station thinks? You never answered my question." Sitting up, he took her slim white hand in his and kissed it. "Shaina McCullough, will you marry me?"

"Well, this isn't quite the way I always dreamed of being asked . . ." She grinned at him suddenly, an expression of pure happiness that made her even more beautiful, if that was possible. "But yes, Brent Tyson, I would love to be your wife." She kissed him hard, surprising him a little, and drew back breathless. "There's only one thing, Ty—what about work? One of us will have to transfer to another station. You know they don't let married people work in the same precinct."

"Well, I wouldn't worry too much about work." His hand reached out to caress a loose strand of hair away from her sweet face. "Actually, I thought we might quit the Peace Officer business and try a new career."

"Quit it?" Shaina pulled back a little, confused. "But you love being a Peace Officer. What other career were you thinking of?"

"Slave Finder," Ty said casually, enjoying the look of disbelief that was growing on her face. "Now, just hear me out, McCullough. I had a chance to talk to some professional slave finders while you were still on Syrus Six. It was Mistress Shy, actually, and her little blond slave. They were partners and work undercover the same way we were."

"Really? I never would have guessed." Shaina looked more surprised than ever.

"Neither would I until she told me. She and L'Mera have been together a long time. Shy guessed about us, what we were trying to do, because she'd been offered the mission to save Paul and had turned it down. She tried to warn us, too, but she couldn't say much since everything was being constantly monitored and recorded. Remember the story she told you about the Executor and her beautiful Glameron that first night?"

"Beautiful Glameron . . . Oh, I remember," Shaina exclaimed.

"Well, that was Faron. He left her for the Chancellor years ago. But apparently they had a falling-out a few years ago and Faron decided to take up where he left off. Remember how weird the vents in the *She-Creature*'s shuttle were? Well, he had them modified to circulate the gas the Kandalar breathe so he and the Executor could have secret rendezvous. Even painted, the whole thing monochrome in her favorite color, just the way the Kandalar like. Only thing was, the Executor wasn't content to have him once in a while. She wanted Faron to come back to her for good. When he wouldn't, she arranged to kidnap Paul, the most important person in his life. She was sure he would come after his son himself, but instead, he and the Chancellor hired us."

"She was saying something about a trap . . . a trap that T'lar sprung too early," Shaina muttered, going pale. Through their link, Ty could hear her remembering the whole awful scene.

"Don't worry, sweetheart." Soothingly he cupped one pale cheek in his hand. "I promise we'll never go back to Syrus Six; it's the heart of the slave trade, but there are plenty of other planets that trade as well." Shaina turned her head and planted a soft kiss in the palm of his hand and he was relieved to see her looking better almost immediately. "What ever happened to old T'lar, anyway?"

"Got taken to the colored chambers. By now I think he's a very fashionable pair of magenta gloves."

Ty burst out laughing. "Serves him right. But getting back to Mistress Shy. She told me she thought you and I made an excellent team and if we ever wanted to get into the business to contact her. She promised to give us a few contacts, help us get started. So I thought . . ." He shrugged. "Money isn't a problem. After Syrus Six we could even afford to buy our own needle. Just imagine, Shaina, going all over the galaxy, hell, the universe if we wanted to . . ." He looked at her hopefully. "That is, if you want to."

"It sounds wonderful, Ty. But are you sure it's what you want? I thought you loved being a Peace Control Officer. I don't know about you, but it makes me feel needed somehow, like I'm performing a vital service."

"I understand what you're saying, but believe me, we'll still be providing a needed service. Do you remember how it was on Syrus Six? The way the slaves were treated?"

"Especially by Masters like Jlle." Shaina shuddered. "What a horrible man." ·

"Oh that's right, you were pretty out of it at the time . . . but I took care of him." Tyson told her about the memory patch and how he had sold Jlle to the ragged slaver headed for the waste-treatment moon. "So our friend Marso Jlle is going to be shoveling shit for the rest of his natural life," he concluded with a grin.

Shaina laughed until tears stood in her eyes. "Oh, Ty, you didn't!" She exclaimed. "Oh how perfect. It's exactly what he deserved."

"I know. But there are millions more out there just like him, Shaina." He took her hand and looked earnestly into her ocean-green eyes. "There's a real need for Slave Finders out there, and not just to bring back the slaves that we get paid to find. Shy told me that she usually has it written in her contract that she gets enough funds to buy at least one other slave on any given mission; the family sponsoring the find agrees to help get the extra slave a place to live, a job, that kind of thing. There's no way we can save them all, but even if we can save a few . . . I think it's worth it. A cause worth dedicating your life to. But it depends on you, of course. If you'd rather not do it, I can be happy staying here and working at different stations. Hell, I can be happy anywhere as long as I have you."

"Ty . . ." Shaina sniffed and wiped at her eyes. "I'd be happy anywhere with you too. And when you talk about being a Finder like that . . . you really want to do this, don't you?"

"I really do," he admitted. "But only if you want it too."

"Then I'm in." Shaina made her decision. "We'll start looking for a needle right after the joining ceremony. You contact Shy and tell her we're getting into the business full-time."

"There's just one more thing." Tyson drew her close and

kissed the sensitive spot under her ear again. "On our next mission, you get to be the slave."

Shaina grinned and arched her neck, shivering at the kiss which promised so much more in the near future.

"I wouldn't have it any other way . . . Master."

Take the plunge with

LORD OF THE DEEP!

On sale now!

1

The Isle of Mists, in the Eastern Archipelago,
Principalities of Arcus

Meg saw the seals from her window, their silvery coats rippling as they thrashed out of the sea and collected along the shore. She'd seen them sunning themselves on the rocks by day and had watched them frolic in the dusky darkness from that dingy salt-streaked window in her loft chamber many times since her exile to the island, but not like tonight, with their slick coats gleaming in the moonlight. Full and round, the summer moon left a silvery trail in the dark water that pointed like an arrow toward the creatures frolicking along the strand, lighting them as bright as day. Meg's breath caught in her throat. Behind, the high-curling combers crashing on the shore took on the ghostly shape of prancing white horses, a pure illusion that disappeared the instant their churning hooves touched sand. In the foaming surf left behind, the seals began to shed their skins, revealing their perfect male and female nakedness. Meg gasped. It was magical.

Her heartbeat began to quicken. She inched nearer to the window until her hot breath fogged the glass. The nights were still cool beside the sea—too cool for cavorting naked in the moonlight. And where had the seals gone? These were humans, dark-haired, graceful men and women with skin like alabaster, moving with the undulant motion of the sea they'd sprung from in all their unabashed glory. They seemed to be gathering the skins they'd shed, bringing them higher toward the berm and out of the backwash.

Mesmerized, Meg stared as the mating began.

One among the men was clearly their leader. His dark wet hair, crimped like tangled strands of seaweed, waved nearly to his broad shoulders. Meg's eyes followed the moonbeam that illuminated him, followed the shadows that collected along the knifestraight indentation of his spine defined the dimples above his buttocks and the crease that separated those firm round cheeks. The woman in his arms had twined herself around him like a climbing vine, her head bent back beneath his gaze, her long dark hair spread about her like a living veil.

All around them others had paired off, coupling, engaging in a ritualistic orgy of the senses beneath the rising moon, but Meg's eyes were riveted to their leader. Who could they be? Certainly not locals. No one on the island looked like these, like *him*, much less behaved in such a fashion. She would have noticed.

Meg wiped the condensation away from the windowpane with a trembling hand. What she was seeing sent white-hot fingers of liquid fire racing through her belly and thighs, and riveting chills loose along her spine. It was well past midnight, and the peat fire in the kitchen hearth below had dwindled to embers. Oddly, it wasn't the physical cold that gripped her then, hardening her nipples beneath the thin lawn night smock and undermining her balance so severely she gripped the window ledge. Her skin was on fire beneath the gown. It was her finest.

She'd worked the delicate blackwork embroidery on it herself. It would have seen her to the marriage bed if circumstances had been different—if she hadn't been openly accused of being a witch on the mainland and been banished to the Isle of Mists for protection, for honing her inherent skills, and for mentoring by the shamans. But none of that mattered now while the raging heat was building at the epicenter of her sex—calling her hand there to soothe and calm engorged flesh through the butter-soft lawn . . . at least that is how it started.

She inched the gown up along her leg and thigh and walked her fingertips through the silky golden hair curling between them, gliding her fingers along the barrier of her virgin skin, slick and wet with arousal. She glanced below. But for her termagant aunt, who had long since retired, she was alone in the thatched roof cottage. It would be a sennight before her uncle returned from the mainland, where he'd gone to buy new nets and eel pots, and to collect the herbs her aunt needed for her simples and tisanes. Nothing but beach grass grew on the Isle of Mists.

Meg glanced about. Who was there to see? No one, and she loosened the drawstring that closed the smock and freed her aching breasts to the cool dampness that clung stubbornly to the upper regions of the dreary little cottage, foul weather and fair.

Eyes riveted to the strand, Meg watched the leader of the strange congregation roll his woman's nipples between his fingers. They were turned sideways, and she could see his thick, curved sex reaching toward her middle. Still wet from the sea they'd come from, their skin shone in the moonlight, gleaming as the skins they'd shed had gleamed. They were standing ankle deep in the crashing surf that spun yards of gossamer spindrift into the night. Meg stifled a moan as she watched the woman's hand grip the leader's sex, gliding back and forth along the rigid shaft from thick base to hooded tip. Something pinged deep inside her watching him respond . . . something urgent and un-stoppable.

Her breath had fogged the pane again, and she wiped it away in a wider swath this time. Her breasts were nearly touching it. Only the narrow windowsill kept them from pressing up against the glass, but who could see her in the darkened loft? No one, and she began rolling one tall hardened nipple between her thumb and forefinger, then sweeping the pebbled areola in slow concentric circles, teasing but not touching the aching bud, just as the creature on the beach had done to the woman in his arms.

Excruciating ecstasy.

While the others were mating fiercely all along the strand, the leader had driven his woman to her knees in the lacy surf. The tide was rising, and the water surged around him at mid-calf, breaking over the woman, creaming over her naked skin, over the seaweed and sand she knelt on as she took his turgid member into her mouth to the root.

Meg licked her lips expectantly in anticipation of such mag-nificence entering her mouth, responding to the caress of her tongue. She closed her eyes, imagining the feel and smell and taste of him, like sea salt bursting over her palate. This was one of the gifts that had branded her a witch.

When Meg opened her eyes again, her posture clenched. Had he turned? Yes! He seemed to be looking straight at her. It was almost as if he'd read her thoughts, as if he knew she was there all the while and had staged the torrid exhibition for her eyes alone to view. She couldn't see his face—it was steeped in shadow—but yes, there was triumph in his stance and victory in the posturing that took back his sex from the woman's mouth. His eyes were riveting as he dropped to his knees, spread the woman's legs wide to the rushing surf, and entered her in one slow, tantalizing thrust, like a sword being sheathed to the hilt, as the waves surged and crashed and swirled around them.

Still his shadowy gaze relentlessly held Meg's. For all her extraordinary powers of perception, she could not plumb the depths of that look as he took the woman to the rhythm of the waves lapping at them, laving them to the meter of his thrusts, like some giant beast with a thousand tongues. She watched the mystical surf horses trample them, watched the woman beneath him shudder to a rigid climax as the rising tide washed over her—watched the sand ebb away beneath the beautiful creature's buttocks as the sea sucked it back from the shore. All the while he watched her. It was as if she were the woman beneath him, writhing with pleasure in the frothy sea.

Captivated, Meg met the leader's silver-eyed gaze. She could almost feel the undulations as he hammered his thick, hard shaft into the woman, reaching his own climax. Meg groaned in spite of herself as he threw back his head and cried out when he came.

She should move away from the window . . . But why? He couldn't see what she was doing to herself in the deep darkness of the cottage loft . . . Could he? All at once it didn't matter. A hot lava flow of sweet sensation riddled her sex with pinpricks of exquisite agony. It was almost as if *he* were stroking her nipples and palpating the swollen nub at the top of her weeping vulva as she rubbed herself, slowly at first, then fiercely, until the thickening bud hardened like stone. She probed herself deeper. She could almost stretch the barrier skin and slip her finger inside, riding the silk of her wetness—as wet as the surging combers lapping relentlessly at the lovers on the beach. A firestorm of spasmodic contractions took her then, freeing the moan in her throat. It felt as if her bones were melting. Shutting her eyes, she shed the last remnants of modest restraint and leaned into her release.

The voyeuristic element of the experience heightened the orgasm, and it was some time before her hands gripped the windowsill again instead of tender flesh, and her gaze fell upon the strand below once more. But the silvery expanse of rock-bound shoreline edged in seaweed stretching north and south as far as the eye could see was vacant. The strange revelers were gone!

Meg tugged the night shift back over her flushed breasts, though they ached for more stroking, and let the hem of the gown slide down her legs, hiding the palpitating flesh of her sex. Her whole body throbbed like a pulse beat, and she seized the thrumming mound between her thighs savagely through the gown in a vain attempt to quiet its tremors and made a clean sweep through the condensation on the window again. Nothing moved outside but the combers crashing on the strand. But for the echo of the surf sighing into the night, reverberating through her sex to the rhythm of fresh longing, all else was still.

No. She hadn't imagined it. The naked revelers mating on the beach had been real—as real as the seals that frequented the coast. Selkies? Could the shape-shifter legends be true? She'd heard little else since she came to the island.

Meg didn't stop to collect her mantle. Maybe the cool night air would cure the fever in her flesh. Hoisting up the hem of her night smock, she climbed down the loft ladder, tiptoed through the kitchen without making a sound, and stepped out onto the damp drifted sand that always seemed to collect about the door-sill. Nothing moved but the prancing white horses in the surf that drove it landward. Waterhorses? She'd heard that legend, too: innocent-looking creatures that lured any who would mount them to a watery death. Real or imaginary, it didn't matter. The people she'd just seen there having sex were real enough, and she meant to prove it.

The hard, damp sand was cold beneath her bare feet as she padded over the shallow dune toward the shoreline. The phantom horses had disappeared from the waves crashing on the strand, as had every trace that anyone had walked that way recently. There wasn't a footprint in sight, and the sealskins Meg had watched them drag to higher ground were nowhere to be seen, either.

Having reached the ragged edge of the surf, Meg turned and looked back at the cottage beyond, paying particular attention to her loft window. Yes, it was close, but there was no way anyone could have seen her watching from her darkened chamber. Then why was she so uneasy? It wasn't the first time she'd touched herself in the dark, and it wouldn't be the last, but it had been the best, and there was something very intimate about it. The man who had aroused her seemed somehow familiar, and yet she knew they'd never met. Still, he had turned toward that window and flaunted himself as if he knew she had been watching, exhibiting his magnificent erection in what appeared to be a sex act staged solely for her benefit. Moist heat rushed at her loins, ripping through her belly and thighs with the memory.

Meg scooped up some of the icy water and bathed the aching flesh between her thighs. She plowed through the lacy surf where the lovers had performed—to the very spot where the mysterious selkie leader had spent his seed—and tried to order the mixed emotions riddling her. Absorbed in thought, she failed to feel the vibration beneath her feet until the horse was nearly upon her. It reared back on its hind legs, forefeet pawing the air, its long tail sweeping the sand a *real* horse this time, no illusion. Meg cried out as recognition struck. There was a rider on its back. He was naked and aroused. It was *him*, with neither bridle nor reins to control the beast, and nothing but a silvery sealskin underneath him.

He seemed quite comfortable in the altogether, as if it was the most natural thing in the world to sit a horse bareback, naked in the moonlight. She gasped and gasped again. The horse had become quite docile, attempting to nuzzle her with its sleek white nose as it pranced to a standstill. She didn't want to look at the man on its back, but she couldn't help herself. He was a beguiling presence. As mesmerizing as he was from a distance, he was a hundred times more so at close range. Now she could see what the shadows had denied her earlier. His eyes, the color of mercury, were dark and penetrating, and slightly slanted. Somehow, she knew they would be. And his hair, while waving at a length to tease his shoulders in front, was longer in back and worn in a queue, tied with what appeared to be a piece of beach grass. How had she not noticed that before? But how could she have when he'd made such a display of himself face forward? Besides, her focus was hardly upon his hair.

Her attention shifted to the horse. At first she'd thought its mane and tail were black, but upon close inspection, she saw that they were white as snow, so tangled with seaweed they appeared black at first glance. But wait . . . what had she heard about white horses whose mane and tail collected seaweed? A waterhorse! The phantom creature of legend that seduced its victims to mount and be carried off to drown in the sea . . . But that was preposterous. Nevertheless, when its master reached out his hand toward her, she spun on her heels and raced back toward the cottage.

His laughter followed her, throaty and deep. Like an echo from the depths of the sea itself, it crashed over her just as the waves crashed over the shore. The sound pierced through her like a lightning bolt. The prancing water horse beneath him whinnied and clamped ferocious-looking teeth into the hem of her night shift, giving a tug that brought her to ground. She landed hard on her bottom, and the selkie laughed again as she cried out. Plucking her up as easily as if she were a broom straw, he settled her in front of him astride.

"You cannot escape me, Megaleen," he crooned in her ear. "You have summoned me, and I have come. You have no idea what it is that you have conjured—what delicious agonies you have unleashed by invoking me." His breath was moist and warm; it smelled of salt and the mysteries of the Otherworldly sea that had spawned him. "Hold on!" he charged, turning the horse toward the strand.

"Hold on to what?" Meg shrilled. "He has no bridle—no reins!"

Again his sultry voice resonating in her ear sent shivers of pleasure thrumming through her body. "Take hold of his mane," he whispered.

His voice alone was a seduction. He was holding her about the middle. Her shift had been hiked up around her waist when he settled her astride, and she could feel the thick bulk of his shaft throbbing against her buttocks, riding up and down along the cleft between the cheeks of her ass. The damp sealskin that stretched over the animal's back like a saddle blanket underneath her felt cool against Meg's naked thighs, but it could not quench the fever in her skin or douse the flames gnawing at the very core of her sex. The friction the water horse's motion created forced the wet sealskin fur deeper into her fissure, triggered another orgasm. Her breath caught as it riddled her body with waves of achy heat. She rubbed against the seal pelt, undulating to the rhythm of the horse's gait until every last wave had ebbed away, like ripples in a stream when a pebble breaks the water's surface.

In one motion, the selkie raised the night shift over her head and tossed it into the water. Reaching for it as he tore it away, Meg lost her balance. His strong hands spanning her waist prevented her from falling. Their touch seared her like firebrands, raising the fine hairs at the nape of her neck. The horse had plunged into the surf. It was heading toward the open sea, parting the unreal phantom horses galloping toward shore.

Salt spray pelted her skin, hardening her nipples. Spindrift dressed her hair with tiny spangles. The horse had plunged in past the breakers to the withers. Terrified, Meg screamed as the animal broke through the waves and sank to its muscular neck.

"Hold on!" he commanded.

"I cannot," Meg cried. "His mane . . . It is slippery with seaweed."

All at once, he lifted her into the air and set her down facing him, gathering her against his hard muscular body, his engorged sex heaving against her belly. How strong he was! "Then hold onto me," he said.

"W-who are you?" Meg murmured.

"I am called Simeon . . . amongst other things," he replied. "But that hardly signifies. . . ." Heat crackled in his voice. Something pinged in her sex at the sound of it.

He swooped down, looming over her. For a split second, she thought he was going to kiss her. She could almost taste the salt on his lips, in his mouth, on the tongue she glimpsed parting his teeth . . . But no. Fisting his hand in the back of her waist-length sun-painted hair, he blew his steamy breath into her nostrils as the horse's head disappeared beneath the surface of the sea.

Meg's last conscious thought before sinking beneath the waves in the selkie's arms was that she was being seduced to her death; another orgasm testified to that. Weren't you supposed to come before you die? Wasn't it supposed to be an orgasm like no other, like the orgasm riddling her now?

The scent that ghosted through her nostrils as she drew her last breath of air was his scent, salty, laced with the mysteries of the deep, threaded through with the sweet musky aroma of ambergris.